Ple
on

T(
or

You

Praise for

T.M. LOGAN

'Smart, intense and with a humdinger of a mid-point twist. I loved it'
GILLIAN MCALLISTER

'Taut, tense and compelling. Thriller writing at its finest'
SIMON LELIC

'T.M. Logan's best yet. Unsettling and so, so entertaining.
The perfect thriller'
CAZ FREAR

'A tense and gripping thriller'
B.A. PARIS

'Assured, compelling, and hypnotically readable – with a twist at
the end I guarantee you won't see coming'
LEE CHILD

'A compelling, twisty page-turner, and that's the truth'
JAMES SWALLOW

'Outstanding and very well-written . . . so gripping
I genuinely found it hard to put down'
K.L. SLATER

'A terrific page-turner, didn't see that twist!
A thoroughly enjoyable thriller'
MEL SHERRATT

'Another blistering page-turner from psych-thriller god
T.M. Logan'
CHRIS WHITAKER

'Even the cleverest second-guesser is unlikely to arrive at
the truth until it's much, much too late'
THE TIMES

TRUST
ME

T.M. Logan's thrillers have sold over a million copies in the UK and are published in 18 countries around the world. His novel *The Holiday* was a Richard and Judy Book Club pick and became a *Sunday Times* bestseller in paperback. Formerly a national newspaper journalist, he now writes full time and lives in Nottinghamshire with his wife and two children.

Also by T.M. Logan:

Lies
29 Seconds
The Holiday
The Catch

TRUST ME

T.M. LOGAN

ZAFFRE

First published in the UK in 2021 by
ZAFFRE
An imprint of Bonnier Books UK
80–81 Wimpole St, London W1G 9RE
Owned by Bonnier Books
Sveavägen 56, Stockholm, Sweden

A CIP catalogue record for this book is
available from the British Library.

Hardback ISBN: 978–1–83877–293–2
Special edition ISBN: 978–1–83877–551–3
Export ISBN: 978–1–83877–377–9

Also available as an ebook and an audiobook

1 3 5 7 9 10 8 6 4 2

Typeset by IDSUK (Data Connection) Ltd
Printed and bound in Great Britain by Clays Ltd, Elcograf S.p.A.

Zaffre is an imprint of Bonnier Books UK
www.bonnierbooks.co.uk

For my agent, Camilla Bolton,
who trusted in me from the beginning

No man chooses evil because it is evil; he only mistakes it for happiness, the good he seeks.

—Mary Wollstonecraft

Bad luck.

That was all it came down to, in the end.

One piece of bad luck that threatened to destroy everything.

He had been so careful. So many precautions, hardly anything left to chance. So much thought and planning and preparation. It was true what they said, though: you can't control everything.

But he wasn't about to let one piece of bad luck dictate his future.

It was time to put it behind him.

Permanently.

TUESDAY.

1

A shape, white and black and grey.

The curve of the spine, the forehead, the tiny snub nose, the perfect feet with toes curled. A shape that holds the promise of new life.

I stare at the grainy image, thumb frozen on the screen of my phone, emotion clogging my throat. The ecstatic caption beneath it written by a woman I have never met, full of optimism and joy and the excitement of approaching motherhood.

So . . . Richard and I have news! Junior has settled in nicely and is on his way. So pleased to be able to tell everyone! Excited!!! #12WeekScan #ultrasound #instamum #instababy #babylove

The knowledge settles like a rock in my stomach. *She's having my ex-husband's baby.* Richard has finally got what he wanted, what we *both* wanted, craved, more than anything.

I feel winded, dizzy, as if I've been kicked in the chest, all the air knocked out of me for the second time in a matter of hours. First this morning's news, and now this.

I lay the phone face down on the table, biting down the ache, the longing, the *wanting*. I stare out of the train window, the Buckinghamshire countryside racing past in a blur of fields and hedgerows. Crops harvested and stalks cut low to the ground, the earth ploughed brown, tendrils of smoke from a distant bonfire curling up into the grey autumn sky. The gentle rock and sway of the train, the vibration rising up through the flat soles of my shoes. The train is taking me back to London, back to my little newbuild house, back to . . .

To what, exactly? An empty home that will be exactly as I left it this morning. Silent and cold. Half the wardrobes newly emptied and half the books and DVDs newly absent; the framed prints and the big corner armchair gone too. Richard left me with most of the furniture at least, that was something. And all of our photo albums; evidently the past is something he wants to leave behind. But somehow I can't do the same. I'm stuck here, stuck in my own past, unable to move on. A prisoner of my own biology. Maybe my time really is up. This is it.

I settle back into my seat, the pockmarked blue material worn smooth by the years, and try to concentrate instead on the low hum of the engine, on the indistinct phone chatter behind me; a group of football fans singing at the other end of the carriage, their voices loud with alcohol.

A young woman makes her way slowly down the aisle, scanning the seats, a pink-clad baby tucked into the crook of her arm. I turn away, avoiding eye contact, looking out of the window again with a silent prayer that she will find somewhere else to sit down. Babies, babies, everywhere I look. It's a mid-afternoon train, too early for commuters, plenty of spare seats further down this carriage or in the next. *Please find somewhere else, anywhere, so I don't have to look at your baby all the way to London.* I sense the woman pass by, walking slowly down the carriage, and let out a guilty sigh of relief.

The rest of the day stretches out in front of me, blank and empty. The rest of the week. Work. Commute. Home. A few glasses of wine, a few shots of vodka. Pulling the duvet up over my head so I don't have to think about anything. Sleeping alone in the big double bed. Next week, next month, next year. More of the same, looking for a reason to continue beyond the unthinking imperative to keep putting one foot in front of the other. *Keep going. Keep going. Keep going.* I feel empty, spent, hollowed out by a hunger that can never be sated. How can it be possible to hope and pray so hard, for so long, and end up with nothing?

I was a fool.

'Hi,' a woman's voice says. 'Is anyone sitting here?'

The young mother is back, hovering next to the set of four seats where I'm sitting alone.

'No,' I say. 'There's no one.'

'Thanks.' Swinging her rucksack into the window seat, she lowers herself gently opposite me. She's in her mid-twenties, wearing a rust-coloured jacket and blue jeans, blonde hair falling to her shoulders. She's pretty, even beautiful, in that way young mothers always seemed to me. She points down the carriage, where the football fans are still going with their half-shouted songs. 'Had to move to get away from those lads. They're passing around the Jack Daniels.'

She moves carefully so as not to jostle the baby in her arm, a tiny thing dressed in a pale pink cardigan and pink shoes with little rainbows on them. Tufts of blonde hair peek out from beneath a pink bow over the top of her head. Her eyes are ocean-blue against perfect white, with long lashes and just the tiniest hint of blonde eyebrows. They lock onto me and a smile spreads instantly across her chubby face, her pink dummy almost falling out, a big gummy grin that dimples her cheeks and lights up her face. Despite myself, despite everything, I feel my own lips curving into a smile in return – but it's been so long that it feels strange, almost unnatural.

'She's absolutely beautiful,' I say. And it isn't just one of those things you say to a new mother, the polite response when their baby is presented to you. It's true enough that *all* babies are beautiful in their own way, to their own parents especially. But this one is unbearably, impossibly cute.

'She likes you,' the young mother says with a shy grin.

'She's very smiley, isn't she?' I say, unable to take my eyes off the baby. '*So* sweet.'

The woman's phone rings on the seat beside her. She checks the screen and silences it.

'How old are yours?' she says.

My smile falters. No matter how many times I'm asked about my own family, I never quite get the answer right. It always sounds like an apology or a defence.

'Me and my husband, I mean ex-husband, we couldn't . . .' I tear my eyes away from the baby in her arms. 'We wanted kids, but it never quite worked out for us.'

'Oh.' The young woman colours slightly. 'I'm sorry. I didn't mean to—'

'It's fine,' I say. 'Really. I'm godmother to my friend Tara's children. She has three boys.'

'This little one doesn't have a godmother yet.'

'What's her name?'

'Mia. She's three months and one week old, today. And I'm Kathryn,' she adds, with an embarrassed smile. 'Hi.'

Her phone rings again and she silences it without answering. Looking closer, she's young to have a baby, not much older than twenty, nearly half my own age. I'm old enough to be *her* mother, I realise with a familiar pinch of sadness. She wears no wedding ring, and her ears are pierced twice – low and high – with unfussy studs in each. She looks like she might be more at home out clubbing than looking after a baby.

But there is something else too, a pulse of unease that she's keeping just beneath the surface.

Her phone beeps with a message, and as she reaches for it the sleeve of her jacket rides up, revealing purple-black skin above her wrist, a line of ugly bruises spreading up towards her elbow.

She sees me looking and hurriedly pushes the sleeve back down again. I give her a sympathetic smile.

'I'm Ellen,' I say. Lowering my voice, I add, 'Is everything . . . OK?'

'Yeah.' She tucks a strand of blonde hair behind her ear. 'Actually, I don't suppose you'd be able to hold her for a minute while I get myself sorted out, would you?'

Yes. No. I would love to hold her. More than anything. Please don't ask me to.

'Of course,' I say, sitting forward in my seat.

Kathryn half stands, leaning over the grey plastic table between us, handing the baby to me. It feels awkward at first and for a moment I think I might drop the baby or she might wriggle free, but she seems quite content to lie back, nestled into the crook of my elbow. She's not heavy, just a warm, solid presence, wonderfully and joyfully alive in my arms, her big blue eyes gazing up, her lips curling into a smile. *Babies love faces*, that was what all the books said. They were hardwired to respond to eye contact and smiles, their own eyes focusing to that first distance between mother and child. The distance between us now. How is it possible to feel a loss for something I've never had and probably never will have?

'You're a natural,' Kathryn says, then immediately puts a hand to her mouth. 'I'm sorry, I didn't mean . . . That was a stupid thing to say.'

I shake my head, unable to take my eyes off the baby.

'No need to apologise.'

Mia reaches out, the tips of her little fingers brushing my cheek with the lightest of touches, tiny points of warmth on my skin. She makes a happy gurgle of delight as I lean a little closer, allowing her fingers to touch my chin, my jawline. I reach over with my right hand and Mia's fingers wrap around my index finger, a tiny clamp, as gentle as a feather. She has the smallest, most exquisite fingernails. I blow a raspberry onto her fingertips and she giggles, a hearty chuckle that warms my heart.

'Nice to meet you, Mia.' I smile down at her. 'My name's Ellen.'

Kathryn has pulled the white rucksack onto her lap. She has a pen in her hand and is busy digging through the contents, rearranging the bottles and nappies packed inside. As she zips it closed, her iPhone starts ringing again, vibrating against the plastic tabletop. The screen displays a man's face, thirtyish, dark ginger hair, stubble, a kink in the bridge of his nose as though at some point it has been broken. The name below the image is *Dominic.*

'Sounds like he's keen to get hold of you,' I say.

'I'd better answer.' She nods distractedly, glancing again at the phone's display. 'Would you be all right with Mia just while I take this call? It's . . . urgent.'

'Sure. Go ahead, we'll be fine for a minute.'

'I'll just be down there.' She gestures over her shoulder, down the carriage. 'I'll be back.'

I look up again and I swear I see tears glistening in her eyes.

'Kathryn, are you sure you're all right?'

'Yeah,' she says, getting up out of her seat. 'Thank you. I won't be long.'

She reaches out and touches her fingertips gently to the crown of the baby's head, as if reluctant to leave her even for a moment. Then she takes her phone down the aisle, towards the end of the carriage, mobile clamped to her ear.

Mia gazes up at me and yawns, blue eyes blinking shut for a moment. I rock her gently from side to side, her wonderful weight in the crook of my arm, the unfamiliar smile returning to my lips. My heart fills my chest, a powerful rush like the strongest drug, a tide of emotion I haven't felt in so long that I've wondered whether it even still exists inside me.

I allow myself to imagine – just for a moment – what it would be like if this little one was mine. If I was returning from the hospital with a baby in my arms, instead of a prognosis even bleaker than the last time. To finally use the little box bedroom for what it had been intended for, saved for: a nursery. Instead of a quiet, empty corner of the house left in stasis like a shrine to a life unfulfilled, to something that will never be. I've imagined this for so long, dreamed of it, of night feeds and cuddles and tiny fingers, walks in the park and first words and bedtime stories. All the little things that parents take for granted. I lean closer to Mia's forehead, breathing in that indefinable soft-sweet baby scent of pure, clean skin and talcum powder and new life. Wondering if Kathryn knows how lucky she is.

There's a shift in the train's momentum, its speed easing as it begins to decelerate into the next station, the last stop before Marylebone. Open countryside has been replaced by busy little villages and roads, church steeples and barn conversions, commuter land on the way into north-west London. I look up to see if Kathryn's on her way back, but she's still hidden from my view in the vestibule connecting the two carriages. How long has she been gone now? Two minutes? Three?

The next stop slides into view. *Seer Green & Jordans*, a little two-platform country station with a footbridge and a small wood-panelled waiting room, a handful of people waiting to board. Kathryn has not reappeared. The train wheezes to a stop in a shudder of brakes, three long beeps as the carriage doors slide open and a few passengers step down onto the platform. I raise myself carefully out of my seat and look around, checking the other way down the carriage in case Kathryn has somehow slipped past while I've been busy with Mia. But I can only see the football fans, all in identical red and white-striped shirts, with close-cropped hair and long legs sticking out into the aisle. The seats across from me are occupied by a small red-faced man in a pinstriped suit, who has managed to spread out his briefcase, laptop, newspaper and raincoat across five of the six seats, as well as the little table. He has not looked over at me once.

'Excuse me,' I say to him. 'I don't suppose you saw the woman sitting here? Did she come past us just now?'

The man glances up, gives a single irritated shake of his head, and goes back to his laptop. I'm about to stand up, to walk down the carriage in search of her, when movement outside catches my eye. A figure hurrying past, right by my window. A blonde woman in a rust-coloured jacket.

Kathryn is walking away down the platform.

2

It takes a second to process what I'm seeing, to make sense of what my eyes are telling me. Is Kathryn suddenly ill? Confused? Is it a prank? Has someone taken her jacket, walked off the train wearing it?

No.

It's her. Blonde hair swishing from side to side as she marches down the platform, hands thrust deep into the pockets of her jacket, head down as if she doesn't want to make eye contact with anyone. I lean over to rap on the window as she passes, the glass cold against my knuckles, the move made awkward by the baby on my left side.

'Hey!' I shout, sensing other passengers turning towards me. 'Kathryn! Hey!'

She looks up and our eyes meet for just a second, long enough for me to see the expression on her face, to notice the tears on her cheeks. She mouths a single word. *Sorry.* Then drops her gaze and hurries on, wiping her eyes and striding down the platform towards the barriers.

A second later and she's out of sight.

An automated female voice comes over the speakers. 'This train for London Marylebone only. Please take care of the closing doors.'

A handful of new passengers have boarded for the final stretch of the journey, hoisting bags into racks and looking for seats. The train doors slide shut with a hiss of finality. This isn't supposed to be happening. It's a mistake, some kind of misunderstanding. I was just going to hold Mia for a few minutes, give Kathryn a moment's respite, then hand the baby back. I don't really know how to look after—

Someone is talking to me.

'Sorry, what?' I turn to face a thin man in a black beanie hat standing next to my seat. 'What were you saying?'

The man points a bony finger at the seat Kathryn has just vacated, her rucksack left behind next to it.

'Is that free?' He's holding up all the other passengers trying to move down the carriage but seems oblivious.

'She just had to make a phone call,' I say. 'She's coming back in a minute. Sorry.'

He stares at me for a moment and then asks the same question of the red-faced businessman at the table opposite, who grunts a reluctant affirmative. The thin man settles himself into the seat, folding his long legs beneath him and taking a laptop out of his rucksack.

The hum of the engine rises as the train begins to move again. Rolling slowly at first, the platform at Seer Green starts to slide by, past a blue-painted steel fence separating the station from the car park beyond, massed ranks of vehicles side by side. Passengers carry bags and clutch tickets as they walk towards the station exit.

I catch a glimpse of a couple of men shaking hands, two middle-aged women embracing; a station worker in a high-vis jacket; a man in a parka, a couple of teenagers walking in; a single figure in a raincoat. I stare out of the window, disbelief fogging my thoughts, as if the train might stop at any moment, as if the situation will put itself right if I just wait a few more seconds. The red-faced man across the aisle is glaring at me with undisguised irritation, his brows knitted together. I return his stare with one of my own, and he drops his eyes back to his laptop.

I throw one last look back at the platform. Perhaps Kathryn was meeting someone here. Then my view is blocked by trees as the train angles away from the station, picking up speed. For a split second I think about standing up and pulling the emergency cord before we've got too far out of the station. Is it a genuine emergency? Is anyone in danger? What's the best thing for Mia?

The baby whimpers in my arms.

'Shh,' I say in a soft voice, rocking her gently. 'Did I startle you? Shh, it's OK.'

Mia settles again and stares up at me with big blue eyes. A long lazy blink and a small smile that makes my heart swell. I'm a calm person; I need to stay calm for the baby's sake. Mia doesn't seem to need anything right now, she isn't crying to be fed or changed or rubbing her eyes for a sleep; she seems happy enough to be held for the time being.

No one else in the carriage seems to be aware of what's just happened. I am on my own with a stranger's baby. Where's the guard or the ticket inspector when you need one? I should find one of them, get them to radio back to the previous station and tell them to keep Kathryn there. The next station's the end of the line – Marylebone – and I can wait there with Mia until Kathryn comes in on the next train. They run every half hour and I have nothing else in my diary for today, nothing calling me home. I could even offer to get straight onto the next train back to Seer Green. Reunite mother and daughter, put all of this right.

There's only one problem with all of that, one doubt niggling at the back of my mind: I'm assuming that Kathryn *wants* to get the little girl back. That she *wants* to be reunited. That this is all some terrible mistake, a momentary lapse of concentration, an exhausted young mother at the end of her tether. A cry for help, perhaps. Postnatal depression?

But what's just happened seemed entirely deliberate. Calculated. Planned, almost. And I saw the look on Kathryn's face as she walked away. A single glance as she hurried down the platform.

I knew that look; I've seen it before. A long way from here, many years ago, in a different life.

Fear.

Fear for herself, or for her baby? Fear of what she'd just done, or what she might be about to do?

I scramble to make sense of the fragments I've gathered in the last ten minutes. A young mother travelling alone. Bruises on her arm. Phone ringing constantly. A brittle, tearful unease she was struggling to disguise, just beneath the surface. Her child left with a total stranger. There doesn't seem to be anything accidental about it: she'd done it to protect the child, somehow. And now that child is my responsibility, for the time being, at least.

Taking Mia straight back to her might mean putting her right into harm's way. Into contact with the father who left Kathryn with those bruises on her arm. Perhaps social services would be able to keep her safe, or perhaps Mia and her mother would end up as two more statistics, two more casualties of a violent, controlling man taking out his rage on a partner who dared to leave him. It's a depressingly familiar story, as old as marriage itself. But what other choice do I have? It's not as if I can take Mia home, back to my little house in South Greenford, is it?

I let the thought sit for a moment, like a forbidden taste on my tongue.

Then I dismiss it. Mia has a mother, and she belongs with her.

The train picks up speed as it pushes deeper into north-west London, streets and shops and houses passing by. My phone vibrates with a text and I shift Mia to one arm as I wrestle it out of my handbag.

How you doing? You OK? Xx

Which is Tara's coded way of asking: *how did this morning go with the specialist? Do you want to talk about it?*

I put my phone face down on the table. Tara can wait. I look up and see the thin man across the aisle staring at me. As soon as I make eye contact with him, he looks down at his phone again. He's wearing black fingerless gloves and is holding the phone at a strange angle, almost vertical.

Did he just take a picture of me and the baby? Or did I imagine it?

He shifts in his seat under the weight of my stare, angling the phone away from me. His laptop is open in front of him. There's something strange about his fingertips, the skin wrinkled and pale. His black beanie cap has ridden up slightly and I notice for the first time that he has no eyebrows at all, the skin above his eyes a strange, mottled-red blank. There's something weird about him altogether, as if he doesn't belong here and doesn't quite know how to act.

I feel my left arm stiffening around Mia's small body, tucking her in a little closer. Now that we're alone together, she feels as delicate as porcelain in my arms, as if any bump or jolt might break her perfect skin, fracture her tiny bones. Every stranger turning into a potential threat.

I tell myself to relax. For the next ten minutes at least, there is nothing that is going to hurt her, nothing will happen to her. I'll take care of her until we get to the next stop – the end of the line – and then find someone responsible, someone in authority, explain what's happened and make sure Mia's in safe hands. I'll do the right thing.

I flip my phone over. I could call 101, ask for the British Transport Police and get them on the case. They'd have officers at Marylebone or nearby, close enough to respond and reunite mother and baby. But – again – that's assuming that Kathryn actually *wants* her baby back. Maybe it *is* postnatal depression, and she was worried she might harm her baby. It would be better to talk to the police in person.

I touch a gentle fingertip to the baby's cheek in what I hope is a soothing gesture.

'What are we going to do with you, little one?'

Mia gives me another gummy smile, a little chuckle. There's something about a baby's laugh that defies words – something perfect and pure and joyful – this human thing she has only just learned to do, an expression of happiness in its original form. It has to be the best sound in the world.

She seems unaware, or undisturbed, by her mother's sudden absence. Perhaps she'll start to fret and cry soon, whimpering in that way small babies do, but for now she seems calm.

What else could help me to get her back where she belongs? I don't even know Kathryn's surname. She has taken her handbag and phone but left the baby's bag, the bulky white rucksack that's full of baby stuff. That means something, doesn't it? That it was deliberate? Another thought strikes me: *maybe the baby wasn't even Kathryn's in the first place.* Had she actually said it was? Did she use the words 'my baby' at any point? I think back to our brief exchange. *No.* She only said 'Mia' or 'her' – or was it 'the baby'? Had she taken Mia from someone else? From a nursery, or a hospital, from someone's house? Snatched her from a pushchair outside a shop, or in the aisle of a supermarket? Then panicked and handed her off to a stranger before she could be caught?

But something about her manner, our brief conversation, makes me think it's unlikely. There was a familiarity between Kathryn and Mia, a connection that seemed genuine.

I lean over and pick up the rucksack. It's deceptively heavy and not easy, one-handed, with the baby snug in my other arm, but I manage to hoist it up and put it down next to me. In one of the mesh pockets on the side is a bottle of formula milk, in the other a half-drunk bottle of Diet Coke. I undo the zip and pull the bag open.

At the top of a bundle of baby clothes is a single sheet of A4 paper, folded once. It's a receipt or delivery note of some kind, a list of baby things, formula milk, bottles, nappies, clothes. I pull it out and frown. The word 'Ellen' is written in looping capitals on the bottom half.

I turn the paper over.

The back is blank except for a handful of words scrawled hastily in the centre, in messy black biro.

Please protect Mia
Don't trust the police
Don't trust anyone

3

I frown at the sheet of paper in my hand. Read the words a second time, turn the paper over to see if there is anything else on it, anything at all. But it's just a computer-printed delivery note from a company called BabyCool.com. Nothing else handwritten, only my name on the front and, on the back, those ten words scrawled in biro. Instinctively, I fold the paper in two and check to see if anyone else has seen what I've seen. But the businessman is tapping on his laptop and the thin staring man is writing in a small notebook, seemingly oblivious to me and everything else.

Don't trust anyone

Perhaps paranoia's a feature of postnatal depression. Is it? I can't remember what I've read. Perhaps Kathryn feared that she might do something to the child herself. Perhaps this is all a cry for help. But not for *her* safety. For the baby.

It occurs to me that there might be something else inside the backpack. I lay the note on the table and begin taking items out of the bag one at a time, setting them on the small table in front of me. Half a dozen nappies, a packet of wet wipes, a tight roll of plastic nappy sacks, two white cotton sleepsuits, vests, scratch mittens and a tiny knitted woollen hat, three bottles of formula milk made up and a small can of formula powder, half-full. Two folded muslin squares, one white and one yellow. Two dummies, still in their blister pack. Some kind of harness – Baby Bjorn – with a complicated set of straps that I recognise as a baby sling. In the front pocket of the rucksack is a new tube of Sudocrem, a travel packet of tissues and a small bottle of sunblock. Another piece of paper, torn from a notebook, with some kind of daily schedule scribbled on it in the same handwriting as the note I'd found with my name on it. A column of instructions down the left-hand side: *6-7 feed/change, 8.30 nap, 10 feed, 11 nap, 12.30 feed/change, 1 nap, 3 feed, 3.30 nap, 6 bedtime routine, 6.45 feed/bed.* A squashy purple octopus with a smiling yellow face, a bell inside that jingles when I take it out of the bag.

Mia's head turns toward the sound of the bell, hands grasping.

'You want this?' I pick up the toy, hold it out to her. 'The octopus?'

Mia coos and clutches the toy to herself, small mouth closing on a soft fabric tentacle.

I survey the train table, covered with the contents of the rucksack. All the paraphernalia needed to leave the house with a baby. Enough for a day out, perhaps? A second day, at a push. Then what? Maybe this was just as much as Kathryn could carry, as much as she could gather in a hurry and pack into a single bag. But there is nothing else which gives a clue to her identity, her full name or where she lives. Nothing to quickly identify Mia to the authorities, to get her back to her family as soon as possible. The daily schedule is curious and I wonder if it's been written for my benefit. But she'd not had time to write it in the minutes that I held the baby. Just my name, and that strange message, after we'd first said hello. I'm at a loss to work out why she has chosen me.

The football supporters at the far end of the carriage are singing another song, the words interrupted by hoots of laughter and shouted obscenities and I make a mental note to give them a wide berth when we get off.

People begin to stand up as the train slows, pulling bags from the luggage racks and shrugging on coats and jackets, an air of purpose filling the carriage as the train approaches its final destination. The red-faced man in the pinstripe suit opposite gathers up his possessions into a briefcase, puts on his jacket and hurries down the aisle, barely giving me a second glance. I begin to repack Mia's bag, putting the spare clothes at the bottom, the formula milk and nappies near the top. One more quick glance at Kathryn's strange note before I slip it into my handbag and slowly get to my feet, making sure to keep a firm hold on Mia.

How do you put on a rucksack when you're holding a baby? Everything – every move, every previously simple action – now seems loaded with extra layers of complexity. Laying Mia very gently on the seat, I swing the rucksack up onto my back, then pass my handbag strap over my head, keeping my eyes on Mia the whole time in case she tries to flip herself onto the floor. But the baby simply grins at me, happily kicking her chubby legs like a little frog learning to swim, and I scoop her up again.

'Come on, you,' I say softly. 'Let's go and find your mummy.'

The strange thin man is still in his seat, scribbling in his notebook in tiny, spidery handwriting. He doesn't seem to notice any of the activity and doesn't look up as I pass. He's dressed entirely in black and dark grey, I notice. Black jeans and Doc Martens, grey sweatshirt and a scuffed black leather jacket. Not a single note of colour; the skin of his face so pale it is almost translucent. Something else strange about him, still nagging at me. Something not quite right.

I step carefully down onto the platform, the air filled with echoing footsteps and thick with diesel exhaust. Marylebone is rich with Victorian red brick, steel girders criss-crossing the glass roof high above. I move away from the train door, look up and down the platform in case Kathryn has somehow managed to get back onto the train at Seer Green and is here right now, searching for her baby, hoping I might catch sight of her rust-coloured jacket moving towards us amid the disembarking travellers. A sea of faces travels down the platform, a group of slow-moving pensioners, a young family on a day trip, shoppers and students and a few suited commuters mixed in. No young women scanning the crowd. No sign of Kathryn.

I look down at the baby in my arms, Mia blinking against the bright light, and begin walking towards the main concourse. At the barrier I reach into my handbag for my ticket, searching awkwardly with my right hand while my left supports Mia. I try to reach into my jacket pocket, just about managing to push down into it with my right hand. Not in there either. Someone tuts loudly in the queue behind me, moving away to another of the ticket barriers. Was it in my trouser pocket? I pat the pockets of my jeans but can't feel its outline. The guard, a smiling fiftyish woman with short dark hair, comes over and gives Mia a little wave.

Should I tell the guard what's happened? Or would she just direct me to the nearest police officer? I'm trying to think of the right words to use but the guard isn't looking at me, she's grinning at Mia.

'Aren't you a little cutie?' the woman says, as the baby regards her with slow-blinking blue eyes. 'Let's give your mummy a hand, shall we?'

She taps her own pass on the sensor and the grey plastic barrier swings open.

'Thank you,' I say, a small bloom of relief in my chest. 'You're very kind.'

The guard gives Mia another one-finger wave.

'Have a lovely day, you two.'

I walk into the main concourse and look for signs to an information point, a ticket office or wherever the station manager might be. Do the British Transport Police have offices in the big stations? I've never seen one in Marylebone, but then I've never really looked either. In central London it feels like anything that isn't a stabbing or a terror alert is a long way down the police pecking order. Is this the sort of thing they would deal with on the spot, like an imminent threat to life? Not really.

Reaching the station concourse proper, I catch sight of my reflection in the window of a shop and I'm momentarily disorientated by the shadowy image of myself with a baby tucked into my arm. It's almost like I'm looking into a parallel life, a parallel universe, where the last round of IVF has worked and I've had Richard's baby. And here I am bringing our daughter home, the wonderful warm little heft of a baby in my arms.

I know that parallel life isn't real. And yet, here I am, with Mia.

With a jolt, I catch another reflection in the glass. Just behind me, keeping pace with steady strides, black beanie hat on his head. The thin man from the carriage is following me.

4

He's walking slowly with a strange, spidery gait alongside a handful of other passengers. Pretending to be looking at his phone while he walks. I think of the bruises on Kathryn's arm. The fear in her eyes. Perhaps this was the boyfriend? Not the broken-nose guy on the phone, but this man? Seeing him among regular passengers just adds to his sense of *otherness*, a sense of not belonging that seems to radiate from him. I quicken my pace.

Further behind me there are shouts, loud and angry, male voices full of protest. Some kind of row breaking out back on the platform. I glance over my shoulder to see the red-and-white shirted football fans held up at the barrier, arguing with the guards – something about tickets – their faces contorted with anger, swigging from cans of lager. The fans shouting, swearing to let them through, their mates joining in the protest, yellow-jacketed platform staff gravitating towards the commotion to calm it by sheer force of numbers.

'Stand back!'

'Open the bastard gate then!'

I walk faster, the shouts from the ticket barrier cutting through the air behind me. Another group of young men approach in a loose group from the opposite direction, a dozen of them in their twenties, jeans and tattoos, blue football shirts. Fists aloft as they shout their songs, belligerent voices echoing off the roof of the station. A shouted challenge as they see the opposition fans held up at the ticket barrier, other passengers skittering to the side, backing off to clear a path between the two sets of fans. Gestures and taunts and more swearing, a hurled can arcing through the air, landing with a flat *smack* and a spray of lager on the platform.

Mia whimpers at the sudden noise. I obey my instincts. I quicken my pace away from the confrontation, avoiding eye contact and shifting my path away from the men, my whole body tensing against the noise and aggression. With a ferocity I haven't felt in years, I feel my right hand curling into a fist in the certainty that I will flatten the first one who dares to lay a finger on Mia.

The football fans pass by, a fug of beer breath and sweat and pungent aftershave in their wake.

I check my reflection in another shop window. The thin guy is still following me.

At the far end of the concourse is the sign for the exit: the remainder of the journey that awaits me. A five-minute walk down to Edgware Road tube, Circle line to Notting Hill, change to the Central line then eight stops to South Greenford and the walk up the main road, through the park to my cold, empty house. I've done the return trip to the specialist so many times these past five years, I can do it in my sleep now. And until half an hour ago, I thought of little beyond taking that last leg of my journey back from the clinic, sitting on the Tube on autopilot, knowing my own stop without even having to look up. It would be easy to let my feet take me there now, following that familiar route.

Easy, but wrong.

Finally, I spot a pair of police uniforms. A couple of armed policemen stand guard, their backs to a tall column in the centre of the concourse. They wear body armour and are bulky with equipment, black straps and pouches and radios, pistols on their thighs and rifles across their chests, index fingers resting against trigger guards. Instead of feeling relief, though, I find myself repulsed by them, by the closeness of these weapons to the tiny life in my arms. I'm no stranger to guns, but this is different.

Still, I'm going to have to talk to them, tell them what's happened. We'll all go to a back office, and I'll give a statement and fill in some forms, and they'll take the baby away from me. I'll hand Mia over and that will be that. Hand her over to these men with their guns, these men equipped for war on the streets.

The thought gives me a cold, empty sensation, a pinch of unease in my stomach.

Today, here, now, I see threats everywhere. I have a powerful urge to take Mia as far away from these guns as possible. And I can't stop thinking about the note in the baby's bag. *Don't trust the police.* But what option do I have? I think we could have been followed off the train, and it seems clear that Kathryn, wherever she is, is in some kind of trouble. I head for the two armed officers, preparing what I will say. *This baby? She's not mine. She was given to me . . .* But as I approach, one of them touches his earpiece, speaks briefly into his radio, and then both hurry off towards the platforms without giving me a second glance.

I turn and watch them go, their equipment jingling as they jog towards the confrontation between the two sets of football fans, which is getting louder all the time. I can't see any other police on the concourse. Maybe the ticket office? But this station isn't a safe place. Guns, shouting, drunks, noise, crowds. Anger. Hooligans. Police on the lookout for knife-wielding terrorists and suicide bombers. I glance over my shoulder: the weirdo from the train is still following me. But it's not just him, this whole place makes me uneasy. There's danger everywhere and I feel exposed – it isn't a safe environment for Mia. Thousands of people coming and going, packed together but oblivious to each other amid the hurry and the rush and the noise. There is a reason why train stations are a favourite target for terrorists.

Not here.

Don't trust anyone.

Kathryn trusted me. She *chose* me.

If I have even a shadow of a doubt, even a flicker, I should trust that instinct to protect the baby. I have to make that decision for her.

I feel the weight of it, having to be responsible for others again.

I scan the station one more time for any other police officers, but see none.

Behind me, the shouting kicks up a notch.

Get away from them, all of them. Put distance between them and you, between them and Mia.

There has to be a smarter, safer way of doing this. I should find somewhere quieter and more controlled. I switch Mia to my other arm and she stares at me, on the edge of tears now, her little body rigid with alarm at the shouting and the noise.

'We're nearly there, Mia,' I say. 'Not long now until you're back with your mum.'

But first I need to put some space between me and the strange man who's followed us off the train, whether it's me or the baby in my arms that he's following. It'll only take a minute to break contact, but I need a helping hand. I approach a stocky fortyish man in a yellow high-vis tabard with 'Station Security' printed on the back, while he's encouraging a homeless man to move away from the cash machines.

'Excuse me?' I say.

The security guard turns, his broad face impassive. 'How can I help?'

'I'm really sorry to bother you but a man's followed me off the train and he's been taking pictures of my baby.' I turn and point at the thin man. 'He's making me really uncomfortable and I just want him to leave us alone.'

'That gentleman?' He points a thick finger, his face darkening into a frown. 'In the black jacket?'

'That's him.'

'Are you both OK?'

'I think so,' I give Mia's hand a protective pat. 'Just a bit freaked out.'

'Wait here, madam, I'll have a word with him.'

He turns and approaches him with his palms up in calming gesture, speaking quietly.

I register the look of surprise on the thin man's face, but I don't wait to see what happens next. I turn away, smile down at Mia and walk towards the big archways that lead out of the station onto Melcombe Place, where the mid-afternoon sun is fighting its way through thinning clouds. I want to lose myself in the bustle of passengers coming and going, to get away from everyone who could be a threat.

I'll do the right thing for Mia, but first we have to go somewhere safe; in the meantime I'll take care of her for just a little while longer.

I walk quickly out of the station and head for the taxi rank without looking back.

5

Melcombe Place is busy with afternoon traffic and there's a short queue at the taxi rank. I join the line, heart thrumming in my chest, keeping my eyes on the station exit in case the thin man emerges before I can get into a cab. There's no sign so far but I know there is a side entrance too – he might go that way instead. Mia squirms a little and I jig her gently in my arm, the muscles already starting to ache from carrying her.

The taxi queue moves with painful slowness, a line of black cabs rolling slowly forward, engines rumbling as passengers get in and then pull away towards the junction with Great Central Street.

Come on, come on.

I'm queuing behind a white-haired couple in their seventies who I recognise from the train, the man in a jacket and tie and his wife in a dress and good shoes, dressed for a London day out, maybe a show. The woman turns around and sees me for the first time, her face softening at the sight of Mia.

'Oh, she is *gorgeous*.' She squeezes Mia's pink-shoed foot. 'Aren't you?'

Mia gives her a wide-eyed smile.

'Come on Mike, let this lady go first.'

'What?' her husband says. 'Oh. Yes, of course.'

He stands aside and gestures for me to go ahead of them.

'Thank you,' I say.

A cab pulls up and the white-haired man opens the door for us, allowing me to clamber in. I slam the door shut and check the station exit again: still no sign of the weirdo from the platform.

'Hi,' I say to the taxi driver. 'Where's the nearest police station?'

'Which one do you mean?'

'Whichever's nearest?'

The driver, a heavy man in his early forties, pushes a button to start the meter running. 'West End Central, probably.' He turns slightly in his seat to look at me, his eyes flicking to Mia and then back again. 'Is everything all right, love?'

'Fine.'

'You sure? Is the nipper OK?'

'We're both fine,' I say, shrugging off the rucksack and settling back into the seat. The cab smells of old leather and a sickly vanilla air freshener. 'Thanks for asking.'

He grunts and puts the cab in gear, the door locks clicking shut as he pulls out into the traffic. I've been in a million black cabs before but never with a baby, and can't work out how to put the seat belt on in a way that would protect both me and her so I just leave it, curling my right hand around Mia's small head instead. The driver is fast, swooping in and out of gaps in the traffic, and I wish he would slow down.

I turn to look through the rear window twice as the taxi makes its way towards Marylebone Road, looking for any signs that the man is still following me. I don't see him, or any black cab he might have flagged down. Switching Mia back to my left side to give my right arm a rest, I let myself relax into the worn back seat as the shops and offices pass by on each side. For the first time, it hits me how surreal the situation is: it's a Tuesday afternoon and I'm in a cab holding a stranger's child, on my way to a police station. Forty minutes ago I had never met this baby, this little person, and now – for the next few minutes at least – Mia is completely and utterly reliant on me in a way that no one has ever been before. Her life is *literally* in my hands, and it's wonderful, a joy – terrifying but somehow the greatest privilege, all at the same time.

It's a little like I imagined it would be to be pregnant and showing, people holding doors open and even giving up their seat for you on the Tube. None of my own pregnancies made it beyond the first trimester. *Unexplained infertility*, the specialist calls it. A shorthand term for when they've done all their tests, and tried all the treatments, and still can't give a reason.

Perhaps today will be the closest I ever get.

It's best not to let my mind linger on that for too long.

After half a mile in stop-start traffic, my heartbeat has slowed to something near normal, the adrenaline wearing off as the taxi winds its way along Edgware Road. I think about Kathryn for a moment, go back over what she had said on the train. Her note asked me not to contact the police. No, that wasn't it. She'd said don't *trust* the police. But that makes no sense. If she's running from *him*, from her abusive partner, why avoid police involvement? I take the crumpled note from my handbag again.

Please protect Mia
Don't trust the police
Don't trust anyone

Unless her partner's a police officer himself – could that be what Kathryn meant? The one who kept ringing her, or the guy on the train? Perhaps one's the ex-husband and the other a new partner. Or maybe they're *both* exes. Kathryn's an attractive woman. But even if one of them is a policeman, I don't see what other options I have. It's not as if I can just take Mia home. Not even for a single night, not even for the afternoon, just to make sure she's safe, just to—

No. I'm not going to do that, however much I might want to.

I need to work out what to say to the police, how to frame it. Just tell the truth, that's all I have to do. It's all I *can* do. No need to add or change anything. I'll go into West End Central police station, go to the front desk and find someone in charge, tell them exactly what happened.

I got on at Aylesbury. I was on my way back from the fertility unit at Stoke Mandeville. Kathryn came and sat down at some point after that. I don't know for sure whether that's where she got on. But she got off at Seer Green and left the baby with me. I only realised she'd got off as the train was about to pull away. Then I found this note in the baby's bag. Why didn't I call someone immediately? I didn't think it was an emergency. I was going to talk to armed officers at Marylebone but they were called away, so I thought it would be better to take her to the nearest police station.

I rock the baby and straighten her little jacket, Mia fidgeting and squirming. Her dummy falls out onto the floor of the taxi and when I pick it up there's dirt and dust on it. I've seen Tara's normal response to this – put it in your own mouth to give it a quick suck to 'clean' it, then give it back to baby – but I don't particularly fancy that considering the likely state of the taxi floor. I drop it in a side pocket of my handbag instead and jig the baby in what I hope is a soothing way.

'Shh, it's OK,' I say gently. 'You'll be back with your mum soon. Shh.'

I'll tell the police everything that's happened, sign the forms and hand Mia over. That's what I'll do.

I gaze down into her little face, the steady sway of the taxi rocking her gently this way and that. Will I ever see her again after today? Ever hold her like this again, like a mother? Probably not. My throat tightens at the thought of it.

The baby is grizzling and fretting now, her smile replaced by red cheeks and a little frown. I open the rucksack next to her and dig around one-handed until I find the packet of dummies, extract one from the packet and pop it into Mia's open mouth. Almost immediately the dummy comes out and I catch it in my hand this time. Mia's cries start to grow in volume, the pitch rising.

I rock her gently in my arms, shifting her up to my shoulder and rubbing her back.

'What's the matter, Mia?'

The baby's cry is sharp and high-pitched, an angry yowl that fills the back of the taxi. I catch the driver looking at me in the rearview mirror, and wonder briefly whether he thinks I'm a bad mother who can't cope. I lift Mia up, turn her wriggling body slightly, sniff her sleepsuit. Clean cotton and the faintest hint of nappy cream. Doesn't smell like she needs changing.

'What do you want, Mia? We're going to be there soon, not long now.'

I present the dummy again and for a moment she calms, sucking furiously, before she opens her mouth to cry again, the dummy falling out once more. I shake my head, shushing her with a gentle voice, frustrated with myself. I always thought I'd be *better* than this. Better at figuring things out. But this feels like an exam I haven't revised for, an interview where I don't even know what the job involves. But I'm *not* an absolute beginner. I've spent enough time with Tara's kids to figure out the answer. I stroke Mia's downy cheek with a fingertip and the baby's mouth moves towards it, seeking it out, her lips forming a desperate little 'o'.

Ah. I remember the other handwritten note I'd found in the backpack. I check my watch – almost 3 p.m. – and scan the street, check behind again, but can't see anyone. No other taxi has followed us from the station.

I can do this. Mia needs to be safe but she also needs to be fed. Cared for properly.

Her cries intensify as she works herself up into a frenzy, a high-pitched wailing that makes every muscle in my body tense. I spot a Caffè Nero coming up on the right-hand side and lean forward towards the driver.

'Actually,' I say through the hole in the clear plastic barrier between me and the front seats, 'could we pull over here, please?'

I know, in my head, that we shouldn't stop. I've already strung this out longer than I should. Screaming baby or not, I should go straight on to the police station and hand her over to the authorities, someone in uniform, social services, some faceless arm of the local council. But the baby in my arms is hungry. I'll feed her, just once, before giving her up. It doesn't seem like too much to ask. I will be a mother to her for just a little bit longer.

It will only be a few extra minutes. That's all.

6

The taxi driver indicates and pulls to the side of the road.

'You sure you want to stop here?' he says. 'Cop shop is a bit further.'

'This is fine, thanks.'

He half-turns in his seat to look at me.

'Do you want a hand with your bags, love?'

'No,' I say, opening the door awkwardly and pushing it wide with my left foot. 'I'm fine, thank you though.'

I pay him and get out, stepping down onto the pavement, careful not to overbalance with baby and backpack.

Thankfully the café is not too busy and I find a table against the back wall next to a willowy blonde woman with a curly-haired boy of around three years old. The boy's playing on her phone while she nurses a large coffee with cream on top. Mia is still fretting and squirming, her little arms and legs pulsing in frustration. I go to the table and unsling the rucksack, pulling out my phone and sending Tara a quick message.

Random question: if at a café, how long do you heat a 200ml bottle of formula milk in the microwave for? X

TRUST ME | 41

I picture my friend, at home with her two youngest sons, probably getting ready for the short drive to pick up her eldest from school. She always keeps her phone to hand – *stops me from going fully baby-mental*, she says – and true to form her replies are almost immediate, three messages dropping in one after the other.

??? 😮
Erm . . .
You OK? X

I frown at the screen and type a quick response.

All fine. Just indulge me?

Mia's hungry cries are coming more frequently now, her little face screwing up in exasperation. I stare at the phone, willing my friend to reply quickly, walking small circles as I jig Mia on my shoulder. Finally a new message arrives with a ping.

Café won't microwave in case baby gets scalded and you sue.
Ask for a jug of hot water to stand the bottle in til warm x

Another message, seconds later.

What's going on? X

I type one-handed, shushing the baby.

Thanks. Asking for a friend

I put the phone down on the table and it pings again almost immediately, then again. I ignore it, pulling the curved bottle of formula milk from the side pocket of the rucksack and giving it a shake.

Five minutes later I'm sitting back down at the table with the bottle in a jug of steaming water, the barista following me with a cup of tea. I keep jigging Mia gently up and down to keep her cries from reaching an ear-splitting level. I grab a muslin cloth from the rucksack and shake the bottle of formula again, squirting a few drops onto my wrist to test the temperature – warm but not too warm. The relief is immediate when Mia latches on to the bottle. I can hear Tara's voice in my head: *keep the bottle tipped up so there is no air in the teat, just milk.* I've fed my godsons from time to time, but it's different when the mother isn't in the next room, when there's no one to hand the baby back to.

Mia begins sucking the milk down in greedy gulps, her whole body relaxing and calming in an ecstasy of feeding, piercing blue eyes focusing on my face as if I'm the only person in the whole world.

While Mia drinks, I glance at the other mid-afternoon coffee-drinkers in the café. There are only a handful of customers. A fortyish guy on crutches, his left leg in plaster up to the knee. A woman in bright yellow Lycra at the counter, studying the cakes and pastries behind the glass. A couple of site workers having a breather over a cup of tea in the corner. A guy in his sixties surrounded by newspapers, pen poised over a crossword.

Calm. Safe. No police, no hooligans, no weirdos from the train. My left arm aches from holding Mia, but it's a good ache.

My phone rings, vibrating against the table, the ringtone loud in the quiet café. Tara's face shows on the screen, but with the baby in the crook of my elbow and my right hand holding the bottle, I can't pick it up. I let it ring until the tune abruptly cuts off.

I smile down at Mia as she sucks busily on the bottle of formula milk, already half finished. I know I need to wind her, to get some burps up, but am I supposed to do that now or when the bottle's finished? I'm not sure. I pull gently on the bottle and it slides out of Mia's hungry mouth, leaving her lips still puckered in a surprised 'o' shape. The blonde woman at the table next to me is leaning over, handing me something.

'Here you go,' she says, holding out a square of soft white muslin cloth. 'You dropped this.'

'Thanks,' I say, shaking it and draping it back over my shoulder, ready for any milk that comes back up.

'Just have a little breather,' I say gently to Mia, putting the bottle on the table. 'Then you can have more.'

But Mia has other ideas, a frown of disappointment clouding her face, eyes flicking left and right, searching for the bottle that was there moments before. Little high-pitched squeaks of desperation burst from her, each a little louder than the last.

'OK,' I say with a smile. 'Maybe you don't want a breather.'

I lift the bottle and Mia latches on again immediately. I've imagined doing this so many times with my own baby. Just this. Nothing complicated or greedy about it. Just this simplest thing, this bond between mother and child, building and strengthening and already so powerful I think my heart might crack at the thought of letting Mia go.

And I *can* do it. These last few years of disappointment, lying awake at night I've half-convinced myself that I don't deserve it, that I'm somehow lacking, that there's *some other reason* why

I can't conceive. Some strange logic that I'd never be a good enough mother. But I *can* do this for Mia, I can feed a baby, sustain her, look after her. I straighten the square of muslin cloth on my shoulder and raise her so she's upright, little chin against my shoulder, rubbing her back in a circular motion. For a moment nothing happens, and I wonder if I'm doing it wrong. Then Mia lets out a single explosive burp, then another, so strident in the quiet café that I'm amazed such a loud noise can come from such a small body.

The woman with a toddler at the next table gives me a grin.

'Best sound in the world,' she says.

'She's a hungry girl,' I say, lowering her back into my arm. Mia's eyes are blinking slowly closed, her belly full, sinking into sleep with her mouth still open in a perfect tiny circle. Her head is warm to the touch, her downy cheeks soft and plump like little peaches.

Children don't make memories, I've read, until they're two or three years old. So Mia will never know me, never remember this in the future. My face will be lost, washed away in time like sand in a rising tide, and she'll never know about this strange day, this beautiful hour we spent together. The thought settles with the weight of sadness in my stomach. I take my phone from the table, unlock it – a missed call from Tara – and snap a picture of Mia. Her beautiful, peaceful face filling the screen. A soft, sleepy, contented baby, warm in my arms. This whole day has taken on an unreal, dreamlike quality, like something I've seen in a film or heard about a long time ago.

Two-thirds of the formula milk is gone. Is that enough? I'm not sure. Mia seems content, so I settle her back. I'm pretty sure you're not supposed to reheat milk for a second go-around. Throw it out, sterilise the bottle, make up new formula with boiled water. I've seen Tara do it a hundred times.

Every mother is a first-timer once. Every mother goes through this, has to figure things out one at a time. I just had a later start, that was all, but I'm a fast learner and—

I catch myself, stop myself. My smile fading.

Mia is not mine.

Stop stalling.

I know what I have to do.

Life is not fair, life is never fair. But self-pity is the purest poison if you let it take hold.

I lay Mia flat on the soft bench seat, perching next to her on the edge in case she suddenly rolls onto her side, and take out the baby sling. I turn it this way and that, trying to figure out the complicated set of buckles and fasteners, to work out whether you put the baby in it before or after you place the straps over your shoulders. After, probably, because it would be easier to lower—

'Do you want a hand with that?'

The woman at the table next to me points at the Baby Bjorn.

'Thanks,' I say. 'Still trying to get used to it.'

'I used to wear it with my jacket over the top.'

'Oh, right.' I shrug my jacket off and slip the straps over my shoulders, tightening and adjusting until it seems about right. 'Could you lift her up?'

'Sure,' the woman says, gently lifting Mia under her arms and lowering her into the sling. 'There you go.'

The woman adjusts the carrier so that Mia is propped up snugly, and I slip my jacket on again over the straps. It's a lot easier than holding the baby in my arms – and means I have both hands free.

'Oh my gosh she's *so* like you, isn't she?' The woman smiles admiringly. 'Just a lovely little mini-me.'

'Yes. I suppose she is.'

I realise that I've not touched my own drink. I take a sip, the tea already tepid, and put the cup back on the table. I wasn't thirsty anyway. I stand up, Mia warm and sleepy against my chest, sling the rucksack over my shoulder alongside my handbag. The baby snuffles, her mouth opening in a tiny yawn, but her eyes don't open.

My heart clenches with what I have to do next.

Outside, I go to the kerb and scan the street for another black cab. St George Street is a fairly busy road; there'll be one along in a minute. I look down at Mia's sleeping face, her chubby cheeks and perfect pink eyelids, a tiny bubble of milk on her lips. My phone pings again in my handbag. I dig it out and see the unread messages from Tara.

You back from the clinic already? X
You OK? School run now but will call when I'm back xx

I try to think of a reply that doesn't sound too crazy, thumbs poised over the screen, and begin typing just as a car door opens wide at the kerb, the door swinging inches from my legs. I look up, a hand instinctively covering Mia's back, as a large man in a black bomber jacket jumps out of the driver's seat. With a jolt of shock, I realise I've seen his face before.

Early thirties, dark ginger beard and a broken-bone kink in the bridge of his nose.

The caller on Kathryn's phone.

7

Before I can react, the man snatches my phone and shoves it into his pocket. He's broad and heavily built, the fabric of his bomber jacket stretched taut over his shoulders and arms. He grabs me with his other hand, his grip digging into my wrist.

'Scream and you're dead,' he says, his voice low. 'Now hand her over.'

'What?' I say, my spine rigid with shock. 'What do you want?'

'Give her to me,' he growls, pulling her closer. He tightens his hold on my arm, his iron grip digging into the flesh beneath my jacket. The bruises on Kathryn's arm. Her ringing phone. Frightened eyes. Her husband – boyfriend, partner, ex, whoever the hell he is – has found us. His breath is sour and hot in my face. '*Now!*'

My head swims with fear, shock rendering me numb for a second before I recover enough to try to shake my arm free. I circle my other arm protectively across Mia's back, holding her close, limbs buzzing with adrenaline.

'Get off me!'

His other hand reaches for the baby, fingers digging under the harness, trying to unclip her, to pull her away from me.

'Give her to me!'

Mia jerks, startled, and begins to whimper. The sound sends a bolt of pure anger through my chest and when he releases my arm to make another grab for the baby I open my hand and throw a palm strike at his nose, thrusting upwards good and hard. He sees it coming and dodges to the side, catching my wrist and wrenching it down to the side. I stamp my heel down on the toes of his boot but it doesn't seem to have any effect.

'What the hell is wrong with you!' I shout. I look up and down the street but there's no one looking our way. 'I'm not giving her to you, get away from me!'

He circles me until he has his back to the café, his bulk hiding us both from the customers inside. His eyes are wide and bloodshot, the pupils dilated, flecks of spittle in the thick stubble on his chin. I try to remember what I have in my handbag, what I could use – attack alarm? Keys? Biro? I open my mouth to scream for help but he slaps a meaty palm over my face, the stink of grease and unwashed skin filling my nose.

With his other hand he opens his jacket to show the black butt of a pistol in his waistband. His fingers curl around it, ready to draw.

'I told you not to scream,' he says quietly. He leans in closer, his breath hot and stale. 'Now *shut up* or I'll put a bullet in you.'

A wave of fear washes over me and I will him to keep the pistol where it is, to keep it anywhere apart from pointing at Mia. I remember something I was once taught: *guns are predictable but people are random.* And maybe this man more than most; he's strong and angry, maybe psychotic. Even a single shot might hit the baby.

'OK,' I say, my voice catching in my throat. 'OK, I won't scream.'

'I don't know who you are, I don't know why you've got the baby. And I don't really give a shit. But you're going to give her to me, right now.' He tries to unstrap her again, a rough hand reaching around under my jacket, the other remaining on the butt of the pistol. 'Christ,' he says under his breath, jostling the baby and pushing her to the side. 'How the hell do you undo this thing?'

I scan the street again, my heart racing, looking for a uniform, a passerby, anyone who might intervene or raise the alarm, call the police. A couple of people at a bus stop further down the street, heads bent over their phones. Cars in traffic, a white van, a cycle courier with earphones in. But no one seems to have noticed us. London: capital city of avoiding eye contact, keeping your head down and minding your own business.

As he hunts for straps and buckles, Mia starts to whimper, her little face turning pink.

'What's the matter with her?' he mutters.

'You're frightening her,' I say. 'You startled her, woke her up.'

Mia's whimpering gathers pace towards a full-blown cry.

'*Jesus!*' The man looks nervously up the street as a traffic warden rounds the corner. 'Just get in the bloody car then, you *and* the baby.'

My hands go instinctively to Mia strapped to my chest, cradling her warm back, the shape of her against my own body.

'Or what?'

'Or I'll shoot you and throw your body in the boot.' He shoves me towards the open driver's door. 'Now take off the rucksack and get in the car.'

I jerk the rucksack full of baby things off my shoulder, and throw it into the passenger footwell then go to open the rear door on the driver's side. Fear pulsing hot in my veins, for Mia, for both of us.

'Not in the back,' he says. 'Get in the front. Can you drive?'

'Yes but not with the baby in the—'

'Just get *in* the damn car.'

I lever myself in gingerly so as not to squash Mia against the steering wheel. He slams my door shut and steps away to get into the back, and for a second he's still on the pavement and I'm behind the wheel of the big BMW, engine running, hands on the steering wheel, one thought leaping ahead of all the rest.

Go.

Now.

Just put it into first and floor it before he can get in. Take his car and leave him behind.

I reach for the gearstick, *P – R – N – D – S* printed alongside it.

Shit. Automatic.

I try to push the gear stick into drive but it won't budge, and a second later the man slides into the rear seat, directly behind me, slamming his door shut.

'You driven automatic before?' he said. When I shake my head, he says: 'Press the button on the gearstick to put it into drive. Take it easy on the gas, it's a three litre. Just take us down to the lights and turn left, nice and steady.'

I roll the seat back to make more space, clip the seatbelt over us both and lower the strap so it tucks behind the baby's back. My heart is thudding painfully against my ribcage. I hear the familiar tone of my phone being switched off as I put the BMW in gear and pull out onto St George Street, feeling the rumbling power of the engine under my right foot. Traffic is starting to thicken up as the afternoon ticks towards rush hour.

'That's it,' he says, 'right onto Seymour and up towards the flyover. Nice and easy. If you try to talk to anyone, if you hit the horn, draw attention to us or do anything stupid, if you so much as buzz the window down I will shoot you, OK? Do you understand?'

With a shiver, I feel the blunt shape of the gun barrel pushing through the seat into the small of my back. At this range any bullet would probably kill both of us but I would also crash the car – so as long as we're moving he won't shoot. I hope.

'Listen,' I say, pulling up at the first set of traffic lights. 'Take me instead. I'll go with you, wherever you want to go. I'll do whatever you want to do, and I won't fight or struggle. But let's leave the baby somewhere safe. I can stop at a café or a shop, somewhere with staff, you can take the keys and I can hand her to someone just like Kathryn handed her to me. I promise I won't run, I swear. I'll go with you but let me make sure she's safe.'

'Just drive.'

'She's just going to make a fuss, make noise,' I continue, my mind bouncing from one idea to the next. A dialogue was better than silence – anything to get a sense of my assailant and his intentions. And more importantly, a chance to get Mia out of harm's way. 'You don't want that, her screaming the place down and drawing attention to us. I'll do whatever you want, but let me leave her somewhere safe. Please.'

'Stop talking.' The gun jabs me harder in the back.

I let another minute pass, trying to push the facts into some kind of logical order, my mind flashing on stories of estranged fathers exacting revenge on their own children. I need to establish a rapport: it'll be harder for him to pull the trigger if he knows my name, if he starts to think of me as a human being rather than a nameless victim. If he remembers that Mia is an innocent. But how did he find us? I should have gone straight to the police station. Delaying was stupid. *Stupid.*

I can smell him behind me, a thin trace of deodorant failing to mask the underlying scents of sweat and unwashed clothes. The interior of the car is a mess, the passenger footwell a rubbish dump of screwed-up fast-food wrappers, polystyrene boxes and drinks cartons. The white rucksack lies on a pile of balled up clothes, and in the rearview mirror I can make out the edge of a sleeping bag on the backseat. The whole car smells fetid and stale.

'What do you want with her?' I say.

I flinch as he jabs the barrel of the pistol hard into my back again.

There's silence for a moment before he speaks.

'Who *are* you, exactly?'

'My name's Ellen Devlin, I'm forty-one, I live in South Greenford, I'm a project manager for an aerospace company.'

'What the hell were you doing in that bloody café anyway? I was about to come in there and drag you out.'

'She was hungry, I had to feed her.'

He points over my shoulder, at a road up ahead.

'Take the next right. The filter lane, there.'

I do as I'm told, guiding the big car into a gap in the traffic.

'Are you going to shoot me?'

'I'm thinking about it.'

I drive on, snatching a glance at Mia in the sling against my chest. She's fretting, whimpering quietly, tiny fists rubbing at her eyes. The warmth of her body radiates through the cotton of my blouse.

'Shhh,' I whisper. 'It's OK, Mia. You can sleep.'

Mia's eyes are heavy but she's still fighting sleep, little grunts and sobs escaping her as she shifts in the carrier.

'You were the one calling Kathryn when she was on the train,' I say slowly. I feel a pang of sadness for Kathryn, at what this man might do when he catches up with her. Is he a jealous ex, out to punish her for leaving him, humiliating him by taking their baby away? 'You're her other half, aren't you?'

'Where the hell were you even going with the baby strapped to you?'

'To a police station. West End Central.'

'Christ,' he says. 'Good thing I found you then.'

'Where are we going now?'

He leans closer, his breath hot against my ear.

'Enough talking. Just drive.'

The right filter light turns green and I accelerate smoothly across the dual carriageway. He's moved the gun away now, I can't feel it jabbing through the back of my seat. I run through the possibilities. We're heading north-west, away from central London. At some point soon we'll have to stop, to get out again. If there are more people around then, all I have to do is get him to draw the pistol, to show it. One witness calling 999 will bring an immediate armed response from the Met.

Unless he is taking us somewhere remote. Somewhere without witnesses.

I shiver, wondering again if he's less likely to shoot while we're moving in traffic, or if he's deranged enough to do it anyway. It's better to act sooner, before he can completely control the situation. As if in answer to my prayers, a police car pulls up at the lights opposite us across a box junction. Two officers in front, a man and a woman in high-vis gear. My pulse ticks upwards. I could flash the headlights at them, get their attention. Maybe they would follow us, pull us over. Or I could turn across the junction, right across their path. I could hit the gas and just aim the BMW at them—

'I know what you're thinking.' His deep voice is inches from my ear. 'And if you so much as give those cops a funny look, the first bullet will blow your spine clean through your chest. Are we clear?'

From behind me comes the unmistakeable *click* of the pistol being cocked, the blunt steel barrel pushing again into the small of my back. I tear my eyes away from the police car and look down. Rocked gently by the motion of the car, Mia is dozing again, oblivious, her head resting against my chest.

'Yes,' I say. 'We're clear.'

The light turns green and I pull smoothly away.

8

We drive in silence for about fifteen minutes before he directs me off the main road and onto a leafy suburban street. He gets out and opens my door and for a moment I consider running, shouting, trying to get away, but even if I could push past him there's no way I can outrun him with Mia strapped to my chest. Instead we switch places quickly, as he watches for passers-by with one hand on the butt of the pistol, before pushing me into the back.

'Now lie down,' he says. 'Flat, along the seat. And keep your eyes shut.'

I lie down slowly across the back seat using both hands to cushion Mia's body against mine. The baby snuffles but doesn't wake.

'Where are you taking us?'

'And stop bloody talking.'

Lying here is uncomfortable, and I have to fold my legs behind the passenger seat, supporting Mia's head to make sure she isn't bumped or startled by the sharp turns and hard acceleration of the BMW now that the man is behind the wheel. The baby sleeps on, oblivious. We're almost face to face, so close I can feel her little warm breaths on my skin. I feel my heart filling again, overflowing with a fierce love, an all-consuming desire to shield her from harm.

This is what Kathryn was trying to protect her baby from. This man. This danger. Dominic.

But he's found us anyway. And it seems clear to me that his interest is the baby: if he can't punish his ex, he will take out his anger on what she loves the most. The only reason he's taken us both is because he couldn't quickly separate us on St George Street. And now I'm a witness, a loose end, someone who could identify him, his car, his movements.

But the realisation brings no fear with it, only a grim certainty that I have no one else to rely on. I have to get myself – and Mia – out of this situation. *Think*. I can smell worn black plastic seats. Oil and dirt and fried food. Something else, dark and earthy. I open my eyes a fraction and can make out street lights and trees upright against the grey London sky. The upper floors of office buildings. Moving more quickly than before, but still stopping and starting with traffic and red lights. I can see Dominic's profile, the angle of his jaw, a trace of dried blood behind his ear. I can't shake the feeling that there is something else familiar about him, but not from today, not from the train. Something about his face, like someone I had seen or known a long time ago. From an old job? Or had I seen him on the TV or a news story online?

I look in the footwell for anything I can use as a weapon. An empty coke can, a bottle opener, a thick AA map book. Underneath the book is a glimpse of white. Slowly, carefully, I reach down and push the map book out of the way. Beneath it is a white phone charging cable. I stretch out my hand towards it and manage to grasp the end in my fingers. If I could somehow loop that around his headrest, around his neck, and pull tight enough he would have to stop the car and if I can keep the pressure on—

'Keep your hands where I can see them,' he says over his shoulder. 'And keep your eyes *shut*, like I told you.'

I drop the cable onto the floor and return my hand to the back of the sling.

I count sets of sixty in my head as we drive; I've counted fifteen minutes when I feel the car slowing to a stop. I hear Dominic's door open, the creaking of metal on metal, then the slam as he gets back in. The car moving off, more slowly this time, taking a series of turns close together and then a long slow loop. From my position, flat on the back seat, I can see the top of a roof, a large building, industrial grey, streaked with dirt and green stains reaching down from the roof line.

Finally, Dominic kills the engine and gestures at me to sit up. We're in a large car park but there isn't a single other vehicle: hundreds of spaces, all empty, just drifts of leaves and plastic bags and other rubbish stirred gently by the early evening breeze. We're parked close to the back door of a large high-sided building with no windows, some kind of warehouse, three or four storeys high. It looks abandoned.

'What is this place?'

As soon as I shuffle out of my seat and climb out of the car, he reaches up and puts some kind of hood over my head. My world goes dark, the cool afternoon air replaced with a reek of dirt and body odour. Something else too, coppery and sharp. His strong grip encircles my upper arm and pulls me forward, Mia's head still just visible through a gap at the bottom of the hood, glimpses of cracked concrete and paving slabs beneath my shuffling feet. The squeal of rusted hinges as a door opens, closes, a change in the atmosphere. A smell of neglect, of wet carpet and rot, stale air and decay, dark carpet tiles under my feet as we move into the building. Sounds are muffled because of the hood but I can hear the soft padding of our footsteps echoing back to us in the silence. Dominic leads me straight on before pulling me into a left turn, then a right, until I feel him pause.

'Stairs,' he says.

I take them slowly, one hand groping for a banister rail and the other around Mia's back in case I stumble, the echo of our shoes tapping back to us against a roof some way above. We turn left at the top of the stairs, another long corridor that smells strongly of damp and mouldering carpet. The flat tapping sound of dripping water. There is another left turn and then he pulls me through a door and slams it shut, the solid *click* of a lock turning.

He pulls me forward again, turns me until my legs are backed up against something.

'Sit.'

I sit back slowly onto something spongy and uneven. I can hear him moving around, putting things down, the click of a light switch. Through the bottom of the hood I can see Mia's peaceful face as she dozes, her head lolling against the baby harness. Then, without warning, Dominic rips the hood from my head and I blink in the sudden brightness. I'm on a stained orange sofa in a large room, the opposite wall made up entirely of glass. The place is – or was – a meeting room of some kind, with a long table in the centre surrounded by orange chairs. Orange fabric sofas against three walls. Above us, circling the room, are poster-sized caricatures of men and women, orange tans and shoulder pads and huge exaggerated grins. Some tattered and ripped, others merely faded with time. A few of the faces look vaguely familiar. Actors? Game show hosts? The whole place has a 1980s faded showbiz feel to it, a sense of former glories long past. It's a mess, strewn with belongings: clothes, plastic bags, sheets of paper. There's an old sofa in the corner with a sleeping bag on it, a small camping stove on the floor beside it with tins of food. Dominic is clearing a space at the end of the long meeting table.

'Put the baby on the sofa over there,' he says without looking at me.

I stay where I am, both hands around Mia's back. I have to keep her close, to make sure we don't get separated.

'She's still sleeping,' I say quietly. 'I can keep her in the sling for a bit longer.'

He pulls the black pistol from his waistband and holds it casually down by his side, staring at me with red-rimmed eyes.

'I'm not going to tell you again.'

I stand and lift Mia gently out of the sling, laying her down against the back edge of the sofa so she doesn't roll off, putting the toy octopus on a muslin cloth next to her. She snuffles and frowns but doesn't wake.

'Now take off your jacket, your shoes and your watch,' he says. 'Empty your handbag on the table and take everything out of the rucksack.'

'Whatever's happened between you and Kathryn, there must be a way to make it right,' I say. 'But you can't take it out on Mia. Please.'

He goes to the sofa and holds the pistol over the baby's sleeping form, the black muzzle barely a foot from her little chest.

My heart rises up into my mouth.

'OK, OK, *please*, I'll do it.'

'This is going to get boring really quickly if you want to have a discussion every time I ask you to do something. And sooner or later, I don't know, my finger might slip.' He mimes the recoil of the pistol going off. 'Boom.'

'Don't,' I say quickly. 'Please don't do that. Please.'

I do as he asks, placing everything on the table.

'Now put your arms out just like you're at the airport.'

He leans in close and pats me down, rough but thorough, running his hands down my front and back, arms and legs, the smell of stale cigarettes strong on his breath. He tells me to sit down again, duct taping my wrists together behind me. He takes off his baseball cap, dark ginger hair flattened against his head. He runs a hand through it, back and forth, raking his fingers across his scalp, then starts to go through my handbag, examining each item as if it might hold some hidden secret. Opening the lipsticks, flicking through the diary, emptying everything out of my purse and feeling inside the bag's fabric lining.

I study him while he works. He is heavy with muscle, thick knots of it around his shoulders and arms. His beard is too long to be smart, but not long enough to be an actual full beard. Ragged and uneven, more like he has simply stopped shaving and hasn't bathed in a while. There are deep, dark shadows beneath his eyes.

'What are you looking for?' I say. 'Because whatever it is, I haven't got it.'

'You're not carrying ID?'

'I'm not at work today.'

'And where do you work?'

'I told you, I'm a project manager for an aerospace and defence company.'

He grunts.

'If you say so.'

Mia gurgles, awake now, and I instinctively try to stand to check on her.

'Sit.' He stares at me, his eyes hard.

Slowly I sit back down as he takes a knife from his jacket pocket. It has a short, wide blade and he goes to work with it on my shoes, a pair of soft brown loafers, prising at the heel and the leather inner. As I watch, he works the blade into a gap and saws back and forth until the whole heel comes free with a snap. He studies it, turning it over in his hand, before throwing it towards an overflowing rubbish bag in the corner.

'Can I at least have my shoes back now?' I say when he is finished. 'Please.'

He throws both shoes into the pile. 'You won't be needing them.'

I swallow hard, my throat dry, absorbing the implication of his words.

'What *are* you actually looking for?'

'You really want to play this game?'

'What game?' I say, trying to keep my voice level. 'I have literally no idea what you're talking about.'

He sighs, unscrewing a ballpoint pen from my bag and pulling out the tube of ink.

'GPS trackers.'

'Why would I be carrying one of those?'

He doesn't reply. Instead, he begins working his way through everything in the rucksack, turning each item over in his hand, feeling the seams, shaking the bottles of formula milk, studying them. Paying particular attention to anything solid. He crushes two of the small tubes of ointment under his boot and crouches down to examine the remnants. Finally, he picks up the empty rucksack and shoves the knife into it, ripping the blade through the fabric, slashing at it, slicing off the straps, cutting into the plastic base, pulling out the lining and opening up all the seams. Prying into each piece of the ruined bag, squeezing it, turning it this way and that, before finally sweeping all the pieces off the table with a shout of frustration.

'Shit!' he shouts.

Mia flinches at the sudden noise, then goes back to chewing on the tentacle of the octopus toy.

His head swivels towards the baby, studying her, his eyes narrowing.

He stands and walks towards her, the broad-bladed knife still in his hand.

9

Mia whimpers in alarm, the sound like a fist clenching around my heart. Dominic stares down at her with something in his eyes that I can't quite read. Anger? Pain, maybe. Or grief. After a moment he reaches out towards the baby with his left hand.

'Don't hurt her,' I gasp. I try to rise in my seat but it's painfully awkward with my wrists taped together behind me. '*Please.*'

He levers the octopus toy out of Mia's grasp, her little mouth opening in surprise. Then her face crumples and she begins to cry, her little legs kicking in frustration.

He ignores her, going back to the big conference table and examining the toy, squeezing it, rolling the fabric of each tentacle between his fingers. He plunges his knife into it and begins sawing back and forth, prising open the cotton seam to reveal the stuffing inside. Mia continues to cry, a broken-hearted wail that makes every muscle in my body twitch with frustration that I can't go to her, comfort her.

Without looking up, he says: 'Get her to calm down, that noise is doing my head in.'

'I think she wants to be held,' I say. 'But I can't pick her up with my hands taped together.'

He puts the toy down with a whispered curse and comes to stand behind me, slicing through the tape with a single stroke. The weapon has a serrated edge, and a ridged metal grip that fits across his knuckles. It's some kind of fighting knife and up close is brutally ugly.

I pull the tape away from my wrists, a few hairs ripping away with it, pick Mia up and hold her against my chest, jigging her gently and trying to shush her.

'Shh, Mia? It's OK, it's all right.'

The baby grizzles, calms for a moment, then gives a short, hiccupping cry that dissolves into more grizzling. She's been fed less than an hour ago. Could she be hungry again already? I lift the baby higher, turn her and give her a sniff.

'She needs a nappy change,' I say. 'She might quieten if I can change her.'

He gestures to the contents of the ruined bag, scattered across the conference table.

'Knock yourself out.'

I find a small changing mat in the pile and spread it out at one end of the table, laying Mia on top of it and trying to remember all the things I'll need in the order I'll need them. Charlie, my youngest godson, is a wriggler, and likes to try to crawl off the changing table, which means you have to have everything lined up and ready at hand before you start. Nappy sack open, three wipes, tissues, Sudocrem, new nappy, hand sanitiser. What else? A new sleepsuit in case of leaks. I start to undress the baby, gently pulling her little arms and legs out of the sleepsuit, grateful that there are no bruises like those that circled Kathryn's forearm.

While I work, Dominic continues to attack the soft toy with his knife, as he swears under his breath.

When I'm attaching the Velcro straps of the new nappy, there is a *thud* as he sticks the knife blade into the wooden table. He comes to stand next to me, looming over us both as I feed Mia's legs back into the sleepsuit. In the palm of his hand a small metal disc, the size and shape of a two pound coin.

'Yours?' he says.

'What is it?'

'What do you think?'

'No idea, I've never seen it before.'

'It's a GPS tracking device,' he says. 'Decent quality, too. Any idea how it found its way inside the toy?'

'Mia had it on the train with her earlier, along with all of her other stuff in that bag. That's all I know.'

He studies me, his eyes narrowing, as if trying to decide whether to believe me or not.

'What I can't work out, is why this place isn't already crawling with cops.' He holds up the coin-sized tracker between his thumb and forefinger, turning it over in his hand. 'If they know where we are, why haven't they kicked the door down ten minutes ago?'

'Maybe they're biding their time.'

He stares at me for a moment before his face creases into a small, joyless smile.

'Nice try, Ellen. But I think not.'

'Why would the police be tracking her anyway?'

'Who else would it be?'

'I don't know.' I shrug. 'Unless . . . maybe Kathryn put it in there so she could find her way back to Mia?'

He grunts. 'Unlikely.'

'Why?'

He shakes his head, frowning.

He lays the GPS device flat on the table and smashes it with the butt of the knife. The metal case comes loose, revealing tiny circuit boards inside. He hits both pieces again, until they are cracked and bent out of shape.

'What are you going to do?' I ask quietly. 'With us?'

'Don't worry yourself about that,' he says, his voice a flat monotone. 'It's best if you don't think about it.'

'It's rather difficult to think about anything else.'

'If you really want to know, I'm waiting for dark,' he says. 'Then the three of us are going to go for a little drive. Somewhere nice and quiet, out of the way.'

My chest tightens, fear settling like a heavy weight on my breastbone.

'Then what?'

He ignores my question.

'Dominic?'

His head jerks up. It's the first time I've used his name.

'I'd advise you to tread carefully,' he says.

'Please just let her go. I'll do whatever you want, but let Mia go. We can drop her off somewhere.'

He shakes his head, a small movement full of finality. 'You don't know who she is, do you?' he says. 'You don't have the first idea.'

'No. But I know she's three months and one week old today and that she should be with her mother. She *needs* to be with her mother.'

'That's not going to happen,' he says, looking away.

'You think just because you're her father, that gives you the right to do whatever you like?'

'I'm doing what needs to be done.'

'Please, Dominic.' I soften my voice, making an effort to lower it. 'You don't have to go down this road. Mia is innocent in all of this, You know she is.'

'Things have gone too far already.' He tucks the gun into the waistband of his jeans. 'Too much water under the bridge.'

'I know you're angry but you—'

'Enough talking,' he says, holding a hand up. 'I have to go and fetch something. You need to put her down now.'

I put some sofa cushions onto the floor and lay Mia gently down on them as she sucks contentedly on one of her muslin cloths. Dominic gestures to me to sit back down in the chair, binding my hands with the duct tape again, then holds something up in front of me. My mobile.

'What's your unlock pattern?'

I tell him and he traces the pattern with a thick index finger. The phone comes to life, the screen filling with a picture of my tabby cat, Dizzy.

'You can't get out of this room, but in case you get any ideas about trying to, just remember that I know everything about you now, OK?' He points at the phone. 'I will come looking for you and I will find you. A day or a month from now, you'll wake up one night and I'll be standing there, at the end of your bed. Do you understand?' He slips the phone into the pocket of his jeans.

'Yes,' I say. 'But I can't look after Mia properly with my hands taped.'

'I won't be gone long.'

He puts the hood over my head again and the world goes dark, the fusty smells of the fabric filling my nose. Dirt, sweat, blood. I sense him leaning in close, his voice in my ear, hard and low.

'Don't move from that chair,' he says. 'Scream if you want, but this whole complex is abandoned and due for demolition next year, no one's near enough to hear you. Miles of corridors and old studios, lots of sound-proofing, car parks on every side. I'm locking this door from the outside and there's no other key.'

I hear his heavy footsteps crossing the room, the sound of the door closing and locking, his steps retreating into the distance and then nothing. Silence apart from the contented gurgles of Mia as she lies on sofa cushions, her little sounds muffled by my hood. I count off another sixty seconds in my head, my whole body shaking with adrenaline and fear, closing my eyes and straining every sense to hear another step, an echo, any noise to suggest he is still close by. Every instinct screaming the same thing: *Go. Get out.*

My hands are taped tightly behind me, low against the back of the chair so it is agonizingly painful to raise myself up to a standing position. Painful, but not impossible. My thighs burning, my shoulders feeling like they might pop out of their sockets, I raise myself up inch by inch until I can roll my body forward and slip my hands over the top of the chair to stand up properly. Breathing hard with exertion inside the hood, the dizziness comes on quickly. *Don't pass out.* I bend at the waist, shaking my head from side to side until the hood comes off and falls to the floor. I pull in a deep lungful of breath, then another, while my eyes find Mia. The baby is cooing to herself contentedly on the sofa, the corner of a muslin cloth clamped in her mouth. I run to her, look her over. She seems OK.

A memory pulses through me. An image as familiar as my own face: the scorching heat of a silent day, drifting smoke, the acrid stink of burning diesel, vultures circling on thermals high above. Broken bodies lying in the desert sand.

Get her out of here.

There is a connecting door through to a small kitchen at the far end of the room. I rush over to it, my shoeless feet almost silent on the rough industrial carpet, and begin awkwardly pulling open drawers with my hands still taped behind me. Old plastic cutlery, brown-stained teaspoons, plastic straws. Nothing with a blade. But there is a row of old glass jars lined up behind the sink, lidless and clouded with age. In the other corner is a broomstick, cobwebbed to the wall. I back up to it and reach for it blindly, grasping it awkwardly in both hands. Holding it up behind me I swing it against the glass jars and in one quick motion sweep them all off the worktop, a succession of smashes – *pop pop pop* – as they shatter on the tiled floor around my feet. The sound is horribly loud in the silence and I freeze for a second, leaning towards the hallway, straining to hear any noise in response. Nothing. I kneel, feeling behind me for the biggest, sharpest piece of broken glass, holding it up and sawing against the duct tape that binds my wrists together.

My arms and wrists burn with the effort. Come on, come on. This is taking too long. I shift position, a shard of broken glass stabbing into the sole of my stockinged foot. Gritting my teeth against the pain, I keep sawing at the tape until I feel the first strand start to give, then the next and the next, until finally I can pull my wrists apart, the black tape still clinging to my skin. I kick more shards of glass into the corner as I go back into the conference room. I hop over to the nearest chair, stabbing pains arcing up my leg, and pull out a piece of broken glass embedded in the ball of my left foot, wiping a smear of blood against my sleeve.

One entire wall of the conference room is taken up with a series of floor to ceiling windows, with a sliding glass door in the centre that leads out onto a balcony overlooking the empty car park. The latch on the metal-framed glass door is broken, the lever snapped off. I haul on the door and feel a fresh surge of urgency as it slides noisily open on its rusted track. Just a few inches. I lean into it and haul again with a grunt of effort, pulling the door open a full foot. It's enough. Outside the air is cleaner, sharp and cold, the light fading fast. The balcony is functional, rust and dirt and drifts of rotting leaves, a waist-high metal barrier around the edge. We're on the second floor, twenty feet above the car park and there's no fire escape – but there is a drainpipe, with supporting brackets holding it to the wall every few feet. I test the pipe with both hands, trying to rattle it from side to side. It doesn't move.

I can put Mia in the sling.

This is the way out.

A sound from below separates itself from the distant hum of traffic. A car. A big engine. I drop to my hands and knees. The BMW is back.

Bent double as I hobble back inside, my eyes search the room. *Shit*. Where is the sling? I had put it on the table, I thought, when I took Mia out of it and laid her on the cushions. I circle the room, pulling aside chairs, checking under the table, pushing aside a sleeping bag and a pile of clothes on one of the sofas. I have to find it. I'm pretty sure I can climb down the drainpipe – I've handled tougher descents before – but not one-handed. Not with a baby in my arm.

Tap. Tap. Tap. Footsteps on the stairs.

I freeze. The sliding door is there, a few feet away. The hood discarded on the floor, back inside the room.

Choose.

Footsteps in the corridor outside.

I could go, climb down, get away, raise the alarm. Find a house, a car, a phone, have the police here in minutes. That would be the smart move. I can just *go.*

But it has to be now. And I'd have to go alone.

10

I stiffen at the sound of the door unlocking, trying to slow my frantic breathing inside the hood. I keep my hands held low behind the chair, as if they're still bound. I can't leave without Mia. By the time I've raised the alarm and police have arrived, Dominic would be long gone, taking her with him.

The big internal door swings open on rusty hinges, closes again. The sound of a bunch of keys dropped on the table. Something heavier put down beside them with a metallic thud. The gun? A rustle of plastic bags. The tearing of a cardboard seal. A soft rustling.

Then silence.

The cut in the sole of my left foot throbs with pain. Have I left blood on the floor? I curl my feet under the chair to hide the injury, my tights torn and sticky with blood. With a jolt of fear I think of the broken glass on the tiled kitchen floor. If Dominic goes in there, he'll know straight away that—

Mia cries out. Once, twice, little squeals of protest.

I sit up straighter, mustering all my restraint not to rise up out of the chair.

'What are you doing to her?' I say, a surge of panic tightening my stomach. 'What are you doing?'

'Shut up,' he grunts.

Mia cries out again, a high-pitched yowl that feels like a knife to my heart.

He swears under his breath.

I plant my feet, get ready to tear off the hood and launch myself across the room at him.

'Leave her alone!' I shout.

Mia's fallen silent.

I flinch as he pulls the hood from my head, blinking as my eyes adjust to the strip lights again.

'Calm the hell down.'

'What did you do to her?' I try to lean around him to see the baby. 'What did you do, you bastard?'

He stares at me for a moment, his bloodshot eyes on mine, grime caked into lines of tiredness around his eyes. Then he moves away, pulling out a chair from the conference table and collapsing back into it.

'She's fine.'

Mia is still there on the sofa cushions, blinking up at the ceiling, little legs kicking contentedly as she sucks on the corner of her muslin cloth. No obvious signs of injury.

I feel my limbs relax slightly.

Dominic takes a remote from the table and turns on the big flat screen TV on the wall, flicking channels until he finds the BBC News. Footage of a cricket match. He took my watch when we first arrived but this must be the end of the national bulletin, so it's coming up to 6.30 p.m. He mutes the sound, pops open a can of Red Bull and takes a long drink, watching the silent images on the screen for a minute before turning back to face me.

'I still don't get it,' he says. 'I don't get *you.*'

'What's not to get?'

'Where you fit into all of this. If you were police, the place would be surrounded by now.'

I shake my head.

'I'm not police.'

He thinks about that for a moment, glancing back to the TV again.

'So who *are* you?'

'I'm no one. I met a woman on a train and she asked me to hold her baby for a couple of minutes while she answered her phone.'

'What else did she say?'

I think back to the conversation. It feels like it happened days ago, not hours, the tingle of adrenaline still keeping me fully present in each passing moment.

'We just talked about the baby, mostly. She walked off the train at the next station and I found that note in the rucksack.'

He picks the note up off the table, reads it again.

'And now here we all are,' he says. His eyes go to the silent TV screen again, the national weather forecast.

'What did you do to her?' I say quietly. 'To Kathryn? Did you shoot her?'

'What?' he says distractedly.

'She was only young, not much more than a child herself.'

'She knew what she was doing.'

'You were calling her on the train earlier, weren't you? Calling her over and over again, trying to find out where she was?'

'Is that what she told you?'

'She got off that train to draw you off. To lead you away from the baby, to protect Mia from you.'

He takes another long pull on the energy drink. 'No.'

'You were waiting for her at Seer Green. You found her, and then you came to find Mia. How did you even know where we were, anyway? We could have gone anywhere when we came out of Marylebone, and you weren't on that train. But you still knew where we'd be.'

He indicates the sling, stuffed into his black rucksack.

'GPS is a wonderful invention.'

I sift through the few facts in my grasp. It is the only explanation that makes sense.

'You were tracking her too?'

'I needed to know where she was going.'

'You were stalking her.'

He snorts but says nothing, turning back to the TV, where the regional London news bulletin is just starting. The presenters, a young blonde woman and a grey-haired older man, stare seriously into the camera, their mouths moving silently as they introduce the first item.

'But she didn't know you'd put a tracking device in the sling,' I continue. 'So you did whatever you did to her and then came to find Mia, finish the job.'

He finishes the energy drink and crushes the can in his fist.

'Sounds like you've got this all figured out, Ellen. So tell me, if you're so clever, why didn't you try to escape when I left you alone just now? I thought you might at least try to get the hood off.'

I curl my bleeding foot further under the chair, glancing again at the half-open door to the kitchen where broken glass is pushed into a corner. 'I didn't want to leave Mia.'

'Someone else's kid, someone you don't even know? I don't get it.'

'That doesn't surprise me.'

He shakes his head in disgust. 'You have no idea what's going on.'

I hesitate. 'So tell me.'

'The less you know, the better. For your own sake. The less danger you'll be in.'

I look at him for the first time, *really* look at him, his bloodshot eyes and sallow skin. Try to see Mia's features in his, in the face of this man who seems set on destroying his own flesh and blood.

'You don't have to do this, you know,' I say. 'Let me take Mia to the authorities, to the police.'

'You really haven't been paying attention, have you?'

'You can just walk away. I won't tell anyone about any of this, about you. I swear.'

'Oh, you *swear*, do you?' His voice is heavy with sarcasm. 'Well that makes everything all right, doesn't it?'

'Just let me take Mia and—'

He shushes me with an outstretched palm. The news report has switched to a reporter standing outside a large redbrick building with a taxi rank behind her, people hurrying past. The screen switches again, to a still that looks like it's been taken from a CCTV camera. The quality is not great, but there is no mistake who is in the picture.

A woman carrying a baby.

An image of me and Mia.

11

He sits up, rigid in his chair.

'*Shit*,' he mutters, stabbing at the volume button on the TV remote as the screen plays grainy black and white footage of me walking out of Marylebone train station a few hours ago.

'*. . . asking anyone who may have seen the woman in the Marylebone area to come forward with any information*,' the reporter says solemnly into camera.

Dominic hits rewind, his attention fully focused on the screen. He runs it back to the start of the bulletin as the two studio anchors introduce the lead story.

'*Police are investigating the abduction of a three-month old baby this evening and the disappearance of a twenty-four-year-old woman. The baby is thought to have been abducted on a journey into London earlier today. Here's Alice Durham with more.*'

The image switches to a young dark-haired reporter standing outside Marylebone station.

'*Concerns are mounting for the safety of Kathryn Clifton, who was last seen in the Amersham area earlier today and was believed to be travelling into London with a baby.*'

The screen changes briefly to a still image of Kathryn, looking younger, smiling in a bridesmaid's dress.

'*Police are also searching urgently for another woman who was captured on CCTV leaving Marylebone station with a baby earlier today.*' The image switches to the CCTV footage of me walking quickly out of the station, Mia in my arms. '*Ms Clifton has not been seen since these images were taken and the police are becoming increasingly concerned for her safety. It's thought that the woman captured in these security camera images could hold vital clues in the disappearance of Kathryn Clifton and the abduction of the baby. Detectives are asking anyone who may have seen the woman in the Marylebone area to come forward with any information. This is Alice Durham for ITV News London.*'

The screen switches back to the two news anchors in the studio as they move onto the next item, about a double stabbing in Tottenham. Dominic hurls the TV remote into the corner of the room, the black plastic case shattering into splinters across the floor.

'Shit!' He shakes his head at the screen, jaw flexing.

'They made it look like I abducted her and did something to Kathryn,' I say, summoning a calmness to my voice that I don't feel. 'That's crazy, that's not what happened at all.'

'Welcome to my world,' he grunts.

'What do you mean?'

'It doesn't matter—'

Finally he turns back to face me.

Freezes.

Stares down the barrel of his own gun, clutched in my out-stretched hand, the remains of the black duct tape still hanging from my wrist.

I circle away from him so that Mia is on my right side, out of the line of fire. The compact bulk of the pistol is solid in my hand, my fingertip curled around the smooth, curved steel of the trigger.

'You should have bound my feet, too.'

He nods slowly.

'Yeah. Guess I should have.'

'Now take three steps away from Mia.' I gesture with the gun. 'Then lie face down on the floor with your hands behind your back.'

He shakes his head.

'I can't let you go, Ellen.'

'I know how to use one of these.'

'I believe you.'

He takes a step towards me. I lower the gun to his leg.

'You asked me why I didn't make a run for it earlier?' I indicate the sliding door to the balcony. 'It's because I had to be sure we could both get away. I knew you'd catch us if I couldn't slow you down.'

'Us?'

'Me and the baby.'

'You're not going anywhere.'

'But now I *can* slow you down.' I take aim at his kneecap. 'In fact, you'll probably limp for the rest of your life.'

'You won't do it.'

'*Lie down on the floor,*' I say, fighting a tremor at the edge of my voice. 'I'm not going to ask you again.'

'Ellen, there's a lot going on that you don't know.'

'I know that Mia and I are leaving this place, one way or another.'

He studies me for a moment.

'Have you ever shot anyone before?'

'You're going to be the first.'

He shakes his head, his hooded eyes never leaving mine.

'You're not going to shoot me.'

'You know, it's a funny thing,' I say, 'but wherever I go in life, there always seems to be a man who wants to tell me what I can and can't do.'

He takes another step towards me.

'Two types of people in this world, Ellen.' He spreads his hands. 'Those who could shoot someone and those who couldn't, and you're definitely in the—'

I steady my aim and squeeze the trigger.

12

I brace myself for the recoil, tensing my forearm against the kick.

But there is only a dull, lifeless *click* as the hammer falls.

Our eyes lock for half a second as I rack the slide back with my left hand to put a bullet in the chamber. Pull the trigger again.

Click.

Muscle memory taking over, I hit the magazine release catch with my thumb and the clip drops out of the pistol's butt into my left palm.

There are no bullets inside.

'For Christ's sake,' I say under my breath.

'Empty,' he says, pulling another of the slim black magazines from his pocket, brass bullets glinting at its top. 'But this one isn't.'

My arms and legs are buzzing with adrenaline, my head spinning, thoughts crowding each other out.

'So in the car when you threatened to shoot me, it was empty then too?'

'You wouldn't have come with me if I'd just asked nicely, would you?' He shrugs. 'I had to get you to co-operate. But I'm not an animal.'

'No, you're just the kind of guy who beats women up. Kathryn had bruises all up her arm, I saw them.'

'You have no idea what you're—'

I sweep the gun up in a quick diagonal arc, cracking him across the side of the head with the barrel. He drops to the floor, the loaded magazine spinning out of his hand. I step over him, reaching towards it, and it's there, inches away when he grabs me from behind, shoving me hard so I slam face first into the door, pain exploding above my eye. I turn and swing out wildly with the pistol again, feeling the ridged steel butt connect with flesh and bone, a groan as he hits the floor and then he's on his hands and knees, a long sticky string of blood between his mouth and the floor. I kick him as hard as I can in the ribs, an *oof* of pain escaping from him as he collapses sideways onto the floor. I've lost sight of the loaded magazine.

Go.

I shove the gun into my jeans and scramble over to where Mia lies on the sofa, still sucking on a corner of her muslin cloth. I gather her in both arms and kick the swinging doors open. A wide corridor full of shadows, almost no light apart from the moonlight slanting in through high windows. In one direction a row of doors fading away into darkness, in the other, a flight of stairs. Which way? I had the hood over my head on the way in but instinct tells me to go left. I head for the stairs at a run, scratchy office carpet beneath my feet, gritting my teeth against the fresh stab of shooting pain that comes with every step. I run to the stairs, taking them as fast as I dare in the semi-darkness. There's something wet on my face, stinging in my eye. Blood. I swipe it away.

An explosive crash – a door handle being hurled back into a wall – echoes through the building. A shout of rage follows it, an animal sound of anger and frustration, hurt and fury, that seems to come from right above me at the top of the stairwell.

I stumble and almost fall forward onto the first floor landing, staggering to keep myself upright, arms wrapped around Mia's body, one hand cupping her hot little head. I recover my balance and run around to the next flight, following the stairwell down and back until I get to the ground floor.

Another furious shout from the floor above. Coming nearer.

'Come back!' he shouts. 'You can't take her! She belongs with me!'

In front of me, the corridor splits left and right. Left is in almost complete darkness. I go right, plunging down a wide corridor studded with closed doors. Another crossroads. I continue straight on, the agony of the cut in my left foot a rolling thrum of pain. I run past a faded sign that says STUDIO 7, half-illuminated in the watery moonlight, an arrow pointing in the other direction.

Thundering footsteps behind me, on the same level now. Closer.

'Ellen!'

Shit. I can't outrun him with the baby, stumbling around in the dark. He knows this complex; he's going to catch up. I pass another stairwell and stop, doubling back, tucking myself into the shadows beneath the stairs, holding Mia close. I squeeze myself into the darkest corner, sliding back to a sitting position, lifting my left foot and feeling along the skin, slick with blood. *There.* I find the edge of another sliver of broken glass, grip it between my bloody thumb and forefinger, and with a silent grimace, ease it out of my flesh.

The footsteps are slower and clearer now. He's almost level with us, the beam of a torchlight sweeping back and forth across the corridor. Mia makes a low contented gurgle that sounds horribly loud in the stillness of the abandoned building.

'Shh,' I whisper into her ear, heart thundering in my chest. I rock her gently and stroke the downy hair on the back of her head. 'Shh, baby.'

Mia coos and squeaks.

I stroke her cheek with a fingertip. My hand brushes something laid over her shoulder. The muslin cloth, half wrapped around her body. I take a corner of it and touch it to Mia's lips.

Please be quiet. Please, Mia.

She instantly latches onto it, falling silent as she begins to suck on the cloth again.

The footsteps slow to a stop and then he's there, maybe fifteen feet away from my hiding place. A shaft of moonlight glinting off steel. The knife. He is turning his head from side to side, listening for the slightest sound. As soon as Mia makes another noise she'll give us away.

The beam of his torchlight probes the darkness a few feet from our hiding place.

I reach into the pockets of my jeans for a coin, a key, anything. All I have is a tube of lip balm. I ease it out and throw it as hard as I can, launching it in a long arc down the corridor. The little plastic tube skitters and clacks in the darkness and immediately the torch beam shifts that way, towards the noise.

'Stay where you are!' Dominic shouts into the dark. 'Stay exactly where you are!'

He runs past, just a few feet away from us.

I can feel the pistol digging into the small of my back, ridged metal against my skin. But even unloaded it's better than nothing, better than bare hands. I count to three in my head and then move away from the corner.

I run headlong into the dark, Mia clutched tightly to my chest, turning through corridors, left and right, purely on instinct, lungs screaming, heart thudding, my foot a symphony of agony with every step. Going as far as possible away from the man with the knife.

A long glass window. *There*. A solitary car in an empty car park. The BMW.

Finally, the door. As I push my way through it another shout of rage echoes down the corridor. I turn right and run towards the distant street lights. Clutching Mia with one arm, I draw the pistol. The night air is cold and sharp, only a full moon and the weak light of a neighbouring warehouse throwing any illumination onto the car park. I'm on some kind of industrial estate, windowless blocky buildings looming up on both sides. No flats or houses.

'Help!' I shout. 'Help me!'

My own voice echoes back to me on the night air.

I run on, cold air burning in my lungs, through the car park, towards a boarded-up security post with barriers lowered on both sides. Running, running, expecting a rough hand on my shoulder at any second. Barefoot, half-dressed, half-blinded from the blood running into my eye, one arm clutching Mia to my chest and the pistol in my other hand.

I dodge around the security barrier and run out into the road.

A pair of headlights approaches, twin halogens dazzlingly bright after the darkness of our escape.

I stop in the middle of the road and raise the pistol.

WEDNESDAY

13

Leon

So close. Close enough to touch. Close enough to reach out and grab her, if he needed to.

To be that close to her – for the first time – gave him a shiver of excitement, of expectation. But not there, not then; there were too many people around, too much potential for disturbance. Of course he had established certain facts already, facts that pointed strongly in this direction. But to have it confirmed gave him a glow of satisfaction. The switch on the train was a surprise, something he wouldn't have predicted, but it didn't change what needed to be done. If anything it made it easier, gave him more options. New options. And it added another twist, another layer of fascination. They would talk about this one for *years*.

Leon didn't grab her. Instead he had watched her walk out of the station and onto Melcombe Place, only half-aware of the tedious security man holding up a hand to him, '*Sorry to trouble you sir but I've had a complaint about your behaviour,*' giving his little pidgin-English lecture on respect for other passengers and allowing people the personal space they need and '*the lady says you were taking pictures without her consent*'. Leon had stopped walking and studied the security guard, a small, thickset man with big hands and a heavy forehead that gave him the look of one of the cave-dwelling Morlocks from *The Time Machine*. He pasted on a concerned expression.

'I'm *terribly* sorry,' he'd said, putting on his best faux-Oxbridge accent. 'Just a bit of a misunderstanding, I think.'

Little people – like this officious security guard, given a tiny bit of power and squeezing every last drop from it – were always impressed by a posh accent, whether they admitted it to themselves or not. A thousand years of hereditary monarchy and the oldest class system in the world had to be good for something. Leon wondered what it would be like to take the stun gun casually from his pocket, hold it to the security guard's thick neck and give him a taste of 50,000 volts right there on the station concourse. He put his right hand in the pocket of his black leather jacket, fingers wrapping around the stun gun's smooth plastic.

It was always comforting to feel the power of it in his hand. The pure elemental force of it, like having a bolt of lightning tucked into your pocket. But unleashing it there wouldn't have been a smart move. Walking through the concourse he'd counted at least six cameras on this area, two pole-mounted, two on the shops and two more on the main exit – not to mention the smartphones carried by every passenger that would inevitably turn in his direction at the first sign of a confrontation.

So instead he had smiled, and nodded, and said sorry.

By the time he had finished apologising and shaken off the Morlock in the high-vis jacket, she was nowhere in sight. Leon hurried to the exit, his thin legs propelling him forward through the crowds of people. He checked left and right, then saw the taxi rank, a small queue of people waiting for black cabs. An old white-haired guy, tweed jacket and tie, was helping her into a taxi. Leon had glimpsed the first half of the number plate but the taxi was already pulling away, a bus coming up behind and blocking his view. Her cab turned right onto Great Central Street and was lost among the afternoon traffic. He had stared after it, still feeling the tingle of excitement.

She was gone, for now.

But it didn't matter. He'd got what he needed.

14

The interview room is a small airless box, a table bolted to the wall and four uncomfortable plastic chairs. I thought there might be one of those two-way mirrors like they have on TV police shows, but there's nothing like that. Just a thin window threaded with wire mesh, four tired grey walls and dirt baked into every surface. It's gone midnight and the police station is quiet around me.

I'm shaking and can't stop, the spike of adrenaline long gone, a crash that's sent my energy levels plunging. My hands shake like an old woman's when I try to pick up the Styrofoam cup of sweet tea. A jittery shake in my shoulders, my thighs, my tapping feet, one of them freshly bandaged by a softly-spoken paramedic. I sit at the small table in a faded blue sweatshirt I was given by the duty sergeant at the front desk. It's rough blue cotton, slightly too big for me – a man's size, probably – frayed at the neck, with slack cuffs and the ghost of a logo that tells me it has probably been washed a thousand times.

I can smell Mia on my skin, my hands, on the collar of my shirt. That sweet, clean, infant scent, a perfume of innocence. My arms feel empty and my skin itches with thoughts of Mia, of where she is, who's looking after – have they fed her again, have they found

Kathryn? They offered me a sandwich an hour ago but I couldn't eat, couldn't even force a mouthful down.

I can't stop thinking about the scrawled note Kathryn left for me.

Please protect Mia.

I've done that, haven't I? I've protected her from harm, removed her from a dangerous situation and delivered her to safety. When we arrived at Harrow police station a few hours ago, an injured woman with a baby in her arms and paramedics in tow, the desk sergeant initially took me for a battered wife fleeing domestic violence. He had smiled kindly and arranged for one of the PCs to bring me the faded blue sweatshirt, flip-flops for my feet and a sweet, milky tea. When I was asked to put all of my possessions in a clear plastic bag – phone, watch, keys, purse, change – before being interviewed, I simply shook my head and indicated the pistol that was already in an evidence bag on the other side of the desk.

'He took everything,' I said. 'Apart from that.'

Mia's gone too now, whisked away by a small, birdlike woman from social services. One minute swaddled in my arms, sleeping in a soft grey blanket provided by the paramedics, the next roused and crying and manhandled into a car seat. I listened with my jaw clenched, fingernails digging into my palms, as Mia was carried away from me through the police station and her crying grew fainter and fainter until it faded to nothing.

That was it, was it? The last time I'll ever see her. I'll never hold her again, the bond built up over the last six hours blown away like gossamer on the wind. I pat my pockets for my phone, to look at the picture I took in the café, before remembering it was taken from me hours before. There was no time to grab it during our escape so I don't even have a single picture to remind me.

Nothing.

The ache builds in my chest, like a bruise spreading outwards, a feeling of loss so overwhelming that for a moment I think I might collapse to the floor, curl into a ball and just cry. Wait for sleep, for oblivion, for a time when I can't feel anything anymore.

But who are you crying for? For Mia, or for yourself?

I know the answer to that one.

Instead I put my palms flat on the cold metal surface of the table, straighten my back and blink the tears away. Six deep breaths in, six out. I focus on what I can feel – the dull throb of pain in the sole of my foot, the rigid band of a headache behind my eyes, the rough cotton of the sweatshirt – and wait for the feeling to pass.

The spherical glass eye of a camera looks down on me from the far corner of the room.

Don't trust the police.

But this was the right thing, the only thing to do. Wasn't it? What other option was there? Abandon her to a violent kidnapper? Take her home? I *know* this is the right thing to do.

Despite that, I still can't shake the nagging feeling that I've let Kathryn down somehow. I'd like to see her again, to explain what happened with Mia, to check they're both OK.

I waved away medical help to begin with, insisting they check Mia over first in case she had any kind of injury. But apart from tucking into another bottle of milk she seemed remarkably unaffected by the last few hours, giggling and smiling up at the green-jumpsuited para-medic as she was examined. Once Mia was checked, the paramedic had disinfected the wounds in my foot – two lacerations from the broken glass – and bound it in a bandage. It's still tender, and pain lances through the sole with every move I make. He also cleaned the cut above my eye and put a plaster over it.

The duty solicitor arrives, an amiable man in his thirties with kind eyes, who introduces himself as Chris Betteridge. He tells me that anything between the two of us is confidential, before asking that I be honest with him. He explains the police caution to me and tells me he's only there to advise, not tell me what to do, but ultimately I have three options: answer the questions; say 'no comment'; or read a prepared statement. I tell him I'm happy to answer any questions they have. Lastly, he tells me my legal rights are ongoing so I can stop the interview as many times as I like if I want further advice, although I get the impression that he'd rather get it done and dusted as soon as possible, given that we're heading into the small hours of the morning. His pep talk complete, he sits next to me filling out a pro forma with various details, while a uniformed PC comes in and takes a saliva sample for DNA, the cotton wool bud soft and strange as it's rolled up and down the inside of my cheek. Then we wait another hour for a pair of detectives to arrive, while I sip a second Styrofoam cup of lukewarm tea.

Don't trust anyone.

My mind scrolls back again over the ten words scrawled on that scrap of paper. Examining each line. The first one a request, the next two instructions. Warnings, distinct and clear.

But I know all too well that fixating too long on one thing is a sure way to get blindsided. I was fixated for so long on starting a family that I hadn't seen the cracks growing in my marriage until it was too late. I was so focused on getting pregnant that I failed to notice the distance growing between me and my husband.

Perhaps I'm looking at this whole situation the wrong way as well.

Perhaps it's not what was written in the note, but what was *missing* from it. It didn't say don't trust *him*, or don't trust Dominic; it didn't refer to him at all – at least not directly. Does that mean something? It said I shouldn't trust *anyone*, but what's that about? The only specific element related to the police.

The door to the interview room opens and two men come in, taking the seats opposite me at the table. The older one is mid-forties, the top button of his shirt undone, tie at half-mast, five o'clock shadow, short dark hair going in all directions. Glasses already halfway down his nose. He looks as if he's been awake for days but he's not unattractive, in a ruffled Willem Dafoe kind of way. The younger one is in his late twenties, slicked-back dark hair, slim and gym-toned in a navy suit and pale pink silk tie. The kind of guy who might hit on you in a bar and refuse to take no for an answer. He has a green cardboard folder which he lays on the table between us. They make a strange pair.

The older one gives a nod of recognition to the duty solicitor before turning his attention to me. He laces his fingers together on the table.

'Hello Ellen, my name is Detective Inspector Gilbourne from the Major Crimes Unit,' he says, 'and this is Detective Sergeant Holt.'

'Where's Mia?' I say. 'Is she OK?'

'She's being looked after,' Gilbourne says with a tired smile. 'She's safe and in good hands.'

'Can I see her?

DS Holt frowns, shaking his head.

'That's not going to be possible, I'm afraid.'

'I just . . . want to make sure that she's all right, that's all.'

'Like my colleague said, she's being looked after.'

'But you need to put special protections in place, she's not safe, her father is—'

Holt cuts me off with a raised hand.

'We'll get to all that in a few minutes, Ellen.'

Gilbourne says, 'You really don't need to worry about the baby anymore, Ellen. The relevant social services teams are doing all they can to get her back to her family, and we certainly all appreciate you bringing her back to us.'

'I was just trying to do the right thing.'

'Of course,' he says, but there's something strange in his tone, something almost apologetic. To his partner, he adds: 'Let's get started, shall we, Nathan?'

Holt busies himself with a boxy black device attached to the table that I assume is some kind of audio recorder. He presses a button, checks the display and then his watch before reciting the time, date and location of the interview.

'Present are DS Nathan Holt and DI Stuart Gilbourne,' he says, 'with Ellen Devlin and duty solicitor Chris Betteridge. First of all, Ellen, can I just check you've received medical attention for your injuries, and you've had something to eat and drink in the last hour, and that you're not in need of any specific medication at this time?'

'Yes,' I say. 'I'm OK.'

'Not in too much pain from your foot, are you?' His face is blank, devoid of emotion. 'Heard you had some nasty cuts.'

'They're all cleaned up and I've had paracetamol from the paramedic, it's fine.'

'Good,' he says, opening the folder on the table in front of him. 'Ellen Devlin, I'm arresting you on suspicion of kidnapping and false imprisonment and possession of a firearm. You do not have to say anything. But, it may harm your defence if you do not mention when questioned something which you later rely on in court. Anything you do say may be given in evidence. Do you understand?'

I swallow and nod, my throat suddenly dry. *They're arresting me.* Betteridge had told me they would but it's still unsettling to hear the words.

'Can you speak up, please?' DS Holt says, gesturing towards the black box. 'For the benefit of the recording?'

'I understand.'

'Right. So how about you tell us, in your own words, what happened?'

15

Dominic

Dominic turned his head towards the weak light over the mirror. He needed to be able to see what he was doing. It wasn't much of a wound, but he needed to close it up to stop infection getting in. He couldn't afford to get sick. And more importantly, he had to blend in better on the street. He still had a lot of work to do and he needed to be able to move around without attracting undue attention. He'd already cleaned and disinfected the area with vodka – the sting enough to make him grip the edge of the sink with white knuckled hands – and now it was time to stitch.

The needle was sterilising in a glass half-filled with more vodka. He fished it out and pushed surgical thread through it. He'd done this before, years ago, but never on himself. *Pain is the price of failure. There's much more pain waiting if you fail again.* The wound was about two inches long; the pistol butt had torn the skin in a straight line, leaving it surrounded by livid purple bruising that was darkening by the hour. With his left hand, he pinched the wound, squeezing the separated skin together over his cheekbone. He gripped the needle in his right hand and pushed the point through unyielding skin, his teeth gritted against a fierce flare of pain.

The B & B was a shithole – cracked plaster hanging from the ceiling, mildew in the corners and a wet dog smell in the corridors – but they let him pay cash which suited him fine, and they didn't ask questions when he walked in, the hood of his sweatshirt pulled low to disguise the blood on his face. He couldn't go back to the studio. Not now. And he certainly couldn't go to a hospital, either. Not where there might be police snooping around, checking treatment records and looking for someone fitting his description. *Fucking police.* He went cold with fury at the thought of them.

Each puncture of the needle brought a new grunt of pain, a low growl at the back of his throat. He stopped to take another hit of vodka straight from the bottle, relishing the rasp as it burned its way down his throat. He stared at his busted-up face in the mirror. He had showered, but he could still smell the smoke in his hair, the stink of petrol splashed onto his jacket and jeans seeming to fill the small room.

He wasn't a violent man. Not normally. His size, his build was normally enough to get him what he wanted, to convince people that confrontation was not a good idea. But sometimes people didn't behave the way you expected them to.

Like the stranger. Ellen Devlin.

Dominic took another slug of vodka and put the bottle back down by the sink.

He pulled a fifth stitch through, cinched it tighter. Unlooped the thread from the needle and tied it off close to the skin. It was an ugly job, the stitches messy and uneven, but it was better than leaving it open. There would be a scar, but he didn't care about that. He had plenty of them already, some of them visible, some not. He found a wide plaster in his first-aid kit and stuck it over the top to cover the stitches.

The pain was a savage throb across the right side of his face, but he deserved it. All of it. Because he had been close. *So* close. And he'd let her get away. He put the vodka bottle to his lips and took another drink, the pain blurring a fraction more as the alcohol hit his empty stomach.

He left the small bathroom and sat down on the single bed with its creaking springs and grey sheets. He picked up his phone and selected the number again. Listened to it ring and go to voicemail. Hung up without leaving a message. Again.

Shit.

He deserved this. All of this. He had been stupid and careless, he'd underestimated her.

He wouldn't make the same mistake again.

16

'It's an extraordinary story,' DS Holt says when I'm finished. 'Quite . . . amazing.'

'I know,' I say. 'But that's what happened.'

I've lain it all out for them, from the moment Kathryn asked to sit down opposite me on the train to when I escaped from Dominic and flagged down a passing van on the street outside. Holt made notes while I was speaking but Gilbourne simply sat and listened, nodding occasionally, hands folded over his flat stomach. The only reaction he's given is an occasional raised eyebrow.

'And he knows where I live,' I say. I think of my captor's threat as he held up my mobile and made me unlock it. 'He's got access to everything in my phone. What should I do?'

Gilbourne's face crinkles with concern. 'Is your husband at home?'

I shake my head. 'No.'

'We do have a few resources for at-risk witnesses, a refuge for victims of domestic abuse, but as you can probably imagine, demand far outstrips supply. They're over capacity already.'

'So what do you suggest I should do?' I say. 'How long are you going to keep me here for?'

'That depends.'

'On what?'

He ignores my question. 'Is there somewhere else local you could potentially stay for a few days? A relative, a friend?'

I think about texting Tara, then immediately remember again that my phone is gone. I don't know her number off by heart. Come to think of it, I didn't know *any* numbers off by heart, apart from my own, Richard's and my mum's landline which she's had since I was a girl.

'There is somewhere I could probably go, for a few days. My friend Tara, as soon as I can get a new phone sorted.'

'Good,' Gilbourne nods. 'That would probably be wise.'

Holt taps his notepad impatiently with the end of his pen.

'Let's get back to the train,' he says. 'Kathryn literally handed you her baby and walked away, and you've had no further contact with her since?'

'She asked me to help for a couple of minutes while she dealt with a personal phone call. I was expecting her to come back at any moment – it never occurred to me that she might get off at the next station.'

'And you had never met her before this, never had a conversation with her, never discussed anything she might or might not be planning to do with this child?'

'No,' I say, looking from one detective to the other. 'Never.'

'Obviously we can check that against mobile phone records.'

I frown. 'Right.'

'To see if you had any contact with Kathryn prior to today's events.'

'I don't understand,' I say. 'I just told you I'd never met her before.'

'So you're saying you didn't plan this with her?'

'Plan it?' I stare at the young detective. 'No, of course not. Wait, so you're saying that Kathryn planned all of this in advance?'

'Didn't she?' Holt says.

'I've no idea, I've already told—'

'This note you said she left in the baby's bag,' Gilbourne says gently. 'You lost it?'

'It was in my handbag.'

'That you left at this place?'

'Yes.'

'And just to be clear, everything else that you had – everything related to the baby – you handed over to the desk sergeant on arriving here, correct?'

'I think so. I mean, Dominic took most of it from me and I left it behind when we ran.'

'I need you to think hard, now,' Gilbourne says. 'Have you surrendered everything? All the baby's clothes, cloths, feeding paraphernalia, dummies, toys, all that stuff?'

I shift in my seat.

'I just took Mia and ran for the door,' I say. 'There was no time to pick up anything else. What do you need all that for, anyway?'

'We need to gather all the evidence we can get for potential lab analysis down the line. Depending on how things pan out.'

'Right,' I say. 'Of course.'

Holt says, 'What about the guard on the train? Could they corroborate what you're saying, did you approach the guard at any point?'

I shake my head.

'There wasn't one that I could see. Isn't there CCTV on the train that can confirm what I've said?'

'Not on Chiltern Line trains, unfortunately,' Holt says. 'And the cameras at Seer Green have been out of action since last winter. But the cameras at Marylebone picked you up getting off with the baby and heading straight for the exit. Tell us again, why didn't you alert the station authorities?'

I cast my mind back to those crucial few minutes when I had stepped off the train with Mia in my arms, a little warm bundle of life in the crook of my elbow. Descending onto the platform into noise and chaos, aggression and alcohol, too many people packed in too close to each other.

'It was chaotic, there were two sets of football fans and it looked as if it was all about to kick off, with us in the middle of it. A lot of hostility. Police with machine guns. And a weird-looking guy who followed me off the train.'

'And he was different from the one you claim abducted you?'

I suppress a bristle of annoyance at his choice of words.

'Yes,' I say. 'Two different men.'

'The first of them, the one on the train, tell me about him.' Holt has one of those posh accents that he's trying hard to disguise but that slides out every so often. A home counties public school voice that he's tried to flatten, coarsen into a generic London accent to blend in with colleagues and suspects alike. Gilbourne, on the other hand, has a natural, soft Cotswold burr.

I summon a memory of the man on the train.

'He was mid to late-thirties, black leather jacket, average height, maybe a little bit shorter than me—'

'And how tall are you, Ellen?' Holt interrupts.

'Five ten and a half.'

'Right,' he makes a note on his pad, taking his time. 'OK. Carry on.'

'He had these really intense staring eyes, dark eyes, black beanie hat on but I think he was bald. He was wearing these big combat boots and he was a bit scruffy-looking, like he'd been sleeping rough. He took a laptop out and when I looked over next, he was taking pictures of me and the baby on his phone.'

'Taking pictures is not a crime,' Holt says.

'Maybe not but it's bloody *weird*,' I say. 'I just wanted to get her away from him, from all of it, to a police station. Somewhere safe.'

'But you didn't do that, did you?'

I cross my arms. 'Being abducted at gunpoint sort of got in the way of my plans.'

'After you'd decided to go to a *café*.' He strings the last word out, his eyes flicking up to mine. 'Then a guy comes out of nowhere, threatens to kill you.'

'He was waiting for me in his car. There'll be CCTV on St George Street, something, won't there?'

'We're checking that out.'

'And the place he took me, the old studio complex, what about that? There must be some evidence there.'

'The fire brigade were called out to it soon after you arrived here tonight, a blaze localised at the back of the building, second floor. By the time they got it under control, the whole wing of the building was gutted. Looks like there may have been some kind of accelerant used. We had a quick look at the scene earlier tonight, there's some evidence there might have been a few tramps sleeping rough in parts of the building. But nothing useful from a preliminary search.'

'He wasn't a tramp,' I say in exasperation.

Gilbourne sits forward in his chair. 'Let's rewind a little back to yesterday, shall we? Before this all happened. Can you tell us about your movements in the hours before boarding that train?'

'Why?'

'You boarded at Stoke Mandeville, correct?'

'No, I had to go back via Aylesbury, some sort of problem on the line.'

'Did that take longer?'

'A little bit.'

'And what were you doing there? Was that a work thing? Seeing a friend? Shopping?'

I have a sudden, powerful sense that he already knows the answer to this question. That he is testing me, probing, trying to catch me in a lie. I feel my anger rising, cutting through the pain and fatigue. I've coped with everything the last twenty-four hours has thrown at me but I'm not about to lay out my medical history in front of these three strangers.

'A personal matter.'

'Which was?'

I stare at him. He still has that half-apologetic, hang-dog expression on his face, as if it pains him to even have to ask.

'Personal,' I say again.

I feel the duty solicitor, Betteridge, shift in his seat beside me.

'Perhaps you could give an outline of your movements, Ellen,' he says. 'In broad terms.'

'I don't see how it's relevant.'

Gilbourne holds up his hands in a placatory gesture. 'I'm sure it isn't, Ellen, but it would be great to have the full picture.' He gives me a tight smile. 'For the sake of completeness.'

I cross my arms and sit back in the chair, the plastic edge hard against the backs of my thighs. 'I had a doctor's appointment.'

'Where?'

I let a beat of silence pass. *Don't let them get to you.*

'The Macmillan Institute.'

'What's that?' Holt says.

I glance at the younger detective, willing him to back down, to apologise, to move on. But he simply returns my stare.

'It's a specialist centre attached to the hospital.' I swallow hard. 'A fertility clinic.'

Holt scribbles another note on his pad, his handwriting a tiny black mass of letters packed closely together.

Gilbourne says: 'And what time was your appointment?'

'One o'clock.' I can feel my face reddening. I want to be out of this room, out of this grim police station. Back in my house with the door locked behind me. I want to shut out these men, these questions, shut them all out. 'It was a follow-up appointment to some previous treatments I've had there.'

'So it wasn't for treatment, as such, but more for . . .'

'Test results.'

Gilbourne nods but says nothing. I recognise the tactic, to leave a silence and wait for me to fill it, but I just want to get this interview over and done with.

'It wasn't good news,' I add quietly.

Gilbourne's face softens. 'I'm sorry, Ellen. That must have been a very hard thing to hear.'

I nod, once, and he lets another moment of silence pass. This time I don't fill it.

'And after your appointment,' he says. 'Did you go straight to the train station?'

'Yes. The 2.11 to Marylebone, via High Wycombe.'

Gilbourne sits back in his chair, glancing at his partner.

'It's understandable, in the circumstances,' Holt says, taking over from where Gilbourne has left off. He clicks his ballpoint pen open and shut with his thumb. *Click-click. Click-click.* 'I mean, I understand how these things can happen. I get it.'

'You understand what?'

'A spur-of-the-moment decision.'

'You mean Kathryn?'

'I mean you.' *Click-click. Click-click.* 'The baby.'

17

I look from one detective to the other, a prickle of unease at the back of my neck.

'I don't like the sound of what you're saying.'

'The urge to *have* that baby,' Holt says, 'to hold her, maybe even keep her. To be a better mother to her than anyone else could be.'

I shift in my seat, the unease turning to frustration and anger.

'That is an incredibly offensive suggestion, detective,' I say. 'You have no idea what you're talking about.'

'I know what it's like to want something you can't have.'

I look at him, this well-groomed, chisel-jawed, confident young man, and wonder if he has ever been denied anything in his entire life.

'I seriously doubt that,' I say.

'I can imagine how strong that urge might be, how powerful, how all-consuming, if you've been hoping for a baby for years.' *Click-click. Click-click.* 'How you must feel when you're told you can't have a child of your own. Then an opportunity presents itself and it seems like fate is finally on your side.'

'Hold on, a few minutes ago you were asking if I'd planned this with Kathryn in advance. Now you're suggesting I took Mia as some kind of opportunistic kidnapping?'

'We're just trying to dig out the truth, Ellen.'

'I've *told* you the truth; I was asked to look after her.' I glance at Betteridge, sitting mutely beside me, but he refuses to meet my gaze. 'This is ridiculous.'

'What happened to Kathryn Clifton?' Holt asks, changing tack.

'I thought that was what you were trying to find out.'

'Where is she?'

'I've no idea.' I frown. 'She got off the train at Seer Green, like I told you.'

'Because she hasn't come forward, which is obviously a serious concern for us. No word from her at all in the last twelve hours, no phone calls, no sightings, no contact with family or friends as far as we can establish. And in the meantime you turn up at the front desk with a child you say she gave to you.'

'You're not seriously suggesting that I somehow took Mia from her, against her will? That's crazy.'

'What I'm suggesting is that you saw your chance on the train and decided to take this baby, to make her yours. Call it a . . .' He shrugs, 'a moment of madness. You saw an opportunity and you took it. This sort of thing does happen from time to time. And it felt so good to have that cute little baby in your arms, a baby you could call your own, so you just took her and walked out of the station.'

'No.' I can feel myself flushing, hating that my body is betraying me.

'That's why you didn't alert a train guard, or go to a member of staff, why you didn't approach uniformed officers on the concourse, you didn't make a call right there at Marylebone. You just walked out with her. But at some point later you panicked, when you realised what you'd done and what might happen to you. Maybe when you saw yourself on the evening news.'

'That's wrong,' I say, arms crossed tightly against my chest. 'That's not how it was at all.'

Gilbourne holds up his hands again, like a referee pausing a boxing match.

'I'm sure you can understand, Ellen, that we have to explore all the possibilities until we can rule each of them out.'

'I didn't do anything to Kathryn, so you can rule that one out right now,' I say, shaking my head. 'Look, I'm exhausted, I've hardly slept, I've told you everything I know and I just want to go home. I don't know what your agenda is, what's going on here. Mia's OK, and that's the main thing, isn't it?'

Gilbourne gives a sympathetic smile. 'Just a few more questions then we'll be done.'

'This Dominic individual,' Holt resumes. 'What's his surname?'

I rub at my eyes, gritty and sore under the harsh strip lighting of the interview room. It feels like I've been in here for a dozen hours already.

'I don't know,' I say. 'I told you that already.'

'Any other identifying information at all? Did he ever actually say he *was* the baby's father? Did he ever say it himself, refer to her as his daughter?'

I think back to the snatches of conversation we had shared.

'I don't remember for sure.'

'It's very important, Ellen.'

I've been replaying Dominic's actions in my mind. Being in the car with him, in the room with him, I felt so sure about his motives. There was clearly violence in him, but had any of it been directed towards Mia? The unloaded gun, the empty threats, opportunities to hurt us both – to kill us, even – not taken? And both he and Kathryn had made the same paranoid assertion, in their own ways: that the police were not to be trusted. Any police? Someone in particular?

'So you're basically the original good Samaritan,' Holt says, clicking his pen again. 'Travelling around and doing good deeds?'

'I was just in the right place at the right time, that's all.'

'Tell me more about the gun,' Gilbourne asks, his voice soft. 'You're familiar with firearms, correct?'

'I wouldn't say familiar, no.'

'What would you say?'

'I know the basics. Not much more than that.'

'But you've handled them before, been trained with them.' He picks up a sheet of paper from his folder. 'Ellen Anne Devlin,' he pauses, glancing at me over the top of his glasses, 'County Tyrone is that? Devlin?'

'My grandfather.'

'Ah, interesting. Omagh?'

'Dungannon.'

'My grandma was an O'Neill, from that part of the world.' He makes a little grunt of satisfaction and resumes reading from the sheet. 'Graduated 2001, twelve years in the navy, currently employed at Global Aerospace as a Project Manager. Married to Richard Sloane, 2013.'

'Yes.' The cut in my forehead starts to throb again.

'Did you want to call him, by the way? Your husband? The desk sergeant said you've not called anyone yet.'

'We're separated,' I say.

'Ah,' he says after a pause. 'I see.'

Holt sits forward in his chair. 'What made you join the navy, Ellen?'

'My dad served on destroyers. HMS Sheffield.'

'Right, a family tradition. Encourage you to follow in his footsteps, did he?'

I stare at him, this arrogant young detective, imagining what it would feel like to throw the rest of my tea in his face.

'He was killed in the Falklands when I was two years old.'

Holt blinks once, twice. But he recovers quickly. 'Sorry to hear that. So, what did you do in the navy?'

'I was on HMS Richmond and then on the Dauntless. Some other roles onshore. I was a principal warfare officer.'

'So you do know your way around guns.'

'I had some small arms instruction as part of my initial training, same as everyone else. But that wasn't my primary role, I barely even carried a weapon outside the practice range.'

'But you're pretty familiar with . . .'

Betteridge, the duty solicitor, holds up a small hand. 'Can I ask what the relevance of this is?'

'Your client was arrested with an unlicensed, unregistered firearm in her possession.'

'And she's explained to you that she only had it to facilitate her escape, from a place where she was being held against her will.'

'So she claims.'

'If I'd left it behind,' I cut in, 'he could have used it on me. Or on Mia.'

'Why didn't you use it on him?'

'I tried, but it was unloaded.'

'You tried to shoot him? To kill him?'

'I was going to put one in his leg, just to slow him down.' The sound is seared into my memory, the empty, impotent *click* of the trigger on an empty chamber. 'I couldn't outrun him while I was carrying Mia, but I didn't realise the gun was empty. I ended up hitting him with it instead.'

'Hard?'

'As hard as I could.'

Gilbourne turns to his partner. 'Have we done a hospital check yet?'

Holt shakes his head, scribbling a note on his pad, and Gilbourne turns back to me.

'Can I get you another tea?' He smiles. 'It might even be hot this time.'

'I'm fine, thanks.'

'OK then. Let's get back to last night, shall we?'

His voice is calm, measured. Friendly. And his smile is almost paternal. But he leaves another long pause for me to speak. I hold his gaze until he finally breaks the silence.

'Why don't you just tell us, Ellen?' His voice is soft, no edge to it. 'Get it off your chest.'

'I *have* told you. I just did.'

'But you've left us with a three-and-a-half-hour window that we can't account for. At 3.06 p.m. we've got you on camera leaving Marylebone with someone else's child, then entering a café on St George Street eleven minutes later, where you stayed for sixteen minutes. After that, nothing. A big blank, until officers are called to Bassingham Road on the King's Meadow industrial estate just before 7 p.m., where they find you running around with the child and a gun, covered in blood. Kathryn Clifton is nowhere to be found, your so-called kidnapper is nowhere to be found, and I'm just struggling to fill in those three and a half-hours, to corroborate anything you've said so far.' He smiles at me, spreading his hands. 'Help me out?'

'I've told you. Everything.'

'Hmm.' Gilbourne frowns, studying me again over the top of his glasses. 'Let's go over it again, shall we?'

18

Dominic

The stitches were a dull, constant throb in his cheek, the whole side of his face tender to the touch. He washed at the cracked sink, the cold water shocking him awake and lighting up fresh lines of pain that radiated from the wound. He patted his face dry with the thin towel. The stitches were still holding, each surrounded by puffy red skin against a darkening purple bruise. He covered it with a fresh plaster but his face still looked a mess. Sleep had come in fragments, a string of blood-soaked dreams from which he'd finally jerked awake after a couple of hours, but there was nothing to be done about that. Time was running out and he had to move soon.

He took her phone from the pocket of his bomber jacket and sat down on the small bed. He wasn't good with technical stuff but he knew enough to get what he needed before she could get home, log into another device and lock the phone or wipe it remotely. There was nothing particularly sophisticated or technical about it. He opened the phone with her unlock pattern, scrolled through a couple of screens until he found the Google Maps app, selected it and watched as it zoomed in on his current location. He tapped the search bar and immediately the screen was populated with all her address searches for this week, last week and prior. Oxford, Northolt, Chiswick.

At the top of the list, with little blue icons next to them, were two words: 'Home' and 'Work'.

He clicked on 'Home' and the map scrolled, pulling out then zooming in again until it came to rest, a spidery route laid out in blue dots from his location to hers. He switched to satellite map and studied the top-down street view. A neat neighbourhood of newbuild houses and small gardens, parallel streets above and below it, not far from the A40.

Claverton Gardens, South Greenford.

He clicked on the car icon.

22 minutes (3.7 miles) fastest route.

It was a postcode, no house number. He came out of Google Maps and scrolled more apps until he found one for Outlook email. He scrolled her inbox briefly, then the list of folders until he found what he was looking for. A recent Amazon delivery confirmation, complete with her full address.

I see you. I know where you live.

He took a screengrab of the address and texted it to the number of the new SIM for his next burner phone. The work address was near Bond Street. He googled it and clicked on the first result. It looked as if she'd been telling the truth about her job, at least. He screengrabbed that as well. It would be useful to keep in reserve in case there were more complications. Still using her phone, he did a search for news stories, scanned the first few results. Just the usual lies and bullshit, half-truths and police propaganda regurgitated by the media. He retrieved a USB drive from his backpack and connected it to her phone, downloading her address book, message history, picture gallery and the contents of her email inbox. With the download complete, he switched off her phone, extracted the SIM card and snapped it in two, before smashing the screen of the phone with the butt of his knife, bringing it down again and again until the mobile was a shattered wreck. He swept the cracked plastic and metal fragments into the small, sticky bin by the bed and took his remaining burner phones out of the backpack – only three left now – unwrapping the nearest one and inserting the new SIM card. He plugged it in to charge.

He emptied the rest of her purse. Credit card, debit card, stamps, gym membership, organ donor card, Costa loyalty card, a few receipts. No driver's licence. No family photos in the little plastic window; no snapshots tucked into any of the pockets. He pressed the soft leather between his fingers, feeling for anything metal sewed into the lining. Picked up his knife and ripped into it, tearing open the lining and separating all the pieces until he was satisfied there were no GPS devices inside. He pocketed the cash and threw the rest into the bin. Better to burn it, to dispose of it properly, but there was no time for that.

The knife had a custom-made sheath that strapped to the inside of his left forearm, so it was concealed but could be drawn quickly. He stood up and strapped it to his arm and put his bomber jacket on over the top.

Finally, he took out a folded picture from his own wallet. He kept nothing digitally, no images, moving from one burner phone to the next without leaving a footprint behind. It was as close to off-grid as he could get, but he hadn't been able to give up this picture, the printed image already starting to wear and crease where he had folded and unfolded it so many times. He allowed himself a moment to stare at the picture, his eyes travelling over her face, her lips, her cheeks, her eyes. He had to get to her before it was too late. Before anyone realised who she was. *What* she was.

He had found her once. He could find her again.

And this time, he would do what needed to be done.

19

DI Gilbourne

Gilbourne took a long drag on his cigarette, looking out over the street lights on Northolt Road.

He liked it up here after hours. The city was asleep, laid out beneath him. The streets quiet, the night air cold and sharp in his lungs, the good people of the city asleep in their beds. He did some of his best thinking up here when it was like this. He was on the fourth-floor fire escape, the door wedged open with a fire extinguisher dragged in from the hallway. It was the only place in the whole building where you could smoke without setting off the fire alarm or having one of the young snowflakes coughing and covering their mouth. The chief had forbidden officers from smoking out the front of any station, anywhere that was visible to the public – it didn't *send the right message*, apparently, to have cops smoking when there was police work to do – so the few remaining smokers congregated at the rear of the building in a scrubby patch of gravel next to the vehicle compound. He didn't mind making small talk with the other twenty-a-day pariahs, but sometimes he liked to have a few minutes alone with his vices of choice.

They were a dying breed. Wasn't that the truth.

He checked the corridor behind him – clear – and fished a couple of pills out of the little Ziploc bag tucked into his wallet, swallowing them down dry. As he was putting his wallet back he heard footsteps behind him and Holt came out holding two cups of dark coffee in identical white mugs. He handed one to Gilbourne and stepped back to the other side of the fire escape, as far away from the smoke as he could get.

'What do you reckon then, boss? About her?'

Gilbourne took another drag on his cigarette, holding in the smoke for a moment. He watched as a lone fox emerged below from behind a row of parked cars. It slinked from one side of the street to the other, its bushy tail held low to the ground, hunched as if ready for attack or escape. Gilbourne followed its progress, elbows on the steel railing of the fire escape, cigarette smoke curling up into the night sky. He had always admired them, these secret city dwellers who had adapted so well to new surroundings. They lived and thrived, bred, roamed and hunted in one of the busiest cities in the world – and they did it largely unseen, under the radar of regular life. They were loners who had made the night their own. Survivors.

The fox stopped, turned, sniffed the air, and trotted off into the shadows.

'You think she's holding something back?' Gilbourne asked, every word emerging with an exhalation of grey smoke. 'Something about last night?'

Holt smoothed his hair, swept back from his forehead, patting a few stray strands back into place.

'Definitely.'

'I'm not so sure. There's something that doesn't quite add up, but I'm not sure it's down to her.'

Holt studied him. 'You believe her, boss?'

'What makes you say that, Nathan?'

Holt took a small sip of his coffee and gave him a shrug. A knowing grin. 'I mean . . . the way you were with her in the interview. Seemed like . . . you know.'

Gilbourne studied his new partner. He was still getting the measure of him: a fast-track graduate with a fancy degree in criminology and forensic science who couldn't get out of uniform quickly enough. Who still wanted every case to be The Big One, with wall-to-wall national media coverage, a career-maker that would propel him up the ladder. Who didn't yet appreciate that a case like that might only come up once in a career, that life was messy and the job was messier, that clean-cut victories were few and far between. The two of them had been teamed up for a couple of months now, Holt on a secondment to Major Crime after nine months on one of the Met's task force operations targeting gang activity. So he wasn't totally green, but he still had a lot to learn – if he ever paused long enough to listen.

There was something about him, though. Was it the cockiness? Like he knew more than he was letting on. He had that young cocksure certainty that he would rise through the ranks, that he would make DI within a couple more years. He'd even had the front to say to his face that he'd be disappointed if he wasn't a detective chief inspector by the time he was forty – a promotion that still eluded Gilbourne for reasons he didn't like to dwell on. Maybe Holt didn't realise he was doing it. Or maybe he did. He wasn't sure.

Just you wait, lad. Wait for the politics and the government targets and the PC quotas and all the bullshit that goes with it. Wait for it to start pressing down on you every day, like you're carrying it on your shoulders every time you get out of bed in the morning. Shovelling the same shit every day, just to keep your head above it, without a word of thanks from anyone. Then we'll see how high you can reach.

Gilbourne was now less than six months away from completing his thirty years in the job, from hitting mandatory retirement. It seemed like a waste to him. He was forty-seven and still had a lot to offer. But maybe it was time to hand over to the fast-track graduates like Holt, the greasy-pole climbers, the politicians, the *shiny people*, and see how they managed. Until then – even though he was within touching distance of his lump sum and final salary pension – he still took pride in the job, in getting a result. Some of his colleagues, older guys who had gone before him, started letting things slide when retirement approached. Started phoning it in, cutting corners. Doing the bare minimum until they could check out.

That wasn't Gilbourne's way.

He was doing the opposite: working harder, putting in more time than before. And he was going to nail this new case fast. Make sure he covered all the angles, got the right result.

He took another drag on his cigarette, pointed at his young partner with the glowing tip.

'You've done some time on property crime right?' He didn't wait for a reply. 'So, answer me this: what's the easiest way into someone's house?'

'How do you mean?' Holt looked confused. 'Like . . . forcing a rear door?'

'Easiest, most straightforward way in? What did you learn in those nine months?'

Holt stared at him as if he was trying to work out the answer to a riddle and didn't want to be caught out.

'I guess a downstairs window, left open?' he said. 'Like, any unsecured window?'

'Nope.'

'Patio doors?'

'Think about the question I've asked, Nathan.'

'I mean, it would depend on—'

'The easiest way into a stranger's house is through the front door, if they've opened it themselves and invited you in.'

Holt nodded slowly, eyes narrowing against the smoke from his partner's cigarette.

'Sure,' he said. 'You mean, kind of like a distraction burglary?'

'Sort of. It's the same with an interview. You're more likely to get the full story if they invite you in. Less effort, less mess, less grief all around. Sometimes you're more likely to get to the truth by being nice than by trying to smash the doors down with a battering ram.'

'Right,' Holt said, taking another sip of his coffee. 'I get what you're saying.'

Do you though? Do you, really?

'Feels to me like there are other factors in play that we might not be aware of. It'll be interesting to see what forensics come up with from the stuff we recovered from the fire. Any joy with the CCTV from outside the café?'

Holt shook his head.

'Not yet. There's a council camera at the junction but it's too far down to pick up activity outside the Caffè Nero. The place opens in a few hours so I'll head down then. Got the trace set up on Devlin's mobile as well, just in case it turns up or she miraculously starts using it again when she gets home later.'

'Did you track down the taxi driver yet?'

'Working on it.'

'Good. I'll cover off the station staff at Marylebone.'

'What about her?' Holt nodded back towards the interview room down the corridor. 'Our little navy wren?'

Gilbourne flipped the cigarette away into the darkness, the glowing tip spinning end over end until it disappeared into the street below.

'We let her think about things for a few more hours,' Gilbourne said, blowing smoke. 'Then we go again.'

'Nicely?'

Gilbourne gave him a half-smile.

'You're catching on, Nathan.'

20

There's another hour in the interview room going back and forth over my story, a short conversation with the duty solicitor after both detectives have left, then I'm led into a frigid cell that's bare apart from a thin blanket and a dull metal toilet in the corner. Finally, I'm woken by the clank of the door unlocking, the desk sergeant informing me that I'm being released for the time being.

Betteridge, the duty solicitor, gave me a card for his firm when he left. He was evasive when I asked what would happen next: that was down to the police and any other evidence they might find. If they could corroborate my story with any of the other parties involved, then the threat of criminal charges would recede. If not . . . they would probably bring me in again and go from there. I should be *prepared for any eventuality*, he had said. Until then, I have to remain in London, keep the officers informed as to where I was staying, make myself available for further questioning as and when required; and I'm prohibited from contacting any of the other people involved in my case. Which shouldn't be difficult as I have no idea who any of them actually were.

There are more forms to sign. The clock above the desk tells me it's nearly five in the morning by the time a taxi is called to take me home. I need to find somewhere else to stay for a few days, but my exhaustion is blanketing everything and all I want to do is lie down in my own bed. It's only as I'm walking up the short path to my front door that it occurs to me I have no keys to get into the house. I'm grateful, for once, for Richard's old habit of leaving a spare back door key in the rockery by the side gate. It's still there, tucked under the third rock from the left. I blow the dirt off it, breath steaming in the cold pre-dawn air.

I let myself in, turn on the lights and stand in my little kitchen. The house is still, silent and cold, and it feels different somehow, as if it belongs to someone else. Maybe to my old life. That life was Richard and marriage and IVF, waiting and heartbreak, month after desperate month, year after year. But that world doesn't exist anymore. It's gone. History.

This is a new world, a new day. A world with Mia in it.

And not just her: a man who wanted to take her away, to harm her. A man who has my phone, who might know where I live. Am I safe here, with the pre-dawn darkness still pressing in around my kitchen windows? I fetch the landline and begin to dial, then stop, my thumb hovering over the keypad, my brain sluggish with fatigue. Slowly, I replace the handset in its cradle. It's only just gone 5 a.m., too early to disturb Tara and wake her boys with a phone call. She gets little enough sleep as it is. Instead I check the chain across the front door, the deadbolt, the patio door and the back door, then check them all again before heading upstairs.

I try to sleep, dropping my clothes in a ragged line across the bedroom floor and crawling under the duvet. But it's already too late, the sun creeping into the bedroom, slanting through the edges of the curtains, rush hour traffic starting up its low hum nearby.

I'm alert to every other sound, every creak of the house slowly warming up, every set of footsteps on the street outside, every car passing by. Try as I might, I can't seem to drift off, even for an hour of sleep. My body aches with tiredness, with the throb of injuries, but my brain is still going a hundred miles an hour and refuses to stop. I'm still wired from a day and night full of confrontation and unanswered questions. The strange black-clad man on the train; Dominic, with his anger and paranoia; the two detectives with their questions.

And now home. Or at least, my house. Our house, as it had been until three months ago. Richard and I had given up our one-bedroom flat on Highbury Park Road five years ago – the flat where we'd first lived together, where we'd dreamed and made plans and returned from honeymoon – in favour of a sensible family home a few miles further out. Five years in this modern end-terrace with its small garden and two-and-a-half bedrooms and a decent primary school nearby, a dozen Tube stops further out of London. Five years waiting for the arrival of a child that had never come. Richard increasingly distant and evasive over the last year, spending more time working late in the office, more time avoiding life at home. More time with the woman who was now carrying his child.

After an hour I give up on sleep and shuffle into the bathroom, standing under the shower for fifteen minutes, letting the hot water pound the back of my neck. I think about Mia, the last time I saw her. The thin, bird-like woman from social services who had taken her away, who had made Mia cry as she manhandled her into the scuffed plastic car seat. Eventually I put on old jeans and a sweatshirt and a fresh bandage on my foot.

It's Wednesday. It's supposed to be a normal working day but I'm owed some time off in lieu so I take the day off, emailing my boss to apologise for the short notice. What else is happening this week? Shopping delivery arriving tonight, Pilates tomorrow, work drinks on Friday night – someone's leaving do that I already know I won't be able to face. As for next week, next month? I can't think that far ahead anymore.

I call my bank and credit card company to cancel all my cards and have new ones reissued. I dig out my old iPhone from the bedside drawer and walk the ten minutes to the high street to buy a new SIM card. Back home I log into my iCloud account, saying a little prayer that the automatic backup has worked as it was supposed to. I feel a little thrum of happiness in my chest as the saved images begin to drop in and there is Mia, tiny and perfect, sleepy and content after the bottle I gave her in the café. One picture. This is all I have of her. But it lifts me, warms me, a bright spot on a dark day.

I call my mobile provider to get my old number transferred to the new SIM. All this practical everyday stuff seems ridiculous, meaningless, set against the last twenty-four hours. I keep flicking back to the picture of Mia, just to remind myself that it's still there and that she really exists. I set it as the new screensaver on my phone, then remove it again, feeling like a thief, a fraud, for having someone else's child on my screen. I'll just keep it in the phone's gallery instead. A secret.

At noon, I give Tara a call. The conversation is full of noise from her three boys, fighting and shouting and screaming in the back-ground all at once, a wall of yelling that makes me hold the phone away from my ear. During a short lull in the mayhem, she tells me that the eldest is off school with a sick bug, the middle one has an ear infection and the youngest, Charlie, a raging case of the terrible twos manifesting itself in some epic potty-training failures.

'This morning he decided to do a dirty protest behind the sofa,' she says, 'just took his pants off and left them there, fully loaded. Not sure I'm ever going to get it out of the carpet. Anyway, how are you? How did it go yesterday? I left you a couple of messages.'

I want to tell her everything, to sit down with her with a glass of wine and go over the whole story from start to finish.

'Sorry I didn't get back to you, it was a bit of a crazy day yesterday—'

There is a fresh explosion of screaming at the other end of the line, small voices rising in competing howls of protest, followed by Tara's exasperated voice asking one of them to stop doing something to his brother.

'Say sorry to your brother,' she says firmly. '*Say sorry.* Or there'll be no TV and no iPad and you'll go to your room until tea-time, do you understand?' There is a pause in the hostilities and an inaudible response from whichever of her sons she's telling off, then she comes back on the line. 'Sorry, Ellen. What were you saying about yesterday?'

I close my eyes and lean against the kitchen wall, hit by another wave of fatigue. I don't even know where to start the story, explain how I went through the looking glass and ended up in a police station interview room. I don't even have the heart to ask if I can crash in her spare room for a few days.

'Long story,' I say instead. 'Listen, it sounds like you've got your hands full. I'll let you go. Give me a call later after the boys are in bed?'

'If they survive until bedtime,' Tara says with a humourless laugh. 'OK, talk later. Take care, Els.'

Maybe I should move into a hotel for a few days instead. I google a few that are local. How long for? A couple of days? A week? I'm in the process of buying Richard out of his share of the house and money's been tight anyway since he left. Can I justify the extra expense? I bookmark the pages to look at later.

There's a message on the answer machine from my mum, the only person I know who still uses the landline. I make a note to call her back later. She's on her own and prone to worry, to catastrophise every situation; I can't remember when I started censoring myself when talking to her, but it's been a while now since I just sat and told her the unvarnished truth. *First the parent lies to the child*, I think, *then the child lies to the parent.*

I find my iPad and search for news about Mia and Kathryn. The latest story on the BBC relates that the baby has been 'found safe and well' but doesn't identify her. Presumably the media is restricted in what they can report because of the involvement of a child whose anonymity is supposed to be protected. The grainy CCTV image of me at Marylebone features lower down the story and I wonder briefly what my mum or Tara – or my work colleagues, for that matter – will make of it if they recognise me. But I haven't got the headspace to worry about that right now. A half-dozen other news websites are all carrying the same basic details and the same quote from Detective Inspector Stuart Gilbourne of the Major Crimes Unit. *'We are still very keen to hear from Kathryn Clifton to confirm that she is safe. If you think you've seen Kathryn, or have any information on her whereabouts, please contact the police on 101.'* But some of the heat has been taken out of the story with the news that Mia is no longer missing; the articles less prominent, lower down the page, the stories more factual and concise. A missing woman is far less newsworthy than a missing infant, I suppose. I scour all the stories for any more information about Kathryn. There is very little, just a few generic facts and a picture that looks like it was grabbed from her Facebook account. No quotes from family members, friends or from a partner. She's twenty-four years old and from Buckinghamshire, but apart from that the story is strangely light on details.

None of them say she is Mia's mother.

It seems weird that there are no pleas from family for her safe return. Surely it must have been her family who raised the alarm that she and Mia were missing? Who else could it have been?

The landline rings with its unfamiliar tone and I reach for the handset, thinking it's my mum calling again. But it's my ex-husband instead: Richard's voice filling my ear, deep and full, as familiar as my own.

I try to be calm whenever we speak, refusing to let him see the scars he's left me with.

'Richard,' I say, wondering whether he's seen my picture in the news.

'I've been trying to reach your mobile but I couldn't get hold of you,' he says, sounding concerned. 'I was going to leave a message. I thought you'd be at work.'

'Day off in lieu today, I've been . . .' It doesn't seem right to tell him, to share this new piece of my life with him. 'Been busy sorting some things out. Mobile's been switched off for a bit.'

'Is everything OK? You sound tired.'

'Fine. Just work stuff.'

A silence, then he clears his throat.

'Listen, Ellen, I wanted to let you know about something, before you . . . hear about it from anyone else.' He sounds reticent, almost apologetic. 'The thing is, I – we, I mean Francesca and me – have got some news and I thought it best that you hear it straight from the horse's mouth rather than—'

'I know, Richard.' I'd rather not hear him say it out loud.

'About her being—'

'Yes.'

'Oh, right.' He doesn't ask me how I know. 'Sorry.'

I close my eyes, force the words out.

'I'm happy for you. Honestly. Both of you.'

'Really?'

'Really.'

'Thank you, Ellen. That means a lot. It just came a bit out of the blue when it happened, you know? I thought it would be better if you heard it from me first.'

'Sure.' I suddenly feel hot, my throat thick and painful. 'Listen, I've got to go, OK?'

I cut him off before he can launch into any more details, and we say our goodbyes. I sit for a moment in my silent lounge, the phone clutched in my white-knuckled hand, blinking tears away. The pain is back, that old familiar sense of failure tightening its rusty barbs around my stomach. In a box somewhere upstairs is a set of framed photos of our navy wedding, with him in full dress uniform, a guard of honour outside the church in my mum's village. We had left the service a couple of years later to start our new life together, to start our family. A man I once thought I would spend my life with; a man who seemed to have his whole life planned out.

By the time I realised I was no longer part of his plan, it was already too late to save our marriage.

I don't know how long I sit there with the phone in my hand. Eventually I go back upstairs to the bedroom and find the old sweatshirt they gave me at the police station, balled up at the end of my bed. I reach into the pocket and pull out a small tightly-folded square of white cloth, the muslin that Mia was clutching when we arrived at the police station. Gilbourne had asked for all of the baby's things – he was quite particular about it. But I'd felt strangely reluctant to hand it over. They didn't *need* it. I decided to keep it instead, just this one little thing of hers.

I sit on the bed, blinds drawn against the gathering dark, rolling the cloth between my fingers, the cotton soft and crumpled, remembering the way Mia had clutched it in her own tiny hands, how it had comforted her. I lift the cloth to my face and inhale deeply, that unmistakeable clean baby smell filling my nostrils.

I think back to the day before, late leaving the hospital, not caring whether I made my train or had to wait for the next one. Not caring about anything really anymore, the deadening finality of the doctor's words blotting out everything else. Walking slowly through the town on autopilot, barely aware of the time, barely aware of the people or the traffic or the daily life going on around me. Just wanting to be on my own, to not talk to anyone or think about anything. I would have missed my train – the 2.11 to Marylebone – except it had been three minutes late, so instead I made it with seconds to spare. I was the last passenger to climb aboard, the carriage door sliding shut right behind me. If the 2.11 had been on time, I would have missed it. I would never have met Kathryn. I would have been spared the trauma of the abduction, the pain of my injuries and the terror of the escape, I would have avoided a bruising interrogation by the police and the criminal charges now hanging over me.

But I would never have met Mia either, never held her, never been there to take care of her.

I was glad the train had been late.

21

Leon

He had downloaded the new pictures and blown them up to A4 size. Now they were tacked to the board above his desk alongside the images of the other women. Alongside the two brunettes: the pretty one and the short one. And the blonde, the one with the piercings. Three girls, three victims. He checked his fingers. There was a faint residue of printer ink so he rolled the white latex gloves off his hands with a *snap* and dropped them into the stainless steel germ-capture pedal bin beside the desk. Plucked a new pair from the large box and eased his long fingers into them, flexing them until the latex was snug against his skin. Then he settled back at his desk and studied the new images. There were three: one in profile as she looked out of the train window, one smiling down at the baby, and one when she was looking straight at the camera, her lips parting, a frown already forming on her face.

She was strange, this one. Tall, athletic, a confidence to the way she walked. Different to the others.

This was his sanctuary, his fortress, his safe space. Fully sound-proofed so no noise could penetrate the walls in either direction, windows painstakingly taped so no light could reach inside. An array of mobile phones lined up and charging on the right side of his big corner desk. This place was what *he* made it, without any interruptions or intrusions from the outside world. In here, he could find his own truth, make his own reality.

His birth name, his baptism name, was Leonard. But no one called him that anymore. His mother had been the last one, and she was long gone. To the few who knew him now, most of whom he kept at arm's length, he was *Leon*. Like the lion. King of the jungle, *Panthera Leo*, top of the food chain. A keystone predator, zoologists called them, because of their disproportionately large effect on their natural environment. He liked that.

His eyes returned to the two large screens in front of him, arrayed with a selection of google search results, social media accounts and an image-handling programme. A third screen had multiple tabs open using the TOR browser that gave anonymous access to the dark web.

But he wasn't using the dark web for this; the open web should give him what he needed. The harvesting software on his laptop sought out internet-connected devices looking for unsecured Wi-Fi; most people were never even aware their phones were doing it. On the train he had used it to harvest the details of the Devlin woman's phone, including her user ID, first name and the networks it had connected to in the last few days, and from there he'd tracked down her social media accounts and gone through the images one by one.

She was on Facebook, posting infrequently until three months ago when her activity dropped to virtually nothing. Before that there had been pictures of her and some predictably handsome drone named Richard Sloane – husband, presumably – together at a restaurant, on a beach, at a back-garden barbecue. But since early June, nothing. Her Twitter account had seen a similar decline in activity, also going back to the same time. Posts on fundraising stuff to do with the Royal Navy and Royal Marines charity. The last post was the second of June. He returned to Facebook and made a note of all the check-ins over the last six months. Then scrolled back through the images posted, clicking on each one and blowing them up to fill the whole of the thirty-seven-inch monitor, studying each carefully for location tags, street signs, menus, landmarks, backgrounds, car number plates, logos, company names – anything that would help him triangulate her location. Noting all the people who were tagged in her pictures for later perusal. There were more pictures of the cat and the husband than her. In one from May captioned 'The two men in my life xx ☺', the husband was lying on his back on the sofa with the big brown-and-black cat sprawled across his chest. Leon suppressed a shudder of disgust as his eyes skated across the image, searching for clues. It was in high-definition, probably a phone camera with ten megapixels plus, a quality that would have been uncommon even a few years ago.

There.

He saved the picture and opened it in the image handling programme, then zoomed in and enhanced it. Highlighted an area below the cat's chin and blew it up another two hundred per cent. Then again.

The cat's tag. It was angled towards the camera, a flat silver disc hanging from its collar. He zoomed in another 25 per cent, sharpened the image, smiled to himself. At normal resolution, you wouldn't have even noticed the careful engraving. But with a little enhancing, it was right there.

Dizzy
46 Claverton Gdns
07791 626957

He switched to another screen and called up Google Maps.

THURSDAY

22

Mia is crying.

A plaintive, mewling cry that cuts right to the bone, right to my core. I can hear her, *feel* her. The cry is swelling to fill the room, the sound squeezing tightly around my heart. Mia needs me. She's afraid, in danger, frightened in the dark. I snap awake. Reach for her, hands searching in the darkness to lift her up and hold her to my chest and—

Mia isn't here.

I lie back down against the pillow, heart thudding against my ribs. The crying was so real, so *near*. Almost as if she was in the room with me. I lie in the darkness, waiting for my heart rate to steady, staring at the outline of moonlight leaking in around the edges of the blinds. It's almost 4 a.m., more than thirty hours now since I last saw Mia. I know she was taken to the hospital for a precautionary check over, but I wonder where she is now. With a foster family? In some council-run facility? Or have they found Kathryn, reunited the two of them?

I shift my legs under the duvet and feel the comforting shape of Dizzy, my tabby cat, curled up at the foot of the bed. Richard had never liked him sleeping upstairs – he claimed his padding about in the night kept him awake – but now Richard's gone and I like Dizzy's company. I'm still not used to sleeping alone, to waking up alone. I sit up, the night-time air cool on my arms, and give him a scratch behind the ears. He doesn't stir but a soft bass purr starts up deep in his chest.

That's when I hear it.

Not a cry this time. A sound. A creak of wooden floorboards shifting under weight. I lift my hand from the velvety fur on Dizzy's head and his purring slowly fades back into the dark. I hold my breath, my pulse ticking faster. Ten seconds of silence spools out, twenty, before it comes again. An almost imperceptible creak, slow, deliberate, the kind of sound Richard used to make when he came back from 'working late' with the new colleague who was now carrying his baby. The kind of sound you make when you're trying very hard not to make any sound at all.

Downstairs.

Dominic's words come back to me.

'*I will come looking for you and I will find you. You'll wake up one night and I'll be standing there at the end of your bed.*'

I reach for my bedside lamp, half-expecting the light to reveal his face glowering at me from the corner of the room, or blocking the doorway, holding the broad-bladed knife.

But I'm alone in the bedroom, just me and the cat. The air seems suddenly colder and I shiver in my pyjamas, a thick wedge of fear lodging painfully in my throat. Very carefully, I lift my phone from the bedside table and type 999, so I just have to hit the green 'dial' button to make the call. The smart thing to do would be to push something heavy in front of the bedroom door, barricade myself in, stay quiet and call the police now.

My thumb hovers over the dial button.

But there's anger behind the fear, too. How *dare* he come to my house? How *dare* he track me down, break in, violate my home? Who the hell does he think he is?

If it even *is* him. Maybe it's just the creak of my little house cooling in the night. Maybe it's some poor creature that Dizzy brought in while I was sleeping, half-dead, trying to make its escape. Or maybe it's nothing all. Just my imagination working overtime, conjuring babies' cries and the sounds of an intruder in the night.

All these thoughts spin through my mind in a matter of seconds as I sit up, listening for the next sound. Nothing. As quietly as I can, I swing my legs out of bed and stand up, pulling on my thick towelling dressing gown. I go around to the other side of the bed, where Richard used to keep an old sawn-off piece of curtain pole for eventualities like this. I just hope he didn't take it with him when he left.

He didn't. It's still there, leaning up against the wall, an eighteen-inch long baton of wood that feels smooth and solid in my right hand. Gripping it tightly, the phone still in my other hand, I move to the door. My heart is beating so fast I feel like it's going to fly out of my chest, my legs tingling with adrenaline. I wait another minute, debating whether to turn the door handle. This is *my* bloody house. I am not going to cower in the bedroom.

I am nobody's victim.

Slowly, carefully, I open the door to the landing as silently as I can. All I can hear is the breath in my throat and the thundering of my heart. I use my phone hand to hit the main light switch, squinting against the sudden brightness as the landing and stairs are bathed in halogen light.

'I've called the police!' I shout down the stairs. 'They're on their way.'

At the top of the stairs I listen again. A creak? A click? Something else?

I take the stairs slowly, straining my ears to hear the slightest sound, hitting the other lights when I get to the bottom. I tiptoe down the hall, breath trapped in my throat, checking the front door is locked and bolted with the security chain on. I check all the rooms, turning all the lights on as I go, every bulb blazing bright in the night to banish the shadows and illuminate the hiding places. The sliding glass door in the lounge is closed and locked. The little dining room with its chairs pushed tightly into the table. The kitchen is last, my narrow galley kitchen with its worktops left and right, a sink looking out over the small garden blanketed in darkness. The iPad there is untouched, plugged in to charge on the kitchen side. I reach the back door that leads out into the narrow alleyway with the garden one side, the street on the other. I test the handle, expecting it to remain firm and unmoving under my palm like the rest.

But the handle gives and the door swings open, a blast of cold night air greeting me.

I stand for a second, frozen with shock, eyes blinking into the darkness – is someone there? A face, a pair of eyes? Movement at the far end of the garden? – before I slam the door closed again and turn the key in the lock. Twisting it all the way around until I hear the metallic *click* of the deadbolt slotting into place. Testing the handle again twice, to make sure it's solid and secure.

Clammy sweat dampens the back of my neck. There is a smell too, faint and fading. A ghost of something sour in the cold kitchen air, sweat and dirt and exhaled breath; then there's fear rising in my throat and I turn back to the hallway raising the baton to strike—

There is no one there.

Heart thudding painfully in my chest, I check the phone in my left hand again, light up the screen up with a shaking hand to make sure the 999 call is only one press away. Listen to the sounds of my house again, straining my ears to pick up any tiny movement. A soft noise on the stairs, descending slowly. Footsteps. I grip the baton in a moist palm. Steps nearing the bottom now. Soft. Padding.

Dizzy appears at the foot of the stairs and walks slowly into the kitchen, winds his way between my legs and sits down by his food bowl. Yawning and blinking slowly up at me. *Early breakfast?*

'Too early,' I say to him, my voice loud and shaky in the silent house. But the cat's calmness relaxes me slightly. If there was someone else still here, he would have sensed it, surely, would be on alert. I check back through all the rooms again anyway, looking behind curtains and anywhere else someone might be concealed. The cat follows me every step of the way until I return to the kitchen and put a few treats in his bowl.

I watch him eat. I've been on my own here every night for three months but I've never felt as alone as I do right this minute. Did I leave the kitchen door unlocked? I was still tired from the previous night at the police station, still strung out and distracted. Maybe I just forgot to do it. Locking up the house at night always used to be Richard's job, one of his night-time tasks, and I'm still acclimatising to his absence. I think for a moment. Maybe it *was* Richard. Maybe he let himself in – he still has a key. But why would he be creeping around in the middle of the night? That wouldn't make sense at all, and he would have mentioned it on the phone earlier – but I text him anyway. Maybe I shouldn't have had that third glass of wine before I went to bed. Maybe I really did just forget to check the back door.

Or maybe someone is still looking for Mia, and he found a way in.

Because he thought she might be here. With me.

Another thought comes swiftly after the first.

As long as he is still out there, Mia is still in danger.

23

I leave all the lights on for the rest of the night. Sleep is an impossibility now, so instead I check all the doors and windows again, search all the rooms twice – even the little box room and the garage – checking under all the beds, then finally shower and dress and put a pot of coffee on. No TV or radio, no Alexa, nothing to mask the sound if someone tries to get into my house again. I make a mental note to buy a couple of deadbolts for the kitchen door and fit them before tonight. Then I scan a dozen news websites for updates on Mia and Kathryn, but there doesn't seem to be anything new beyond what they were running yesterday. Kathryn is still missing. The unnamed baby is barely mentioned, almost a footnote to the story now she has been found. The CCTV image of me no longer features on most of them.

I wait until 7 a.m. to make the call. He picks up after three rings, answering with a single word.

'Gilbourne.'

'Hello, Detective Inspector, it's Ellen Devlin.'

A moment of silence.

'Ellen,' he says, his voice rising with surprise. On the phone he sounds younger. 'Hello.'

'Sorry to call so early, but I need to talk to you.'

'Everything OK?'

'Erm, yes. I think so. For now, anyway.'

It's not entirely true. I can't shake the sense that someone is behind me, whenever I stand with my back to the room, whenever I'm near an open door, as if someone is going to burst through it any moment. The sense that someone is following me, watching me. Waiting for me.

'Are you sure?' he says. There is a rustling noise before his voice comes back clearer. 'Where are you?'

'I'm at home.'

'You're safe?'

I feel a little glow of appreciation, that his first thought is for my well-being.

'I'm fine,' I say. 'Is now a good time?'

There is another pause on the line. He's breathing heavily, I realise, breaths punctuating each word as if he's just climbed a steep flight of steps. I'm about to say more when his voice returns, cutting through the silence.

'Sorry Ellen, can I call you back in literally one minute?'

'Sure,' I say. 'Of course.'

He rings off without another word and I stand in the middle of my kitchen with the phone in my hand, staring out at the empty garden. Another area that was always Richard's domain, the mowing and weeding and pruning the little apple tree at the end. There's a six-foot fence on all three sides. Was that how the intruder had got in, pulling themselves up and over a fence panel? I can't see any obvious signs of damage, but one side borders the street – that would be the obvious place to come over. Dizzy sits on a fence post at the far end, surveying his domain, blinking slowly at me in the weak autumn sunshine. On a clear morning it's the one place that always catches the sun as it rises between the trees.

A minute later, the phone vibrates in my hand.

'Hello again.' Gilbourne seems to have got his breath back. 'What's on your mind, Ellen?'

'Sorry to wake you, inspector.'

He grunts with something like amusement.

'I'm a long way from my bed, don't worry about it.'

'I need to ask you something first.' I take a sip of coffee. 'Am I still a suspect?'

'The investigation is ongoing.'

'But do you think I was lying in the interview on Tuesday night?'

There is a brief silence at his end of the line, an exhalation of breath or maybe cigarette smoke.

'Officially or unofficially?'

'Whichever is nearer the truth.'

'Unofficially, no I don't think you were lying. But we have to shake every tree to see what falls out of the branches, if you know what I mean.' His voice lowers a little. 'Apologies if Nathan came across as a little bit . . . over-zealous. He's quite new to the team and he's still trying to make his mark.'

I'm momentarily thrown by his honesty. I'd expected some kind of mealy-mouthed official line about keeping all options open; not that he would actually *answer* my question.

'Thanks, Detective Inspector. I appreciate your candour.'

'One of the upsides of being in your last few months in the job – your boss doesn't bother to haul you over the coals anymore when you bend a few rules,' he says, a smile in his voice. 'Was there something you wanted to tell me, Ellen?'

I tell him about the previous night, the noises in my house and finding the kitchen door unlocked. My feeling that someone had been creeping around downstairs while I slept.

'Are you sure you're OK? Did you see anyone?'

'I thought I might have seen someone through the kitchen window when I came down. A face.'

'Can you describe them?'

I think for a moment, summoning the memory. In the early morning sunlight, it barely seems real. Had it been real?

'I don't know, it was fully dark outside, I had all the house lights on and I was a bit dazzled. A bit freaked out too, if I'm honest.'

'Do you think it was a man or a woman?'

'Man, I think. I don't know. It was so fast, then they were gone. Sorry, I'm not being very helpful, am I?'

'Don't worry about it. Any CCTV on your house that might have caught him?'

'No.'

'Did he take anything?'

'Don't think so.'

'Anything at all? Are you sure?'

'My iPad was right there on the kitchen side, charging overnight. But they left it, they left everything.'

'Anything in your house that might identify them? Anything they might have dropped on their way out?'

'No.'

'They didn't force entry? You're able to secure the property, are you?'

'I think they must have picked the lock on the back door. There's no damage, I'm going to buy some deadbolts to put on it today.'

His voice takes on a slightly brisker tone.

'OK, Ellen, you should call 101 and make a formal report, I can give a nudge to a couple of the lads on the burglary team to make sure they follow up with you. They can give you a crime number for the insurance claim if you discover anything has been damaged or stolen.'

'I don't want to make a claim, it's not about that.' I pause, not sure how to proceed. 'That wasn't why I was ringing.'

He clears his throat. 'So what's on your mind, Ellen?'

'This is . . . it's going to sound a bit mad.'

Instantly, his voice takes on a reassuring neutral tone again.

'Why don't you let me be the judge of that, Ellen.'

'I just feel like – sorry if this sounds crazy, but I've been going over and over it in my mind for the last few hours. I think whoever came into my house was looking for Mia.'

There is another pause on the other end of the line.

'OK. What makes you say that?'

'It can't be a coincidence.'

'Go on.'

'What I mean is, I'm forty-one years old and I've never had my house broken into. Not once. Not in this house, not in our flat in Highbury, not in my place before that. Not in service accommodation in the navy, not even in three years at university when I lived in some quite dodgy areas.'

'You've been lucky.' On his end of the line I can hear the sound of his footfalls, distant traffic noise, as if he's outside. 'But I get it, I think it's understandable. Ellen, the baby's on your mind, it's a pretty intense experience you've had. I can see why you might want to see a link between the two things.'

'Barely twenty-four hours after this thing happens with Kathryn and Mia, someone gets into my house and is creeping around in the dead of night? There must be a connection, don't you think? What are the chances of that just being coincidence? The guy who abducted me, he took my phone, he knows where I live. He told me he'd find me if I talked to the police.'

'Can you stay somewhere else for a few days?'

'I'm not running away. And if I'm in danger, then so is Mia, right?'

He is silent for a moment.

'I'm not really sure what you want me to say, Ellen.'

'Do you really not think they're connected?'

'I suppose it's possible.' I can hear the sound of a car door slamming shut and the line at his end is suddenly quieter. 'But honestly? I can't imagine what the link would be. Unless he just got a kick out of frightening you, which is why I'd urge you to stay with a friend for a few days.' .

I lean against the kitchen worktop, looking out of the window. Dizzy has jumped down from the fence and is stalking a magpie that sits in the highest branches of the apple tree. There is one question, the only real question that needs an answer, pushing all others from my mind.

'Why would he be looking for Mia?' I say. Finally voicing the suspicion that's been growing in my mind with every passing hour. 'Is Kathryn her mother, or is she a nanny or something? Are her parents famous, or rich? What does Dominic want with her?'

'I can't tell you that.'

'But you know, do you? You know something?'

'I . . . I'm afraid I can't discuss that with you either, Ellen. But I can assure you that she's safe.'

He tells me he has a meeting with his boss, so I ring off and sit in my silent kitchen. I was hoping that he would be able to reassure me that my instincts were wrong, that I was overreacting, putting two and two together and making five. Maybe that they had arrested Dominic, or identified the weirdo from the train. But the conversation with him doesn't reassure me at all. In fact, it only prompts new questions. I pull up the single picture of Mia on my phone, stare at it for a moment until I feel a lump start to build in my throat, an ache in my chest. It's like a drug, an addiction, I know it's bad for me but I can't stop looking at her face.

Stop. Just stop.

I need to get out of the house. I kill an hour walking to the high street and buying a couple of deadbolts from the little hardware store, sticking to the busy roads on the way back and checking over my shoulder every few hundred metres. Back home again, I'm glad of something else to think about as I measure and mark up and put the screws into the top and bottom of the kitchen door, feeling marginally better as I slide both bolts home with a *thunk* of metal on metal. I make another pot of coffee and look for something else to distract me. My eyes fall on a stack of unopened mail that I have piled on the kitchen table and I sift through it. A handful of flyers for takeaways and local tradesmen. A thick letter from Richard's solicitor and a thin one from mine. Two utility bills. A credit card statement. I don't bother to open any of it. All mundane, pointless, meaningless.

I push the stack to one side and sip my coffee, thinking back to where this all started. A train carriage. Mia. Kathryn. A strange guy sitting down opposite me, taking pictures. It wasn't a coincidence that he had suddenly appeared – there *had* to be a connection. At the time, my first instinct was that he was following *me*. Because that was a natural assumption, wasn't it? Photographing *me*. But I was wrong. Mia's the key. She was the reason. All of the strange things, all the craziness started the moment I took her in my arms.

The fresh jolt of caffeine clears my head a little. I find a pen, turn over one of the junk mail flyers and begin to write.

Train guy – photographs – why? – follows – how does he know Mia?

Dominic – father? – GPS tracker – who is tracking? Didn't harm. Burglary?

Police – Gilbourne/Holt – know Mia's ID – burglary not connected? Theories?

Kathryn – gives baby away – mother? Or not hers? Doesn't trust police – still missing

And below that:

Mia – who is she? Why do they want her? Parents? Family?

I stare at the list until my coffee cup is empty again, trying to draw links and connections. But it's like trying to complete a jigsaw puzzle when half the pieces are missing. I hold the flyer in both hands, squinting at each word, willing my caffeine-infused brain to make the leap. Thinking back to another piece of paper I had held in my hands on Tuesday afternoon, a scribbled note left for me to find. Black biro on white paper. Ten words, nothing else. The detectives told me to recount the words precisely, *exactly*, for any clues that might help them.

I said at the time that I didn't have anything else to tell them. Except there *was* something else. There was one other piece of information that I didn't think to mention. It hadn't seemed relevant at the time. The note had been written on the back of a receipt, an A4 delivery note like you got with a gift when you ordered online. What was the name of the company? I close my eyes, coaxing the memory to the surface, reaching for it.

BabyStuff? BabyLove?

BabyCool.com. That was it.

I reach for my mobile and find the list of recently-dialled numbers. My thumb hovers over the *call* button next to Gilbourne's name. But did he believe me about the stranger in my house? Was his concern real? Or is he starting to think I'm just a bit mad? *It's understandable, Ellen, the baby's on your mind, it's a pretty intense experience you've had.*

I put the phone down again. This is probably nothing. But I can check it out, then let the police know either way. I unlock my iPad and go to Google.

24

I close my eyes and clear my mind, the way I've done since I was a little girl trying to remember the last day with my dad. Reaching out for the memory, trying to visualise again the piece of paper I had pulled from Kathryn's bag. It was a delivery note, a computer-printed list of items: a sling, a packet of muslin cloths, a tin of powdered baby milk, a few other items. All the stuff in the bag that she'd been carrying with her. I'd only glanced at it for a second; it hadn't seemed important at the time. Now I try to summon the other details to mind, dragging fragments of memory to the surface. I remember the paper was crumpled, the top left corner torn off where a staple might have been, the vague outline of a dirty shoeprint across it. A delivery address in the top right. One of those quaint village names with 'Little' in front of it, like they have on *Morse* or *Midsomer Murders*. I feel like it's *M-i* something. Two or three syllables. Miston? Milhaven? I try to focus, try to find the stillness that I use to block everything else out. Take a deep breath in, hold for five, deep breath out, hold for five. Repeat.

Little Milton? I open my eyes and google it. There is a village called Little Milton south-east of Oxford. That seems like it might be a possibility. But it's tiny and out on a limb, only a few hundred people, and doesn't seem like the kind of place someone of Kathryn's age would choose to live. I write the name on the pad next to me, then delete the search term one letter at a time until other results appear.

Little Mill? Another small village, this one near Pontypool. Kathryn's accent had been flat, southern, Thames Valley. No Welsh intonation. And it was a long way away, hours by car or train. I write it on the pad anyway and go back to the search results.

Little Minster? A hamlet to the west of Oxford. Nearer to London. I stare at the results for a moment, write it on the pad and delete the search term. It doesn't sound right either.

Mia's muslin cloth is there in front of me on the kitchen table. I pick it up, roll the creased fabric between my fingers, remembering again the way she had clutched it. I hold it to my cheek for a second, inhaling the soft baby smell, feeling for a moment as if I'm back on the train with her warm in the crook of my elbow. A memory bobs to the surface and I put my hands back on the keyboard, adding one letter to the search term.

Little Missenden?

It's in south Buckinghamshire. A Wikipedia page describes it as 'a village and civil parish on the River Misbourne in the Chiltern Hills, situated in between Great Missenden and Amersham.'

Great Missenden has a direct rail connection to Marylebone station in London.

I feel a tingle of recognition, of excitement. *This one.* This address. In my mind I see the address on the paper more clearly now, although whether this is just hope filling the gaps, I don't know. But it *feels* right, this place. It fits. If I can talk to Kathryn's family, I can find out what's going on and if she's OK. I need to tell her what happened myself and get answers to some of my own questions, closing the loop on this strange couple of days in my life. I need to know that Mia is safe. There is a whisper at the back of my mind too – *you just want to see her again, to hold her in your arms one more time* – but I push it away.

According to Google Maps, Little Missenden is about twenty miles north-west, outside London, beyond the M25 towards Oxford. Forty minutes or so by car. I select the satellite image and study the layout of the village. Two pubs, a cricket club, a church, an infant school, a crossroads. A scattering of houses stretched along the two roads, running east–west and north–south, the whole thing surrounded by cultivated fields, brown and green in the satellite image. The curve of the Chiltern Rail line just to the north, parallel with the main road as it snakes its way south-east towards London. I can't remember a street name from the delivery note but the village looks like one of those small places where everyone goes to the same pubs and knows everyone else's business. I could just ask around, find someone who knows her. I find myself wishing I still had her white rucksack, the one she'd left on the train – it would have been a useful starting point for conversation.

The thought gives me an idea. I change into work clothes, a mid-blue trouser suit and white blouse, cover the healing cut above my eye with concealer as best I can. I rummage in the back of the wardrobe until my hand falls on the handbag that my former mother-in-law bought me last Christmas. Garish purple and black leather, not really my thing at all but I didn't have the heart to take it to the charity shop. I pull off the label and throw a few things inside, a packet of tissues, some pens, a couple of lipsticks that are almost used up, a pack of paracetamol, an old purse full of receipts and expired train tickets. I send the Google Maps directions to my phone, put some dry food in Dizzy's bowl and grab my coat and keys. I check all the windows are closed, upstairs and down, go out the back to check the side gate is bolted, then lock the back door and push both of the new deadbolts across again, top and bottom. I triple-check that my front door is locked, rattling the handle to be absolutely sure, then look up and down my cul-de-sac too, scanning both ways for any suspicious parked cars I don't recognise. Nothing.

The roads are busy but the worst of rush hour has passed, and traffic is merely heavy rather than gridlocked. It helps that I'm travelling against the flow, going out of London rather than in, and I make good time. Twice I think I spot a dark BMW following me, turning with me, staying two cars behind. But just as I'm squinting in the mirror to make out who's behind the wheel, the car slides smoothly down a slip road. Ten minutes later I wonder if I've seen the same car in traffic behind me, only for it to pull past with a roar, a woman behind the wheel. I tell myself that BMWs are not particularly rare in this part of the world, and make an effort to stop looking in the rearview mirror. The sign for Little Missenden – *Please drive carefully through our village* – appears at the roadside just before 11 a.m.

I drive through the centre and I'm heading out the other side before I even realise it, out into open country again. I do a U-turn in the driveway of a large manor house and drive back into the village, more slowly this time. Little Missenden is chocolate-box cute, old houses and ivy-clad cottages clustered around a well-kept village green. An old parish church with the flag of St George fluttering against the cold autumn sky. There are two pubs but the Red Lion is nearer, a whitewashed country inn with big brick chimneys at each end near the centre of the village. I park up next to an old red phone box, grab the handbag from the passenger seat and head inside.

The pub is quiet and dark, a low ceiling, thick wooden tables and chairs, padded benches lining the walls. A smell of roast dinners, real ale and open fires. Only a few other patrons, an older couple in Gore-Tex jackets and walking boots, a few middle-aged men watching horse-racing on the TV. A log fire burning low in the grate with a large dog sprawled in front of it, chin on its paws. There are two staff behind the bar. One is barely out of her teens, elbows on the till, thumb-typing on her phone. The other is an older man, early fifties, hair thinning back to almost nothing, writing in careful capitals on a specials board. I order a Diet Coke and wait until he's poured it before setting it down on the bar in front of me.

'One-sixty please, darlin'.'

'Thanks,' I say brightly, reaching for my purse. 'Actually, I don't know if you can help me with something?'

'I'll do my very best, love.' He indicates the thick gold wedding ring on his left hand. 'But just to let you know, I'm spoken for.'

I nod and smile as if this is the funniest thing I've heard all week. 'That *is* a shame.'

He cracks a crooked smile. 'Just teasing, young lady.'

'I'm actually looking for someone, was wondering if you might know where I can find her?' I hold out my debit card and he gives me the card machine to tap it against. 'I got chatting to someone on the train yesterday, going into London, but when she got off she left her handbag behind. I was going to just stick it in lost property at Marylebone but then I remembered she'd said she lived in Little

Missenden and since I've got a lunch meeting in Amersham today, I thought I'd just drop it off on my drive through.'

The lie feels unconvincing on my tongue, even though it contains shards of truth. I put the handbag down next to my drink and the landlord gives me a blank look, his belly straining against a grey Lacoste polo shirt.

'What was her name, this woman?'

'Kathryn.'

He leans on folded arms against the varnished wood of the bar. 'Kathryn *what*?'

I start to wonder if this was the wrong place to start. I'll try the other pub next, The Crown, then the post office, if there is one.

'She's probably early twenties?' I say. 'Blonde, maybe five foot five? Could have sworn she said she lived here in the village.'

He starts shaking his head and is about to speak again when the young barmaid cuts him off.

'D'you mean Kathryn Clifton?' she says. 'Skinny, pretty?'

'That sounds like her. Don't suppose you've got her number, have you? I could give her a ring, drop the bag over to her on the way to my meeting.'

The girl shakes her head. 'Haven't got her number.'

'Is there someone who might—'

'But she only lives around the corner.' She gestures with a thumb.

My pulse ticks up a notch. The barmaid is about to say more, then sees the landlord giving her daggers and the words die on her lips.

'I can drop the bag around to her,' I say. 'I don't mind, honestly. If you just point me in the right direction, I can go.' I give him a smile. 'Do my good deed for the day.'

'We'll make sure it gets back to her,' the landlord grunts. 'It's no bother.'

'Really, I don't mind. I've got time before—'

'You a journalist?' he says suddenly, his expression darkening.

'What? No.' I try to adjust to this sudden change of direction. 'I'm just . . . someone she met on the train.'

'Because that family's had more than enough with journalists spreading their shit around trying to sell papers, if you know what I mean.'

'I don't really read a lot of papers,' I say. 'And I promise you, I'm not a journalist.'

'Still, probably best if you don't go knocking on doors,' he says, all traces of warmth gone from his voice now. 'Not after what happened to her sister.'

'OK, thanks.' I hand the bag over the bar to him. 'Who's her sister?'

Without asking, he reaches out, snatches the handbag and stows it away under the bar, out of sight. He ignores my question.

'And your name is?'

'Ellen,' I say. 'Ellen Devlin. Tell Kathryn I said hello.'

I take my Diet Coke to a side table by the door and sit with it for ten minutes, pretending to be absorbed in my phone. If they're going to return the bag to her, now would be the time, before the lunch-time rush kicks off. If they *have* a lunch-time rush. But neither the landlord nor the barmaid are going anywhere, although the landlord catches my eye a couple of times as if he's still trying to get the measure of me.

My drink finished, I walk out of the Red Lion and back to my car. I'm parked on the street with a good view of the front of the pub, next to an old-style red phone box. A tractor passes, huge tyres thick with mud, squeezing between parked cars and the pavement in a rumble of diesel. Five minutes later, the barmaid appears with the garish purple-and-black handbag slung over her shoulder, thumbs moving over the screen of her phone. I slide down further in the driving seat but she doesn't even look up, just turns towards the centre of the village and sets off down the footpath. I watch her progress as she walks away. I could follow her on foot but it would be conspicuous in this sleepy Buckinghamshire village on a Thursday morning. The car is a marginally better option.

Little Missenden has two main streets that meet at a staggered crossroads. I turn the car's ignition and wait to see which way the barmaid will turn, watching her amble down the path, still absorbed in her phone. Once away from the pub she stops, checks over her shoulder and then casually unzips the bag, fingering quickly through the contents, taking things out and putting them back again. She takes out the purse and unzips it, checks up and down the street again, opens all its pockets and flaps. Frowns, drops it back in the bag and zips it shut again. Keeps on walking.

She reaches the crossroads and turns left, disappearing from sight. I put the car in gear and pull out to follow her.

25
Leon

When he was out, Leon wore two pairs of gloves: long fingerless gloves over translucent skin-tight latex underneath. It was hard to see the latex pair unless someone was really close up, and Leon didn't let people get too close. At his own place he just wore the latex but it was better to disguise them when he was out – and in any case he preferred to leave no trace of himself behind. Better to move through the world like a ghost.

He washed his hands, snapped on a new pair of gloves and dimmed the lights a little. Sat back in the leather desk chair to study his victim board, covering most of the wall in front of his desk. Four unlucky women. Two blondes now, two brunettes. Leon liked to know about the victims – to *really* know about them – that was what set him apart, made him different from the rest. Not just who they were before they died, but who they loved, how far the ripples of their murder spread. To really appreciate the true impact on their families and friends, on their colleagues, on society. Especially when the cases remained unsolved, when the guy responsible was still out walking the streets, continuing with life as if nothing had happened. Continuing to hunt.

Leon smiled.

His eyes moved from one victim to the next, over the words and numbers beneath each picture. Dates of birth, of death. Place of discovery. Name. Age. Address. Occupation. An exclusive club with only four members. The third victim was special though, different – there was something about her that he couldn't put his finger on.

So he did what he had always done, in time-honoured tradition. Maybe not time-honoured, exactly, but an updated version: emails and texts to family members from multiple sources – a refund, an invitation, a letter, an apology – messages on WhatsApp, direct messages on social media, all looking reasonably genuine and carrying the same link with the same payload. All the parents had to do was click on that link once, on any of their devices. It didn't matter if they ignored, blocked, deleted most of them, because sooner or later they would click on one in a moment of distraction, or tiredness, or boredom – and then he was in. The payload delivered a small piece of malware giving him remote access to that device, and from that point on he was no longer on the outside looking in.

He was on the *inside*.

He hadn't even been looking for it, not exactly. He just wanted to get inside their heads after their daughter had been taken. Get the inside track.

That was how he had found out. They'd used coded terms at first, even with each other, but over time it became clear that there was something in their family that no one else knew about. Something they had kept hidden.

A terrible, dangerous secret.

A baby.

The shiver of excitement was still fresh. The thrill of discovery, of knowing before anyone else, being in the unique position to do something about it. The knowledge of the danger she represented, the danger she would be in.

The baby is the answer, the thing around which all the rest of us are in orbit.

She was the key to all of it.

And that was why her picture was destined to end up on his wall.

26

I drive slowly, the engine grumbling in third gear. The staggered junction is little more than a trim triangle of grass, a carved wooden signpost across the way pointing to nearby villages, a black-painted barn on the left and a high stone wall facing me on the far side. I steer through the slow turn and catch sight of the barmaid further up the road. Beamond End Lane. The road is narrower here and the footpath has disappeared so she's walking along the road, beside a neatly-clipped hedge. Still on her phone. I brake and pull in again behind a Mercedes estate parked on the left.

If she's spotted me, she gives no sign of it. About a hundred metres up she crosses the road and walks into a driveway, disappearing from view. I pull out again and drive closer, slowing to a crawl as I pass a row of ivy-covered cottages that ends in an open wooden gate, a sign for Silverdale Barn. The drive leads into a courtyard where a couple of cars are parked, a two-storey barn conversion on the far side. Two front doors on the ground floor. Flats? The barmaid is trotting up a wooden staircase at the end of the barn, to another door on the first floor.

There. She knocks on the door and I pull away again in case she turns and sees me.

Another barn conversion stands opposite, with another large courtyard. No cars, no animals, no signs of life in the windows. Hopefully they are at work, at whatever City hedge fund or investment bank that means they can afford to live in this little corner of home counties paradise. I pull into the courtyard, gravel crunching noisily under my car tyres, and kill the engine. Grab the AA map book from the back seat of my car and open it across the steering wheel to give the impression of a wayward traveller, angling the rearview mirror so I can see the barmaid at the top of the wooden staircase. She's talking to someone, but she's side-on to me so I can't see who's answered the door. I say a little prayer that it's Kathryn, that she's standing on the doorstep bouncing Mia on her hip, that she'll look at the handbag and shake her head, wondering what's going on. *Nope, sorry, the bag's not mine, never seen it before.*

The barmaid hands over the bag, gives a little wave to whoever's at the door and makes her way down the staircase again. I watch in the mirror as she ambles across the courtyard towards the road, towards me, before turning left to retrace her steps to the Red Lion. She's back on her phone again, head down, thumbs flying over the screen.

I give her a minute to get to the crossroads before unclipping my seatbelt. I'm about to get out of the car when there is more movement in the mirror. The front door to Kathryn's flat opens and a man steps out, moves back to talk for a moment, hands over a card to someone in the doorway. He is wearing a dark suit and tie. He turns to go and I feel a cold wash of unease as I recognise him: slim build, sharp haircut, strong jaw.

Detective Sergeant Holt.

That can't be good news. I look past him, expecting to see DI Gilbourne emerge from the flat behind his partner and follow him down the steps. But he doesn't. Holt is alone. The door shuts behind him and he hurries down the wooden staircase. He takes out his mobile and puts it to his ear, pulling open the door of a black Ford Focus parked in the courtyard. The arrogance of our last meeting is gone – today he looks shifty, almost surreptitious in the speed of his walk and the hunch of his shoulders. He gets into the car, still talking on the phone. *Did he hear the exchange at the front door just now? Did the barmaid mention my name when she handed over the bag, or was Holt the one she actually talked to?* It could mean more trouble for me, if he was. I slide down a little lower in the driver's seat, hoping the young detective hasn't seen me. Holt guns the Ford's engine and turns out of the courtyard in a spray of gravel, disappearing down the road.

I wait five minutes, to be sure that Holt and the barmaid are both clear and gone. While I wait, I take out my phone and google 'Kathryn Clifton'. There's only one bar of reception here and there's a lag while the results page loads. She has accounts on Facebook, Instagram, Pinterest. Some links to posts for a university magazine from a couple of years ago. A few other hits, but nothing particularly controversial. I google 'Kathryn Clifton sister'. No news stories, no obvious controversy, nothing out of the ordinary.

I frown and put my phone away. If journalists have been causing trouble for her and her family, surely there would be evidence of it on the internet somewhere? Isn't Google the place none of us can escape, where everything lives forever? The landlord's words come back to me. *Probably best if you don't go knocking on doors, not after what happened to her sister.* Maybe I'd be breaking some sort of rule about not contacting witnesses. The duty solicitor mentioned something about that on Tuesday night but I was so exhausted by that point that I can't remember the details.

And I'm here now. In for a penny, in for a pound.

I get out of my car and walk across the road into the courtyard opposite, past the sign for Silverdale Barn. I climb the staircase quickly and knock twice on the smart wood-panelled front door, a large silver three at its centre. I hear the thudding of heavy footsteps from inside, quick and urgent, and the door is opened by a muscular young guy in tracksuit bottoms and a black vest. He's somewhere in his mid-twenties, dark hair shaved close to his scalp and a full sleeve of tattoos up his left arm, patterns and skulls and Celtic swirls accentuating the swell of muscles. There is a scattering of stubble across his jaw, dark circles under his eyes.

'Can I help you?'

'Hi,' I say. 'Is Kathryn home?'

He frowns at me, leans out to look down the outside staircase. Checking if I'm alone.

'If you're looking for that other policeman, he just left.' When I shake my head, he says abruptly, 'What do you want then? Are you a journalist?'

His voice is deep, confident, public school vowels smoothing off all the rough edges.

'No.' That question again, twice in the last twenty minutes. 'I'm a friend of hers.'

'Have you seen her?' His red-rimmed eyes narrow, as if he's trying to work out if he recognises me. 'Do you know where she is?'

'I was kind of hoping she'd be here.' I gesture at him. 'You're her . . . flatmate?'

'Boyfriend.'

'Right.' My memory flashes on an image of the dark bruises on Kathryn's arm. 'I'm Ellen, by the way. You must be . . . ?'

'Max,' he says reluctantly.

'Nice to meet you, Max.' I hold out my hand to shake, but he doesn't reciprocate. 'I'm a friend of hers, I was wondering if you'd seen her since Tuesday afternoon? That was when I was with her.'

There's a deep red blush rising up his throat.

'I saw her last on Monday morning.' He sniffs. 'We didn't exactly part on the best of terms.'

'Has she been in touch at all since then?'

'I've already told that cop all of this. Why should I tell it all again to some randomer who just turns up on my doorstep? Why do you want to get involved, anyway? I've never seen you before.'

I throw a look down towards the road, where a pair of horses and riders are clip-clopping past.

'Can I come in for a minute, to talk? I can explain.'

He crosses his arms and leans against the doorframe, tattooed bicep bulging against his knuckles.

'I don't think so.'

He moves to close the door but I put a hand against it to stop it shutting all the way.

'I want to help,' I say quickly through the gap. 'To find her. And I want to help the baby, too.'

He stares at me, keeping his expression neutral. 'What baby?'

'Mia.'

'Don't know what you're talking about.'

But he says it too fast, his face betraying him, his blank expression slipping. Just for a second. A moment of surprise.

'I think you do, Max,' I say. 'They were together on Tuesday. That's what Detective Sergeant Holt was just talking to you about, wasn't it?'

'How'd you know his name?' He frowns, his heavy forehead bunching. 'That cop?'

'I've talked to him too.' I sense him withdrawing again, putting more pressure on the door. 'Listen, I was at the pub just now, the Red Lion, and the landlord mentioned Kathryn's sister? I wondered if you'd heard from her too, if you'd spoken to her recently?'

He freezes, the red rising further up his cheeks, his jaw clenching and unclenching. '*What?*'

'Has DS Holt already spoken to her?'

'No.' His voice is low and flat with an undercurrent of barely-controlled rage. 'I think you should go now.'

I take a business card from my purse and quickly write my mobile number on the back of it. I hand it to him and he studies it, front and back, as if he's not quite sure whether to hurl it back at me.

'If you give me your number too, Max, I can let you know if I hear—'

But he's already closing the door.

I walk down the steps and across the courtyard. In the silence of my car I sit and think about what Max had said, replaying his lies in my head. *Don't know what you're talking about. What baby?* Was he aware of the role played by Dominic, the angry ex-boyfriend, in the events of these past few days? After a few minutes, I type 'Seer Green' into the satnav, and make the short drive to the small train station where Kathryn got off the train on Tuesday.

It's another picturesque Chiltern village, a few miles nearer to London. Why didn't she get off in Great Missenden, which was nearer to her flat? Was that where she got on? And what was here? There's a pub, a church, a primary school. Not much else. I park at the little train station and walk up onto the platform through open ticket barriers, staring down the two parallel tracks carving their way through the Buckinghamshire countryside and flanked by trees on both sides. It's a little two-platform stop that looks like it hasn't changed much since the 1950s, I guess mostly used by commuter-belt workers heading in and out of London. Was Kathryn meeting someone? Or avoiding Dominic, waiting for her at the end of the line in London? And most important of all, why leave Mia behind?

On the drive home, I can't stop thinking about Holt visiting Kathryn's flat without Gilbourne. The way he'd looked when he left: furtive somehow, as if he didn't want to be seen. Max lying about Mia. His reaction when I asked about Kathryn's sister. I'm still trying to decide whether I should ask Gilbourne about her as I pull up on the drive of my house, still mulling it over as I find my front door key and fit it into the lock.

The side gate *slams* in the wind, the wood banging against the frame like a gunshot. I flinch, my pulse spiking. I'm sure the gate was bolted when I left. I push it open carefully in a creak of hinges and walk around the little block-paved path at the side of the house, cold fingers of unease at the tip of my spine. I stop at the edge of the garden.

The kitchen door has been kicked in.

27

I can see through the busted door that the kitchen is a mess.

Run. That's my first instinct. *Get away.* Go to Tara's house, to a hotel, anywhere but here. I take a step back towards my car, engine still ticking as it cools on the drive. But at the gate, I stop, the heat of shame rising up from my chest, the prickle of frustration and anger. I've never run away from anything in my life. I've stood and faced everything head-on. This is *my* house. *My* home.

Heart thumping in my chest, I turn back around and walk over to the patio to look in through the kitchen windows. Cupboards and drawers hang open, pots and pans and cutlery and food strewn across the floor. The lounge is worse. Through the closed patio doors I can see books and DVDs scattered everywhere, chairs knocked over, the sofa cushions ripped and scattered. The drawers of my antique writing desk pulled out and upturned, contents spilled. A bookcase knocked down, framed pictures lying in shattered glass, dark earth spilled across the carpet from pot plants knocked to the floor. There's no sign of Dizzy and I look around the garden in case he's waiting for me but he's nowhere to be seen. He's a smart little guy – he would know when to run and hide, where to wait out the storm.

I can't see anyone inside. Phone in my hand, I step carefully into the kitchen and listen, waiting, straining my ears to hear any sound of movement. But the house is silent, as if it is exhausted, broken by this ordeal. The kitchen door hangs drunkenly, half off its hinges, fragments of wood and plaster from the wall scattered just inside on the kitchen floor. I'm about to try to push it closed when I remember I shouldn't touch anything: my house is a crime scene now, there might be fingerprints. Evidence.

Gilbourne's words ring in my ears again, the scepticism in his voice when I had called him about last night's intruder. *'The baby's on your mind, it's a pretty intense experience you've had. I can see why you might want to see a link between the two things.'*

I'm not imagining *this*.

There is a spilled bag of rice near the kitchen door, grains scattered in a long white arc across the tiles, and I step over it into the hallway. It's the same in here, coats thrown across the floor, their pockets pulled inside out. I pick up a few books and magazines spilt from the side table onto the stripped wooden floorboards, feeling something hard at the bottom of the pile. My iPad. I check the lounge again. The TV is still here, too.

I stop at the foot of the stairs, listen again with my phone in my hand. Silence.

One careful step at a time, I go slowly up the stairs. A faint smell of something here, of exhaled breath and disturbed air. The same faint scents as last night when I found my kitchen door unlocked, earthy and dark. Did I know they would come back for a second visit? Maybe. Perhaps I've just been in denial.

All four doors off the landing are open and it is clear that none of the bedrooms have been spared. The master bedroom is a riot of clothes on the bed, on the floor, bags and shoes and coats, all the drawers and wardrobes open. My bedside drawer is open and scattered beneath are my passport, a few credit cards and a small box of jewellery that includes a few items inherited from my grandmother. Diamond stud earrings that I haven't worn in years, a silver chain bracelet. Still here.

When I go into the little box bedroom that looks out over the garden, all my fear turns to angry tears, a hard weight brimming behind my eyes.

Last night I was terrified at the idea of my home being invaded while I was upstairs. My sanctuary, my refuge from everything, being violated by a stranger. I've had an uneasy feeling all day that someone might be watching me, following me. Last night they left the house untouched but were close enough to hurt me if they wanted to. Today I was far away, safe, when they returned – but it's still much worse, because of what they've done to this room.

It's the room we once decorated as a nursery, sunshine yellow walls and soft cream carpet, one feature wall papered with circus animals. Neutral yellow, not pink or blue. Ready for pine furniture, a cot and a wardrobe and maybe a chest of drawers with a changing table on top. This would have been the baby's room, and then when he or she got big enough we were going to move them into the spare room to make way for a sibling, maybe two. Richard and I decorated it together one weekend, Radio Two on and sunshine streaming through the window, me in the first trimester of the only natural pregnancy we managed to conceive. I was already allowing myself surreptitious visits to Boots and JoJo Maman Bébé to buy a few sleepsuits and vests and scratch mittens and all the things I knew I shouldn't – but I wanted to dive into it, to be fully immersed in it, to be properly ready. Ignorant of what was to come. That was before the worst years started, before the brutal cycles of IVF and the endless waiting, hoping, praying, wondering in sleepless hours whether I had somehow cursed it – cursed my pregnancy – by buying baby clothes too far in advance.

I haven't been into the nursery for months and normally I keep the door shut. It's a snapshot of a life that will never be, a museum exhibit, preserved in aspic and frozen in time.

Now it's in an even worse state than the rest of the house. Everything is torn, opened, strewn on the floor. Drawers pulled out and turned upside down, smashed, the wood splintered and snapped. Everything opened, emptied, ripped. Hurled against walls and stripped of their contents. The destruction downstairs is methodical; but this is on a whole different level. It looks like venom. Like anger.

The tears spill then. I'm furious at myself, but I can't help it. I cuff the tears away with the heel of my hand, not wanting to look at the ruin of the nursery but unable to look away. I pick the little doll off the floor and set it on the small painted chair by the door. It doesn't make sense. There is literally nothing in here worth stealing. Nothing of value. I haven't even set foot in the room since . . . I don't know when. Maybe the summer, a few months ago. I nudge the shattered remnants of a wooden drawer with the toe of my shoe. Then I begin setting some of the furniture back upright to clear the floorspace a little.

And I realise there *is* something missing.

The half-dozen sleepsuits – soft white cotton never worn or washed – are gone. The little nought to three month vests are gone.

The scratch mittens and a few other items of baby clothing, bought years ago during those furtive visits to Boots, all gone.

A thought pushes its way through the anger and fear: this is all about Mia. But she's never been here in my house, not even once. Did they see the little nursery in the box room and connect it to her? Did they take the baby clothes as the next best thing, as evidence of her presence here? That doesn't even make sense. Or was someone trying to send me a message? I have no idea what the message might be, apart from the fact that it somehow relates back to Mia.

Everything relates back to her.

In the bathroom I find a box of tissues among the bottles and creams knocked off the shelf, dry my eyes and blow my nose. I go into the spare bedroom last, survey the damage there. More of the same, wardrobes open and searched, everything flung to the floor, blankets and old clothes and pillows piled up to complete the wreckage of my house.

I'm about to go back downstairs when I notice something. *Feel* something. A draught. A breeze. Just a touch of cold autumn air coming through an open window across the room. Pulling the sleeve of my shirt over my hand to avoid messing up any fingerprints, I shut the window and turn the key in the lock, making sure the latch is fully down. I need to call 101, and when I've done that I'll call Gilbourne as well.

I turn to leave the room and immediately freeze in place, the breath stolen from my chest.

There is a man standing behind the door.

28

I register two things in the first split-second of shock.

He is dressed all in black.

His face is covered with a balaclava.

Pure liquid terror rushes from my stomach down to my toes, a wash of fear so powerful it almost knocks me off my feet. My mind fills with an image of the stranger from the train two days ago. Thin build. Staring eyes. Fingerless gloves. *He's found me.* We stare at each other for a moment and he takes a step forward into the room, a black spider unfolding itself from the shadows.

A masked stranger in my house. A stalker. Maybe a killer.

I move towards the open door but his left hand shoots out and slams it shut, the sound of varnished timber hitting the doorframe like a shotgun blast in the silence. He shakes his head slowly – *no* – his eyes two pinpricks of light inside the balaclava. In the mask he looks like a terrorist, an assassin – but there is a familiarity in the way he moves, in the articulation of his limbs. I scan the jumble of items on the floor at my feet for something I can use to defend myself with; blankets and sheets, clothes, pillows. Nothing solid, nothing that might do damage.

He takes another half-step towards me and I back away, further from the door, holding up my hands in a calming gesture.

'Take whatever you want,' I say, my voice taut. 'And just go.'

His eyes take me in. A predator sizing up prey.

'Not. Yet.'

His voice is smooth, calm, both 't's' pronounced clearly and precisely. As if he's happy to take his time.

'Just go, please,' I say. 'I won't call the police, I won't try to stop you.'

He snorts.

'Put your phone on the bed.'

I'd forgotten I still had my mobile in my hand. I lean down and drop it onto the bare mattress without taking my eyes off him. He scoops it up in one fingerless black glove and switches it off, puts it up on top of the wardrobe.

I take a step back, away from him.

'Keep it,' I say. 'There's an iPad downstairs too, some money in my purse, jewellery in the master bedroom. It's all I have that's worth taking.'

He gestures at the mess on the floor, his eyes narrowing. 'What? You think *I* did this? You think *I* broke into your house?' Anger shimmers beneath his words.

'You're here, aren't you?'

'No,' he snaps. 'This was *not* me. I didn't do this.'

'I believe you, I'm sorry.' I have to keep him talking. 'I just assumed—'

'I simply came over to take a look at your place for background and I saw your back door was open. I thought someone might be hurt.'

Background? I think. *What is he talking about?* He has a black rucksack on his back, big enough to hold all the baby clothes that have disappeared from the room next door.

'OK,' I say.

'I was about to leave but then you came back and caught me by surprise.'

'That makes two of us,' I say.

Is he carrying a weapon? I can't see one.

He moves forward again, edging me back towards the corner, his black-clad frame blocking the door, sucking all the light from the room.

'Someone did quite a number on your house though, didn't they? What do you think they were looking for?'

'What do you mean?'

'Clearly they were searching for something.'

'They?'

He shrugged.

'Whoever did this. You must have something they want.'

'What are you talking about?'

'Did they find it, I wonder?'

He's testing me, I realise. Checking to see if I give the right answer, or try to fool him with the wrong one. If I tell the truth, I can't trip myself up.

'I have no idea, I don't even know what *it* is. All that I've found missing so far are some baby clothes.' I want to say *in the nursery* but it sounds foolish, ridiculous, a word I haven't said out loud for a long time. 'They were in the little box room.'

He stares at me for a moment, his eyes narrowing. Weighing up my answer. Finally, his cheeks stretch beneath the black wool of the balaclava in what I assume is a grin.

'This just keeps getting better,' he says. 'You don't even know who the child is, do you?'

'Child?' I frown. 'You mean Mia? How do you know about her?'

'I know a lot, Ellen. About you. About her. All kinds of interesting details.'

I back away again, towards the window.

'How . . . how do you know my name? How did you know where I live?'

'I'm good at finding things out. It's what I do.'

'You're the guy from the train,' I say quietly. 'The one who sat down at the table opposite me.'

The weirdo who took photographs, followed me off the platform.

'I wanted to help her, to help Kathryn,' he says tonelessly. 'I want to help you, too.'

'Help me with what?'

'You handed the baby over to the police, did you?'

'Of course.'

'You trusted the police.'

'Yes.'

He sighs and shakes his head. 'Mistake.'

'Why?' I say. 'What do you mean?'

'They let him get away once already.'

'They let *who* get away?'

'The husband. Don't you know? It's always the husband.'

'I don't understand,' I say, thoughts tumbling around in my head. 'Kathryn's husband?'

He sighs, as if disappointed. 'The one who wants to take her away. To take the baby away.'

'Tell me,' I say, desperation creeping into my voice. 'Please. Why was it a mistake to hand Mia over to the police?'

He moves closer. I take another step away from him and almost stumble on a cardboard box that has been thrown to the floor. He is close now, close enough that I can smell him, sickly-sweet sweat and a tang of bleach beneath it.

'Because,' he says, leaning into my face, 'it will make her easier to find.'

His fists are clenching and unclenching by his sides, as if he is struggling to control himself. Black fingerless gloves, just like on the train. I notice for the first time that his fingertips are covered too, in smooth transparent latex, like a surgeon.

No fingerprints. No DNA.

Fear wedges in my throat like a splinter.

'Why are you wearing gloves?' I say quietly.

He doesn't answer. His cheeks broaden beneath the balaclava again but the smile doesn't reach his eyes and it's gruesome, false, as if he learned it by rote from watching TV. *Think*. There are two ways out of this room. Through the door to the landing or out of the window, dropping down onto the back patio. Both shut. If I run for the window, will he try to stop me? Of course he will.

There is a third way out of this room, I realise with a cold certainty: carried out on a stretcher or zipped into a bodybag. An image pops into my head of crime scene officers in white boiler suits standing here later this evening, or tomorrow, or next week. Examining, photographing, looking for clues. Sifting through the wreckage of my house as they try to connect victim and killer. The scene jolts me as if I've just grabbed a live wire.

I am nobody's victim.

I nod towards the closed door, as if expecting it to open at any moment.

'You know, my husband will be home any time now.'

He glances to the door – just for a second – and I put my hands in my jacket pockets, wrapping the dark fabric around myself as if for warmth or protection.

His eyes narrow.

'No.' His tone is flat, matter-of-fact. 'He won't. Don't do anything stupid, or I will have to hurt you.'

I ignore him, my fingers finding the bunch of keys in my jacket pocket. My hand closes around them, a single straight key sticking out from the bottom of my fist. I must have done this a dozen times walking alone at night, hearing footsteps behind me on a dark street, working late or becoming separated from my friends after a night out. I never actually had to use them, though, never found out if it could make a difference. I am about to find out. Two inches of brass that might give me a fighting chance to get out of here if I can catch him off guard.

He takes another step towards me.

'I can't have you running to the cops, Ellen.'

I ease my hands back out of my pockets, keys clutched painfully tight in my right fist. The key is facing away from him so he can't see it. A navy self-defence class comes back to me. *Focus on the vulnerable areas with a hammer strike: eyes, nose, throat.* I roll my weight onto the balls of my feet, ready to raise my right hand and bring it down in his direction. A thin sliver of skin is visible at his neck, where the balaclava ends. The flesh looks pale, vulnerable, deathly white against the black of his clothes. It makes a good target.

Now. I raise my right hand high and swing it down but he darts away at the last moment and I miss him by inches. He's backing up, holding out a hand.

'Stop!'

'Don't like a victim who fights back, do you?'

I swing again, backing him towards the corner. With a speed that surprises me he brings his own right hand up and there is something in it, rectangular and metallic. He raises it to my neck. There is an instant of shock and then a white-hot, paralysing pain, fierce agony like I have never known before, lighting up every nerve ending in my body like I'm filled with freezing fire. I am falling backwards.

Then, nothing.

29

He liked to listen to her in the dark.

If he closed his eyes, he could almost imagine himself there, in the house with them, in the room with her. Just the two of them. Her little hand in his. Five tiny fingers, curled softly in sleep.

The woman was there most often, talking to the baby. Playing music designed to stimulate or soothe the infant brain.

But he preferred it when the door closed, when the woman's voice faded away, when it was just the two of them. He would listen to the baby's gurgling laugh, her coos and chatter. He listened to her breathe. Short, shallow breaths in and out of little lungs. Sometimes he listened to her cry. But she didn't cry often. She was a good girl.

Hacking the Alexa in her room made the little gadget so much more useful.

Helpful for so many things.

For listening in.

Feeling like a part of the family.

30

DI Gilbourne & DS Holt

Gilbourne took two of the pills from the small plastic bag and held them in the palm of his hand.

Twenty years ago he could go a night without sleep and it would barely touch him. Ten years ago, even. Crime scene, search, door to doors, arrest, interview, doing the briefings, grab an hour of sleep along the way, plenty of coffee and he could keep rolling. That sleep-deprived first or second or third day after you got the call, pushing and pushing until you could finally charge your suspect.

But he wasn't that man anymore. The years had left their mark on him. With the ranks of frontline officers increasingly depleted and not enough new blood coming through to replace them, with the ever-growing expectation from the top brass and the know-nothing politicians above them, the thin blue line was getting thinner all the time. Everyone was stretched to the limit and beyond. And everyone had their breaking point.

His eyes were gritty, his head thick with fatigue. He *needed* this. It was just about staying sharp, that was all. It was what the victims deserved, what their families deserved. He shook a third pill out of the clear plastic Ziploc bag and threw all three into his mouth. Found an almost-finished takeaway cup in the driver's side door and washed the pills down with a grimacing mouthful of yesterday's coffee.

He opened the car door and poured the rest of the cold coffee onto the lay-by's cracked grey tarmac. The country air was a cold slap in the face as he got out of his car and he pushed his hands deep into the pockets of his raincoat. Holt was waiting for him a few metres away, the younger man with his head down, talking earnestly on his mobile. Seeing his approach, Holt hurriedly finished the call and slipped the phone into his pocket. Somehow, he looked fresh and ready to go despite the hours they'd been putting in this week. He looked keen. Excited, even. What was that saying? *Youth is wasted on the young.*

Gilbourne nodded a hello to his partner.

'What have we got, Nathan?'

'Called in two hours ago by a woman walking her dog. Uniforms came down to check it out and found the body just down there, in the stream near those trees.' He pointed into a stand of beech trees further off the track.

'Come on then.'

The two of them set off up a rise out of the lay-by, an unofficial path where the grass was trodden flat up the bank's gentle incline. It levelled out at the top, the path disappearing into trees. There was a uniformed officer in a high-vis jacket standing sentry by the first oak tree, at the top of the bank. Gilbourne showed his ID and stopped to take a brief look back.

A country road between Beaconsfield and Amersham, curving away in both directions. Quiet. You'd probably hear approaching traffic from a fair way away, before you saw it at least. Or before they saw you. It was early afternoon but only two cars had passed since he had parked up a few minutes before. Trees on both sides made for good cover and concealment. He estimated the distance from the lay-by into the trees at five or six metres. It was up a slope, but even so a reasonably fit man carrying a body – assuming the victim was average size and weight – could probably cover that distance in six to eight seconds. Which didn't make him hopeful about witnesses driving by and catching their killer in the act.

All in all, it was a good spot. Well-chosen. The best they could probably hope for was dash cam footage that might have caught any cars parked in the lay-by over the last couple of days.

Holt waited for him, his face alert with excitement, pointing further into the trees as he caught up.

'It's just down there,' he said. 'There's a dip in the ground but you can't see it until you're virtually on top of it.'

'The Thames Valley boys been all right about handing this over?'

Holt nodded. 'No bother at all. They seemed happy about it.'

Gilbourne allowed the younger detective to lead, pushing through low bushes and stepping over logs rotting on the ground. The ground was muddy, the path slick with autumn rain and the air heavy with the smell of moss. About twenty metres from the road they reached another couple of uniformed officers, thumbs hooked into their stab vests at a cordon of blue and white police tape, the outer perimeter put in place to stop anyone else stumbling into the scene. There was no media presence yet, but with the number of police vehicles pulled into the lay-by behind them, it was only a matter of time. He made a mental note to give the force press office a heads-up when he was on his way back to the station later.

'Did she disturb anything, the dog walker?'

'Don't think so,' Holt said. 'They've got her in a patrol car back at the lay-by.'

'Did you ask her?'

'I assumed the uniforms checked that with her, and they didn't pass on anything to me.'

Gilbourne took out packet of Marlboros from his pocket and lit one with his Zippo, taking a long drag on the fresh cigarette. He had seen too many crime scenes messed up by over-zealous bystanders, putting their hands on the victim, contaminating good sources of DNA and trampling trace evidence into the ground in a misplaced effort to help. He'd even had one screwed-up scene where a guy tried to give mouth-to-mouth resuscitation to a neighbour who'd been dead for more than twenty-four hours. That had taken some untangling.

'Let's not assume, OK, Nathan?' He blew smoke upwards into the air. 'Have another chat with her, double-check she didn't touch anything or let the dog near the body.'

The younger detective took half a step away from the smoke and seemed about to protest, but decided against it.

'You want me to do that now?' he said.

'In a minute. Let's have a look at the scene first.'

Yellow and black crime scene tape was strung between trees to create the inner perimeter, a small square scene-of-crime tent at its centre. The tent's flap was pinned open and they could see a pair of feet, one shoe on and one fallen to the side. Stepping plates had been laid on the ground to create a common approach path, leading away from the tent to the edge of the inner cordon. The plates – ridged metal squares that stood proud of the ground – didn't follow the trodden path through the woods. Instead they went up and to the side, an awkward route that would have been chosen as the least likely to have been taken by the suspect, to prevent trampling of evidence by investigators.

Gilbourne could feel the tingling buzz as the pills started to kick in, lighting up his nerve endings, making everything sharper, clearer; the muted colours of the day that little bit brighter. Was it even the pills, or was it something else? The buzz of the scene, the mental challenge of putting the pieces together, the thrill of the chase? Maybe a bit of both.

He was going to miss this.

He nodded a hello to the lead SOCO, Fiona Whyler, as they approached. She was in white crime scene overalls, masked and hooded and with one booted foot on either bank of the small stream.

'Stuart,' she said with a small wave. She stepped back onto the near bank and made her way carefully along the stepping plates to the crime scene tape. She had a pale, milky complexion, a few strands of red hair escaping from the hood of her overalls. She smiled, crow's feet crinkling at her eyes. 'Thought retirement had caught up with you by now.'

'Still a few months off my thirty, Fiona,' Gilbourne said with a smile.

'Feels like you've been saying that for the last three or four years,' she said. He indicated the white crime scene tent behind her. 'How are we doing?'

'Well, we've got a female victim, early twenties, looks like at least two stab wounds to the back, possibly others. Fully clothed.'

'Weapon?'

'Nothing yet. The size of the wounds suggest we may be talking about a broad-bladed kitchen knife, something like that. Something big.'

'Defensive injuries?'

'Not that I can see on an initial examination.'

'Was she killed here, or somewhere else?'

Whyler shrugged, eyeing his lit cigarette with something like hunger. 'Ask me again in a couple of hours' time.'

'I don't suppose you're going to help me out with an approx. time of death, are you?'

She shook her head. 'Not yet, we need to do more work. I'd be guessing.'

'So what's your best guess?'

'I don't guess, Stu, I'm a scientist. That's why they give me this nice white suit.'

Gilbourne clasped his hands together in front of him. 'Just for me?'

She stared at him for a moment, then blew out a breath. 'The body's been lying half-in, half-out of that stream for an unknown number of hours which will have accelerated bodily cooling rates and messed with various other things.'

Gilbourne nodded, waiting.

'OK,' she said finally. 'OK. If I had to guess, I'd say more than twenty-four hours, less than forty-eight. And probably leaning towards the higher end. But *don't* quote me on that.'

'You're a star, Fiona.'

'When the PM's done, you'll be the first to know. But for right now, that's the best I can do.'

She glanced back at the scene to where one of her white-suited colleagues was securing clear plastic bags over the victim's hands to preserve any forensic evidence under her fingernails.

'I'd best get back to it.'

'Thanks, Fiona. I appreciate it.'

Gilbourne watched her go, taking a last drag on his cigarette before nipping off the burning end with his thumb and forefinger and putting the butt into his jacket pocket. He stood for a minute, taking in the scene.

* * *

Holt waited, saying nothing. They had only been partnered up for a few months but he knew this was Gilbourne's *thing* and that he was not to be interrupted. One of his quirks, trying to get his head into the mindset of an offender so that he could visualise the time of the offence, see the problems they might have encountered and where mistakes might have been made. He had told Holt to imagine committing the crime himself – to imagine the details, the practicalities, the specifics – if he wanted to pinpoint the most likely sources of evidence. Holt had listened politely, nodded, agreed. But it sounded more like superstition and old school *Columbo* bullshit to him. In modern policing, securing a conviction was much more likely to hinge on DNA, maybe above everything else. DNA to move from arrest to charge, DNA to get a case to court, DNA to convince juries who had spent half their lives watching *Prime Suspect* and *Dexter* and *CSI Miami*.

DNA was the key. Holt knew that better than anyone.

Finally, Gilbourne nodded and turned to his partner. 'So, Nathan. You think this is the primary scene?'

'Too early to be definitive,' Holt said, 'but my gut instinct would be no. Not sure how you'd get the victim to come down here voluntarily. There's nothing really to see, it's not on the way to anywhere, it's not a short cut. Kind of a dead end.'

'They could have been forced to come down here, against their will.'

'Maybe,' Holt chose his words carefully, knowing he was being tested. 'But I don't know. I just can't see it. The primary scene is more likely to be a vehicle, a property, where the injuries were inflicted. This is the secondary, the disposal site.'

Gilbourne nodded. 'I'm inclined to agree with you. And what do you deduce from the choice of this place as a secondary crime scene?'

'Well, they'd need to know the area,' Holt said. 'I mean you wouldn't lug a body up here from the road without knowing it in advance. From back there, you can't tell what it's like in terms of visibility, foot traffic, options for concealment. Could be the boundary to someone's back garden or the ninth hole of a golf course, for all you can tell. You wouldn't know it's a good spot to dump a body unless you'd already been here.'

'Maybe our killer just got lucky with his location?'

'No, I reckon he's local. Or has local knowledge.'

'Agreed,' Gilbourne said again. 'Come on, let's have a chat to the dog walker.'

They were turning to go when Whyler called to them.

'Stuart?' she said, pointing to one of her white-suited SOCOs, who was picking his way along the stepping plates to the edge of the inner cordon. He was holding something in a clear plastic evidence bag. The officer stopped and held out the bag in his gloved hand, clear plastic over a credit-card sized rectangle of pink and white. A driver's licence, edges smeared brown with mud, but the name and picture still visible.

'Christ,' Holt said, looking closer. 'It's her.'

31

The twin burn marks on my neck are covered with a large plaster. The pain has slowly subsided to a low throb around a numbness that extends down to my shoulder blade and up into my jaw. A stun gun, the paramedic said, delivering a high voltage shock on contact with the skin. Illegal, highly dangerous and readily available on the internet. There is apparently no way of knowing what level of shock I was given, but she said I'm lucky the injuries aren't more severe: she once saw a stun gun used in a street robbery and the victim suffered a heart attack. I had been lucky, too, that I only banged my head on the windowsill as I fell. She advised me to go to hospital for a proper check-up, but it seemed like overkill to me.

By the time help arrived the house was empty, of course, no sign of my attacker apart from the destruction he left behind. The uniformed officers who turned up, a couple of well-meaning young constables with beards and big arms, noted down my limited description of the intruder and took my statement about the events of this afternoon. They were more interested in the assault; the fact that nothing of any particular value had been stolen seemed to blunt their interest in the burglary. I tell them everything I can remember, including the words that are now branded onto my brain.

You handed the baby over to the police.

Mistake.

It will make her easier to find.

The expression in his eyes when he'd said it, the flash of anticipation. Was that what it was?

The two young officers made a note about Mia but I saw them exchange a look, I could tell they didn't really know what to make of my story and whether I was concussed in some way. They'll likely write this up as assault and robbery on a householder, and there's no space in that story for a baby that wasn't here and isn't mine. A detective from CID would be in touch, they said, to talk about evidence recovery, checking for fingerprints and DNA. In the end I gave up trying to explain it to them.

Now they've gone, I call Gilbourne instead. I need him to get a warning to Mia's parents. I phone him three times, the call going through to voicemail each time.

Despite everything, I find myself missing Richard at times like this, not because he was great at fixing doors, or mending furniture – or any kind of DIY, to be honest – but because it was always easier to face things together. As a team. To have someone to talk to, be close to, to share the trouble.

Instead, I call Tara from the wreckage of my kitchen as I watch a locksmith secure the back door with plywood and new deadbolts, just a temporary fix until I can get it properly replaced. I'm telling her that I'm going to check into the nearest Premier Inn when she cuts me off.

'Absolutely not,' she says. 'You're coming to stay with us.'

'That's really kind of you, Tara, but I know you've got your hands full with the boys and I don't want to put you in danger from—'

'No excuses, the spare bed's already made up and I'm opening the wine now. I'm not taking no for an answer, so you might as well get yourself over here.'

My heart swells at the compassion in her voice. 'Thanks, T.'

*   *   *

She greets me on the doorstep with a deep, enveloping hug, her smile turning to shocked concern when she sees the dressing on my neck and the fading bruise over my eye.

And so I find myself in my best friend's spare bedroom with nothing but an overnight bag, a cat carrier and the clothes I'm standing up in. This is it: the sum total of what my life amounts to now.

I put my stuff on the bed and open the cat box to coax Dizzy out. He steps out slowly, cautiously, sniffing the unfamiliar air and rubbing his furry face against my knuckles.

'Just for a few days,' I say to him. 'Then we'll be back home.'

I turn and find we're being scrutinised from the doorway. Three boys arranged in height order, tallest to shortest. Tara's sons are used to seeing me on a regular basis – I'm godmother to all three – but the sight of Dizzy is a rare novelty for them. My cat positions himself at the end of the spare bed like a grumpy sphinx, eyeing the three boys with suspicion.

Noah, Tara's oldest, is a serious six-year-old who likes *Bake Off* and memorising flags of the world and has always seemed older than his years. He takes a few tentative steps into the room and looks at up me, big chocolate-brown eyes behind his Spiderman glasses.

'Can I stroke her?'

'Sure.'

He considers my answer for a moment, his face solemn, still standing at arms-length from the cat. I rarely have the boys over to my little house – it's always easier to babysit at Tara's, where all the boys' stuff is – and he's only seen my cat once before.

'What's her name?' Noah says.

'Dizzy.' Originally called *Daisy*, I explain in a roundabout way, until a first visit to the vet had revealed certain undeniable male characteristics.

'Will he bite or scratch me?' Noah asks.

'No,' I say with a smile. 'He's just a bit nervous around small people, but if you're gentle, he'll be fine.'

Noah turns to his brothers, hands up like a teacher getting the attention of his class.

'You have to be nice to him,' he instructs the younger boys as they crowd around to stroke the cat. 'Because he's sad about not being at his own house.'

They each take turns stroking Dizzy carefully, even the smallest of the three siblings, Charlie, who's a bit of a loose cannon at the best of times. Dizzy sits and takes it all with the patience of a saint, eyes front, ears up, big paws tucked beneath his chest. Not purring, but not growling either.

Lucas, the middle son, stares up at me after he's taken his turn.

'We're not allowed pets,' he says.

'We are,' Noah corrects him. 'We've got Baby Shark.'

'Fish don't count.'

'*Do.*'

'*Don't*,' Lucas says, as if he's ready to fight his corner on this important point of principle. 'Because you can't stroke them.'

Noah gives Dizzy a final little stroke.

'Are you going to live with us now?' he says. 'And your cat?'

'Just for a little while,' I say. 'Maybe a day or two.'

Tara calls up the stairs to summon the boys for their tea and I'm reminded as they stampede out – just like I am every time I visit – how far our paths have diverged over the last decade. Tara and I met in the navy, in the first week of training at the Royal Naval College in Dartmouth, homesick and disorientated by the sudden segue from student life into a military environment. Both graduates whose dads had been in the service, both competitive and sporty. She had done eight years and I had done twelve, but after she left the navy for a career in journalism we had stayed in touch. Then, once I rejoined civilian life, we ended up living close enough for Friday drinks, meals out, cinema trips. We were chief bridesmaid at each other's weddings, thoughts turning to families of our own in our early thirties. She got pregnant within months of coming off the pill and our lives started to diverge more quickly, like railway lines splitting at a set of points. One son became two, then three, Tara's life shifting to accommodate the continuous demands of night-feeds and nurseries, of maternity leave, weaning, potty training and school runs. We've worked hard to keep in touch, to remember why we first became friends, but it isn't always easy. Since Richard left, she's been the one I've confided in more than anyone else.

With the boys' tea finished and Tara's husband, Dave, watching *In the Night Garden* with them in the playroom, Tara opens a bottle of Pinot Grigio and pours two sizeable glasses. She sits me down in the lounge and I tell her about the last three days, starting with my appointment with the fertility specialist and going through every-thing that has happened since. Tara nods, eyebrows raised as I talk, and refills both our glasses when they get low.

I've almost finished the story when my phone rings. I answer, expecting someone from the burglary squad.

'I just got your message,' Gilbourne says, sounding breathless. 'Where are you? Are you safe?'

'I'm all right,' I say. 'Just a bit shaken up.'

'Listen, I've managed to get you a place in secure accommodation. It's mostly used as a halfway house for victims of domestic violence, but it's tucked out of the way and you'll be safe there. I've talked to the manager personally and there's a room for you tonight. Can I give you the address?'

'That's kind of you, Inspector, but I think I'm OK.'

His voice takes on a firmer tone. 'This is not negotiable, Ellen. You could have been seriously injured or worse. You need alterna-tive accommodation until we catch the guy who did this.'

'I'm not at home.'

'Right, well that's good,' he says. 'You're sure I can't persuade you though?'

I wonder again if I'm putting Tara in danger just by being here. Maybe it would be better for her if I was somewhere else, away from her boys.

'Where is it, this halfway house?'

'Burnt Oak. Not too far from you.'

'And they have a bed spare?'

'I can call them back right now to secure it for tonight.'

Tara catches my eye and very firmly shakes her head. She puts one hand over mine, pointing at me with the other.

You're staying right here, she mouths silently. *With us.*

She squeezes my hand gently and I feel a lump come to my throat.

'Ellen,' Gilbourne says. 'Are you still there?'

'I'm here,' I say. 'It's very kind of you, but it won't be necessary.' His concern gives me a little glimmer of warmth. It seems he's going above and beyond the call of duty. 'I appreciate you taking the trouble though.'

'As long as you're sure,' he says with a sigh. 'You can call me Stuart, by the way. So I've had a chat with the two officers who came to your house this afternoon. You said you weren't able to describe or identify the burglar. Is that correct?'

'No, I said he had a balaclava on.'

'His face was covered the whole time?'

'Yes,' I say. 'But I know who it was.'

'What? How?'

'It was the guy from the train on Tuesday.'

'Christ, Ellen.' The firm tone is back. 'Why didn't you tell them that?'

'I tried,' I say. 'He was looking for Mia. He was looking for her on the train that day, that's why he followed me. He was in my house on Wednesday night and he came back today. He's still after her. He claimed that he wasn't the one who ransacked my house, that it was someone else and that they were looking for something in particular.'

There is a moment of silence at the other end of the line.

'He said that?' Gilbourne says slowly. 'He said he was looking for her?'

'He said I shouldn't have handed Mia over to the police,' I summon his words from memory again. 'Because it was going to make her easier to find.'

'I see.'

'What does that mean, Stuart? Why would he want to find her? What's going on here?'

He hesitates again, and I can hear the sound of a lighter sparking at the other end of the line.

'It's not a good idea for you to get involved in this, Ellen.'

'I'm already involved, whether I want to be or not.'

'You've seen the danger, what might happen,' he says quietly. 'You could have been killed today. You need to take a step back, let us do our jobs.'

'In the last three days I've been followed, abducted, burgled and attacked in my own home. I don't think taking a step back is up to me anymore. And I can't protect myself unless I know what's going on. So are you going to tell me, or do I have to figure it out for myself?'

I hear a deep exhalation of breath at the other end of the line as he blows smoke from his cigarette.

'Listen,' he says finally. 'Can you come in? We should talk face to face.'

'I left the car at my house, I didn't trust myself to drive. The paramedic told me to rest.'

'OK, all right.' His voice goes quieter as if he's got a hand cupped around the mobile. 'How about I come to you?'

I give him Tara's address in Harrow.

'I'm on my way over,' he says, and hangs up.

32

I go upstairs to unpack and check on Dizzy. By the time I get back downstairs, Tara has already let Gilbourne in and the detective is standing in the big parquet-floored hallway. Charlie, the youngest son, is keeping his distance, peering out at the stranger from behind Tara's leg, but Noah and Lucas are sizing him up, staring at him with unalloyed admiration. I can see in Noah's eyes that this is pretty much the most exciting thing ever: a cat *and* a real-life policeman in his house on the same day.

'Where's your gun?' Noah says.

Gilbourne smiles down at him. 'I don't have a gun, but I do have this.' He reaches into his pocket and produces a black leather wallet, flips it open to reveal his Met Police ID. He hands it to the boy. 'Warrant card. Much better than a gun.'

Noah stares wide-eyed at the ID, then back up at Gilbourne.

'I'm going to be a policeman,' he announces seriously, 'when I'm big.'

Gilbourne ruffles the boy's brown hair gently. 'Good for you, son. What's your name?'

'Noah,' he says. 'I'm going to catch the bad men.'

'Well, Noah, I think you'll make an excellent policeman.' He gives the boy a wink. 'In fact, I'll put in a word for you with the chief constable.'

Gilbourne looks a little fresher, his eyes brighter than the last time I saw him. Maybe it's just because it's not the middle of the night, under the anaemic fluorescent light of the police interview room, but he seems younger somehow. He's had a shave, his dark hair is brushed back, and although the top button of his shirt is undone, the knot of his tie is only slightly below it. Maybe not a rumpled Willem Dafoe. Maybe more like a well-travelled James Franco with a few more miles on the clock.

I look past him, to his car parked at the kerb. 'You on your own today?'

'DS Holt is looking into a couple of other leads.'

Tara shows us through into the dining room, a pine table set with six high-backed chairs. It's the one room that she likes to keep clear of the boys' stuff, banishing toy cars and games, action figures and scooters.

'Can I get some drinks?' she says. 'Tea, coffee? Something stronger?'

We both decline.

'I'll leave you to it, then.'

I shut the door behind her and sit down opposite Gilbourne at the dining room table.

'You're a big hit with Tara's boys.'

'They're nice lads.'

Somehow it's on the tip of my tongue, the question people have asked me for years, a casual inquiry with the potential to slice through scar tissue and re-open old wounds. 'Do you have children of your own?'

'Four girls,' he says. 'Twelve, fifteen, eighteen and nineteen.'

'Oh,' I say. 'That must be—'

'How are you really, Ellen? Shouldn't you be in the hospital?'

'I've been better,' I say. 'But it's all superficial. Nothing they'd do at the hospital that I can't do for myself.'

He gives me a sympathetic smile. 'You've had a rough week.'

'What's going on, Stuart?'

'I thought you were owed an apology. For us giving you such a hard time in the interview the other day. And for the way DS Holt behaved with you.'

'I thought giving people a hard time was what you did every day of the week?'

He shakes his head and places both hands palm-down on top of a black leather folder. His hands look strong, broad and tanned.

'And I just wanted to see how you were doing.' He looks suddenly reticent, as if he might be having second thoughts about coming here. 'And to reassure you that we will do everything we can to catch the person who did this to you.'

Being here with him feels a million miles away from the air-less grey room at the police station. That little interview room – much the same as a wood-panelled courtroom or a high-vaulted cathedral – felt like it was designed to make you feel small, insignificant, to intimidate you into honesty. But Tara's dining room is neutral ground and it's almost as if Gilbourne's just a regular guy, someone's husband, a friend, a colleague, and we're simply having a chat.

'I appreciate your concern,' I say, grateful that he's changed his tune since Tuesday night. 'But you didn't come here just to tell me that, did you?'

Gilbourne leans closer, elbows on the pine tabletop. He smells of chewing gum, minty, the cigarette smoke a musky undertone, not unpleasant. He unzips the black leather folder on three sides and opens it out on the table.

'We've got hold of CCTV images which corroborate certain elements of your story.' He pulls a sheet of paper from the folder and slides it across the table to me. A colour image of a man, dark jacket and jeans on a train station concourse. 'Do you recognise this individual?'

I study the image. The quality's not great but it's clear that he's thin, wearing a black jacket, black beanie hat, rucksack, para boots. A flash of memory from this afternoon, his hand coming up to my neck, agonizing pain lighting up every muscle in my body. I suppress a shiver.

'That's him.' I push the paper away. 'He was on the train on Tuesday and he attacked me at my house today.'

'You're one hundred per cent sure it was the same man at your house?'

'Ninety-nine per cent.' I swallow hard on a dry throat. 'How did he find me?'

'We're looking into that, but let's just say he's got form for it.'

'So you know who he is?' I feel a glimmer of relief that finally, *finally*, he believes me. 'What's he got to do with Mia?'

He stands up, goes to the dining room door and opens it a crack. Looks out into the hallway and closes the door again before coming to sit back down at the table.

He holds out a hand. 'Can I have your mobile?'

'Why?'

'Please?'

'I'm not recording this conversation, if that's what you think.'

'Just indulge me,' he says with a shrug. 'For two minutes. I'm getting paranoid in my old age.'

I take my phone from the pocket of my jeans and hand it over to him. He studies it for a second and finds the power button, switches it off. Lays it face down on the table between us.

'What I'm about to tell you is strictly off the record, OK?'

33

Gilbourne rubs his face with both hands, looking suddenly older in the soft light of the dining room.

'I'm not exactly flavour of the month with my boss at the moment and I shouldn't really share anything else with you,' he says. 'But I'm going to anyway, because a) my boss is an idiot and b) I want to keep you safe, and frankly I'm worried that you're going to put yourself in more danger if I don't give you a little bit of background.'

'I understand,' I say. 'And it's appreciated.'

'This is a live investigation, so I need your word that this won't go any further. Not to your friend.' He gestures with a thumb towards the closed door. 'Not to anyone.'

'OK,' I say. 'You've got it.'

He considers me for a moment, taps the printout with his index finger. 'This individual's name is Leon Markovitz. Thirty-six years old. Last known address in Camden. Former tabloid journalist convicted in 2013 on various charges relating to phone hacking, burglary, breaches of privacy and bribing of public officials. Served three years in jail and then spent some time in a secure psychiatric unit after his release. No newspaper would touch him with a bargepole when he came out so he re-created himself as one of those true-crime fanatics, podcasts and what have you. He was one of our prime suspects in a serious criminal investigation last year, one of my cases. Arrested and questioned on two separate occasions.'

'Questioned about what?'

'A series of extremely violent offences – he had certain information about the victims and about the circumstances of those crimes. Information that was deliberately *not* put into the public domain, to separate the responsible party from the various internet nutters who ring in wanting to give a full confession. Facts that *only* the perpetrator would have known. Unfortunately the investigation ended up . . . falling short in other areas. In the end we didn't have enough to charge Markovitz.'

'Surely you've got an address for him? You could—'

Gilbourne holds up a hand. 'Bear with me for a minute.' He leafs through the papers in his folder. 'As I mentioned, we've been doing a trawl of CCTV, including on St George Street where you said you were abducted on Tuesday afternoon. Camera coverage is patchy there but we did get an ANPR hit very close by that might be significant.' I frown at the acronym soup and he adds: 'Automatic number plate recognition.'

'The BMW?'

He pulls another A4 sheet from the leather folder and slides it across the table to me. This one is not a blurry CCTV image taken from a distance, but a close-up head and shoulders of a man against a green background. A police mugshot like you'd see in a news report or on TV. An angry, hard face. A dark ginger beard, buzz-cut short hair. Thick neck. Nose kinked in the middle from some long-ago break.

An unpleasant buzz of fear loosens my stomach. I cross my arms over my chest.

'That's him,' I say. 'Dominic. The guy who abducted us on Tuesday.'

He stares at me for a moment but doesn't contradict me. I realise after the words are out of my mouth that I said *us* and not *me*. As if there is a bond, a promise, a connection between Mia and I that is more than just chance.

'This mugshot was taken earlier this year,' he continues. 'Dominic Church, twenty-nine years old. Before all this he had convictions for assault, robbery, possession of drugs. We haven't managed to track him down again yet, but it's only a matter of time.' He slides over the other image until the two are side-by-side on the table in front of me. Two violent men. I shudder at how close I've been to both of them in these past few days. 'Him and Markovitz have something in common.'

'What?'

'Dominic Church was questioned over the same case – he was our other prime suspect. In fact, we looked at whether they were working together, and that is still an open line of enquiry. But he also slipped through our fingers.'

'So . . . someone else was arrested, then? Convicted?'

Gilbourne shakes his head, suddenly unable to look at me.

'No. As I said, it's still a live case. Still *my* case, unless my idiot boss decides to shuffle the deck to please the chief. I've not got long left on the force but I've sworn to the victims' families that we'll get a result before I leave.' He taps the mugshots with his index finger again. 'As far as I'm concerned, these two are still prime suspects, so if they try to make contact with you, if you see either of them again, if you even *think* one of them is following you, do *not* engage with them. Do not approach. As you already know, these are both very dangerous individuals. Whatever you do, don't trust either of them. And promise me you'll let me know. *Immediately.*'

A memory floats up out of nowhere, like a flash of déjà vu. The scrawled instructions of Kathryn's note: *Don't trust anyone.*

'OK,' I say. 'I'll let you know.'

He puts a hand over mine, the skin warm against my fingers. It's been months since I've felt a man's touch and I'm suddenly aware just how much I've missed this small intimacy.

'I can't stress how important that is, Ellen. For your safety. I've put a request in for renewed surveillance on both of them but until then you need to be extra careful.'

'How long until the surveillance starts up?'

'Within the next twenty-four hours, hopefully, as soon as the chief super approves the overtime.' He gives me an apologetic shrug. 'Form filling and red tape. Sorry.'

I look down at his hand and he moves it away.

'All right, but I still don't see what this has to do with Mia.'

For a moment I think he's going to tell me more. Then he drops his gaze and starts gathering the sheets of paper back into the leather folder. Zips it shut briskly and stands up.

'I've already told you much more than I should have.'

'Have you found Kathryn yet?'

He ignores my question. 'She should never have involved you in this.'

'But she did.'

'Yes,' he says quietly. 'She did.'

I think for a moment. 'The case those two men were suspects in, Church and Markovitz, did it have anything to do with Kathryn's sister?'

He stops and his head turns toward me again, his eyes finding mine. 'What?'

'Her sister. It's connected, isn't it?'

His voice is flat, neutral, some of the warmth leached away. 'What makes you say that?'

For a moment, I consider lying to him. Keeping this to myself. But he's gone out of his way to help me, to tell me things he probably shouldn't have, and I feel bad holding anything back from him.

'I went to Kathryn's flat,' I say. 'Talked to her boyfriend.'

'What . . . ?' He frowns in exasperation. 'This is what I'm talking about, Ellen. You do things like this, it will put you in more danger. How did you even . . . know where to find her? When were you there?'

'Earlier today. I saw DS Holt as he was leaving and—'

He puts both palms up like he's stopping traffic. 'Hold on, *Nathan* was there?' He sits back down again, his frown deepening. Clearly, this is another unwelcome surprise. 'On his own? You're absolutely sure it was him?'

'Yes.'

Gilbourne's face darkens and I can almost see the gears turning, surprise turning to disbelief. Disbelief turning to suspicion. He's about to say something else when his phone rings and he snatches it from his jacket, answering in monosyllables.

'What?' he says, turning away from me. 'You sure? Where? Give me that again.' He flips open a notebook with his free hand and scribbles something on it. He ends the call and stands up, checking his watch.

'Stuart—'

'I have to go.' He hesitates for a moment, then places a hand lightly on my arm. 'Look after yourself, Ellen. And please remember what I said.'

My head pulses with unanswered questions. But he's already gone, striding down the drive and onto the dark street outside.

34

DI Gilbourne

Gilbourne watched from a safe distance, the smoke of his cigarette curling up into the evening sky. He was out on the station's fourth-floor fire escape again, taking the opportunity of a short break from phone calls and interview notes and spooling through hours of CCTV footage. He had watched Holt pull into the car park five minutes ago, choose a space in the far corner and sit in his Ford Focus, mobile glued to his ear. His partner was gesturing with his free hand as he talked but he wasn't getting out of the car, just talking, talking.

Gilbourne's first cigarette was burned almost down to the filter so he shook out another one from the packet and lit it off the burning butt, grinding the first beneath the heel of his brogue. Why was Holt skulking out here in a dark corner of the car park where his colleagues on the second floor couldn't see him? Maybe a personal call? A girlfriend? But Holt had never been shy of bringing his personal life into the office before; in fact he seemed to revel in it, wanting to let it be known that he was a player with two or three women on the go at any one time.

There was something else going on with him. And why was he going rogue, going back out to interview Kathryn Clifton's boyfriend without telling him? Without telling his DI, his partner, the senior investigating officer on this case?

Gilbourne watched as Holt finished his call and held the phone against the steering wheel, now two-thumb typing a message or an email. Gilbourne dialled the young detective's number and put the phone to his ear, listening as it connected and started to ring. He watched, from his vantage point on high, as Holt reached into his jacket and pulled out another phone, his normal phone, looked at the display for a second and then touched the screen. Gilbourne's ear filled with the sound of his partner's recorded voice.

'Hello, you've reached the voicemail of Detective Sergeant Nathan Holt, please leave a message and I'll—'

Gilbourne ended the call and watched as Holt slipped the handset back into his jacket, returning his attention to the other phone. *Two* phones. His regular mobile and . . . what? A burner phone that couldn't be traced?

His own mobile rang in his hand and he checked the display before answering.

'Rhodri,' he said, flipping the half-finished cigarette away. 'How's life treating you?'

'Can't complain.' The pathologist's voice was slow and deliberate, soft Welsh vowels that always seemed at odds with the cold scientific facts of his profession. 'I've got some preliminary findings on your PM, Kathryn Clifton. Is now a good time?'

'Of course.'

Gilbourne stepped back inside and headed for the lifts. He wedged the phone between his cheek and his shoulder and pulled his notepad from his jacket pocket, flipping it open to a clean page.

'Right then,' the pathologist said. 'I've estimated time of death at between 4 p.m. and midnight on Tuesday.'

'Don't suppose you can be more specific than that?' Gilbourne always asked, and the answer was almost always the same. 'It would really help if we could narrow the window down a little.'

'Afraid not, Stuart. The location of the body in the stream, plus various other factors related to the temperature gradient between body temperature and ambient temperature, make it impossible to give a more precise determination. She's received three stab wounds to the back, injury depth consistent at around thirteen centimetres with some bruising around the entry wounds suggestive of a blade being pushed in right to the hilt. One weapon. Two of the wounds penetrated the heart – either one of them could have been the killing blow. Death would have been fairly rapid.'

Gilbourne reached the lifts, pressed the button. Both were on the ground floor. He considered the tightness of the belt around his stomach, another notch away from where it should be. He turned and pushed through the door into the stairwell instead.

'Anything else you can tell me about the weapon?'

'Wide blade, forty-six millimetres from side to side. Injuries inflicted with a fair degree of accuracy which might suggest some anatomical knowledge. The stab wounds are clinical, deliberate, between the second and third ribs. Not random. Certainly not a frenzied attack.'

'So the blade – maybe a kitchen knife?'

'Or some kind of fighting knife, perhaps.'

'Injuries in the back,' Gilbourne said, his voice echoing in the dimly-lit stairwell. 'Victim taken by surprise?'

'Possibly. There's some bruising on the lower right arm but from the colouring I'd say it's older than the stab wounds, maybe one or two days prior to death. And there are also a couple of superficial burn marks on the back of the left hand. Two identical marks fifty-one millimetres apart.'

'Like cigarette burns?'

'No, the skin's not broken. I would think probably a taser, or a stun gun. Consistent with some kind of electroshock device.'

Gilbourne stopped on the stairs, remembering what Ellen Devlin had told him about the attacker she'd confronted in her house.

'The victim might have been incapacitated first, before she was stabbed?'

'Would explain the lack of defensive wounds.'

'Killed at the scene, or somewhere else?'

'From the small amount of blood at the scene, I'd say somewhere else. These were sizeable wounds but blood deposition was minimal where she was found.'

'What else?'

'No evidence of sexual assault.'

'DNA from a possible perpetrator?'

'None that we can find.'

'*None?*' Gilbourne repeated. He could feel the small hairs standing up on the back of his neck. A tick of something in his veins, not excitement. *Recognition*. 'No blood, saliva, nothing?'

'Lots of blood on the victim's clothing. All of it belonging to the victim.'

'Are you sure?'

'We've not been able to recover any other traces.'

'So, no contact DNA, no defensive wounds, nothing under her fingernails.'

'Correct.'

Gilbourne was silent for a moment. He began walking down the stairs again, from the third floor landing to the second floor.

'Stuart?' the pathologist said. 'You still there?'

Gilbourne could almost feel the tiny pulses of electricity surging in his brain, connections being made. The case that had hung over him for more than a year, the investigation he knew better than anyone else, the hunt that had driven him to the edge and almost derailed his career. The case he *had* to solve before his time on the force was up.

'I'm here,' he said quietly. 'Just thinking.'

'Anything you want me to clarify?'

'Does it remind you of anything?' Gilbourne said. 'The lack of evidence, lack of DNA, the victim profile, the area the body was dumped?'

The pathologist left another beat of silence before answering. He wouldn't use the nickname – Gilbourne knew Rhodri thought it was just a bit of tabloidese – stooping to that level offended his sense of precision, of science.

Eventually Rhodri said, 'You mean similarity to unsolved cases.'

'I mean the Ghost.'

Gilbourne could almost hear the tut of disapproval on the other end of the phone line. 'Yes . . . and no. Some similarities but some significant differences too.'

'But it could be?'

'It's possible, or a copycat. There was something unusual though, a definite departure from previous victims. We've got some residue on the skin suggestive of heavy plastic sheeting which infers the victim was wrapped, post-mortem, then the wrapping was removed when she was dumped. Possibly she was wrapped up to avoid DNA deposition in a vehicle, then unwrapped after she was dumped to accelerate decomposition.'

'He never did that before, did he?'

'We didn't find that residue on previous victims, no. He also didn't shock any of the victims with a stun gun. May suggest he's being more careful. If it is the same perpetrator.'

'Or that he's learning, honing his technique, getting better at it,' Gilbourne said. 'All the signature aspects are consistent – lack of DNA, age and gender of the victim, evidence of pre-planning, the area where the body was found. He's forensically aware and he's done this before.'

The pathologist grunted reluctantly. 'I'd tend to agree with you on the last point – I don't think it's his first time. But three attacks in the space of three months and then he disappears off the radar for a year before killing again? What kind of offender pattern is that?'

'I knew he'd do it again,' Gilbourne said firmly. 'It was just a matter of time.'

'So where's he been for the past year?'

'Trying to keep his nose clean, maybe. Trying to find out if he could just stop, walk away from that part of who he is. But the victim alone, if nothing else – her connection to the case. There's no way on earth that's a coincidence.'

Rhodri paused again, considering his answer. 'I suppose I'll leave that to you, Stuart. More your territory than mine.'

Gilbourne checked his watch. 'Thanks Rhodri, appreciate you turning this one around so quickly. I've got to go.'

'I'll email the full report to you now.'

'And could you copy in my partner?'

'Already done.'

Gilbourne thought he'd misheard. He stopped on the second-floor landing, where the four major incident teams were housed in a set of open-plan offices, but didn't pull open the door into the main area.

'I'm sorry, say that again?'

'DS Holt, correct? He's been in touch with me twice already asking for the results to be expedited and emailed to him as soon as I had anything. As *a matter of extreme urgency*, he said. A real keen bean, that one.'

'Yes,' Gilbourne said, a strange feeling turning over in his stomach. 'He certainly is that.'

Gilbourne thanked the pathologist again and rang off. Then he opened the door onto the second floor, and walked quickly through the bustle of ringing phones and inquisitive voices, over to the corner that was home to MIT 3. He nodded to a few other colleagues on the team, but Holt was not at his desk. Gilbourne sat down at his own workstation and called his partner's mobile again.

This time he answered.

'Nathan,' Gilbourne said without preamble. 'I've just had the headlines through on the PM from Rhodri Lawson. Need to brief the team. Are you nearby?'

He paused, waiting for Holt to say *Oh yes, boss, I've already got the post-mortem report.* To say *I asked for it to be sent over asap.* Or maybe *I didn't want to waste time.* But Holt didn't say any of that.

'I'm five minutes away,' he said instead. 'What's the story, boss?'

Gilbourne paused, trying to detect any hint of deceit in his partner's voice. Any suggestion that he was hiding something. What *was* the story? Was Holt playing games, trying to get one over on his partner? Trying to climb the career ladder, go over his head to win brownie points from the DCI? Or was it something else?

Answers to those questions would have to wait. Because if he was right – and Gilbourne felt in his bones, in his blood, that he *was* right – then the results of the post-mortem were bigger, much bigger, than any of that.

'I'll tell you when you get in,' he said.

FRIDAY

35

Dominic

He preferred the night. The twenty-four-hour places when there was no one around. He could get what he needed and get away quickly, disappear back into the dark before anyone knew he was even there.

He tugged the brim of the baseball cap down low, keeping one eye on the flood-lit forecourt and listening for the approach of other cars as he filled the tank of the BMW. He drew in a heavy breath sharp with petrol fumes, pulling it deep into his throat, his lungs. He had always loved the acrid smell of petrol, the burn, the headrush when you leaned in close. And it was better, purer than his own stink, unwashed clothes and the pungent tang of fast food. Too many days sleeping in his car.

Initially he'd stayed in the cheapest B & Bs, moving on every few days when he felt the press closing in. Staying on the move was supposed to be a temporary thing, but with the house gone, he mostly slept in the BMW if he couldn't bed down in a derelict building for a day or two. Sometimes it still amazed him how far he'd fallen. How fast. Most of the time he tried not to think about it. He just had to keep moving, keep ahead of them. Stay under the radar.

He was screwing the petrol cap back on when a small red car pulled up at the next pump along, loud voices and music with a heavy bassline puncturing the early morning silence. Glancing up, he saw four teenagers crammed into the little Nissan, two boys in front and two girls in the back seat, fast food in their laps. Coming off the back of an all-nighter, judging by the pallor of their skin and excitable chatter. The driver, a tall, reedy youth in a black jacket, looked up and saw him, their eyes meeting for a split second before Dominic ducked his head and turned away. He was acutely aware of the plaster covering the ragged stitches on his face, the livid bruising darkening the flesh around it. It drew unwanted attention.

He locked the car and strode across the forecourt, pulling the collar of his jacket up, keeping his face under the brim of his baseball cap as he slid his credit card into the handheld machine at the counter inside. Cash was a better option – it left no trail – but all his accounts were deeply in the red. There was a beep as the card was declined. He reached for a second card. Declined. He found another in his wallet, feeling his shoulders relax slightly as the payment finally went through. He took the receipt without a word and stalked back towards his car, giving the red Nissan a brief glance as he reached into a pocket for his keys.

Two of the teenagers had their phones up, pointing at him.

The driver stood by the car and one of the girls leaned out of the window. Filming. Photographing. Keeping their smartphones on him as he crossed the concrete to his BMW. Dominic felt his jaw tense with a familiar flash of rage, the breath hot in his nostrils. The old tingling in his fists.

The driver was typing now, thumbs a blur over the screen, lines of concentration creasing the pallid skin of his forehead. Dominic shifted his direction and walked up to him.

'What are you doing?'

'Hold on a second.'

'Give me your phone,' Dominic said, holding out his hand. 'Now.'

'What?'

'Give it to me.'

The youth stood his ground. 'Don't think so, mate.'

Dominic thought for a moment about the broad-bladed jungle knife strapped to his forearm in its sheath. Self-protection. It could be in his hand in less than a second, the grooved handle nestling in his palm. The satisfaction of seeing this arsehole's face if he drew it.

Not here. Too many cameras.

Instead he reached out and ripped the phone from the teenager's hand, turned it around to study the screen. A looping video of him paying at the desk inside the garage, then walking across the forecourt, a clear shot of his face with its angry purple bruising.

'Hey!' the teenager tried to grab it back, but Dominic held him off easily with one large hand against his bony chest. He scrolled down to look at the caption below the video.

SPOTTED! #Killer #ChurchGuilty #TheGhost

It was already posted and live, out there on the internet for the world to see.

The teenager struggled against his grip. 'How does it feel?' he said, his voice high and tight with false bravado.

'How does *what* feel?' Dominic said.

'To have killed those women and got away with it.'

Dominic could feel a flush heating the skin of his face. Those months seared onto his memory, the accusations that had followed him ever since: a household name for all the wrong reasons. Arrested and held for four days straight, questioned over and over again. Returning to a house half-emptied by police forensic officers, besieged by journalists camped on his front lawn. Months on bail as work dried up, months of headlines, evidence mounting day by day, the police a whisker away from charging him but never actually crossing that threshold.

And now this. Limbo. A grey half-life where the unconvicted guilty live. Only one way out.

There was no good answer to the kid's question. Instead, Dominic swung the mobile into the edge of the concrete pillar, shattering the screen, smashing it again and again and again until shards of plastic and metal fell from his hand onto the floor at their feet. Ignoring the teenager's cries of protest, he grabbed the lapels of his jacket, lifting the younger man onto his tiptoes up against the Nissan.

'Psycho! Let go of me!'

The other teenaged lad was scrambling out of the passenger side of the Nissan, his hands up in supplication – *hey hey hey come on now mate* – but Dominic could barely hear the reedy voice. The anger was churning and boiling up at the back of his throat, threatening to choke him.

'You want to know how it feels, do you?' he growled into the teenager's face. 'How it feels when your life turns into a fucking hashtag?'

'You're a nutter, you're—'

Dominic reached up to his own cheek and tore the plaster away, pointing to the mass of black and purple bruising beneath, the ugly, jagged wound crudely stitched.

'*That's* how it feels,' he said, pointing to his cheek. 'Every. Fucking. Day.'

He pinned the flinching teenager a moment longer before dropping him back to the asphalt.

One of the girls in the car began to scream.

Dominic got into his car and gunned the engine, her cries ringing in his ears as he drove away.

36

I call in sick again at work. There is a twinge of guilt as I dial the number, but I've been ground down by Tara's insistence that I take at least one more day off. The ache in my neck has subsided and the cuts above my eye and in my right foot are healing OK, but when I tell my boss what happened yesterday she tells me to *take as long as I need*, her voice full of concern. So instead of getting the Tube to Bond Street, I help Tara get the boys ready for nursery and school, helping them dress and filling bowls with cereal. Lucas and Charlie currently have two days a week at nursery as Tara tries to pick up some freelance feature writing. Her plan is that when the youngest is three and the other two are in primary school, she'll go back to journalism part-time.

In a tearful moment a few months ago, she drunkenly confessed to me that sometimes – most recently when the boys were in a state of near-constant warfare and she was zombified with exhaustion– she's felt a fierce flash of hatred for her husband Dave when he walks out of the door for work in the morning. When he *waltzes off down the drive to his car and escapes*, was how she described it. She told me how jealous she felt, how she loved her boys more than life itself but still sometimes yearned to be back at work.

'To be out there, on deadline, just myself and the story to worry about,' she'd said to me as we tucked into a second bottle of Friday evening wine. 'Even the worst possible assignment. Even a midnight deathknock on the dodgiest council estate in England. Sometimes I'd kill for that.'

She had immediately apologised to me, but I waved it away. She was just being honest. And I understood – I would kill for what she had, too.

With the boys dropped off at nursery and school we find ourselves back at her house, in her kitchen, waiting for the kettle to boil, low autumn sun slanting through the windows. The house is strangely quiet without her boys and it feels unnatural, almost unreal, without their constant noise and chatter, the burble of the TV, their high voices raised in play or protest.

After Gilbourne left last night I had googled Leon Markovitz and found a link to his podcast series, *Inside the Killing Mind*, reading the accompanying text with a rising sense of unease: *We delve deeper into the psychopathic brain than you've ever been before. Remember, you're never more than a stone's throw away from a psychopath.* Scrolling through dozens of episodes over the past few years, each one focusing on a different UK murder with a particular interest in psychopaths, serial killers, spree killers and gangland murderers. Fred and Rose West. Michael Ryan, who shot sixteen people in a single afternoon in Hungerford. Dr Harold Shipman, the UK's most prolific serial killer. Peter Sutcliffe, the Yorkshire Ripper. Angus Sinclair, the World's End murderer. Robert Black. John Christie. And on, and on, and on.

'So how are you doing, Ellen?' Tara takes two mugs from the cupboard and spoons in instant coffee. 'And don't just say "OK" because I'm not letting you get away with that.'

'I'm all right, I suppose.'

'How are you *really*?'

'Well.' I blow out a heavy breath. 'I've had better weeks, if I'm honest.'

'Come here.' She pulls me into a hug and I'm enveloped in the smell of her almond shampoo and the musky perfume she always wears, even on a school-run day. I feel my defences start to falter and suddenly I'm on the verge of tears. I try to wipe them away before she can see but it's too late.

Tara gives my back a gentle rub. 'I'm worried about you, Ellen.'

'I'll be fine.'

'Tell me what I can do to help.'

The kettle clicks off and she releases me to make the drinks, stirring milk into both mugs and handing me one. I follow her into the conservatory and she asks me for a full update on my conversation with Gilbourne.

'I can't, Tara. He said the details were confidential because it's a live investigation. I'm not allowed to tell anyone else.'

'Yeah but this is *me*, Ellen. I'm not a random person in the street.'

'I promised him.'

'So why did he tell you this stuff?'

'He said he was worried about me after what happened yesterday,' I shrug. 'Thought I would be safer if I knew some of the details.'

'Seems like it's a bit above and beyond the call of duty.'

'What do you mean?'

She shakes her head. 'He drives out here in an evening, gives you confidential info and swears you to secrecy like it could get him in trouble if anyone finds out. D'you think he would have done that for just anybody?'

'Probably? I don't know. I think he's actually a nice guy, despite first impressions.'

'He's got a soft spot for you.'

I frown. 'He's just doing his job.' I sip my coffee for a moment. 'Is this your idea of trying to cheer me up?'

'And he's quite good-looking in a been-round-the-block-a-few-times kind of way. You can tell he's a bit of a player.'

I shake my head at her, but I'm smiling. 'Do you really want to help?' I say.

'Of course.' She puts her coffee down on the table. 'Anything.'

'You did a stint on the *Daily Mail*, right? Before the boys came along?'

'Longest three years of my life,' she says with a grin. 'Toughest newsroom in the country.'

She had put her English degree to use after leaving the navy. From newspaper journalism she had shifted into magazines and was currently on a career break as a staff writer for *Jane's Defence Weekly*, with a specialism in the naval sector.

'Are you still in touch with anyone you worked with at the *Daily Mail*?'

'Some of the other specialists, yes. Education, health, the social affairs bod. Not so much with the general news guys.'

'How about the crime desk?'

'There wasn't really a *desk*, more like two blokes with a couple of phones each. But I'm still vaguely in touch with one of them, yes.'

'Do you think you could ask him a favour?'

I explain to her what I've found out about Kathryn Clifton, the way the locals in Great Missenden referred to her sister and the look Gilbourne gave me when I mentioned her. How he closed the subject down.

'Kathryn's boyfriend, Max too – his reaction when I asked about Kathryn's sister. He was . . . weird. I thought he was going to really kick off, take a swing at me. But then he just shut the door. I googled the sister, all kinds of different combinations, but nothing came up that seemed relevant. Which seems weird because surely whatever happened would appear on a news site, a webpage somewhere?'

'Could be a married name?'

'Perhaps. I was thinking there might have been one of those EU privacy removal things to scrub her name from the Google results?'

Tara wrinkles her nose.

'Maybe, but they don't make that easy. Takes time and effort.'

Dizzy appears from under the side table, moving slowly and sniffing the air, likely checking the coast is clear of small boys for the time being. He jumps up beside me on the sofa and I scratch him behind his ears, his deep purr starting up on cue.

'Well then, I thought there might be some kind of legal restriction on reporting? An injunction or something?'

'There would need to be a sound legal reason for an injunction, a plaintiff with a lot of money and the high-powered lawyers that will buy you. Like those premiership footballers who got super-injunctions when they were sleeping with each other's wives, so you can't name names or even report the fact that there *is* an injunction. Victims of certain crimes get anonymity too. But I can message my guy at the *Daily Mail* and see if it rings any bells.'

'Thanks, Tara.'

'He'll want to know why I'm asking.'

'I'm sure you can spin him a line that's plausible. Just don't mention me.'

'It might set some hares running. He might start doing some digging of his own.'

'As long as he keeps us in the loop, that's OK by me.'

She picks up her phone, selects a few options and begins typing a message. I stroke Dizzy's head while she types. My cat has established himself on a soft grey blanket at the end of the sofa, his big paws kneading the material while he purrs contentedly. He seems to have settled in OK and I'm amazed how well he tolerates being pursued and grabbed by Tara's boys, none of whom has discovered how sharp his claws are yet. He's even making use of the long-neglected cat flap left behind by the house's previous owners.

My own mobile buzzes with a text. An unrecognised number. I unlock it and read the words, the breath catching in my throat.

Mia is still in danger

Tara leans over and looks at my screen.

'What the hell?'

Before I can reply, the phone buzzes again as a second message appears below the first.

And so are you

37

There is a shiver of cold fear at the back of my neck as I type a reply.

What danger? Who is this?

I press send and try to think of who the message could be from, who knows enough about Mia and what's happened this week. Not Gilbourne, I had his number stored in my phone. Holt would show as unrecognised, but why not just call me? Perhaps it was Kathryn getting back in contact – if somehow she'd got my number? I will my brain to make a connection that's just out of reach, just beyond the edge of my vision.

My phone buzzes again.

She needs your help

I put a hand over my mouth. My heart's thudding painfully in my chest, all the fear of Tuesday rushing back. I knew the danger wasn't over, I felt it in the marrow of my bones. I type another reply.

Who are you?

Tara puts a hand on my shoulder.

'Are you all right, Ellen? You're shaking.'

'I don't like this,' I say. 'Something's wrong. It's really wrong.' I press the number and select the *call* option, putting the mobile on speaker so that Tara can hear too. It connects and rings four times before going to an automated female voicemail, the robotic voice tinny and loud in the silence of the conservatory. I hang up, dial again. Voicemail again. This time I leave my name and ask that my call is returned as soon as possible.

Tara gives me a look.

'Doesn't want to talk, I guess.'

A minute passes, then another, as we both wait for another text to arrive. Nothing. I stare again at the string of messages, stand up and pace up and down the tiled floor.

Tara says, 'Did you give Kathryn your number?'

'We didn't have the chance to exchange numbers.'

Another couple of endless minutes pass, and I sit down rigidly on the sofa, a drumbeat of fear in my chest. *Mia is still in danger.* I picture her little face, her soft round cheeks, big blue eyes, tufts of silky blonde hair. People still want to hurt her. How could anyone want to do that to such a sweet, innocent child? My mind flashes to last night, the conversation with Gilbourne, the pictures of two desperate men laid side by side. Which of them wants to hurt her? Maybe both?

'I've scared her off by ringing the number,' I say to myself, shaking my head. 'Shouldn't have done that. It was stupid.'

The phone buzzes twice in my hand and I flinch with shock.

I can explain everything

But she doesn't have much time left

'What does that even *mean*?' I stare at the words, pushing down the panic rising in my throat. 'That she doesn't have much time?'

I send another text, my hands shaking.

Call me on this number. Please tell me. I can help

This time there is no delay to the replies.

No

Has to be face to face

'Yeah, right,' Tara says. 'The mantra of stalkers and weirdos worldwide. I'm calling the number.'

She leans over to see my mobile and begins to tap the digits into her own phone.

'Wait,' I say quickly. 'A call from another number might spook her again.'

She stops, her thumb poised over the green 'call' icon.

'We don't even know if it is her. Could be anyone. Who have you been giving your number out to?'

'I don't know.' Something clicks in my brain. 'Hold on, remember I said I went for a drive yesterday, trying to find where Kathryn lived?'

I type a one-word message.

Max?

'Who's Max?' Tara says.

'Kathryn's boyfriend. I met him yesterday, wrote my number on a business card but he wouldn't give me his. He was very suspicious, definitely knew more than he was letting on.'

Good guess

I'm about to type a reply when two more messages arrive.

Meet me, Rectory Park. Kids play area. 11 a.m.

Just you, no one else

I check my watch: just after 10 a.m. I'll need to get back to my house, pick up my car. It'll be tight, but I can make it if I don't hang around.

'Wait,' Tara says with a frown. 'You're not actually going to go, are you?'

'Yes. I have to.'

'You don't *have* to do anything. This could be anyone. Someone who knows they can use Mia to push your buttons. This is like . . . I don't know, like psycho Tinder, only without names or photographs – for all you know it could be the guy who was waiting for you in your house yesterday. Maybe he wants to hurt you again.'

'He had the chance to do that yesterday.'

'Yes, and he did, he hit you with 50,000 bloody volts,' she says, her voice rising in exasperation. 'Men like that get a kick out of this stuff, controlling, manipulating, leading you up the garden path. What if it isn't Max?'

'What if it is?'

'He didn't volunteer that name, you offered it to him.'

'I know,' I say. 'You're right, it could be anyone. But what if something does happen to Mia? And I could have helped her, but I didn't? If I just sat here in your conservatory, drinking coffee? He says time's running out for her.'

A memory pulses through me, like a half-remembered nightmare. The stink of burning diesel, burning tents, acrid black smoke billowing up into the bright blue African sky.

I type a two-letter response.

OK

Tara leans over and studies the chain of messages again.

'We should at least tell your police guy, Gilbourne,' she says. 'Better still, let the police handle it full stop.'

'If he wanted the police, he'd have called them already. I can fill Stuart in later.'

I stand up, putting the name of the park into Google Maps. It's a couple of miles west, nearer the M25 and the Buckinghamshire border. In the direction of where Max lives with Kathryn.

Tara finishes her coffee and stands up too. 'Come on then, let's get to it.'

'Where are you going?' I say.

'I'm coming with you.'

'No,' I shake my head. 'He said I had to go alone.'

'Well of *course* he wants to get you on his own, Ellen. But he won't see me, I'll hang back at a distance. I can be discreet when I need to be.'

'You are many things, Tara, but discreet is not one of them. I'll be fine.'

'Like you were fine on Tuesday? Like you were fine yesterday?' She indicates the marks left by the stun gun on the side of my neck. 'I don't trust you not to do something silly. It could be a trap, it could be anything. I don't like it, I don't like it at all.'

'It's in the middle of a park – it'll be full of people. Nothing's going to happen. And anyway, you need to pick up the boys.'

She checks her watch. 'Not for ages yet. Loads of time until then.'

'I'll be fine.' I touch her arm, give it a reassuring squeeze. 'I need to do this.'

She holds my gaze for a moment, then gives me a slow nod. An admission of defeat. 'Have you got an attack alarm?'

'Somewhere at home.'

'Take mine.' She goes into the kitchen and returns moments later with a small metal cylinder, the size of a small aerosol. 'Unlock tab's here, press the button here to deafen yourself and everyone else in a fifty-foot radius. Best held at arm's length, next to his ear.'

'Thanks, Tara.'

She drives me to my house on Claverton Gardens, pulling up in front of my Citroën. We both get out and she comes around to my side, gives me a hug.

'Can I persuade you out of this?'

'No.'

'Then look after yourself. Stay in that park, don't go off anywhere with him. Call me if you need anything.'

'Yes, Mum,' I give her a smile.

'Silly mare,' she says. 'You know what I mean.'

I pull away from the embrace.

'I'll text when I have news.'

It's 10.35, so I still have a few minutes to play with. I go through the side gate and do a quick check on the back door that was repaired with sheets of plywood yesterday. Through the kitchen window I can see the mess of my house – waiting for a visit from police to dust for fingerprints – but the back door at least seems to be holding. By the time I come back around to the front of the house, Tara's big Nissan people carrier is gone.

The mid-morning traffic is not too bad but I push it anyway, blowing through a couple of amber lights on the way to Rectory Park. At each junction stop I check my phone for more messages from the unrecognised number. But Max – or whoever it is – has gone quiet for now. I pull into the car park with a couple of minutes to spare, slamming my door shut and scanning the surroundings. The small car park is two-thirds empty. The park itself is a well-kept playing field the size of three or four football pitches. Beech trees lining two sides, a scattering of people, young parents out with pushchairs, older couples walking slow circuits. There is a chilly autumn wind in the air and I belt my raincoat and thrust my hands into the pockets, feeling the comforting smooth shape of Tara's attack alarm in my right hand, mobile phone in my left.

I walk quickly towards the play area on the far side, a fenced in oval with slides, swings, roundabouts and sandpits, plus benches for weary adults. I feel exposed on the open ground. I suddenly wish I hadn't persuaded Tara out of coming. But the message had been quite specific.

The playground is busy with people pushing preschool age children on swings, standing next to climbing frames, dusting off toddlers in the sandpit. I study each of them to see if anyone stands out, if any are flying solo without a child in tow. Maybe Mia is here too? But of course she'd be too young for this playground. I quicken my pace anyway, summoning a picture of Max from memory: mid-twenties, tall, muscular, short dark hair and a left arm full of tattoos.

My phone buzzes with a text. Tara.

You OK? What's happening?

I type a quick reply as I walk, looking up every so often, keeping my eyes peeled for anyone who looks like Max.

Yes. Lots of people here. Can't see him yet

I open a low gate to get into the playground, find an unoccupied bench and sit down. It's one minute past eleven. I study each of the adults in turn again. Lots of mums, a few dads, some grandparents too, overseeing a couple of dozen small children. Maybe a hundred and fifty metres to the car park entrance, two smaller entrances off side roads to the left and right. A stand of trees to the left, next to a circuit of outdoor gym equipment: parallel bars, balance beams, monkey bars, all empty. I should be able to see Max coming from a long way off, but there's no sign of him yet. At least this is a public place and there are witnesses here.

Time slows to a crawl. One of the young mums catches my eye and gives me a strange sideways look, as if to say *what are you doing here, childless woman*? I flash her a smile and pretend to be looking at my phone, checking the time again: 11.06 a.m.

Another text from the unrecognised number drops in.

Stand up so I can get a better look at you

I stand quickly, scanning the car park, the other entrances, the row of trees behind me. Studying the adults in the playground again. No sign of Max: he's playing with me, observing me from a distance. Checking that I'm alone.

I text back.

I'm here. Where are you?

Three messages, seconds apart.

Hillingdon Road car park. 11.30
Level 9
If you're late, I'm gone

38

Patience is the hunter's friend.

Because the true predator is set apart not by brutality or size, nor by stealth or agility or speed. Not even by cunning or appetite. It is patience that separates true-born hunters from all the rest. Not the killing blow but the stalking that precedes it, a willingness to wait for the perfect moment, to let the prey come closer. To do the work for him. It comes from confidence, from experience, from a supreme certainty in his own abilities. From the ability to predict how prey will behave, how a target will move and react in the field.

This is why he holds off, always keeping the prey in sight, always within reach. Savouring the anticipation.

He stalks. He follows. He watches and he waits. But not for much longer.

She is almost ready.

It is almost time.

39

Level nine of Hillingdon Road car park is the top floor, the roof, open to the sky. I speed all the way there, jumping a red light and overtaking against traffic, and by the time I swing the car past the white-painted LEVEL 9 on the concrete pillar I'm sweating. The dashboard clock says 11.32 a.m. *Shit*. Two minutes late.

The roof level is bright after the low-ceilinged concrete gloom of the lower floors and I squint as I drive out into the daylight. Like the floors below it, level nine is split into two halves, one lower and one higher, connected by a sloping ramp that leads to the highest point. In the centre of the level, there is a low circular brick structure, a door with signs to a stairwell and lift. There's a low concrete barrier all the way around but it's barely four feet tall, not enough to stop someone going over if they are determined to.

Or if they are pushed.

I drive slowly along the rows of vehicles, looking for a driver behind the wheel of one of them. Nothing. I follow the long curving ramp up to the higher level and go all the way to the end, checking cars left and right. But I seem to be alone up here. Ahead of me, the top level of the car park finishes in a dead end, a blank wall that marks the building's highest point. I spin the steering wheel in a quick three-point turn and head back down the ramp to the nearest space, reversing in so I'm looking down the two rows of cars towards the exit.

Is he a no-show? Something must have spooked him, put him off. Or maybe he's already left because I'm a couple of minutes late. But surely I would have seen his car on the way down? If he was even *in* a car. If he was even here at all.

Tara texts me again asking for a progress update but I ignore her message. I need to keep alert.

I decide to stay in my car until I know what's going on. I hit the central locking, hearing the reassuring *chunk* of all the locks engaging. Leave the engine running in case I need to get out of here in a hurry. The dashboard clock clicks over to 11.34 and I type another text, holding the phone against the steering wheel.

I am here, Max. Where are you?

A full minute goes by without any response. I keep my eyes up in case he drives in.

Get out of your car and walk up the ramp to the highest level

Everything about this situation is bad. Absolutely everything: the height, the isolation from the street and the fact there's only one way in and out for vehicles. The attack alarm, with its 120-decibel scream, is next to useless up here; its noise will simply be carried away on the wind and dispersed before it can reach anyone on the ground – even if they could get up here fast enough to do anything about it, which seems unlikely as we're at least a hundred feet above street level. I'm fully aware of all these facts. And yet here I am. *Mia is still in danger.* I think of her in the café three days ago, eyes closing into a contented sleep in my arms, a tiny bubble of milk on her lips.

Move.

I kill the ignition, get out of the car and go to the boot. Under the carpet is the spare tyre and tools that go with it. I pick up the wrench, a foot-long steel tool angled at one end, and slip it under my coat. Grip it with my left hand through the pocket. Slamming the boot shut, I scan my immediate surroundings. This level is mostly full, maybe a hundred cars and only a few empty spaces. No people that I can see, no cars that I recognise. I force my legs to start walking slowly, cautiously, up the ramp. The wind whips at my hair, blowing it across my face, flattening my trousers against my legs. It's stronger up here, on this concrete platform, a cold whistling slap that makes my eyes water. The sky is a mass of iron-grey clouds rolling low overhead.

At the top of the ramp I pause for a moment, tucking strands of hair behind my ear again. There is a tingling in my stomach, something like nausea, but I swallow it down and will myself to keep moving forward.

There is an empty space at the very end of the row. No car parked there. I circle to the other side of it, as far from it as I can get. The wind flattens my raincoat against my body, the ridged steel of the wrench outlined against the fabric. My heart is thudding painfully in my chest now. I keep walking towards the blank wall, towards the drop into the street far below, even though all my senses are screaming at me. *Run. Go. Get back in your car and drive away. Now.*

Somehow, I reach the end, leaning around to check the empty parking space. But there is no one there, just an eddy of litter spiralling in the wind, blowing round and round, up and over the parapet into empty air. The offices and shops and streets of Hillingdon spread out below me, railway lines cutting through the sprawl. Maybe this is another test to make sure I'm alone, Max observing me through telescopic sights. Maybe he's gone already and I'm alone up here.

There is a tingling at the back of my neck, the fine hairs standing up. Movement behind me. A shift in the light, a figure rising, slipping between two parked cars. Emerging from behind a big SUV, moving out into the centre of the pitted concrete lane.

But it isn't Max, or Kathryn.

It's Dominic Church.

40

I'm trapped.

Behind me is a dead end, a low blank wall. Beyond it, a hundred-foot drop. In front of me is Dominic, standing between me and my car. He looks even worse than he did three days ago. He's wearing the same black bomber jacket and blue jeans but there is a large plaster on the cheekbone below his right eye, the skin around it puffy and bruised. Big fists at his sides, the fingernails crusted with dirt. In my head I hear Gilbourne's voice: *convictions for assault, robbery, drugs.*

Dominic's lured me up here to throw me off the roof.

'*You,*' I say finally, taking out the wrench from under my coat and gripping it in my right hand. 'Don't come any closer.'

'You going to hit me again?' He walks slowly towards me. 'Because I've had just about enough of being hit for one week.'

The gap between us is only five or six metres or so, close enough for him to reach me in a few strides. All the terror of the last time I saw him is flooding back – but at the same time I'm furious with myself because I should have guessed, should have *known* it was him. The anonymous contact, checking I wasn't followed to the park, the isolation of this spot. It all fits with the way he behaved on

Tuesday, the way he tore Kathryn's bag apart, looking for tracking devices. Next-level paranoid.

I heft the wrench. 'I will if you come any closer.'

'Look, I just want to talk.' He slows his pace. 'How about you put that thing down?'

'How about you back off? Why didn't you tell me who you were?' The wind is icy on my cheeks and threatens to carry my words away. 'Why did you let me think you were Max?'

'Would you have come if you thought it was me?' He shakes his head. 'Of course you wouldn't.'

No, because you're a violent kidnapper who threatened to kill me. But I don't want to aggravate him any further. Neither of us speak again for a moment but he's clearly agitated, on edge, and the wrong words could set him off.

'Why did you say Mia is in danger?' I say. 'That I am in danger?'

'Because it's the truth.'

'But Mia's safe now, she's with—'

'She's not safe. She's in more danger now than ever, and there's only one thing that will change that.'

'What?'

'If I tell you, you're going to have to trust me first.'

'After what you put me through?'

He stares, bright green eyes studying me, as if seeing me for the very first time. A gust of wind almost pushes me sideways but he is as steady as a rock, feet planted shoulder-width apart, black jacket flattened against the slab-like muscles of his shoulders and chest.

'Kathryn made a good choice,' he says, 'when she picked you. The right choice. I understand that now.' He nods. 'She trusted you and now you're going to have to trust me.'

Gilbourne's words come back to me. *Do not engage. Do not approach. Whatever you do, don't trust either of them.*

'I can't think of one reason why I should.' I indicate the healing cut above my eye. 'You kidnapped me, attacked me. Fifty-fifty you've been in my house too.'

He frowns. 'Someone broke into your house?'

'Twice.'

He shakes his head emphatically. 'That wasn't me.'

'That's exactly what the other guy said.'

'I have no reason to lie.'

'You have *every* reason to lie.'

'What did they take?' He takes another step towards me. 'When they broke in, what was stolen?'

'Stay back!' I move away, backing into the low concrete wall. 'I told you to stay back.'

'You've got this all wrong, Ellen, you've got *me* wrong. I could have killed you three days ago, could have killed you and Mia both. There were a dozen opportunities to do it, but I didn't. Ask yourself: why not?'

'You were waiting for nightfall, so you could get rid of us under cover of darkness.'

'I was. But I was going to drive you out into the countryside and leave you somewhere so you couldn't identify me straight away, couldn't stop me taking Mia to safety.'

'*Safety*?'

'I wasn't going to harm you, or her. I swear on my mother's life.'

I edge sideways along the wall, inching nearer to my car and ready to burst into a run if he makes another move towards me.

'I'm leaving now, Dominic.'

'You're going to run away again?'

'I've never run away from anything in my life.'

'You ran away to your friend's house to play happy families with her three little boys.'

I flinch, stopping in my tracks. 'How did you know I was staying with Tara?'

'I had your phone, remember?' He shrugs. 'Your whole life was on there, birthdays, addresses, diary, messages. She was your most frequent contact. I've been keeping tabs on you.'

The sound of a car engine rises up from the ramp below and Dominic's eyes flick to me, then in the direction of the sound. He slides back into the space between the two big SUVs. The new arrival, a small white Volkswagen, pulls into a vacant spot below us and we both watch as a young woman gets out and hurries to the stairwell at the centre of the level. While Dominic is distracted I circle around and further away from him, putting me a few feet closer to my own car.

He emerges from his hiding place once more, moving closer, cutting off my line of escape again.

'Just ask yourself how you'd feel,' he says, his voice low. 'If something happened to one of those little boys.'

Noah, Lucas and little Charlie. A cold stab of fear slides between my ribs.

'Is that a threat?'

'It's a hypothetical. Someone's come after you twice already, who's to say they're going to stop? They found you once, why couldn't they find you again?'

'You lay a finger on any one of them and I'll—'

'*Me?* I'm not talking about me. I'm talking about whoever's doing all this.'

'Leon Markovitz?'

'Possibly.'

'If not him, then who?'

'You wouldn't believe me if I told you. All I can say is that I think we both want the same thing, you and I. But I've run out of options. You're the only one who can help her now.'

He comes closer and for the first time I notice a desperation in his eyes, an anguish, that I hadn't seen on Tuesday. His big shoulders slump and his chin drops, the dark circles heavy under his eyes. He looks exhausted, bone tired.

'Will you help Mia?' His voice is barely above a whisper now. 'Will you help me?'

It occurs to me that he's never actually told me what his interest is in all of this. In the handful of hours we spent together on Tuesday, I assumed he was Kathryn's ex-husband or rejected boyfriend, out for revenge. But I didn't ask for the truth, and he never offered it.

'Who are you, Dominic? Tell me, and I'll think about it. Tell me the truth: is Mia your daughter, are you not allowed to see her anymore? Is that what it is, a restraining order? Are you Kathryn's ex, denied access to your own flesh and blood?'

He looks at me for a long time, his eyes filled with a plunging sadness I've not seen there before. Eventually he shakes his head.

'No,' he says. 'Mia's not my daughter. And she's not Kathryn's either.'

41

'So who are you?' I say, trying to recalibrate everything according to what Dominic has just told me, to assemble all the different fragments of this puzzle. 'And if Mia's not *your* daughter, who is she?'

'It'll be easier for you if you don't know. All you need to know is that she is in terrible danger, she's out there, she's defenceless and we have to get a warning to the people looking after her. You have to get her back. You're the only one who can help me, because you'll be able to get close to her. They won't let me anywhere near.'

'Then you should tell this to the police, they can—'

'We can't trust the police!' There's a sudden fury to him, anger crackling like a surge of electricity. He gestures to the car park around us. 'Haven't you got that yet? You're not listening to me! Why do you think I'm like this, why do you think I'm constantly looking over my shoulder? Why do you think I have to bring you up here, to check you weren't followed, to check you're not working with them right now? The police messed up everything from the start. If it wasn't for them none of this would have happened. Their investigation was screwed from the beginning and then they tried to fit me up, tried to make me take the fall for it because they couldn't do their jobs properly. Such *bullshit.*'

I swallow hard on a dry throat. All the calm, the fatigue in his posture has gone. Instead there's a furious tension in the set of his jaw, in the ridged knuckles of his clenched fists. Can he even distinguish the truth anymore? Can I trust anything he says? The wrench still clutched in my right hand feels small and light and useless against his anger, and I'm suddenly aware again how close we are to the edge of the roof. He could probably pick me up with one hand if he decides to throw me off.

'Kathryn said that too,' I say quietly. 'About the police.'

'Damn right,' he growls. 'She had a gut feeling for what was going on.'

I need to calm him down, avoid setting him off again. Keeping my voice soft, I say, 'Is that why she ran?'

'She's a smart girl, she knew Mia was in danger. It's been days now since I heard from her. She's not answering her phone, she's not been back to her flat.'

'You think something has happened to her?'

He stuffs his hands deep into his jacket pockets. 'It's not like her to be out of contact. Something's not right.'

'You said in your message that Mia doesn't have much time left. What did you mean?'

'It's only a matter of time now before they find out who she is. *Exactly* who she is. A day or two, maybe not even that. And there's someone out there who will kill her to make sure that doesn't happen. Who will make her disappear.'

'I want to understand, Dominic, but it all sounds a bit . . .'

'Crazy?'

'Yes.'

'Did you think Kathryn was crazy?'

Worried, certainly. Stressed out, definitely. But crazy? No.

'She didn't seem crazy to me,' I say, realising abruptly that he's now talking about her in the past tense. The thought jars me out of my train of thought for a moment. 'She was just . . . scared out of her wits.'

'Kathryn understood the danger, that's why she took Mia. That was the reason she was running, the reason she handed her over to you, a total stranger, when she felt them closing in.'

'*Who* was closing in?'

'You don't need to know. That doesn't matter.'

'It does to me.'

He sighs and crosses his big arms over his chest. 'I can't risk you relaying every word I say straight to the police. Gilbourne's already got his hooks into you, I can tell.'

'No, he's just been trying to help.' Before I can stop myself, I hear myself defending the detective inspector. 'He's been very kind, actually. Helpful.'

'You can't trust him. You can't trust any of them, they're all as bad as each other.'

'He said the same thing about you.'

He barks out a short, humourless laugh. 'Of course he did. But here's the thing, Ellen: you've got to work out whose side you're on, who you're going to believe.'

'Why do I have to be on anyone's *side*? I'm on my own side. I'm on Mia's side.'

He stares at me for a long moment, bloodshot eyes unblinking. 'She needed you a few days ago, and she needs you again now.'

'So how do I help her?'

'Her grandparents – you have to warn them. They think they're safe, shut in behind their walls and gates and cameras, they think they can keep *her* safe, but they can't.'

'I thought she was with social services?'

He shakes his head.

'Back with family, which makes her a sitting target. They need to get her out of there, take her somewhere else. Somewhere no one knows.'

'You could tell them that yourself.'

'I tried. But we're not exactly on speaking terms anymore. Haven't been for a while.' He blows out a breath. 'I went up there to warn them yesterday and they wouldn't even let me onto the property.'

'That doesn't seem completely surprising, if I'm honest.'

'We've got history, but they don't know you. They might listen to you, if you tell them you met Kathryn on Tuesday. If you tell them who you are.'

'OK,' I say. 'I'll try. Can you give me a name, an address?'

'Just like that? You don't want to think about it a little longer?'

I shake my head. 'I'll talk to them.'

'Thank you, Ellen.' His lips barely part when he says it, as if it's been so long he's forgotten how to form the words. 'Thank you.'

'How do I find them? How do I reach you, for that matter?'

'You don't.' He shakes his head, the moment of gratitude vanished on the wind. 'I'll call you. As of now, that burner phone is done, finished. I never use the same one for more than a day or two.'

'Give me your new number then, I can call you.'

'And have you pass it straight to Gilbourne so he can track my every move? I don't think so.'

I feel a prickle of annoyance push through the fear, his assumption that I will pass everything on to the police. Which is what I *should* do, I suppose. But I don't want to challenge him again, not when he's let his defences down for the first time.

'So where is she?' I say instead. 'Where's Mia?'

He glances over his shoulder, eyes scanning the rows of cars, before his hooded eyes come to rest on mine again.

'About ten miles north of here there's a village called Prestwood Ash. Right in the sticks, middle of nowhere.'

'Near Little Missenden?'

He gives me a strange look but seems unsurprised that I know the name. 'It's about another three miles north of there, further into the Chilterns.'

He's interrupted by a car engine revving hard in low gear, tyres squealing as it climbs the ramp onto the roof level. I look over and see a blue Nissan people carrier accelerating hard between the rows of parked cars, the driver clearly visible.

Tara. She has followed me after all.

She is sitting forward in the driver's seat, her head turning this way and that as she searches for me. Our eyes meet and I shake my head – *I'm OK, back off* – but it's too late. She guns the engine into the turn, accelerating up onto the ramp towards us and aiming the people carrier at Dominic. He's seen my gesture and he's already backing away towards the stairwell, a look of disappointment and disgust on his face.

'The *one thing* I asked you to do was come alone.' He's shaking his head. 'I thought I could trust you.'

'You can.'

'I thought you wanted to help Mia, but you've got your own agenda just like all the rest.'

'I will help, if you tell me where she is!' I say to his retreating back. 'The address! Please?'

He stalks away, pushing through the door to the stairwell, and then he's gone.

42

DS Holt

The old woman wasn't going to let him go upstairs.

He could tell, as soon as the first words were out of his mouth. As soon as he'd seen her face, blank, staring, shell-shocked with grief. Already numbed with the worst news that any parent could hear. Now she stood just inside her thickly carpeted hallway, staring at him, skinny arms slack against her sides, eyes red-rimmed with crying. He looked past her. There was a wide sweeping staircase against the far wall, curving up to the first floor. Mia was up there, Holt knew, up on the second floor in one of the six bedrooms. He'd already noted the security system beside the front door, reasonably old, a small black and white monitor displaying the camera feed from the gate intercom, a straight live feed without a recording facility. The dogs, thankfully, were locked away in a side room for the time being.

'It's just routine, madam.' He still had his wallet open in his left hand, his warrant card there. He hadn't actually anticipated the woman would be difficult about it, that she'd actually say no. It wouldn't take him long to do what he needed to do. 'It's kind of a double-checking process that will assist us in the—'

'I can't cope with this, not today. We just need to be on our own together. I'm sorry.'

For a moment, Holt thought about telling her the real reason for his visit. Or he could try telling her they had no choice – that he had a warrant, or a court order or some other fictitious piece of paper – but he didn't think she'd care. Not with the news they'd just received.

'It'll literally take a few minutes,' Holt said. 'Then I'll be out of your hair.'

'We've always dealt with Detective Inspector Gilbourne up to now,' she said, her voice regaining some of its strength, some of its Merseyside lilt. 'He's been very good to us, very understanding. He advised us not to let anyone get close to her unless we knew them well and trusted them completely. And he said it would be Monday, not today.'

'If you can just let me—'

'And besides, Mia is asleep and we've only just got her down. I don't want to put her through it again today when she was so upset the first time around.'

The husband appeared from the back of the house and Holt suppressed a sigh of frustration. He was a bit older than his wife, mid-seventies, tall and bald with a bushy white moustache that contrasted with the flaring-red complexion of his skin.

'What's this all about? Angela, what's going on?' He turned to Holt, staring at him like a tradesman who had just trodden dog shit into the carpet. 'Have you got anyone in custody yet?'

'I'm afraid not yet, sir, but I can assure you that we're giving that our full attention. We have teams of officers working on the case as we speak. I was just explaining to your wife the reason for my visit.'

'And what did my wife say?'

'I said *no*,' the woman barked, her voice cracking on the last word.

'Well.' The husband turned to him. 'There's your answer, detective. You've upset my wife, now please leave.'

Holt's phone rang. Gilbourne again. He couldn't ignore him for a third time.

'DS Holt,' he said.

'Nathan, where the hell have you been? I've been trying to get hold of you for the last hour.'

'Sorry boss, was interviewing witnesses earlier and my phone was still on silent, I didn't realise.'

Gilbourne's voice was loud with anger and he had to hold the mobile away from his ear.

'You're not a bloody librarian, Nathan. You do not put your phone on silent. Ever. Your colleagues, your teammates, need to be able to reach you at all times. I need to be able to reach you. *At. All. Times.*' He enunciated each word individually. 'Even if you think you're a cut above all of us. Do you understand?'

Holt gave the woman a nod and stepped back out through the open front door. She seemed glad to get him out of the house, pushing the door closed behind him. He went out to the smooth stone porch, turned away.

'Yes sir.' He looked down the long gravel driveway, where the black iron gate out to the road still stood slightly ajar. 'Of course, will do.'

There was a pause, then his senior officer's voice came back quieter.

'What's going on, Nathan?'

'Nothing,' Holt said smoothly. 'Nothing's going on, Stuart. Just finishing up here and then I'll be right with you.'

'I need you to get to South Ruislip to reinterview Sienna Parker's parents. Give them the standard spiel, see if anything new shakes loose in light of recent developments, any possible links between her and the new victim. How quickly can you be there?'

Holt was ready for this one, had thought about what he would say. He looked round at the front lawn, the willow trees lining the drive, the stone wall around the edge of the property.

'I'm just at Marylebone, sir,' he said. 'The station manager found some additional footage from Tuesday afternoon. There was no one from the tech team available so I just nipped over to pick up the DVDs.'

'Anything worth seeing on there?' Some of the anger had gone from Gilbourne's voice. 'Anything we don't already know?'

'Not sure, I'll have a proper look when I'm back in the office.'

'OK, get yourself over to Ruislip and keep me updated.'

Holt ended the call and turned back to the front door to find the woman standing there in the doorway, eyes narrowed. She hadn't closed the door after all; she had been eavesdropping on his call.

She gave him a look that said *I see you. I hear your lies.*

'Marylebone?' she said.

Holt flashed her a smile, which she didn't return.

'Thanks for your time, Mrs Clifton. I'm so sorry for your loss.'

He crunched across the gravel to his Focus, feeling her eyes on his back every step of the way.

43

By the time Tara has pulled up in her car and jumped out, it's too late to follow Dominic down the stairwell – even if I wanted to.

'Are you OK?' my friend says, her face flushed. 'Who was that guy? Was it Max? He looked like a right thug.'

'I'm fine, just a bit shaken up.' I try to give her a smile. 'You weren't supposed to follow me.'

'I was worried. Someone has to keep an eye on you, especially after the week you've had.'

She explains that she followed me all the way from the junction out of my little estate, slipping into traffic behind me and keeping her distance all the way to Rectory Park. Watching as I waited for a rendezvous that didn't happen, then tailing me all the way to Hillingdon. It helped that people carriers were pretty much ubiquitous in this part of commuter land.

'It was like being in *Charlie's Angels*,' she says, clearly still buzzing with the thrill of the chase. 'Almost lost you when you were speeding but it turns out I'm *really* good at following people. Discreet.'

'Apart from that last bit, with the squealing tyres.'

'Sorry about that. I lost you on the high street then had to check every single floor of the car park. When I realised he'd got you on the top floor I freaked out a little bit. God, I was worried about you, and when I saw—'

'Listen,' I say, 'you need to do something for me right now, I will tell you why in a minute. You need to call Noah's school, and the nursery.'

The smile slides off her face, muscles slackening in alarm.

'Why?'

'Just do it, just check they're all OK.'

'You're scaring me, Ellen,' she says, blinking fast. 'What's happened, what are you talking about?'

'Just to be safe. Call them.' I put a hand on her arm. 'Do it now.'

She's torn between asking me more questions and making the calls. But after a moment she turns away from me, dials a number and puts the phone to her ear. I watch her talking urgently, waiting, pacing the concrete deck as the wind whips around us. Then she's nodding, but I can't quite hear what she's saying. I hate myself for giving my friend this scare and I hate that everything seems to be spinning out of control, but I can't ignore the threat.

When she turns back to me, her face is pale. She wraps her arms around herself.

'They're fine,' she says quietly. 'Noah's about to go into lunch, Lucas and Charlie are having outdoor play. They're all fine. What's going on, Ellen? Should we call the police? Are they in danger?'

I explain to her what Dominic said to me, that he knew her boys' names and where I was staying.

'Then we should tell DI Gilbourne,' she says. 'You've got to report this, he'll know what to—'

'No,' I say quickly, Dominic's angry words still ringing in my head. 'Not yet.'

'What are you talking about?'

'I'm not sure who we can trust right now. Let's just get back first, pick your boys up and take them home.'

Tara's eyes are wide, phone still clutched in her hand as if she's expecting it to ring at any moment. She looks at her watch.

'Does this guy know where the school is? The nursery? Oh my God, was he the one who abducted you, the one with the gun?' When she sees me nod, she adds, 'We should definitely call someone.'

'I'll do it,' I say. 'I'll speak to them. But let's get out of here.'

'I'll pick up Lucas and Charlie first.' She moves towards her car. 'Then Noah.'

'Come on,' I say, reaching for my car keys. 'Let's go together.'

* * *

I dial Gilbourne on the hands-free as we're driving back but get his voicemail. I remember the look of concern in the detective's eyes last night and it occurs to me that he will probably be upset with me for going to the meeting on my own. Or for going at all. I also remember the fresh, clean smell of his aftershave, the way it felt when his hand was on my arm. The warmth of his touch.

I shake the thoughts away and concentrate on keeping up with Tara as she weaves in and out of traffic on the way to the boys' nursery.

Little Charlie has to be roused from his post-lunch nap when we finally get there. As Tara carries him out he flops like an exhausted baby monkey, his head against her shoulder, unaware of any break in the normal routine. Lucas is delighted to be picked up from nursery early and even lets me hold his hand as we walk out to the car park. We make the five-minute drive to Noah's infant school in three minutes and park up on the street next to the playground. Tara doesn't want to let go of Charlie or leave him in the car for even a second, and he's happy to be carried over to the tall slatted steel fence that separates the pupils from the outside world. Lucas wants to see as well so I lift him up onto my hip. He's only four but he's surprisingly chunky, nothing like the featherweight of having Mia nestled in the crook of my arm. The thought of her gives me a lurch of fear, the sense that she is somewhere out there, still vulnerable, exposed to a violent world. Unprotected from someone who wishes her harm.

Lucas gives me a shy smile as I hoist him up and we all look into the playground filled with sturdy outdoor play equipment and a couple of hundred small children wearing coats over forest green jumpers, with dark grey trousers and skirts. The sun has come out and the crisp autumn air is full of the excited shouts and squeals of young voices, an excited hubbub of sound as if everyone's trying to be heard above everyone else.

'Are we looking for Noah?' Lucas says.

'Yes, can you see him?'

'Has he been bad? Is he in trouble?'

'No.' I manage a smile. 'He's not been bad.'

The three of us scan the playground, children running and playing, weaving in and out, jumping and stepping over complicated shapes and numbers painted onto the tarmac. A handful of adults on patrol amid the throng of small people. A couple of times I think I spot Noah's red coat but it's not him. I can't see him anywhere.

A block of dread is growing in my chest, a solid mass expanding with every second that I scan the playground. Trying to process it, to figure out how this can have happened if we drove straight here? How can Dominic have got here before us? What did he do?

Because Noah is not here.

44

A voice in my head whispers: *this is your fault.*

'Where is he, Ellen?' An edge of panic is creeping into Tara's voice. 'I called the school literally half an hour ago, why isn't he out here? He should be here.'

'Maybe he's inside?'

She shakes her head.

'Not on a day like this, when the sun's out. I'm going to find a teacher,' Tara says, hurrying away towards the school's front entrance. 'Call the police, Ellen, we need to—'

'There.' Lucas points over to the far side of the playground, into the furthest corner. 'Over there, look.'

We both turn to see where his little finger is pointing. Two small figures sitting on a white-painted log near the kitchen block. Noah with his friend Rakim. They appear to be playing some kind of card game, two small bespectacled boys facing each other, laying cards in the space between them. Relief floods through me like a shot of morphine.

'Your eyes are better than mine, Lucas,' I say. 'You've got eagle eyes.'

He grins up at me, pleased to be the one to spot his brother first. Tara hurries back to the fence, not satisfied until she's laid eyes on her oldest son herself. She turns to me, her face still white with fear, and I can tell she doesn't want to frighten the younger boys.

'I could say he's got a doctor's appointment,' she says quietly.

'Looks like he's OK,' I say. 'He's safe here, isn't he?'

Lucas says: 'Has Noah got to go to the doctor's, mummy?'

'Shush a minute, darling.' Tara stares for a moment longer, studying her son as he plays, checking the side gates, studying the adults in the playground, teachers and lunch-time supervisors on patrol. The familiar faces of people she knows, people she has chatted to at parents' evenings, in the supermarket or on the street. Everything seems to be as it should be. 'We'll pick Noah up at normal time,' she says finally. 'Hey, who wants strawberry milkshake when we get home?'

When we get back to her house, she makes drinks for the two younger boys, and I sit making Lego spaceships with Lucas while Charlie plays a complicated toddler game with various teddies, action men and uncannily real-looking dolls unloaded from a box in the corner of the lounge, burbling to himself all the while. I can't stop thinking about Mia, what she'll be like when she's their age. Wondering whether she will be serious like Noah, competitive like Lucas or a little comedian like Charlie. Wondering whether she will even have that chance.

Dominic's chilling words won't leave me alone.

There's someone out there who will kill her. Who will make her disappear.

I stay with the boys while Tara collects Noah from school. When they return, I go upstairs to the spare bedroom and call Gilbourne again but his phone is still going straight to voicemail. Dizzy is curled up on one of my jumpers at the end of the bed, one eye opening as I sit down next to him. The sound of the TV in the lounge floats up the stairs and a few minutes later Tara appears in the doorway, a cup of tea in each hand. I'm just about finished packing the few clothes that I have into my overnight bag.

'What are you doing?' she says.

I take one of the teas from her, steam curling from the mug.

'I need to go, Tara.'

'Where? What are you talking about?'

'It's not right, me staying here. I'm putting you and your family in danger. I shouldn't have come,' I say. 'I'm sorry.'

'There's nothing to be sorry for.'

'I hadn't realised before, but I can see it now.'

'But . . . your house is still a mess, isn't it? I thought they wanted you to leave it until they could check for fingerprints or whatever?'

'I'm going to a hotel for a few days. I know Noah was OK earlier but just the thought of him, you know, of something happening to him . . . I couldn't bear it.'

She nods, pulls me into a hug.

'Dave's on his way back from work early,' she says. 'I'm glad it's the weekend. I might keep them off school and nursery next week. Keep them here with me.'

'I'll tell the inspector what Dominic said today, maybe they can send someone to keep an eye on the house, get a patrol car to drive by or something.'

'How long will you be in the hotel?'

'Just for a few days I think, until the house is sorted out.' I want to say *until this is over.* 'Until . . . everything is back to normal.'

She releases me from the hug but keeps her hands on my shoulders.

'Are you sure about this? I don't think you should be on your own, Ellen.'

'It's only a mile down the road. Not far.'

'I'm worried about you.'

'It'll be all right. The boys have to be your priority.'

I put my jacket on and carry my bags downstairs into the hall, retrieving the cat box from the cupboard under the stairs and whistling for Dizzy. It's nearly food time so it's only a moment before his little face appears at the top of the stairs and he begins descending, keeping a cautious eye on the nearest small boy as he gets to the bottom.

'Where are you going with the cat box?' Tara says.

'I need to take this young man to the cattery.'

'Rubbish, he can stay with us. The boys love him, don't you boys?'

Noah gives a double thumbs-up. 'Can we keep him *forever*?' he says.

'Not forever, Noah,' Tara says gently. 'Just a few days.'

I give Dizzy a scratch on the top of his big solid head. 'Be good,' I say to him.

He blinks up at me, purring his deep rumbling purr. I crouch down to Tara's eldest son.

'Noah, I need you to do something for me, OK? I need you to look after Dizzy until I can take him back to my house. Make sure everyone is nice to him. Can you do that?'

'Doesn't he want to go with you?'

'Yes, but I'm going to stay in a hotel for a few days, and cats aren't allowed. I need someone to make sure he has two sachets of his food every day and a little dry food for lunch. Will you remind your mum to give him his lunch?'

'OK.'

'Promise?'

He nods solemnly, eyes wide behind his red and black Spiderman glasses. 'Cross my heart,' he traces a shape over his little chest, 'and hope to die.'

'Thank you, Noah. You're a good boy.'

I kiss the top of his head and stand up. At the front door, Tara puts a hand on my arm, her face still full of concern.

'Are you sure about this?'

'It's the way it has to be, Tara.'

'Text me when you get settled in.'

'Will do.'

'Hey, I nearly forgot,' Tara says, lowering her voice and checking that her boys are safely out of earshot. 'While I was waiting at the school gates, I had a call back from my guy at the *Daily Mail*. Bit of a sleazebag but he's got some good contacts in the Met. He was rather cryptic on the phone, said Kathryn Clifton's sister had lifetime anonymity because of what happened to her. Does that make sense to you?'

'Not sure. What else did he say?'

'That he would deny ever having the conversation with me if I mentioned it to anyone else. But he said there was something I might want to see, promised he'd email a link through when he had a minute. Sounds interesting. I'll forward the email to you when I get it.'

45

Leon

Leon counted only one camera at the entrance. Directly over the keypad where the intercom was housed in a small steel box, looking directly into the driver's side window of any vehicle pulled up at the gate. Any serious system would cover multiple angles but this one was typical of the kind of thing installed on a house like this: mostly for show. It was an even bet, he thought, whether that single camera even worked. From his vantage point he had a partial view of the front of the house, and inspection through the telephoto lens had not revealed any further cameras over the front door.

The front gate was wrought iron – eight feet of curved metal topped with a row of spearpoints – set in concrete posts that formed part of the perimeter wall running around the entire property. The wall was visible on Google Maps but he'd checked it out anyway, walking the outer rim at dusk. It was in reasonably good repair without any obvious weak spots but there was one section at the back, well away from the road, where trees had grown up too close on both sides and a couple of oaks offered a way over.

He had always liked to climb.

There were a number of other weaknesses in the system. The gate opened via an infrared sensor activated by dashboard transmitters mounted in the three cars, the husband's Range Rover, her Mercedes A-Class and the little Toyota that belonged to Mrs Kelsall, the help. There was also a coded keypad below the intercom and of course a remote gate release that could be activated from anywhere with a phone signal, via a security app. All three of them had the app on their phones, which was a mistake because it opened the whole system up to human frailty – in this case, a re-used password that almost made it *too* easy once he'd found his way into Mrs Kelsall's mobile.

Any security system was only as strong as its weakest link.

So the gate itself was not a problem. The camera wouldn't help them much. But that still left the dogs, which made it tricky for any approach on foot. Two Doberman Pinschers that roamed the grounds inside the eight-foot walls at night and most of the daytime, too. Leon hated animals. *Hated* them. And he hated dogs most of all, big, stupid bastards with their oily, greasy fur, their dripping saliva and foul, stinking breath.

That was why he was grateful to Detective Sergeant Holt; seeing him loitering around the house had given Leon an idea.

46

I go by my house for fresh clothes on the way to the hotel, filling a carrier bag with food, a pint of milk, some fruit, biscuits and energy bars. I step carefully around the mess in the kitchen, taking care not to touch any surfaces, pulling my sleeve over my hand to open the fridge. I've been told to leave things as they are until the police can come around to dust for fingerprints and look for other physical evidence.

The house seems both familiar and foreign, a place I used to know better than any other that now bears a permanent stain of intrusion. Another harsh lesson on top of the one I've already learned these last few years: *what you yearn for, you cannot have. And what you have can be taken from you in an instant.*

The Premier Inn is on the edge of a small retail park off the north circular, a bland newbuild for business travellers and people on their way to or from somewhere more interesting. I check in with the bored twenty-something guy on reception and take my things up to a small, boxy room on the first floor. Purple and cream décor, a bed, a desk, a low table and an armchair by the window. Functional. Just the basics, nothing more.

I pull the heavy curtain open. The view is of a small windswept car park, two-thirds empty, chain-link fence backing onto a railway embankment. A white plastic bag circling, tossed around by the wind. The first spots of rain darkening the tarmac. First Tara's house, now here, every step taking me further from what I know, further from home, from my routine, my life. But I can't go back, not yet. I have to move forwards, push through and keep on going. Until Mia is safe. Until I'm *sure* she's safe.

Unpacking my overnight bag, I lay out what I have on the double bed. Three changes of clothes, a second pair of shoes, phone, charger, a small toiletries bag, my handbag and its various contents. I check through the handbag, pull out the folded muslin cloth and hold it to my nose. Her scent is still there, that beautiful sweet baby smell that makes my chest ache. It's fading though, and I wonder how much longer it will be before it's gone for good.

I plug my phone in to charge and type 'Prestwood Ash' into Google Maps. The image zooms into south Buckinghamshire, a small collection of streets around a village green, not far from Little Missenden. I switch to satellite view and pinch the screen to zoom out. It's surrounded by woods and fields, nestled deep in the heart of the Chiltern Hills. Forty minutes by car. Away from London, away from noise and traffic and people. But is it safe? Can it be safe if Dominic knows she's there, if he's already tried to get to her? Who else knows?

I need to speak to Dominic again, assuming he hasn't switched to a new phone already. He told me he was going to dump it but I find the number for his burner phone anyway, the one he used earlier today, and spend a few minutes composing a text, something that might persuade him that he can trust me.

I want to help. Please tell me how to find her. Just the address

No reply. I ring the number, only to be greeted by an automated female voice.

'*Sorry, this number is out of service.*'

I curse and throw the phone on the bed. He's likely already destroyed the SIM card and dumped the phone. I suppose I could sit around here and wait for him to contact me again. Or I could take the initiative, get on the front foot. I wasn't sure of a sur-name for Mia's grandparents, but I could start with Clifton and see where that led. I remember a favourite quote of one of the instructors at the Royal Naval College, who taught the leadership element of the officers' course. *A good plan, vigorously executed now, is better than a perfect plan next week.* The words have always stuck in my memory for some reason. It's better to crack on with what you have, rather than waiting and waiting for everything to line up in perfect order. Do I even *have* a good plan? Maybe not, but I'm certainly not going to sit around in a hotel room waiting for my phone to ring. I grab my keys and coat and head out.

*   *   *

As I drive north out of London, I turn the question over in my head. Did I mean what I said to Dominic, when I agreed to talk to Mia's grandparents? Was I just saying whatever I needed to say, to get away from him in one piece? Maybe. But beneath that there is something else. I want to know if what he said is true, to judge for myself if Mia is safe. I told Dominic I would talk to them – and I will. To warn them. All I have to do is find her.

Prestwood Ash is a small, picture-perfect Chiltern village nestled in a shallow valley. Huge oaks and horse chestnut trees tower on both sides of the road as I approach, branches touching overhead as if I am driving through a dark, forested tunnel. The satnav announces that I've reached the village, a speed limit sign urging drivers to stick to twenty miles an hour, the trees giving way to hedgerows, then walls and fences, then a neat village green with large houses set back behind gates and walls. I drive around for a few minutes, taking it slowly, getting a feel for the place. Three and four cars on shaded driveways, Range Rovers and Mercedes, Audis and a couple of Aston Martins. A tennis court in the garden of one house, a triple garage next door, an outdoor pool covered for the winter; landscaped lawns and tall wrought iron gates. Everything about it says *money*.

It's not quite what I had envisaged. I thought there would be somewhere I could go, a meeting place with people I could ask. But there is no pub, no post office, no starting place for a conversation that might lead me to the right house. I even thought I might catch sight of Mia through a window, maybe in a pushchair being taken for a walk. But it's almost six o'clock on a Friday evening and a sharp autumn shower from the darkening skies seems to have cleared the streets of people, if there were even any out in the first place. Maybe this isn't the kind of place where you walk even when the sun's shining. I circle the village twice, driving in and out of the long main road before doing a U-turn in a farmer's track and going back through, looking for a car seat strapped into a car, a stroller in a porch, a glimpse through a window. Nothing.

An elderly man walking a dog emerges from the woods at the end of the lane. I wait for him to come level with my car and buzz my window down.

'Excuse me,' I say, 'I'm a bit lost, could you help me? I'm looking for the Clifton house.'

His eyes narrow slightly, the lines of his face pinching into a frown as he clocks me for an outsider. He bends awkwardly down to my window.

'Who?'

I repeat the question and his frown deepens.

'Sorry.' He shakes his head. 'Can't help you.'

Turning around again, I drive back up the main street and pull over next to a teenage boy on a bike. He's maybe thirteen or fourteen, leaning on his handlebars and intent on the screen of his mobile phone, and he barely removes one earpod for long enough to listen to my question before shaking his head *no* and putting it back into his ear.

A single street lamp flickers hesitantly into life, throwing a narrow wash of pale light that only serves to emphasise how dark the rest of the street has become as night falls. I'm starting to get the feeling that Prestwood Ash is one of those places you see on the news sometimes, the kind of place where *everyone keeps themselves to themselves*, where you might know your immediate neighbours to say hello to but not many beyond that. No pub to bump into people, no shop to trade gossip at the till, most residents happy to stay cocooned inside their own little bubbles of wealth, with their walls and gates and gravel driveways. I take out my phone and google the village name again in frustration. This is *definitely* the place. One of these houses. There can't be more than a few dozen here, fifty at most. But which one? I get out of my car and go to the nearest gate, a driveway leading up to a large whitewashed house with a thatched roof.

I press the buzzer and a woman's voice barks a single word in response.

'Yes?'

'Hi, I wonder if you can help me, I'm looking for—'

'Not interested, thank you.'

The intercom clicks again: the conversation is over. I walk down to the next gate, the next intercom, press the buzzer. A dazzling halogen security light comes on, half-blinding me, but there is no answer at all from inside the house. The next one has never heard the name Clifton and the occupant of the one after that – an older man by the sound of him, with a thin, reedy voice like a frightened bird – threatens to call the police if I press the bell again.

It's almost fully dark now, windy, wet and cold out – all factors working against me, against the stranger at the gate. I could keep knocking on doors in the hope of striking lucky or finding someone who knows Kathryn's family. But almost all of these houses have gates with intercoms, cameras and keypads to keep visitors at arms' length. I get a strong sense that the residents of Prestwood Ash are pulling curtains and locking doors, hunkering down, shutting themselves up in their multimillion pound houses for the night. But there's still a little time left. I've got to try.

I'm starting up another tree-shaded driveway when I register the sound of rapid footsteps behind me. A heavy, unfriendly tap on my shoulder. A man's voice.

'Hey!' the voice says. 'What the hell are you doing here?'

47

I turn and recognise him instantly. Tall and heavily built with a sleeve of tattoos visible through his white shirt, dark hair cropped close to his scalp. Kathryn's boyfriend, Max, faces me at the head of the driveway.

'I asked you a question,' he says. 'What are you doing here?'

'Trying to find someone.'

He stands close, *too* close, pure aggression in the set of his shoulders and the jut of his chin. 'You are one of them, aren't you?'

'What?'

'A reporter.' His eyes narrow. 'Trying to stir up shit and print lies about people.'

'I'm not a reporter. We met the other day, remember?'

'And now you're knocking on my mum's door.' He jerks a thumb back over his shoulder towards one of the other houses on the street. 'You can't go around harassing people in their own homes.'

'I wasn't harassing anyone, I was just trying to find out where—'

'Who do you work for? The *Sun*? *Express*?'

He moves still closer and I smell his sharply pungent aftershave with a base coat of sour sweat. He's got to be sixteen stone at least, the kind of guy who's used to impressing and intimidating people with his size, his bulk, using it to get what he wants. I take a step back away from him – further from the street, from the anaemic street light – and he comes forward again, nostrils flaring. I go to move around and past him but he puts out his big arms and now he's crowding me, blocking my path back to the pavement. There's no one else around, dusk is falling fast, and for the first time I feel a shiver of unease flash up my spine. I think of the attack alarm in my handbag, slung over my shoulder, wondering if anyone will respond if I trigger it.

'Let me through,' I say, trying to make it sound more like an instruction than a request.

'You don't get away that easily. Not until I've seen some ID.'

'Can you let me pass, please?'

'Show me your ID.'

'I'm not going to do that.' I reach into my handbag.

'Then you ain't leaving.' He jerks his chin at my handbag. 'What's in the bag?'

'Nothing very interesting.'

'OK I'll just report you for harassment right now then.' He pulls a mobile from his pocket and before I know what he's doing there's a camera flash. 'I'm *sick* of you people.'

'Did you just take my picture?'

'Going to make sure everyone knows who you are.'

'This is ridiculous.'

'I've got another idea,' he says. 'How about—'

Another voice cuts him off. A male voice, calm, neutral, reasonable. 'Is there a problem here?'

Half over his shoulder, Max says tonelessly, 'No problem, mate.'

There is a crunch of footsteps on gravel as the figure approaches and I feel the relief and gratitude wash through me as a familiar face appears at Max's shoulder.

'Everything all right?' Gilbourne asks.

'Everything's cool,' Max says, without taking his eyes off me. 'We're just having a chat.'

'Why don't you take a couple of steps back, sir.'

Max turns on him angrily, his expression darkening as he registers the warrant card open in Gilbourne's hand, the photo ID and Met Police crest.

'Eh?'

'Just take two steps back, sir, and we'll get this all sorted out, shall we?'

'She's harassing people.'

'It's all right. She's with me.'

'What?' Max's face creases with confusion. 'What do you mean?'

'We were actually just leaving, weren't we Ellen?' He gives Max a nod. 'Have a good evening, sir.'

He turns and heads back out to the pavement. Max doesn't try to stop me as I follow.

When we're safely out of earshot, I say: 'Max seems to have some anger issues.'

'Yeah. We've been keeping an eye on him.'

'Is that why you're here? Because he's a suspect?'

Gilbourne gives me a sideways glance as we walk beside the village green. He has his hands in his pockets and his pace is slow, casual, as if he's in no hurry to be anywhere else.

'To be honest, Ellen, I'm more interested in why *you're* here.'

There doesn't seem to be any reason to lie.

'You know why. I'm looking for Mia.'

'And what do you plan to do when you find her?'

'Warn them. Tell them about Dominic Church, about Leon Markovitz, about people coming after her.'

'You think they don't know about all of that already?'

I blow out a breath. 'I have to do *something*. I have to know that she's safe.'

He considers my answer for a moment. 'So have you found her?'

'Not yet.' When he doesn't reply, I add, 'Is this where you tell me to back off, keep my nose out of it again?'

He looks across at me and sighs. 'I don't think you're the sort of person who takes kindly to being told what to do, Ellen. I'm just worried about you, that's all.'

'I'm fine. I can't just sit on my hands waiting for news.' Something occurs to me. 'But you know where she is, right?'

'I do, yes.'

'How about you tell me, off the record? Since I've driven all the way out here.'

'You know I can't do that, Ellen. It would be breaching about six different rules.'

'I thought you weren't bothered about breaking the rules now and again?'

'I'm bothered about the victim's family,' he says. 'They need privacy.'

We reach my Citroën; his black Alfa Romeo is parked right next to it. He leans against the door of his car and slides a cigarette out of a packet of Marlboros. I've been trying to decide for the last few hours whether to tell him what happened at the rooftop car park today. But now we're here, together, and I can still feel the tingle of relief that he defused the situation with Max. I make a snap decision.

'I spoke to Dominic today.'

Gilbourne's eyes widen, the lighter pausing on its way to his cigarette.

I update him – in broad outline – what Dominic told me earlier. 'He said she's in danger, she's a sitting duck. He asked me to talk to her grandparents, persuade them to take her somewhere else.'

Gilbourne blows out a lungful of smoke with an exasperated sigh.

'Well of *course* that's what he wants, Ellen. He tried to take her from you and failed. He's tried to get to her there, and failed again. So he wants Mia to be out in the open, unprotected, where he can try to get to her for a third time. She's much better off where she is.'

'So, should she have police protection at the house, some kind of security?'

'I offered that to the family but they declined. They're private people. Her grandfather in particular is quite a . . . strong-willed character. Knows what he wants.' He gestures at me with his cigarette. 'He's not the only one. You don't give up, do you?'

'I can't get Mia out of my head.'

He takes a deep drag, blows grey streams of smoke through his nose that drift and dissipate on the evening air.

'I don't get you, Ellen. You don't have skin in this game, Mia's not your flesh and blood. You could have walked away, but you didn't.'

For a moment, I think about telling him a story I have only ever shared with Richard. About the memories I can't shake, the guilt that pulls me down with invisible anchors. About the first time a complete stranger had put her baby in my arms.

A decade ago, a different time, a different life.

He says, 'Why are you putting yourself at risk?'

'Because sometimes you just have to do what you think is right, and damn the consequences.'

'Amen to that.'

'So let me help you.'

'You can help me by staying safe.' He drops his cigarette onto the tarmac and grinds it beneath his shoe. 'Listen, I've got to get back to the station, let's catch up tomorrow. And Ellen?'

'Yes?'

'Look after yourself.'

'Thanks for earlier.' I gesture back over my shoulder. 'With Max.'

He nods, gives me a half-smile.

'You're welcome.'

He drives away and I watch as his Alfa Romeo accelerates into the distance and then, as the road curves away, is gone. I get in my own car and sit for a minute, thinking about what he said. He didn't *specifically* say I couldn't keep looking for Mia. *He wants Mia to be out in the open, unprotected, where he can try to get to her for a third time.* The least I can do is tell Mia's grandparents what Dominic is planning.

I resolve to come back in the morning. And even if I have to knock on every door in the village, I'm going to find her.

SATURDAY

48

There is a buzzing by my ear. I jerk awake, wreathed in sweat, a moment of terror as I realise I have absolutely no idea where I am. A dark room, almost pitch black, just a thin line of light to my right side. Not my pillow, not my bed. Not my house. I twist onto my back, heart drumming against my ribs—

The hotel. It's OK. I'm OK. The door is shut, the room is quiet. No one in the shadows behind the door. No one here but me. My phone, on the bedside table, buzzes again. Two texts from Tara.

Morning. How's the hotel? Sleep OK? T x
Check your email x

It's 6.09 a.m., I guess she's up early with the boys. I let go a deep breath.

My head throbs from lack of sleep. I swing my legs out of bed and pull the blackout curtain halfway open, squinting as grey morning light floods the room. I flick the little kettle on and pour a sachet of instant coffee into one of the mugs on a pull-out tray below the desk. Check the chain is still secured on the door and get back on the bed, unplugging my phone from the charger. There are a few emails from work which I ignore.

And there at the top of my inbox is a forwarded email from Tara, with a message from her at the top.

> *Hope you're OK. Dizzy fine. See below. Call me if you want ANYTHING. Take care, T xx*

Below it, the original message from Matt Simms, Crime Correspondent at the *Daily Mail*. Sent to her just after 10 p.m. last night.

> *Hey Tara,*
> *Great to talk earlier, really good to hear from you. Brilliant to hear you're looking for freelance stuff, will mention your name to a few buddies. Here's the link to that unsolved case I mentioned on the phone:*
> *www.dailymail.co.uk/news/uk/crime/alkj8lpoa9bqtrd*
> *Let me know when you want to go for that drink 😊*
> *Matt x*

I click on the link and a new browser window opens on my phone, the screen filling with a headline from the MailOnline.

Has The Ghost Struck Again?
By Matt Simms, Crime Correspondent
A WOMAN attacked and left for dead could be the latest victim of a serial killer dubbed the Ghost, according to police.

Detectives are appealing for witnesses after a 30-year-old woman was subjected to a 'sustained and brutal' attack in a London park. The victim is believed to be in a critical but stable condition in hospital.

A Metropolitan Police source said, 'It's very possible these three cases are linked – the latest attack bears all the hallmarks of previous crimes. We need to stop this man before he strikes again.'

The killer, dubbed 'the Ghost' on social media after police were left baffled by the lack of physical evidence at his crime scenes, has evaded officers for more than three months. Murder detectives have reportedly been unable to find ANY fingerprints, fibres or traces of DNA that could help them narrow the search before he strikes again.

Police have been hunting the killer since late August after previous attacks which left two women dead.

The kettle clicks off but I ignore it, scrolling down through the text of the story, trying to work out what this might have to do with Mia. There are more details of the two previous victims, Sienna Parker, aged twenty-four, and Louise Taggart, twenty-nine. Both sex workers from the Northolt area, killed two weeks apart, both found in woodland off the same stretch of the A40 in north-west London. There are head-and-shoulders pictures of both women in happier times, both young, pretty, smiling. No anonymity for them in death.

There's more background, more comments from the unnamed police source, thinly-veiled speculation that the perpetrator had not realised his third victim was still alive when he dumped her, and somehow she was still clinging to life when she was found by passersby a short time later; that the killer may have been disturbed in the act of disposing of the body, before he could check his latest victim was dead; hope that she might be able to identify her killer if and when she recovered. Not a whole lot of concrete progress in terms of finding the person responsible, the vacuum filled by yet more disposable speculation on social media that he was a forensic scientist or some kind of CSI expert turned killer, like the fictional Dexter from the eponymous TV show.

Lower down, far below the unnamed – and possibly made-up – quote from 'a Met Police source', is an attributed quote and a name I recognise instantly.

Detective Inspector Stuart Gilbourne, who is leading the hunt for the Ghost, appealed for potential witnesses to get in touch: 'Somebody will know the man who's done this. He's a neighbour, a colleague, maybe even a friend. Any information you have, however insignificant you think it might be, could be key to the investigation. We're also very keen to speak to the owner of a dark blue or black estate car seen in the vicinity on the night of the attack.'

There's a phone number to ring, and a description that says the suspect is thought to be a white male between thirty and forty-five, around five eight to five ten, average build, dark hair. It doesn't exactly narrow it down much; there must be a million men that fit that description in greater London alone. There's no photofit image of a suspect, which presumably means no witness managed to get a good look at him. It sounds like the police were desperately short of leads and clutching at straws. I scroll back up to the five-word headline at the top of the story.

Has The Ghost Struck Again?

What's that thing Tara always says about headlines with a question mark at the end? *The rule is, ninety per cent of the time it means the answer to the question is 'No' – but the headline and the story are just too juicy not to publish.* It's one of those flippant things she says and I'm never sure whether she means it or not. But this story feels like it might be an exception to the rule. Reading the text for a second time, it *feels* true. It makes a sick kind of sense that this guy would keep on attacking women until he was caught. It makes sense that he wouldn't stop.

At the little desk, I pour water from the kettle into the mug, the *tink* of the spoon against white porcelain the only sound in the silence of my hotel room. The plastic bag of food I brought with me from home sits on the desk – bananas, apples, biscuits – but I can't face any of it. My appetite has disappeared. Caffeine's the only thing I can summon any enthusiasm for right now.

I scroll to the bottom of the story on my phone, tapping on a headline that links to a more recent piece. An image of two grey-faced couples, the women holding up framed pictures of smiling young women, the same head-and-shoulders images used in the previous story.

Families' Plea For Justice As Ghost Probe Hits Dead End

By Matt Simms, Crime Correspondent

GRIEVING families of two women murdered by a suspected serial killer are demanding justice on the anniversary of the first attack.

Detectives admit they are no closer to finding an attacker dubbed 'the Ghost' after it was revealed he had left no DNA, fingerprints or other physical evidence behind. He is believed to be responsible for a string of vicious attacks that left two women dead and a third fighting for her life.

The families of Sienna Parker and Louise Taggart made an emotional appeal today for renewed efforts to track down the killer.

Jacqui Taggart, mother of victim Louise Taggart, said, 'We want justice for our daughter. Every day that goes by, every family birthday, it just gets harder knowing she isn't here. Someone out there has information that will help the police bring our daughter's killer to justice – I would just ask you to please, please pass that information on to the police.'

Andrew Parker, father of Sienna Parker, said, 'The police promised us they wouldn't stop until they found the man who took our daughter away from us. But one year on, we're no nearer to knowing what happened. It's been a living hell.'

Murder detection figures for the Met make worrying reading. Until 2015 detections remained stable, with only 5 to 10% of cases unsolved. But since then the proportion of unsolved killings has risen as high as 26% in the capital. Police insiders have blamed a shortage of detectives and forensic science provision, alongside increased demands on police.

A Met Police spokesman said, 'Behind every unsolved murder there is a family looking for answers. That's why this investigation is ongoing and why detectives will continue to pursue this offender until he is brought to justice.'

There's no mention of DI Gilbourne anywhere in the piece. Perhaps he was taken off the case, or maybe just shifted on to other live investigations that came up in the meantime. There's nothing from the family of the other victim either, the only mention is a single line near the bottom of the story. 'The family of the third victim declined to comment.'

I look up from the screen, a feeling of nausea rising up from my stomach. No wonder Gilbourne couldn't tell me more about the case he's working on. It also explains Max's reaction when I went to Kathryn's flat in Little Missenden, why he virtually slammed the door in my face: Kathryn's sister was the third victim of an attacker who was never caught.

49

I pour two thimble-sized pots of UHT milk into my coffee and send a WhatsApp message to Tara.

Can you talk?

The coffee is strong and bitter, but the kick is almost immediate as the caffeine hits my bloodstream. I stir in half a sachet of sugar to make it a little more palatable and take another sip. A selfie pops up in reply to my message: Tara on her sofa, birds-nest hair and bleary-eyed from sleep. Charlie, her youngest, is on her lap, thumb clamped in his mouth, both of them wrapped together in a large blue blanket. They look so cosy together I can't help but smile, despite what I've just read. The message below the picture reads:

Not right now, deep into Paw Patrol. But can text.
You read Daily Mail story?

Yes, grim. The three attacks definitely connected then?

It's not actually confirmed on the record by police.
Daily Mail and all that

I take the coffee back to bed, tucking my legs under me and wrapping the duvet around myself. My phone buzzes with another message from Tara.

> *Looks to me like the story is solid. Simms is a sleazeball*
> *but he's a good operator. Good contacts. If Met had*
> *squashed the connection theory he wouldn't still be*
> *touting it around a year later*

> *So Kathryn's sister was third victim of this guy?*

> *He wouldn't say it out loud or put on email, got*
> *very cagey. But I used my charms*

The message ends with an emoji of a laughing/crying face. I type another message.

> *How did he know her name?*

> *Wouldn't say. My guess: £££*
> *changed hands with a police contact*

> *So she recovered then if still got anonymity?*

> *Assume so*

I wonder what it's like, having to live your life knowing that the man who attacked you is still out there, carrying on as if nothing has happened. Recovering from terrible injuries, all the while worrying that he might be watching you, stalking you, ready to strike again if the mood took him. Ready to finish the job he'd already started. I also wonder how this story managed to pass me by when it first happened, when it was making headlines like this one. It rings a vague bell, but it was around the time of our last go at IVF, when I was focused on that to the exclusion of almost everything else – even Richard's affair, I realised later.

I read the whole news story again, more slowly this time, lines jumping out at me as I scroll down.

'. . . *woman attacked and left for dead . . .*'

'. . . *sustained and brutal attack . . .*'

'. . . *bears all the hallmarks of previous crimes . . .*'

My mind spins back to Thursday, to Leon Markovitz in my house. Lying in wait for me, his face almost totally covered by a balaclava. Fingerless gloves with latex gloves beneath them. '*Murder detectives have reportedly been unable to find ANY fingerprints, fibres or traces of DNA.*' And there was something else odd about the way he looked, something I noticed on the train but was too preoccupied with Mia to fully take in.

His eyebrows. Shaped and plucked, perfect fine lines. No, not *shaped* but gone completely. Plucked out and drawn in again. His head shaved tight to the scalp. No hair or eyebrows to leave a trace at a crime scene. I remember his podcast, *Inside the Killing Mind*. The retelling of dozens of sadistic murders in graphically gruesome detail, for a large online audience. Victims – mostly women – stabbed and strangled, their bodies battered and violated and dismembered. Buried in shallow graves, disposed of as if their lives were nothing, meant nothing, had *been* nothing. How deeply could you immerse yourself in that world before it started to have an effect on you? How long before it started to distort the lens through which you viewed everyday life? A shiver flashes through me as I remember the encounter in my spare room, his black-clad form emerging from behind the door, dead eyes flat and unblinking in the moments before he raised the stun gun to my neck. The split-second of helpless fear, of agonising pain before I blacked out. I pull the duvet closer around me, willing the memory away.

No matter. The article has given me an idea. I finish my coffee, the last mouthful already tepid, and send another message to Tara.

Thanks for this. Really helpful xx

> *No prob. You going to tell me*
> *what's happening?*

Soon. Need to ask you another
favour though in meantime

> *Of course. Anything to distract me*
> *from Paw Patrol* 😊

I send her a longer message telling her what I need, and there's a ten-minute wait before she replies to say she'll see what she can do. I finally put down the phone and lay back into the scratchy cotton pillows, still damp with sweat, staring at the ceiling of this anonymous hotel room.

There's something else nagging at me, scratching at the edges of my consciousness. Kathryn's sister is the missing piece of the story, silent, anonymous, unrepresented. An absence, never named, never pictured, a victim who has maintained her silence. I started off with the assumption that Kathryn was trying to protect her own child. But there's been something sitting quietly at the centre of the story in front of me, something so obvious I can't believe it's only now that I've finally seen it.

I grab my phone again and scroll to the top of the story, below Simms's by-line, where the date is listed. Time slows as another piece slides into place, and I have the feeling I knew this already, had known it as soon as I read the first lines of the article.

The date on the first news story is September 14th just over a year ago.

And Mia is three months old.

50

The inside of Langtry's, a basement bar away from the bustle of Kensington High Street, is cool and dark. It's not busy, just a few office workers enjoying a lunch-time drink, and a handful of tourists taking a break from the shops. I find who I'm looking for sitting alone in a booth against the back wall, two high-backed wooden benches facing each other across a ring-stained wooden table. He's in his late thirties, a couple of days' stubble on his cheeks and dark bristly hair cut the same short length all over. 'You'll recognise him from his by-line picture online,' Tara had told me earlier. 'Just add ten years and twenty pounds to bring him up to date.' He's scrolling on his phone as I walk up, a half-drunk pint of bitter on the table in front of him.

'Hi,' I say, and slide into the booth opposite him.

He looks up in surprise, already shaking his head in apology. 'Sorry, love, that seat's taken.' He glances around the bar. 'I'm waiting for a friend, she's due any minute.'

'You're Matt, right?' I stay where I am. 'Matt Simms, *Daily Mail*?'

He sits up a little straighter in his seat, eyes narrowing. 'Sorry,' he says again. 'Who'd you say you were looking for?'

'My name's Ellen Devlin. I'm a friend of Tara Richardson.'

'I'm supposed to be meeting Tara for a drink.' He checks his watch. 'Like, now.'

'I know,' I say, holding my hands up in apology. 'Sorry about that, I asked her to ask you. I wanted to meet you face-to-face but I didn't think you'd do that for a total stranger.'

'Tara's . . . not coming?'

'Afraid not, but she said to say hi from her, and thanks for the chat yesterday.' I flash him a smile. 'Can I buy you a drink instead? Then I'll explain.'

Simms shrugs as if he's still trying to decide whether he's annoyed about being played. 'Err . . .'

'Pint of London Pride, is it?'

The reporter looks down at his pint glass, still half-full. 'Why not?' he says.

I get up to fetch the drinks, watching his reflection in the mirror behind the bar. He straightens his tie, tucks his shirt in and runs a hand through his hair, patting down the unruly strands before taking a generous gulp of his bitter. When I return to the booth, with another pint for him and a large tonic water for myself, he seems to have gathered his wits and greets me with a grin.

'Cheers Matt,' I say, clinking my glass against his.

'So, Ellen,' he says, leaning back and spreading both arms along the back of the booth. 'It was you who wanted to know about the Ghost, was it? Not Tara?'

'You wrote a couple of pieces about the victims and their families.'

'If you want to complain about a story in the paper you need to use the proper channels, go through the managing editor, he deals with all that—'

I take a sip of my drink. 'I don't want to complain,' I say.

He looks at me dead-on, straight in the eyes, looking for any flickers of deceit. 'Are you recording this, Ellen?'

'No, I'm not.'

'So you're a journalist? With the *Express*, are you?'

'No, I'm a friend of Tara's from way back. We were in the navy together.'

He takes another pull on his first pint, still studying me over the top of his glass. 'Well, if Tara's vouched for you, that's good enough for me,' he says finally. 'So what's your interest in that story? There's not been anything new on it for ages.'

'I know the sister of one of the victims. And . . . I think that story, the Ghost, is about to blow up again.'

'OK.' He raises an eyebrow. 'You've got my attention. What makes you say that?'

'Can I ask you a few things about the case first? Strictly off the record?'

'Sure, you can ask.'

'You contacted the family of the third victim, right?'

'A few times.'

'So when it says in your story that someone "declined to comment", does that mean you couldn't actually get hold of them, or . . .'

'I tried, but they weren't interested. Went out to the house myself the first time but never got past the gates. Sent a casual a couple of times after that, it's a right ball-ache to get to from here, you can waste half the day going there and back.'

'A casual?'

'One of the general news grunts, given three or four casual shifts a week,' he says as if this should be obvious. 'New guys, paid on a day rate rather than a permanent contract.'

'Right,' I say with a nod. 'So you know where the family lives?'

'Makes the doorknock more straightforward if you know which door you need to knock on.' He gives me a wink. 'I mean, yes, I managed to get hold of the parents' address.'

'How'd you do it?'

'Does it matter? Anyway, like I said to Tara on the phone, the name of the third victim is covered by anonymity, so I can't really discuss it with you.'

'I already have her name, I'm not asking you for that.' I run a finger around the rim of my glass. 'I'm just intrigued. Tara said you were a good operator, one of the best. She speaks very highly of you, how you get stories that other reporters can't.'

Simms shrugs, but allows himself a small smile. 'Called in a few favours, that was all. Then it was just a case of making some calls, asking the right people the right questions, wearing out the shoe leather the old-fashioned way.'

'The thing is, Matt . . . I really need to see them. I know they're in Prestwood Ash, but I don't have a street address.'

'And you think I'm going to hand it over, do you?'

I lean forward, my hand inches from his on the stained wooden table. 'I need to see them urgently, Matt, and I would really appreciate your help.' When he doesn't respond, I add, 'Please?'

Simms leans forward on the table too, his head close to mine. The move is familiar, almost intimate, and brings with it the smells of exhaled beer and old clothes not properly dried from the rain.

'Love your perfume, by the way,' he says. 'You smell *amazing*.'

'Thanks,' I shift back a little in my seat.

'So, Ellen Devlin,' he says. 'If I give you their address, what's in it for me?'

51

'How about if I said I had a story for you?' I say. 'A great story, an incredible one.'

'About the Ghost?'

'I can't tell you right now, but I promise you it will be worth it. Soon.'

Simms lifts his glass to his lips. He's well into his second pint now and I can sense the alcohol starting to kick in, the gentle loosening of his shoulders, a relaxation in his jaw. He glances at the bar, where a crumpled middle-aged man is hunched alone on a stool, nursing a pint of his own. The guy looks at Simms, then at me, then at Simms again, before going back to his own drink with an envious shake of his head. Simms notices it too and smiles, returning his attention to me. He takes another sip of beer, puts the glass down so close next to mine that our hands almost touch.

'All right, if you mention this to anyone, I will deny ever having this conversation. I will deny ever meeting you.'

'Understood. But I won't say a word, I swear.'

He checks that no one is in earshot before leaning forward again.

'The third victim was Zoe Clifton, eldest daughter of Gerald and Angela Clifton.' He picks up his phone, scrolls through a few screens, lays it face down on the table and pulls a pen from his jacket pocket, scribbling on the edge of his beer mat. 'That's where you'll find them.'

I turn it around, study what is written there and tuck it into my handbag.

'Thanks, Matt. I really appreciate it.'

'So, this great story – give me a clue,' he says. 'A starter for ten.'

I lace my fingers together on the table in front of me. 'In your piece, it doesn't mention if there was a . . . sexual element to the attacks.'

He frowns at me over the top of his glass. 'Because there wasn't. According to the police, anyway.'

'But you would have included that? I mean there wouldn't have been a reason to leave it out of the story, would there?'

'*God* yes, I would have included it,' he says. 'Absolutely. Why do you ask?'

'Tara said victims of sexual offences get lifetime anonymity. So I assumed that because victim number three wasn't named in the media, she had—'

'No, the granting of anonymity was a police decision, because of the circumstances of the case and the nature of the attack, she was deemed to be an especially vulnerable witness. The Met line was that putting her ID out there would jeopardise her safety, and therefore jeopardise their ability to bring her attacker to justice.'

'Because the Ghost might come for her again?'

'If he knew where to find her. The family got an injunction as well, preventing her from being named in the media. Belt and braces job, kind of overkill really. Excuse the pun.'

'Do you know much about the women he attacked?'

'Well, victims one and two were street prostitutes working in and around Uxbridge. Both involved with drugs, both users, and Louise Taggart had been nicked a couple of times for low-level supplying as well. I was never able to nail much down about Zoe Clifton, but she had a flat in the same area. Some suggestions she was also on the fringes of sex work, but I couldn't stand that angle up. Family never wanted to talk, but let's just say it had the makings of a cracking story for us.'

'How do you mean?'

'Mr and Mrs Clifton are loaded – their house is like something out of *Country Life*. It's the kind of story my editor loves: pretty, posh, privately-educated girl, the apple of her parents' eye, drawn into a life of vice. A shame the parents never wanted to play ball on an exclusive – fully anonymised, of course. Thought I'd wear them down eventually but they blanked me every single time. Thankfully, no one else got the story either.'

I take a small diary out of my handbag, flip to a blank page at the back and write the words UXBRIDGE FLAT? in capitals.

'Was there ever a suggestion that the Ghost was linked to any other attacks?' I say. 'Any other murders?'

'We had a couple of sniffs here and there but never anything definite. Nothing the cops would even go near confirming.'

'Not even off the record?'

Simms gives a definitive shake of his head. 'Nope. Not even then.'

'So, this guy, this Ghost, he attacks three women in the space of a few months, and then stops? Does that make sense?'

'I think the third one might have freaked him out. The first two, he kills them. Then for whatever reason he messes it up with victim number three. She survives. And knowing she was out there, knowing there was a living witness, he just wanted to crawl back under his rock. That's my theory, anyway.'

'Didn't the police ever make any arrests?'

He takes another swallow of his pint of bitter, wiping his mouth with the back of his hand.

'They pulled a few guys in. But the investigation had a weird feel to it, like it never really got off the ground, you know? Like they were late to the party and never caught up. Zoe's estranged husband was arrested and it seemed like they were pretty sure he was their man. I mean, ninety per cent of the time it's the partner, right? Or the ex.'

'So what happened with him?'

'He looked guilty as sin – at least on the circumstantial evidence – but they never charged him.' Simms grins at me. 'Poor old Dominic had the media camped on his front lawn for a fortnight, lost his job into the bargain. Then his house. Ruined the bloke.'

My glass is frozen in mid-air, an inch from my lips. Very slowly, I put it back down on the table.

'Say that again.'

'He lost his job, he was freelance and all his clients dropped him when he was linked to—'

'Not that bit.' I hold a hand up, unsure whether I've misheard him. 'Dominic Church?'

He nods.

'The police thought he was the Ghost?'

'Still do, I think. They had a theory that he wanted revenge on his ex, but to cover his tracks he made it look like she'd been the victim of some random serial attacker. The cops couldn't make it stick, though – some sort of balls-up with the evidence, a technical-ity. They never had enough to charge him.'

I sit back on the bench seat, staring at a point over his shoulder. 'My God.'

'Are you OK?' he says.

'Dominic Church was Zoe Clifton's estranged husband?'

'They'd split up about six months before she was attacked. There was another theory that Zoe was in a relationship with the Ghost – that he was a new boyfriend – and when she found out what he'd done, he tried to kill her. That in fact the Ghost knew all three vic-tims personally, and they weren't random at all. But the police never found any new boyfriend and we couldn't stand that line up.'

'Where did the boyfriend theory come from?'

'A few of the cops. The family.'

I sit for a moment, trying to process what this means, taking a gulp of the tonic water and wishing there was gin in the glass too.

'What about Leon Markovitz?' I say. 'You know he was arrested too?'

Simms gives me a twisted smile. 'Who told you that?'

'Someone who knows. You've heard of him, though?'

'Everyone in the industry's heard of him: Leon's a walking, talking cautionary tale. Total fruit loop.' He took another pull on his beer, index finger raised in admonition. 'You want to stay *well* away from him.'

'You're not the first person to tell me that. Did you work with him?'

Simms frowns in mock offence. 'Him? God no. Heard some pretty scary stories about him on the grapevine. We never crossed paths though, he was *News of the World*, then *Sunday People*. Went off the deep end when he got banged up.' He tapped a finger against his temple. 'Several screws loose, that bloke.'

I indicate his almost-empty pint glass. 'Can I get you another?'

'Anyone would think you were trying to get me drunk.' He raises an eyebrow, reaches into his jacket and hands over a business card embossed with the black and white crest of the *Daily Mail*, just a mobile number and email, no landline. *Matthew Simms, Crime Correspondent*. 'Unfortunately, I have to get back to the grindstone before my news editor starts jumping up and down. Give me your number and I'll drop you a message if anything else comes up.'

We both stand up and I type his number into my phone to send him a blank message. I get the feeling he's about to lean in for a peck on the cheek, Parisian style. But I pocket his business card and hold out a hand instead.

'It was good to meet you, Matt.' We shake hands, his skin clammy in my palm. 'I'll be in touch.'

52

I stop outside High Street Kensington tube station and take the beer mat out of my handbag. An HP16 postcode is scribbled in biro in one corner. I put it into Google Maps and it zooms to a location east of Prestwood Ash, maybe half a mile out of the village. But it looks as if there's nothing there, just green space on the computer image. I zoom out and back in again. Nothing. It occurs to me that Matt Simms might be a world-class bullshitter who has spun me a line just to get me off his back. He wouldn't be the first tabloid journalist to have a tenuous relationship with the truth. I replay our conversation in my head, sifting through it, trying to judge the truth of his words.

Switching to satellite view, I catch my breath and say a silent apology to the reporter. Because it's there: a single large house, set in its own grounds with a long driveway curving away from the road, the faint outline of a wall surrounding the entire property. I can see why Gilbourne wasn't worried about me stumbling on their house through blind luck when I was in the village yesterday, why he didn't push harder for me to stop what I was doing. This house is not even *in* the village, it's in between Prestwood Ash and the next one down the road, St Leonard's. Out on a limb. Private. Isolated.

I walk down the steps into the bowels of High Street Kensington tube station, heading for the northbound platform.

* * *

When I arrive, the wrought iron gates are shut. I pull off the little hedge-lined country road into a gravel driveway, the tall black gates topped with a row of spearpoints and recessed into a high stone wall set back from the side of the road. A large marble panel tastefully engraved with two words: THE GRANGE. A black metal keypad is set into the wall and I buzz my window down to reach it, the steel call button cold and smooth beneath my fingertip. The intercom buzzes and I wait, looking into the square plastic eye of a camera set above it. The camera's eye stares back, but there's no response. I press the buzzer again, wishing that I could have phoned ahead rather than just turning up at the gate unannounced. I can see one corner of the house from where my car is pulled in, three storeys of white stone just visible through the trees. But it's quite a way back from the road, too far away for me to make out any movement. I'm about to press the intercom buzzer one last time when there is a click and a female voice comes through the speaker, an older woman, a single word so quiet and reedy it sounds like it's coming from a thousand miles away.

'Yes?'

'Mrs Clifton, my name's Ellen Devlin, I'm so sorry to just drop in on you like this, but I was hoping I could have five minutes of your time. It's important.'

A pause.

'It's . . . not a good time at the moment.' Her voice is flat, toneless. 'Sorry.'

'Please, Mrs Clifton, I would have called but I don't have your number. I really need to talk to you.'

'I don't have anything—'

'It's about Mia.'

Another pause. Longer this time, seconds stretching out.

'What are you talking about?' she says finally, a trace of worry lifting it above the monotone. 'What do you mean?'

'I looked after Mia for a short time on Tuesday. For a few hours.' When there is no reply, I add, 'I met your daughter Kathryn on a train, and she asked me to take care of her.'

The voice has fallen silent again. I've said too much, too quickly. *Damn.* I lean a little closer to the intercom.

'Mrs Clifton?'

With a metallic *click*, the wrought iron gates part in the middle and swing slowly open on silent hinges. I put the car in gear and make my way up the curving gravel drive with wide green lawns on both sides, edged with tall trees along the boundary wall. The drive leads into a gravel turning circle in front of a house which is every bit as impressive as the satellite image suggested it would be, a Georgian manor house in creamy-white stone, neatly-clipped lawns and gravel paths on every side, low hedges giving onto a tennis court, a large patio, an orchard off to the far side. Two large fierce-looking dogs gallop up to my car as I pull in, staring and barking, teeth bared. At a signal I can't see or hear, they run off towards the front door.

I park next to a Mercedes with a baby seat strapped into the back and make my way to the front door, gravel crunching beneath my shoes. A tall, dark-haired woman is already standing in the half-open doorway, arms crossed over her chest. She's in her mid-sixties, expensively dressed in grey and black, the soft lines of her face shadowed with fatigue. A small silver crucifix hangs on a chain around her slender neck. The two dogs sit at her feet, staring at me with their tongues lolling.

'Are you a reporter?' she says as I approach.

'No.'

'He told us to expect reporters, sooner or later. The detective inspector.' She has the faintest trace of a Liverpool accent, the vowels softened but still there. She sizes me up for a moment or two, before pulling the door open wider. Her eyes are puffy and red, a balled-up tissue clutched in one hand. 'You'd better come in.'

She dispatches the dogs back out into the grounds with a single command and I follow her down a silent hallway, my feet sinking into the deep cream carpet, into a large L-shaped sitting room with views out onto the gardens at the back of the house. Framed paint-ings line the walls, broad canvas landscapes and a couple of abstracts, wide splashes of colour that contrast with the dark furniture. A grand piano stands alone in the corner, abandoned, its keyboard shut. A pair of shotguns are displayed in an ornate glass-fronted case. Despite the brightness of the afternoon, the room is in semi-darkness. Cur-tains half-closed and blinds pulled down against the cold autumn sun. She points to a corner of the room and I realise there is a man there in the shadows, slumped in an armchair. He is around her age or perhaps a little older, with a thick white moustache, his head bald except for a neat semi-circle of white hair at the back and sides. There is a large book open across his lap. A photo album.

'My husband,' she says quietly. 'Gerald.'

He nods vaguely in my direction but doesn't say anything.

She gestures to a long leather sofa and I sit down. She remains standing in the middle of the room, squinting against a single shaft of sunlight slanting in through a gap in the curtains, motes of dust suspended in the air.

'I'm Angela, by the way. I've got some coffee on; would you like a cup?'

'Thank you.'

She disappears back into the hallway, her footsteps silent on the thick carpet. Distant kitchen sounds reach me from a long way away. Apart from that the house is utterly still, as if it has been frozen in time like an old photograph. I glance at her husband in the corner again, but he is simply staring at the book in his lap and seems to have forgotten I'm here. Family portraits line the mantelpiece showing him and his wife with two young women. I recognise Kathryn. She's pretty – very – but the woman in the picture next to her is on another level, like a Hollywood film star. Long dark hair, flawless skin, laughing brown eyes.

There is no sign of Mia anywhere. None of the usual debris of small children that Tara battles on a daily basis, no brightly-coloured plastic, no toys, no high chair pushed into a corner.

Dominic Church said she would be here.

Dominic Church is a liar.

I'm suddenly overcome by a cold wash of fear, a terrible sense that I'm about to discover something unbearable.

This is a house in mourning, a family shell-shocked with grief. And Mia is not here.

Angela returns and hands me a steaming cup of coffee in a white china cup. She sits straight-backed in the armchair opposite me, hands on her knees, blinking rapidly as if she's fighting hard to hold it all together.

'So, Mrs Devlin,' she says quietly. 'You met Kathryn. Tell me what happened.'

I gather myself and describe the events of Tuesday afternoon as briefly as I can, from the moment Kathryn sat down opposite me on the train to my arrival at the police station several hours later, barefoot and desperate, with Mia in my arms. When I'm finished, Angela's face is creased in concern and she is wiping away tears with a balled-up tissue she has pulled from the sleeve of her cardigan.

'How was Kathryn?' she says. 'When you spoke to her, how did she seem?'

'She was scared,' I say. It might not be what Angela wants to hear but she deserves the truth. 'Scared for Mia, and for herself. But she was determined, too. She knew what she was doing.'

'She rang me,' she says. 'As she was getting off the train, she called me and said Mia was safe, she was with someone safe. So that was you.'

I nod, holding her gaze. 'Yes.'

'She wouldn't say who it was, she said 'people' might be listening in. Asked me to drive over and pick her up, take her to Marylebone by car. But when I got to the station she was gone. Vanished. No sign of her at all.'

'Angela,' I say as gently as I can. 'Where's Mia now?'

She seems not to hear me.

'I should have listened to her,' she says, more to herself than to me. 'Should have talked to her, *believed* her.'

A drumbeat of fear in my head. 'Isn't Mia here with you?' I ask again.

'I still can't believe she's gone,' she says softly. 'My baby.'

My heart is suddenly in free fall; all the blood draining from my chest. I have to grip the coffee cup tightly to make sure I don't drop it. *Mia is not here.* Images flicker in front of my eyes. A curl of white blonde hair. Tiny white fingernails. A little bubble of milk on rosebud lips.

The breath is stuck in my throat.

'Who's gone, Angela?'

She closes her eyes on fresh tears that roll down her cheeks unchecked.

'You must have been one of the last people to see her alive. My little girl. My beautiful Kathryn.'

53

I blink, trying to think of the words. But there are none. Of course there aren't. I had known the police were trying to find Kathryn but I'd somehow convinced myself that she was lying low, keeping her head down until the danger had passed. Hiding, perhaps, or maybe still running. But not this.

'I'm so sorry, Angela,' I say quietly. 'I didn't know. The police didn't tell me.'

She swallows hard, suddenly looking older and frailer than before.

'Three days we hadn't heard from her. Three days since . . . she got on that train. You keep on hoping, you know? Even though your mother's instinct tells you everything is wrong. I had a text from her on Tuesday night saying she wanted some time to herself, she was going to go off to our weekend house in Norfolk for a few days and not to worry if she was out of contact. But I knew it wasn't right, it didn't sound like her at all. She was *always* on her phone. I knew straight away that something terrible had happened. I knew.'

'Someone else sent that message?'

She nods, finding a fresh tissue in her pocket and wiping her nose and eyes. 'Whoever did this was trying to cover their tracks, the police think. The post-mortem said she was probably already . . . she had already passed away by then.'

I reach out and cover her hand with mine, her skin papery and cold under my palm.

'I don't know what to say, Angela. I'm just so, so sorry for your loss. I only spent a little time with your daughter but she was a lovely young woman. She wanted to protect Mia.'

'The detective inspector came to tell us last night that they'd found a body in the woods near Seer Green. I had to go in today to do the identification.' She indicates her husband, still sitting wordlessly in the shadows across the room. 'We both went, but Gerald couldn't do the formal bit. I did it.'

I try to make sense of her words, trying to stitch together fragments of a larger canvas. An image returns to me, of Leon Markovitz on the train, looming over me, only moments after Kathryn had got off. She separated herself from Mia because she knew danger was close by. Perhaps she didn't know who, exactly, but she drew that danger away from the baby all the same. Sacrificed herself. Did Markovitz turn back and go after her again after losing me in the station?

'I can't imagine how hard that must have been.'

She pulls the tissue from the sleeve of her cardigan again, wiping her eyes. 'Do you have children of your own, Ellen?'

'Always wanted them, but it never quite happened for me and my ex.'

'I was a late starter, an older mother, nearly forty when I had mine. Always wanted girls. I was lucky, blessed with my two.' She shakes her head slowly, not seeming to see me. 'All the things you worry about when they're little, when they're growing up, all the hazards and dangers you learn to be aware of, cot death and meningitis rash and choking on food, steep stairs and open windows. Then it's cars on the street and open water and talking to strangers and a million other things. By the time they're adults you fool yourself that the worst dangers are over, that you've got past it, you've succeeded in navigating all those hazards and you can let them get on with it. But really it's harder than when they were little, because you can't protect them anymore. You can't hold them close and shield them like you used to, and the danger's still out there. It's just changed.'

A sound cuts the air between us. A little moan, a tiny grunt of a baby turning, shifting in her sleep, and for a second I think I've imagined it. *Mia*. But then Angela stands and walks to a bookcase by the door, turns up the volume on a white plastic baby monitor and listens for a second. The sound fades away and Angela sits back down in her armchair, bringing the monitor with her.

'Mia?' I say, a glow in my chest.

She nods, looking at her watch. 'She's due a feed soon. She's a hungry little monkey.'

I wait for a beat to pass before speaking again.

'Angela, I met someone who said Mia was still in danger,' I say slowly. 'But I think he was trying to trick me, to get me to convince you to leave here. To leave this house, take Mia away with you.'

'What are you talking about?'

'Dominic Church. He said . . . Mia would still be at risk as long as she stayed here.'

'He's got a bloody nerve after how he treated Zoe.' Angela's fists clench in her lap. 'Still trying to control her life, control Mia's life, even now. Trying to tell us what we should and shouldn't do. Kicking him out of her life was the best decision she ever made.'

'How's Zoe coping, Angela? She's heard about Kathryn?'

Angela turns her head to look away, the skin tight along her jaw. A ringing reaches us from somewhere else in the house. A landline phone, its noise echoing down the hallway, intrusively loud against the quiet. It trills six times but she makes no move to go and pick it up.

Abruptly the trilling stops and silence is restored, falling like a blanket over the house.

Angela speaks without looking at me. 'Yes, I've told her,' she says. 'Come with me.'

It's a statement rather than a request. She pockets the baby monitor and stands up to lead me out of the lounge, down a long hallway lined with wooden picture frames perfectly spaced, one after the other. Images of Kathryn and Zoe as children together; a proud little girl hugging her baby sister, then kneeling on a sandy beach, at a school sports day, in fancy dress, cheek to cheek in paper Christmas hats, as teenagers with reluctant smiles for the camera, then Zoe in a black graduation gown arm-in-arm with Kathryn wearing her mortar board at a jaunty angle. Angela leads me past a book-lined study and another reception room, wooden floorboards creaking beneath our feet, past a downstairs bathroom and into another corridor.

'This is the annexe,' Angela says over her shoulder. 'It's just down here.'

At the end of the corridor is a single closed door, plain white, a viewing window set into it. She opens the door and I follow her into a large white room, sash windows looking out on the lawn on two sides. The sharp smell of antiseptic in the air. The room is dominated by a high single bed, metal-framed and complicated as if it's come from a hospital ward, machines and monitors beeping and clicking beside it. Two monitors, one on top of the other, numbered displays in green and red.

In the bed, there is a young woman. Dark hair fanned out on the pillow behind her, her skin so pale it is almost translucent. There is a tube running into the back of her hand and a sensor clipped to the end of her thumb trailing a wire out of sight. A slow and steady *beep beep* from a screen next to the bed.

Her eyes are closed.

'This is my eldest, Zoe.' Angela goes to the bed and touches the back of a hand gently against her daughter's cheek. 'We had this annexe converted when we brought her home from hospital so she could be with us, after it happened. She's much happier here at home. I won't leave her, and I won't leave Mia either. So we won't run away, no matter how Dominic Church might try to frighten us away. We stay here. All of us, together.'

A woman in a starched blue nurse's uniform appears from a side room. She's fortyish and has a kind face, her dark hair pinned carefully back. Angela gives her a nod.

'Why don't you get yourself home now, Michelle? See you on Monday morning.'

'Thanks, Mrs Clifton.' The nurse peels off latex gloves and drops them in a yellow bin in the corner marked *Medical waste – for incineration*. She gives Angela a soft smile. 'If you need me to come in tomorrow though, just let me know. It's no bother.'

Michelle takes her coat from the back of the door and leaves the way we came in, her footsteps clicking into the silence.

'She's very good,' Angela says when the room is quiet again. 'Very experienced. She spent a lot of time getting Zoe settled, those early months. Making sure she was comfortable, getting her routines going. In fact, Michelle was the one who first realised.'

I move closer to Zoe until I'm standing by her bed, her palm laid flat on the crisp white bedsheet just inches from mine. The beeping of her heart monitor is the only sound in the room, steady and hypnotic, each pulse a gossamer thread keeping her tethered to life. *I'm still here. I'm still here.*

'Realised what?' I say, looking up at her mother.

'That Zoe was pregnant.'

54

Angela tells me the whole story. A moonless night in September, just over a year ago, Zoe finishing an evening shift of outreach work with vulnerable women on the streets of north London. Walking home alone when she was grabbed, beaten, knocked unconscious, her balaclava-wearing attacker intent on strangling her until he was disturbed in the act, chased away by a group of students returning from a night out. One of the students was a first-year medic who gave Zoe mouth-to-mouth resuscitation until the ambulance arrived.

'Her heart stopped twice on the way to the hospital,' Angela says. She is sitting in a chair by the bed, holding Zoe's hand, her thumb tracing the line of a pale blue vein on the back of her daughter's hand. 'But they managed to bring her back both times. Those first twenty-four hours were unbearable, the worst. Thinking every minute that we were going to lose her; then trying to keep her alive in the first few days, bouncing between that and the hope that she might actually regain consciousness. But her brain had been starved of oxygen for too long – there was too much damage.'

I put a hand to my mouth, the weight of tears heavy behind my eyes.

'I'm so sorry, Angela.' The words feel hopelessly inadequate. 'For both of you. I can't imagine . . .'

'The media had a version of the story by then,' Angela continues, 'saying it was this serial attacker the police couldn't catch, this 'Ghost' who was still on the loose, filling in the gaps in the story they didn't know by suggesting that Zoe was a sex worker like the other victims. That subtext of *just another prostitute*, as if that meant they all deserved it in some way. Every headline as if she was being attacked all over again. And we couldn't help her, no matter what we tried.' She pauses, takes a deep breath. 'You feel so helpless, as if you can't do what a mother is supposed to do. But after a couple of months, after this room had been kitted out, we brought her back from the hospital so she could be with us, at home. We thought it might help her recovery.'

I look at her daughter's pale skin, long lashes beneath closed eyes, the slow pulse of a vein at her neck, wondering whether there might be any kind of recovery for her. Whether she might ever hold her own daughter in her arms, feed her, smile at her, wonder at the miracle of life that she had made. If there was anything that could bring her back from this existence, suspended somewhere between life and death, or whether the Ghost had taken it all away from her forever.

Angela says, 'She always looked for the good in people, always believed the best in them.'

'How far along was she,' I say quietly, 'when you realised she was pregnant?'

'About twelve weeks.'

'And it wasn't . . . from when she was attacked?'

Angela shakes her head. 'The police did their tests, didn't find anything.' Without looking at me, she adds, 'And no, we never thought about abortion. We never even discussed it. When you see life hanging by a thread, you want to cling to it, nurture it. Gerald was convinced she would miscarry anyway, but Mia had other ideas.'

She describes the move to a private wing of St Mary's Hospital in Paddington at thirty-seven weeks for a planned caesarean section, a healthy baby delivered and both mother and daughter returning to the big house in Prestwood Ash a month later. A guest room converted into a nursery, grandparents taking on the role of parents.

'I didn't even know she'd been seeing anyone after her and Dominic split up; she was quite secretive about things like that. Kathryn knew something was going on but the only thing she could get out of Zoe was that it was early days, and she couldn't talk about him yet. That it was . . . complicated.' She brushes a strand of hair off her daughter's forehead. 'And then all of a sudden, the relationship was over. He was history. She was so upset, but she still wouldn't talk about it apart from to say he wasn't a good person and she wished she'd never met him. I told her she should come over and spend the weekend at home with us. But that night she was attacked.'

'And the police never tracked down her boyfriend?'

'They investigated, they pulled her private life apart, but they never came up with a name and whoever he was, this boyfriend never came forward. Never volunteered himself.'

'Do you think it's because he's the one who tried to kill her?'

Angela nodded. 'Just like he killed those other two women. And now he's taken Kathryn from us too.'

'You think it's the same man?'

'He knew her. He knows *us*.'

Dominic. His name reverberates in my head, crowding out everything else. A man who had been at the heart of this family, who knew them all.

'The message he sent from Kathryn's mobile,' I say, 'about your holiday home?'

Angela nods. 'How else would he know something like that, except from Zoe?'

'Did the police . . .' I can't think of a sensitive way to put it. 'Are they going to take a sample of DNA from Mia? See if they can track him down that way?'

She nods slowly. 'They did it once already but there was some sort of problem with it. They're going to take another sample on Monday.'

A high-pitched sigh cuts through the silence and Angela takes the little baby monitor from her pocket, the display popping with green lights as it transmits the tiny voice to us from somewhere else in the house.

'She's awake,' Angela says, with the ghost of a smile. 'Would you like to see her?'

'Yes, I'd like that.' My heart swells in my chest at the thought of seeing Mia again, a sunburst of warmth right at my core. 'I'd like it very much.'

She gives Zoe's monitors one more check and kisses her gently on the temple, then leads me back out to the entrance hall. I follow her up the grand curving staircase, each step wide and shallow as it sweeps up to a first floor landing lit by a chandelier. The staircase continues upwards to a second floor, another landing, past bedrooms and bathrooms, a library and a home gym, the little voice on the monitor burbling and chattering all the way. At the end of the landing, Angela opens a door and beckons me through. The nursery is at least five times the size of the little box bedroom at my house, with every conceivable gadget, toy and labour-saving device for new parents. It's tastefully decorated in yellow and pale blue, one wallpapered wall busy with images of colourful tropical birds. Angela pulls up half-closed blackout blinds on two tall windows, bathing the whole room in afternoon light.

'It's a little bit different to when I was growing up with my brothers and sisters in Toxteth,' she says, leaning down into a cot in the corner. 'Back then it was five to a room, two in each bed and the littlest in the bottom drawer.'

She lifts the baby up onto her shoulder, supporting her head and whispering into her ear. Tiny hands clutch the folds of her grandma's cardigan. A soft white sleepsuit, tufts of blonde hair standing up off her head as she gurgles happily. Angela walks over to me and turns around so I can see her face, this little miracle baby.

Mia.

55

'This little one is the only thing that's keeping us going,' Angela says, jiggling Mia gently on her shoulder. 'Such a happy baby, just like her mum was.'

Mia gives me a gummy grin, her chuckle lighting up the room, and at the sound of it I feel my heart lift. Angela sees me and her expression softens.

'Would you like to hold her for a minute, while I get her feed ready?'

I nod. Angela smiles and hands Mia over to me, settling her gently so she nestles in the crook of my elbow. I rock her slowly from side to side, that perfect weight in my arm, soft and warm and beautiful. Mia looks up at me with her big blue eyes, smiling and giggling, a little hand reaching up to my face, tiny fingertips brushing my cheeks. A little bundle of life, pure and untainted, untouched, this one good thing that has survived in the midst of so much tragedy and grief.

Angela takes a clean baby bottle from the cupboard and puts it into a Perfect Prep machine next to the changing table. She presses buttons on the machine's display and it whirs into life, preparing a formula feed for Mia.

'Sometimes I just come in here and sit with her and cry,' Angela says. 'She's all I have left of my girls, now. Of either of them. I look at Mia and I see my daughters. It doesn't matter how she came to us, the circumstances.' The machine beeps and she takes out the bottle, screws the lid on, shakes it and squirts a little milk onto her wrist. 'I wasn't sure, before she was born, whether I'd even be able to look at her. But as soon as I saw her, as soon as I held her, it was love. I knew, right from that first minute.'

The emotion comes out of nowhere, rising higher and higher, a tidal wave, a tsunami that I'm powerless to stop. And just like that I'm crying, tears rolling down my cheeks.

'Sorry,' I say. 'I'm sorry, Angela, it's just, she's so, so beautiful. And with what happened to Zoe. It's all so sad.'

I'm smiling through my tears, and Mia is smiling back at me.

'She likes you,' Angela says. 'I think she remembers you.'

She shakes the bottle of milk, tests the temperature on her wrist again, nodding to herself.

'Right then, Miss Mia. Tea-time.'

She settles herself in a big armchair next to the cot and I pass Mia back to her, supporting her head with my right hand. Angela gives the bottle one last shake and puts it to Mia's lips. The baby latches on immediately and begins enthusiastically guzzling milk, tiny hands across her chest, blue eyes blinking up at her grandmother.

'Could you pass me one of the muslin cloths?' Angela indicates the chest of drawers. 'Top drawer on the left.'

The drawer is full of neatly folded muslins and I unfold a pale pink one from the top of the pile.

'She likes to suck on the corner of these, doesn't she?' I lay the cloth gently across Angela's shoulder, ready for any milk that might come back up. 'My godson was the same, he was still doing it until just before he started school.'

Angela smiles and returns her attention to Mia as she feeds.

I look around the room at the cot, the changing table, the little fabric books and toys, the play mat, all the paraphernalia of new life. Mia is safe here, with the people who love her. This is where she belongs. I think of my little box bedroom at home that will never be used, a hollow opening up inside me.

I'm glad I made the trip here, but it's time to go.

'Ellen?' Angela is looking up at me, tears glistening in her eyes. 'Thank you. For what you did for Mia.'

I nod, try to give her a smile. 'I'm just glad she found her way home to you again.'

She smiles back and it is the saddest smile I have ever seen. 'So am I,' she says. 'So am I.'

She pulls the half-empty bottle of formula from Mia's mouth and switches the baby to an upright position on her shoulder, rubbing her back with a circular motion.

'I should go,' I say. 'I've taken up enough of your time already.'

Angela stands up, still gently rubbing and patting Mia's back.

'I'm glad you came, Ellen. I'll show you out.'

Following her down the second floor staircase, I say, 'So you kept Mia a secret when she was born?'

'We knew it would get out eventually, but we wanted to keep her to ourselves for as long as we could. No more intrusion, no media, no speculation about my daughter carrying a murderer's child. As long as she was secret, she was safe. With us.'

'But they did find out.'

'Paperwork was filed from the hospital and somehow the detectives still working on the case became aware of it. Straight away, one of them came to the house, said he wanted to take Mia away with him, put her into care or some such nonsense. Took a DNA swab there and then, said he would fast-track it through their lab.'

'Detective Inspector Gilbourne?'

'Not him, the younger one. That detective sergeant.'

I feel a shiver of unease, the small hairs standing up on my arms. 'Holt. Nathan Holt.'

She nods. 'He was talking about taking Mia away, putting her into some sort of protection programme. But it was a ridiculous idea. A three-month-old baby, going into hiding with strangers looking after her? We're her family, her blood, we can protect her better than anyone. We told him no, point-blank. Then he said we could have a twenty-four-hour police presence at the house, as if that wouldn't attract exactly the sort of attention we didn't want! Advertising the fact with a police car at the gate, ridiculous. I don't like him at all. Arrogant sort. You can tell he's the kind used to getting exactly what he wants. I never wanted them to do the damn DNA test in the first place.'

'Why not?'

'Because Mia is *ours* – a part of our family. No one else's. I wanted to keep it that way. As long as she was anonymous, she was safe. But as soon as you start talking about DNA and paternity, she becomes a target – which is exactly what happened.'

I look over at Mia, drowsing half-asleep against her grandmother's shoulder 'You can't put the genie back in the bottle.'

'Precisely.' Angela resumes gently rubbing Mia's back as we continue down the stairs. 'And the whole thing with them getting a DNA sample . . . there's been something off about it right from the beginning. Something strange.'

'In what sense?'

She is silent for a moment before replying.

'I don't know exactly. DS Holt was here again yesterday wanting to see her, wanting to take another swab. Someone rang him as he was leaving and Holt told them he was in central London. Just flat-out lied about where he was, cool as you like, as if he's got some other agenda, goodness only knows what that might be.'

'Seriously?' I think about Holt, aggressive and jumpy the very first time I met him, in a police interview suite. Interviewing Kathryn Clifton's boyfriend alone. Working behind his DI's back. 'DS Holt?'

We reach the bottom of the stairs and she leads me into the big hall, pulling open the front door for me, Mia still propped on her shoulder. The two dogs trot up to her and sit obediently at a single word of command. I take one last look at Mia's little apple-cheeked face, at her slow-blinking blue eyes, wondering if I will ever see her again.

'Something's not right about him,' Angela says. 'But Kathryn must have been in touch with him secretly, over those last few days. He must have convinced her of the danger, because she got it into her head that someone was going to take Mia away. On Tuesday morning she came over to babysit and just took her. The two of them were gone before we even realised. That was the last time I saw Kathryn.'

I step out into the darkening afternoon, a cold autumn wind snatching at the hem of my coat. The sun is gone, replaced by a blanket of grey clouds stretching from one side of the sky to the other.

'Her note said not to trust the police,' I say. 'Why do you think she said that?'

'She trusted Holt at first, but then . . .' She tails off. 'By the time she took Mia and ran, she didn't know who to believe.'

'And what do you think?'

'You know the media stories about the Ghost being a scientist or some forensic expert?'

'Because he doesn't leave trace evidence behind. No DNA.'

'That's it. Seems to me, a police officer would have that expertise too.'

56

Human tissue is surprisingly resilient.

It's not just a case of digging a hole and putting the body in. Bones can yield DNA profiles decades after death, hundreds of years after. Even buried under a ton of concrete, hard tissue will still yield a profile if it's ever found and retrieved.

Acid is effective. Unfortunately though, rather hard to come by in sufficient quantities without raising suspicion.

If not acid, pulverisation can do the job nicely. Pulverising the bones into dust. But the forces involved are colossal. Just ask the poor bastards charged with finding bodies in a collapsed building.

Ultimately, incineration always comes out as the best option. Ashes to ashes. Dust to dust.

Grind up the bones and scatter what remains over open water to aid dispersal.

The main issue is with the size of the subject: portability and movement, volume of tissue, bone mass and residue, the time involved in the burning process.

Which is why it's so much easier when the subject is a baby.

57

The gates close smoothly behind me as I head back out onto the country road that leads into the village. I drive the half-mile into Prestwood Ash and pull over in a lay-by next to a little country church, turning off the ignition and letting my head fall back against the headrest.

Deep breaths. In through the nose, out through the mouth. Spending time with Angela – hearing about her daughters – was heartbreaking, and it's almost impossible to comprehend that so much tragedy can descend on one family. And yet somehow she keeps going, keeps putting one foot in front of another. Keeps doing the best she can for Mia, for her family. She is as tough as they come.

I start the car again and drive on, through the tunnel of over-hanging trees, up and over the undulating Chiltern Hills through one village after another. Switching channels on the radio as a distraction, not really hearing the music, unable to settle on anything for more than a minute or two. Spots of rain spatter my windscreen as I drive south and east, picking up the main road back towards London, crossing under the M25 and hitting Saturday afternoon football traffic that ebbs and flows with a tide of cars and buses.

I'm a couple of miles away from my hotel when I realise I'm being followed.

A dark saloon, a few cars back, is shifting lanes to follow me. It's smooth and subtle, nothing to attract attention and on a normal day – in a normal week – I wouldn't have noticed it there at all. I change lanes again, filtering left at the last minute to leave the elevated section of the A40 and drop down onto city streets away from my route back to the Premier Inn. The dark car indicates and follows, *calm as you like,* and I finally get a glimpse of the driver. Male. Late twenties. Stubble. Dark baseball cap and sunglasses despite the gathering dusk. Angela's words in my ear. *Just flat-out lied about where he was. As if he's got some other agenda.*

Holt. Who had been in contact with Kathryn before she ran. A decision she had paid for with her life.

How long has he been following me? A few miles at least. Maybe more than that, maybe from the start of this journey back in Buckinghamshire. He could have been waiting in the lane outside Angela's house. How did he know I'd be there? And what will he do when I stop?

For a moment I think of googling the nearest police station and pulling up outside but just as quickly dismiss the idea. He *is* the police. And more than that, I'm tired of being stalked and followed, of constantly looking over my shoulder. There's a lump in my throat, a painful mixture of fear and anger, as I make another turn, right at a junction. Again, he slides into the lane behind me, one car back. I'm still heading in the wrong direction, away from where I need to go, compounding my sense of creeping dread.

As the next set of traffic lights approach I slow down and let a gap grow between me and the car in front. I dawdle on the green light, dropping down into third gear, then second, the driver behind me hooting furiously that I'm holding him up. When the traffic light turns orange I stamp on the accelerator and speed through the junction with the engine screaming, the car behind me forced to stop on red, his horn still blaring. I check my rearview mirror and feel a pulse of relief as I see Holt is stuck behind the angry driver, both of them receding behind me.

When the road curves out of sight, I brake hard and turn left into a busy shopping street, accelerate to the next junction and then take another left into a supermarket car park. I find a spot facing the road and kill the engine, sliding down in my seat. My heart is thumping, my hands slick with sweat on the steering wheel. Sure enough, thirty seconds later the dark saloon car roars past with Holt hunched behind the steering wheel. I don't think he's seen me but I'm not going to wait to be sure, reversing out quickly and returning the way I came.

I keep one eye on my mirrors all the way back.

* * *

I've eaten nothing since breakfast but the thought of sitting in the hotel restaurant – alone, exposed, surrounded by strangers – makes my palms itch. Instead I call in at a Tesco Express near the hotel, grabbing items with barely a glance and dropping them into my basket. A ready-to-eat pasta salad from the shelf. Crisps, flapjacks, chocolate chip cookies. Comfort food. I add a bottle of red wine and take it back to my hotel, fighting a powerful urge to ignore the food and get started on the wine straight away. I need a drink.

In the car park of the Premier Inn, I find a space in the corner with a view of the main entrance, checking all the cars around me and keeping an eye on the main entrance to the hotel. I can't see Holt's dark saloon car anywhere. But I do see a side entrance leading into the car park, a fire exit by the looks of it, slightly ajar after a staff member steps out for a cigarette break. After ten minutes, when there's been no one suspicious coming or going from reception, I lock my car and walk quickly to the fire exit. I find myself in a side corridor away from main reception, quickly orientating myself. *Ignore the lift. Take the stairs.* On my corridor, I pull the stairwell door open a few inches, just enough to get a look each way. My room is only five doors away. The corridor looks clear, still no sign of Holt. I reach into my handbag and my fingers find the attack alarm that Tara gave me. Next to my keycard for the door. I hurry to my room and let myself in, a breath of relief pushing from my chest as the door slams shut behind me.

Silence. I flip on the lights and put the Tesco bag down on the desk, checking the bathroom in case there's anyone hiding in there. It's empty. I flip the security latch on the door, check the fisheye view of the corridor through the peephole, then take off my jacket and shoes, finally feeling some of the tension in my neck and shoulders start to ease. It feels better to have a solid door between me and the outside world.

I can't stop thinking about Angela's haunted expression as she sat with Zoe in the annexe, as she told me about her shattered family, weighed down with tragedy and grief. Circled by an unseen predator, who was waiting even now for his moment to finish what he started more than a year ago. Because it seems logical to assume that both her daughters were attacked by the same man. The same man who now wants to kill Mia – the clue to his identity he unknowingly left behind.

Holt. Markovitz. Church.

One of them is the Ghost.

My hunger has disappeared but I make myself open the pasta salad anyway, picking at it in its container, pouring wine into a plastic tumbler which doesn't leave my hand until it's empty again. The wine is a French Grenache, velvety and dark on my tongue, and I'm deep into my second cup and thinking about a third when an unfamiliar ringing breaks my train of thought.

It's the hotel phone beside the bed, a little red light flashing below the keypad. *Reception?* I hadn't asked for a call.

'Hello?'

Silence. Broken by the sound of breathing from the other end of the line, slow breaths in and out.

'Hello?' I say again. 'Who is this?'

The voice is precise, careful. Refined.

'Have you figured it out yet, Ellen?'

I recognise the voice instantly, my stomach turning over.

Leon Markovitz.

I grab my mobile up off the bed. No missed calls. Plenty of charge. So why is he calling on the hotel landline? Before the question is even fully formed, the answer comes to me: to show he knows where I am. To show me he's in control.

Nowhere is safe.

'Figured what out?' I manage to say.

'What happens next.'

'How did you find out where I am?'

'You left a trail about a mile wide, Ellen. Not difficult to follow, not difficult at all. So how do you like the hotel? Nice view from the window?'

58

I reach over to pull the curtain aside. The car park below is a pool of deep shadows. A figure steps out of the darkness in the far corner, into the cone of half-light thrown by one of the street lamps. Dark clothes, a heavy coat, black hat and gloves. Mobile pressed to his ear. He doesn't wave, doesn't gesture at all. But he's staring *right* up at my room, directly at me. I step back from the window and hit the light switch, not wanting to be outlined against the dark, an unpleasant bump of adrenaline tingling in my stomach.

'What do you want, Leon?'

'We never finished our conversation the other day.'

I rub at the fading marks on my neck from our last encounter. 'Because you hit me with a stun gun.'

'Yes, apologies for that.' His voice sounds loud and close, as if his lips are pressed right to the mouthpiece. 'That wasn't my intention. But I had to. You didn't give me any choice. You attacked me, you were going to run off and tell the police.'

'You were in my house!'

'I was trying to help.'

'I don't need your help, Leon. Please just leave me alone and don't call again.'

'Listen to me for a minute: the person who broke into your house on Wednesday night. You were alone. He could have attacked you, made you give him what he was looking for. But he didn't do that, he slipped away into the night.' He pauses for a second and I can almost feel his hot breath on my ear. 'Why do you think he did that?'

Is he talking about himself? I've heard about people who refer to themselves in the third person; it's a sign of extreme narcissism, of dangerously large ego, an inflated sense of their own importance. The traits of a sociopath. And an associated trait: that they're fluent liars.

'I don't know, Leon, why *did* you do that?'

A sigh comes down the line. 'It wasn't me. But somebody thought you weren't going to be home on Wednesday night. He was spooked when he realised you were still in the house So he came back the next day when he knew you wouldn't be there.'

I inch closer to the window so I can see out into the car park again. At least my room is on the first floor. Leon has moved closer, his dark outline visible among the shadows directly underneath my window. The ego that prompted him to call me on the hotel phone direct to my room – to surprise me, unsettle me, show me how clever he is – has also given me an opportunity, I realise. I pull up the keypad on my mobile and press nine three times, my thumb hovering over the green *call* button. If I can keep him on the landline and somehow direct the police here, they might be able to arrest him before he can get away. Box him into the car park, where there's only one way in and out.

I press *call*, 999 on the display. I don't put it on loudspeaker in case he hears it when the call connects.

'I know about you, Leon.' Matt Simms's words come back to me: *Total fruit loop. Psycho. You want to stay well away from him.* 'I know what you've done.'

He ignores me. 'Did you tell anyone your house would be empty that night?'

'No,' I say. 'No one. Not even my best friend.'

'What do you think he was looking for?'

Keep him talking.

'For the baby,' I say quietly. 'For Mia.'

'So you know she's in mortal danger.'

The call on my mobile connects and a tinny female voice asks me which service I require.

'The police,' I say loudly. I leave a pause before adding, 'They told me about the Ghost.'

The tinny voice replies but I can't hear her properly. 'The police are incompetent,' Leon says in my other ear. 'Their investigation into the Ghost was riddled with it, mainly because your *friend* Detective Inspector Gilbourne is an incompetent, old-school cop desperate to cover up his own failings. Desperate to conceal the fact that the case was botched from the start when he let Dominic Church slip through his fingers. Church is a clever guy, I'll give him that. But trust me, I've been researching and writing about his kind for almost twenty years, I've lived their cases, lived their crimes, and I know a psychopath when I see one.'

'So where do you fit in, Leon?'

'I can help you.'

'*Help* me?'

'We can help each other. I protect you from Dominic Church, you can get to the baby, take her somewhere safe. Church is never going to allow that second DNA test to be done.' He pauses, his voice dropping lower. 'Which means her time is almost up. And if she disappears, the story disappears with her, do you see?'

'What on earth makes you think I'd want to help you?'

'Because it's the only way, and because you're a good person, Ellen. I trust you. Can you trust me?'

I raise the mobile and hear the police operator's voice again, loud and insistent as if she's repeating herself.

– street address or location if you are in immediate –

'You attacked me, Leon,' I say. 'Now you've tracked me to the Northolt Premier Inn and you're threatening me again.'

'Of course I'm not threatening you, I'm trying to—' He stops abruptly, and when he comes back on the line there is a note of disappointment in his voice. 'Who else are you talking to, Ellen?'

'You're in the car park at the back of the building and you know I'm on my own here.'

He sighs audibly down the line.

'You're in way over your head, Ellen. And that child is going to pay the price.'

There is a soft *click* as the hotel phone goes dead.

I put the mobile to my ear and give the police operator my details again, telling her about Leon's previous attack at my house. She asks me to stay on the line until officers can be sent to check the area, and not to open the door to anyone. I chance another look out of the window, but the car park is empty. No sign of Leon down there.

Sitting in the dark, mobile phone pressed to my ear, everything boils down to two options: go or stay. Wait for the police and then get out, get to my car and take my chances, knowing he's out there somewhere close by. But go where? Or I can sit tight, stay here until the morning, hope that a visit to the hotel by uniformed police will convince Leon to stay away. Keep the door locked and the security latch on until daylight, hope he doesn't get into the hotel in the meantime, hope he doesn't get up here to my—

There is a sharp knock on the door.

59

I freeze, a chill creeping over my skin. The knock comes again, louder and more insistent this time. I can't believe how fast he's got up here from the car park. Maybe he just called the landline to confirm where I was.

'He's here,' I whisper to the police operator. 'He's at the door.'

'Do *not* open it, under any circumstances,' the voice comes back. 'Units are en route.'

'How long?'

'A few minutes. Stay calm and stay on the line, madam.'

I check for the third time that the security latch is flipped, muting the TV into silence. Creeping nearer in bare feet, I squint through the spyhole, the fisheye lens distorting the corridor into a crazy hall-of-mirrors version of reality. There's a dark-clad figure with his back to the door. He turns to knock again and I feel a wash of relief, every muscle in my body relaxing in unison.

It's DI Gilbourne. He knocks once again and this time I open the door.

'Hey, Ellen. I was just passing and I thought I'd check in with you, make sure everything's all right.' He stops, studying my face. 'Are you OK? You're white as a sheet.'

'Leon Markovitz,' I say quietly. 'He found me, he knows I'm here.'

'When?' Gilbourne says, his eyes narrowing.

'Just now. He was downstairs, phoned me from right outside my window.'

'Markovitz was *here*?'

I nod and he raises a finger to his lips. He walks noiselessly down the corridor to where it turns at a right angle, then does the same on the other side, before checking the stairwell and the fire exit door.

'All clear,' he says, returning. 'Who are you on the phone to?'

He takes over my call to the police control room and tells them he'll meet the uniformed officers as they arrive.

'Wait here,' he says to me. 'Don't open the door to anyone except me, OK?'

He gets out his own phone and heads back to the stairs as I shut the door. I sit down at the little desk again, top up my wine and take a heavy swallow, my hand shaking as the adrenaline slowly recedes. I hate to admit it to myself but I feel safer with Gilbourne nearby and I'm glad he's here. Not because he's a police officer, or a man. Because he's an ally. Because it means I'm not on my own, even if it's only for a little while.

He knocks on the door ten minutes later, his deep voice full of concern, and tells me they've done a sweep of the whole site and the surrounding area, finding no sign of Markovitz or his car.

'Are you OK?' he says. 'You looked a bit shaken up before.'

'I'm all right,' I say. 'I think. Thanks for . . . you know. Coming over. I appreciate it.'

He nods, smiles, but says nothing.

'How did you know I was here?'

'I didn't. I called in at Tara's house on my way home and she told me.' He gestures over his shoulder with a thumb. 'Listen, I'm going to stay downstairs for a bit, in my car. Keep an eye out in case he turns up again. I don't like the idea of you being here on your own if he comes back, especially after what happened the other day.'

'Do you think he will come back?'

'Hard to say, he's a very unpredictable guy. Better safe than sorry though. You sure you're all right?'

I feel another rush of gratitude for this man, a warmth spreading in my chest. Standing there in a hotel corridor with his tie askew, his day of stubble, the fresh clean scent of his aftershave.

'I appreciate it, Stuart, but you don't have to stay. Saturday night, I'm sure you've got other places to be. Better places.'

He gives me a wry grin and shrugs his shoulders. 'Not really. Married to the job, that's me.'

I almost don't say it. But then I jump in before I can change my mind.

'Well, if you are going to hang around for a bit, you might as well be in the warm rather than freezing down in the car park.' I indicate the open bottle of French red on the desk. 'Either way I could use some help with this bottle of wine, otherwise I'm going to end up drinking it all myself and that never ends well.'

'Shouldn't really, I'm driving.' He smiles again, his eyes crinkling at the edges. 'But I can stay with you for a bit if you like, in case Leon reappears.'

'I'd like that. Thanks.' I gesture to the armchair by the window and he turns it around to face the room, sits down.

'So,' he says, crossing one leg over the other. 'What did Leon have to say this evening?'

I outline the conversation, Leon's offer to protect me from Dominic Church while I somehow spirit Mia away to a safe place.

'To *protect* you?' Gilbourne gives a disbelieving shake of his head. 'After assaulting you in your own house with a potentially lethal weapon? I find that a bit hard to swallow.'

'Me too.'

'To be honest, Mia will be a lot safer when both of them are off the street. Both him and Church. That's as simple as I can make it.'

'Can't you just arrest them?'

'Once we get a DNA match – definitely. Until then, we don't want to spook either of them, risk them disappearing off the radar, dropping out of sight for good. We've been keeping an eye on them these last few days, waiting for one of them to make his move. Dominic's tried to persuade you to talk the Cliftons into leaving the property at Prestwood Ash. We believe Leon burgled your house, looking for information that would lead him to Mia, and he's obviously tracked you here to this hotel. We still haven't discounted the idea that they're working together.'

'So let me help you. To bring them to you, to keep Mia safe. I could ask to meet them, arrange a time and a place where you can grab them both.'

'Ellen, I don't want you exposed to any more danger than you have been already. And I suspect they'd be wise to an approach like that – not that I don't appreciate the offer. But you've done enough already.'

I look at him over the top of my wine, wondering whether to tell him about my conversation with Angela, trying to gauge how close his partnership with Holt really is. At the police station they seemed like very different men; Gilbourne calm and sympathetic while Holt was aggressive and impatient, full of his own self-importance. *Good cop and bad cop*, I suppose. But it feels like there's more than that between them, a deeper division. Do they like each other, professionally? Personally? Do they get on?

'You should probably know something else.' I tell him about my visit to Prestwood Ash this afternoon, and if he has questions about how I found the Clifton family, he keeps them to himself. I relay Angela's concerns about DS Holt and the way he's been with Mia. 'Also, Holt followed me this evening, on the drive back here.'

'He *what*?' Gilbourne frowns, sitting forward in his chair. 'Are you sure?'

'I assume you didn't ask him to do that?'

'No.' He stands up abruptly, paces to the window and back. 'No, I didn't. You're absolutely sure it was him?'

'Yes. Angela Clifton said he came to their house on his own, talking about taking Mia away, doing DNA tests. She said she got a really weird vibe from him. Didn't like him at all. And I have to say, I know what she means.'

Gilbourne is not looking at me anymore. He nods slowly, as if just realising something for the first time. 'What else did Angela say?'

'She thought Holt was in touch with Kathryn too, before she ran.'

He sits back down heavily in the armchair. 'I see.'

'When Kathryn got off the train on Tuesday, when she left Mia with me, do you know if someone intercepted her at Seer Green? All this time I was thinking it was Dominic Church, but do you think it might have been DS Holt?'

Gilbourne shakes his head. 'We've still not got a clear line on what happened to her when she got off that train. The pathologist thinks she died on Tuesday, between 4 p.m. and midnight, which leaves us a lot of time still unaccounted for.'

'What about CCTV at the station?'

'There's one camera up there but it's not worked for years. Not really a lot of call for CCTV at these little country stations.' He sits forward in his chair. 'Listen, are you sure it was Nathan following you today?'

'He had a baseball cap and sunglasses on but I'm pretty sure, yes.' I nod, slowly. 'He was driving a dark coloured Ford Focus, grey or black.'

'Standard issue pool car for use by MIT detectives.' He sighs, looks at me, looks away. He takes a pack of cigarettes from his jacket, flips it open with his thumb, closes it again and replaces it in his pocket. Finally his eyes come back to mine. 'I shouldn't be telling tales out of school, but . . . ah, Christ.'

I let the silence spool out for a few moments but he seems reluctant to fill it.

'What is it, Stuart?'

'Nathan's been . . . strange these last couple of weeks. Jumpy. On edge. I really don't know what's going on with him.'

'How long have you worked together?'

'A couple of months. He was seconded in from the human exploitation task force.'

'Exploitation as in street prostitution?'

Gilbourne glances up at me, then looks away. 'Amongst other things, yes.'

With an unpleasant sick feeling in the pit of my stomach, I remember the news articles I read this morning.

'All three victims of the Ghost were linked to street prostitution, two sex workers and Zoe Clifton, who was an outreach worker with a charity that tries to help women get off the streets and put their lives back on track.'

He doesn't acknowledge me.

'Ellen, can you do me a favour?' He reaches out to me and his fingertips come to rest lightly on my forearm. 'If Nathan—' He stops himself, his voice suddenly thick with emotion. 'If DS Holt contacts you, follows you, turns up at your door, you need to let me know straight away. Promise me you will?'

'OK,' I say quietly. I feel safe for the first time in days. 'I will.'

Gilbourne still looks shell-shocked, all the colour drained from his face.

'You know what?' he says, eyeing the half-empty wine bottle. 'Maybe I will have that drink. Just one glass.'

'Afraid I haven't got glasses, just plastic beakers.' I fetch another clear plastic cup from the bathroom and fill it with the Grenache.

He shrugs. 'I don't suppose it makes much difference, really.' He taps his beaker gently against mine. 'Cheers, Ellen Devlin.'

We both take a drink.

'I'm not going to get you in trouble with your boss, am I?'

'To be honest,' he says, blowing out a breath, 'I'm past caring what my boss thinks.'

60

We sit in silence for a moment, me on the bed and him by the window in the armchair. The TV is on mute and it suddenly feels very quiet in this little hotel room, the two of us together with an open bottle of wine on the bedside table. Gilbourne shifts in his seat, putting his beaker on the floor.

'So tell me about you, Ellen,' he says, his head cocked slightly. 'You're a bit of an enigma.'

'Not much to tell, really.'

'Why do you care about Mia so much? You could have walked away, but you didn't. That's a rare thing.'

'Is it?'

'Believe me, I've been around the block enough times to know more than I ever wanted to about human nature. Most people would have handed that baby over at the first opportunity and never looked back, been glad to get away. Or they wouldn't even have volunteered to help in the first place. But not you.'

'Just trying to do the right thing, that's all.'

He studies me, eyes locked on mine as if he can see right into my soul, until a frown creases his forehead.

'There's more to it than that though, isn't there? Don't tell me there isn't.'

I take a breath. I realise I'm about to open myself up in a way I haven't done for years, tell him a story that only my ex-husband and my best friend have ever heard.

'There is, yes,' I say finally. I take a swig of heavy red wine, feel the warm buzz as the alcohol hits my bloodstream. 'There's more to it. The truth is, it's not exactly the first time I've been in that situation.'

Gilbourne frowns. 'Really?'

'Not on a train. Somewhere else, a while back.'

'When you were in the navy?'

I nod silently.

After a moment, he says gently, 'What happened, Ellen?'

I sit back against the headboard so I can face him properly, begin telling him about one day a decade ago when I had still been in uniform, all the memories, the images, still as fresh in my mind as if it happened last week. Operation Ellamy, 2011 – as Libya tore itself apart in a bloody civil war, civilians were caught in the crossfire and the Royal Navy was dispatched as part of the UN-backed intervention to protect them. I had been leading part of the humanitarian relief effort that went alongside, flying in food and medical supplies to refugees using helicopters from HMS *Ocean*.

'On the second day we found a makeshift refugee camp on the outskirts of Benghazi.' Now I've started telling him, I find I can't stop, the story picking up its own momentum. 'A couple of hundred civilians displaced by the fighting, terrified they would be singled out as rebels by government forces. I wanted to take them out on the helicopters, take them back with us onto the ship for a few days until the situation had stabilised. Until it was safer. We'd had reports of mass shootings.'

'But you couldn't take them?'

I shake my head. 'I was overruled by my commanding officer. He told me it wasn't our mission. We were to provide "relief not rescue", he said, and if we started pulling civilians out, a trickle would turn into a flood and we'd be overwhelmed. But the civilians, they thought we were there to rescue them, to take them somewhere safe. They all started gathering around the helicopters. When they realised we weren't going to take them . . . it was awful. They knew the government forces were close, what would happen if they found them. One of the mothers . . .'

My throat is thick. Gilbourne gives me a sympathetic smile, waits for me to continue. I take another mouthful of wine, swallow it down painfully.

'One of the mothers had a baby only a few months old. She made her way to the front of the crowd and she was talking to me non-stop in Arabic, wouldn't leave me alone. She singled me out, not because I was in charge but because I was a woman, I think she thought I would be a mother too. When she realised we were leaving, she . . .' I pause to take another breath, determined to keep my voice steady. 'She handed her baby over to me. She gave me her little boy, told me his name was Hassan, just put him in my arms and backed away. I guess she thought I'd be able to keep him safe. And so I'm standing there, surrounded by my guys and a crowd of desperate civilians, the rotors are turning on the helicopters, dust flying everywhere, and I'm right in the middle of it all holding this tiny baby blinking up at me with his big brown eyes. It was just crazy.'

'So what did you do?'

The tears are heavy behind my eyes. 'I'd been told point blank we couldn't bring civilians out. *Relief not rescue*, like my CO had said. So I handed her little boy back to her. She was crying and pleading and the interpreter was telling her we'd be back the following day with more supplies. We got on the helicopters and flew back to the ship.' I take a deep breath, blow it out again. 'When we flew back in the next morning, we could see the smoke from miles away as we came in. One of the pro-government militias found them during the night. They'd torched everything that would burn and killed everyone they could find.'

'Jesus,' Gilbourne breathed.

'Men, women, children. All of them. Lined them up and shot them. Hunted down anyone who tried to run. I found the mother's body in a drainage gully at the edge of the camp. She'd tried to hide, tried to shield Hassan, to cover his body with hers.'

He lets the silence spin out for a long moment before replying, his voice quiet. 'I'm sorry, Ellen.'

I shake my head. 'None of it made any difference. All of our ships, all the helicopters and planes and personnel, all of the assets we had, none of it made *any* difference to those people. When my tour was up, I put in my papers to resign.'

'You did what you could.'

'But it wasn't enough.' I look down at the floor, still trying to put the memory back in its place and close the door on it, knowing that I'll dream about it tonight anyway. 'That's why I wanted to help Kathryn. It sounds stupid but I thought, maybe this was my chance to put things right. To do the right thing.'

'You've done more than enough already,' he says. 'You brought that child back to her family.'

I pour the last inch of wine into his cup, sitting on the desk chair so I can reach.

'The DNA test on Mia,' I say. 'How come it hasn't been done already?'

'The grandparents were reluctant at first. They had to give consent for DNA to be taken from a minor, and I think they just thought they were going to be able to keep her a secret forever. When we finally persuaded them, Nathan went out there to take an initial swab but . . . There were issues with it.'

'What kind of issues?'

'The lab kicked it back to us as invalid, which can mean any number of things.'

'Such as?'

'Theoretically,' he says, 'it might indicate the sample had been interfered with in some way. Rendered unusable. I mean, people think DNA is infallible, that it's some kind of magic bullet, they watch *CSI Miami* and think it solves everything like *that*.' He snaps his fingers. 'But the reality is that it's not always straight-forward, sometimes things get messed up. Hence we're going back on Monday to try again with another sample. I probably should have just overseen the whole process myself, right from the start.'

'So it's possible that Holt tampered with the first sample?'

Gilbourne stares into his wine, swirling it slowly in the bottom of the cup.

'Well,' he says slowly. 'Yes. I suppose it's *possible*. But I can't imagine why he'd do that.'

'Angela Clifton doesn't trust him.'

'No,' he says. 'She doesn't.'

I push on, emboldened by the wine.

'She thinks he's got his own agenda.'

'Meaning?'

'I don't know.' I'd been turning it over and over in my mind on the drive back from Prestwood Ash – the strength of Angela's suspicion, of her instincts about the young detective sergeant. 'Maybe he's trying to protect someone, or the opposite? Make the evidence point in a different direction, at least.'

'Hang on, Ellen.' He frowns, lines bunching on his forehead. 'That's a pretty bloody serious allegation.'

'I know it is.'

'Have you got any solid evidence to back it up?'

I ignore his question.

'Of course, there is another possibility.'

'Which is?'

'*He's* the one. He's Mia's father. The Ghost.'

'Now hold on a minute, that's a crazy—'

'But then I don't get why he'd be worried about a DNA match. Surely your DNA only ends up on a computer if you're arrested or convicted of something? If you're a criminal.'

Gilbourne takes his cigarettes from his coat again, takes one out of the packet, puts it between his lips but doesn't light it. After a moment he takes it out again, rolling it thoughtfully between his thumb and forefinger.

Finally, he says: 'It's not as simple as that.'

'Isn't it?'

'You're thinking of the main national DNA database. But there's also a resource called the police elimination database, which has the profiles of serving police officers and civilian staff like CSIs. So their DNA can be discounted in case of inadvertent contamination of a crime scene.'

'So Holt's DNA is already on file?'

He gives me a reluctant nod. 'And as soon as Mia's DNA's uploaded and cross-referenced against the databases, if the father is on there too, we'll get a familial match and we'll have our prime suspect.'

'Good,' I say.

'Amen to that.' He puts down the unlit cigarette and swigs his wine again. 'Do you want to know something weird? Twenty-nine years I've been on the force, I've got one of the highest solve-rates in the division and this is the only unsolved case of my whole career. Haven't been able to get my head around the idea of this last job hanging over me after my thirty years is up – that the Ghost would still be out there somewhere, unpunished. But this is the last possible outcome I would have wanted. The idea that it might end up being a fellow officer. My own *partner* . . .' He runs a hand through his dark hair, leaving tufts of his fringe standing up. 'I just can't see it. I can't believe it would be.'

I look at him, sitting in the armchair by the window in his crumpled suit jacket, one leg crossed casually over the other. Pale blue eyes – *thoughtful* eyes – that crinkle at the edges, square jaw shadowed with stubble. A strong hand cupping his wine, veins standing out against tanned skin. In some ways he reminds me of my husband, in others he's as different from Richard as it's possible to be.

'What will you do,' I say quietly, 'when you leave the police?'

'Honestly?' He fills his cheeks, blows the breath out. 'I have no idea, being a police officer is all I ever wanted to do. Joined at eighteen, right out of South Bucks Grammar. I only ever imagined myself doing this, I've tried to visualise it but I can't see myself doing anything else.'

'I always imagined myself being a mother,' I say, the words tumbling out before I can stop them. 'I thought that at some point, sooner or later, it would be inevitable. When I came out of the navy I built everything around that idea, tied everything to it. So when it didn't happen it was like there was a big hole in the middle of my life. Some days I didn't really know what the point was anymore. I felt like such a failure. I started thinking it was payback, karma, for what happened in Libya, for not saving that little boy.'

Gilbourne gives me a sympathetic smile. 'Maybe it will still happen.'

I shake my head. 'I'm forty-one years old, Stuart. I've been through two rounds of IVF, my marriage is over, and I don't think I have time to start all over again.'

'I'm sorry,' he says, holding my gaze. 'How long have you been divorced?'

'Separated for three months,' I say. 'Divorce will be finalised next month.'

'Snap,' he says. 'But I'm a little bit ahead of you.'

'How long?'

'About a year ago.' He adds, 'Join the Force, get divorced.'

'Do you see your children much?'

'Every other weekend.'

'That must be hard.'

He shrugs, finishing the last of his wine. 'It is what it is. My own fault, mostly. Never gave my wife enough time, or my girls, I was always too busy with the job. Always gave that priority. Didn't real-ise what a failure I was as a father until it was too late.'

I sit forward on the chair again, leaning closer to him. Catch a hint of his aftershave, fresh like the ocean. 'You're not a failure, Stuart.'

He colours a little, then lifts his eyes to mine. 'Neither are you,' he says. 'Neither are you. In fact, you're the most—'

And then I'm kissing him, my lips meeting his, not even really knowing what I'm doing, only that I *am* doing it and it feels good. It feels right, and it's been so long since I kissed someone properly that I can't believe how much I've missed it, the intimacy of it. The surrender of two lonely people to each other, each of us looking for a glimmer of light in the darkness.

He pulls away, the whisper of his stubble against my cheek.

'Ellen, I—'

I kiss him again, longer this time, a deep slow kiss as he leans into me and I'm surrounded by the smell of him, the *taste* of him, mint and red wine and the faintest hint of cigarettes that makes me think of stolen teenage kisses from a lifetime ago. My skin feels alive with him, electricity flashing up and down my spine and as I pull away this time I'm breathless.

His forehead rests gently against mine, his palms cupping my cheeks. When he speaks again, his voice is breathy and low, barely above a whisper. 'Do you want me to stay?'

In answer, I kiss him again.

SUNDAY

61

He's gone when I wake up, and in the first delicious moments after I open my eyes I wonder if I've dreamed the whole thing. Lying there in tangled sheets, enjoying the half-awake warmth of the duvet, I close my eyes again and remember. Not a dream. Flesh and blood reality. The edge of a hangover lingers but it doesn't matter: this morning is the first time in a long, long time that I have woken without a feeling of dread for what the day holds.

The room is dark, the thick blackout curtain blocking all but a tiny slice of daylight. His scent lingers on the pillows and when I breathe him in it's as if I can still feel his touch on my skin, the way he held me afterwards, one arm curled around my back, a finger tracing up and down the line of my spine. As if we'd known each other for years. As if we'd done this a thousand times before. I've not been held like that in so long, a feeling of being totally safe and secure, protected from the world.

I sit up and reality creeps back in, bringing the guilt with it, the feeling of transgression, of crossing a line that shouldn't have been crossed. Of doing something that can't now be undone. I unmute my phone and check the time. It's almost 10 a.m. On the desk, between the empty wine bottle and my handbag, is a note written on the top sheet of a hotel stationery pad. Looping handwriting that is at once strange and yet familiar.

Didn't want to wake you. Can I see you tonight? Take care and stay safe – remember what I said.
- S x

Despite the guilt gnawing at me, I can't help but smile as I re-read the note, a little pulse of happiness in my chest. *Can I see you tonight?*

I send him a text.

Thanks for your note, the answer is yes. Call me when you can x

I search through my handbag for a couple of paracetamol. It takes an age to find the packet but I eventually track it down in a side pocket and swallow two down with a handful of tap water. I've been taking a lot of these the past few days and make a mental note to buy more. I could do with some cash too. I scan the room. Something's different about the desk this morning, but I'm still too fuzzy-headed from lack of sleep to remember what. I smile. Maybe it's just the empty bottle of wine and the handwritten note, Stuart's tie still hanging over the back of the chair. I fold it up and put it in my handbag to return to him later.

I shower and dress, going downstairs for breakfast, taking time to check the corridors and stairs in case Leon has returned. But it feels better in daylight, safer, the normality of people in the restaurant queuing for their coffee and fruit juice and full English breakfasts. By the time I get back up to my room it's gone 11 a.m., the day stretching out in front of me.

Part of me wants to tell Tara about last night but it doesn't feel right, not yet, I want to keep it for myself a little while longer. Instead I send her a WhatsApp asking how everything's going and she responds with a picture of Dizzy, my cat, sitting on Noah's lap. Noah is grinning as if he's just won the lottery.

Dizzy settled in OK then??? x

Says he's moving in with us now ☺x

We trade some more messages back and forth and she makes me promise to call her later. But the glimmer of well-being I woke up with is gradually melting away, every message from Tara a fresh reminder of the tragedy that's descended on the Clifton family. I wish I had a phone number for Angela, so I could at least check she's OK today.

Talking things over with Stuart last night, I'd convinced myself that Holt was involved with Zoe's case somehow, that he was hiding something. But a new day has brought new doubts, a nagging sense that there is more going on just beyond my eyeline. Dominic Church has dropped out of sight since I met him on Friday. Stuart's team is looking for him, so how does he connect to all this and what's he planning? Does he know another DNA sample is being taken from Mia tomorrow? Leon's chilling warning returns to me, his voice soft and precise on the hotel landline. *That child is going to pay the price.* All of my certainty has melted away in the cold light of a new day.

I call Matt Simms to ask if he has a number for Dominic, a workplace or a last known address, but the call goes to voicemail so I leave a brief message.

I think about Kathryn, her flat in Little Missenden, my confrontation with her boyfriend Max on Friday night. Something was *off* about him too, his aggression, and I wish I'd asked Angela about him and how he fits in. He knew both sisters, he knew the Clifton family – could he be the Ghost? Was that why Zoe wouldn't tell her sister about the new man in her life, why the relationship had been a secret – because she'd been seeing her sister's boyfriend? Had he bribed or blackmailed Holt into botching the DNA test to cover up his involvement? I think back to Holt's solo visit to see Max on Thursday. Come to think of it, both men seemed cut from the same cloth – both good-looking white guys in their twenties, same private-school home counties inflection, both gym-toned types who clearly looked after themselves. Did they know each other from way back? I make a mental note to flag this to Gilbourne. And I will visit Angela again to give her an update.

I go down to the car park and within a few minutes I'm on the A40, making good time heading out of London in the Sunday morning traffic. Thinking about Max and the barely-contained violence in his words, his posture, his whole attitude when he had confronted me in Prestwood Ash on Friday night. A man on the edge.

I'm halfway to the village when my phone pings with a new message in its hands-free cradle on the dash. I expect to see Matt Simms's name on the display, but it's an unrecognised number. I click on the message.

Mia's almost out of time

I start a reply, then delete it and simply call the number, panic swimming through me. It rings out. I end the call and text instead, holding the phone against the steering wheel as I drive.

Who is this?

Don't make the same mistake twice.
He's already on his way

In answer to my question, at the end of the text he's signed it off as if he's writing an email.

Leon

Do you mean DS Holt? Is he the one?

I push down on the accelerator and pull out to overtake the car in front. I've just pushed the phone back into its cradle when it rings, the Bluetooth-connected speakers bouncing the sound around inside my car.

'Ellen?' Gilbourne's voice is taut with tension. 'Tell me you're still at the hotel.'

'No,' I say, overtaking a van. 'I'm in my car.'

'Listen to me very carefully, Ellen, do you trust me?'

'Yes. Of course.'

'I need you to turn around and go back to your hotel, lock the door and wait until I call you back. Do not open the door to *anyone*, do you understand? Not the manager, not DS Holt, no one at all, until I let you know it's safe and give you the all-clear.'

'What's happening, Stuart?'

There is a pause on the line, road noise, traffic, muffled conversations in the background.

'Dominic Church has shaken off his surveillance and he's on the move. I have units out looking for him but I need to be sure you're safe in case he comes for you.'

'This is it, isn't it?' Pressure is building at the base of my throat, the pain rising into my larynx. 'What about Holt? Where is he?'

'I don't know,' Gilbourne says, almost shouting with frustration. 'He's not answering his phone.'

'Where did they lose the surveillance on Church? Where was he?'

'Ellen, you need to go back to the—'

'Just tell me!'

There is another pause on the other end of the line. Engine noise, the pitch rising, a siren wailing close by.

'The last ANPR hit we had for his car reg was on the A40, heading north-west out of London.'

'You mean he's going towards Prestwood Ash.'

'We don't know that for certain but we've got the situation under—'

I hit end and push the accelerator flat to the floor.

62

I speed the rest of the way there, breaking limits on every single road, my hands in a death grip tight around the wheel. I can't sit in a locked room waiting for the phone to ring: I have to know that Mia is safe. I flash through Prestwood Ash and hit the country road out the other side, pushing up to seventy miles an hour before standing on the brakes as the turn-off for The Grange comes into view. The gates are open and I skid into the driveway in a slew of gravel, almost clipping the wall as I accelerate through and on up to the house.

There's a black Ford Focus in the driveway, parked at an angle opposite the Mercedes and the Range Rover I saw yesterday. There are no police cars. No uniforms, no flashing lights. No helicopters buzzing overhead. Just the wind high up in the trees, bare autumn branches swaying against a gunmetal grey sky. The sound of dogs barking furiously comes from somewhere around the rear of the house. I jump out of my car, shoes crunching over the gravel, looking into each of the cars in turn. A doll discarded on the back seat of the Mercedes; no movement behind any of the windows at the front of the house. The front door itself is ajar, only a few inches, but it's enough to see a thin slice of the dark hallway beyond.

Is Dominic Church here? *Someone* is here.

I stop in the doorway, strain my ears for any sound.

Nothing. Just the wind, tree branches clicking and scratching against each other next to the high stone wall. I reach into my handbag for a weapon but there is only the attack alarm, the noise-maker, which will be useless in a place as isolated as this. My fist closes around my bunch of keys instead.

I take another two steps, pushing on the front door. All my instincts tell me not to call out, not to alert anyone to my presence. Instead, I listen again for any human sound, any movement or conversation.

Silence. Even the dogs have stopped barking.

I push on the door again and it swings noiselessly open. There are no lights on and the hallway is dark even though it's barely noon. I stand completely still, willing my ears to pick up some-thing, anything from inside, straining to hear the sound of a baby's cry from somewhere deeper in the house. But the only sound is the insistent, steady tick of a grandfather clock opposite the front door. Apart from that, The Grange is utterly, completely still, as silent as a funeral.

I step over the big stone threshold and move around the door. And that's when I see him.

Gerald is lying on his back in the hallway. His jaw and the left side of his face almost completely blown away, the thick cream carpet beneath him a mass of red. A double-barrelled shotgun lies on the floor next to his hand.

I know instinctively that it's hopeless but I force myself to kneel beside him anyway, putting two fingers against the big carotid artery next to his windpipe. His skin is still warm to the touch but there is no pulse, no sign of life. He's gone.

He's lying on his back, only a few feet from the front door. I try to picture it, imagine him suspicious, on edge, arming himself from the gun cabinet in the lounge when he hears the ring of the doorbell. Pulling the front door open and being shot immediately, barely a chance to register the gun in Dominic Church's hands. No chance at all to defend himself.

I'm not going to let the same thing happen to me.

I pick up the shotgun, remembering the first time I met Dominic Church, only five days ago. Can it really be only five days? *Don't make the same mistake twice.* With blood thumping in my ears, I press the barrel release lever and the gun clicks open, revealing the circular brass caps of two shells, side by side. Loaded. Neither have been fired. Gerald didn't even have a chance to get a single shot off. I snap the gun shut again, the polished walnut stock smooth against my palms.

Where the hell are the police?

Still crouching, I lay the heavy weapon across my lap and dial Gilbourne's number on my phone. An engaged tone comes beeping back into my ear. *Shit.*

A sound. A voice. What was that? Faint, from somewhere else in the house, from above me, the first floor?

Mia?

I have to move. I slip the phone back into my pocket. With multiplying terror at what I'm going to find in the rest of the house, I heft the gun in both hands and make my way upstairs, my shoes sinking into the thick carpet. On the first floor landing I wait, listen again, straining my ears to pick up the slightest sound.

Still nothing. The master bedroom is empty, the bed neatly made, the room tidy, nothing that looks out of place. *Keep going.* I go to the spiral staircase to the second floor and move quickly up it, expecting the blast of a gun with every step that takes me higher. There's a very particular smell in my nostrils, growing stronger the higher I go. Oil-sharp and acrid. Dangerous. The stink of petrol.

A sick, metallic taste blooms on my tongue. Fear.

With the shotgun raised to my shoulder, I go to the first door on the right, the nursery, saying a silent prayer. *Please. Just this. This one life. I will never ask anything again, but please let Mia be spared.* Using the muzzle of the shotgun, I nudge the door open.

Angela is lying just inside the doorway.

She is on her side, curled into herself. The side of her blouse torn by a shotgun blast, the carpet beneath her stained dark crimson red.

Oh no.

Oh no.

Panic is rising in me, heat flowing up to my face. I kneel by Angela's side, touching my fingers to her neck in search of a pulse. It feels intimate, almost intrusive, to be touching her as she lies here when we had not even shaken hands yesterday. There is a pulse, weak and thready, but still there. Unconscious but still breathing, her airway clear. There's still a chance.

I ball up a bedsheet and press it to her wound.

'Hold on, Angela. I'm here and help's coming.'

I pull out my phone and dial 999, covering her with a blanket as I wait for the call to connect. A part of me had known I'd find Angela here in this room as soon as I saw her husband's body in the hall. I knew she would fight to defend her granddaughter, guarding the entrance to the nursery. And so she has. The stink of petrol is stronger here, almost overpowering, the floor and furniture stained dark with it. It is splashed everywhere, up the walls and curtains. The smell transports me back to that day in Libya, seeing the corpses scattered in groups, in ragged lines, in ones and twos, dark blood soaked into the dust beneath them. Civilians, all. Men, women. Children.

The call connects and I ask for an ambulance, giving the details as fast as I can.

'Is the attacker still in the house?' the operator is saying. 'Are you in immediate danger?'

'I don't know.'

'How many victims?'

'Two. One dead, one injured. Both gunshot wounds.'

I realise as I say it that they won't send paramedics in now until armed police have cleared the house and neutralised any threat.

'Anyone else hurt?' the operator says.

'Not sure.'

I step over Angela's prone form and move further into the room but it is a wreck, everything turned over, drawers emptied, baby clothes and sheets and bottles of formula milk strewn across the floor. My eyes search out the wooden crib in the corner. It is on its side, broken in on itself, the wooden bars snapped, the mattress upended and laying beneath the frame. Something else. Small. Delicate. Pinned beneath the cot, motionless. Lifeless.

The 999 operator is still talking but I can't hear him anymore.

No. No. No.

A sob rises in my throat as I realise what it is.

A tiny arm sticking out from under the bedding.

63

I stumble to the overturned cot, my eyes blurring with tears.

A drumbeat hammers in my head, Kathryn's unspoken plea and my own promise. *Please protect Mia. Please protect Mia.* I knew there was danger, and I've failed her. We've all failed her. So many wasted lives. Kathryn, who sacrificed herself to protect this child, all that she had left of her sister. Angela and Gerald, shot by the man who almost killed their daughter a year ago. Zoe, locked in an endless sleep in the white room two floors below.

Less than twenty-four hours ago I was here with Mia while she giggled and smiled, Angela cuddling her granddaughter, talking to her, feeding her. I held Mia myself, felt the warmth of her little body, the touch of her tiny fingers on my cheek.

Now she's gone. All gone.

I let my phone fall to the floor, pulling the frame of the upturned cot away as gently as I can to reach the tiny body beneath. Moving the broken slats and shifting the frame of the cot to the side so I can lift the mattress away. Touching her arm as gently as I can, I feel for a pulse at her wrist but there's nothing, the skin waxy and smooth, the fingers already stiffening in death. I push the mattress away to move more of the weight off her. This most innocent victim, the only innocent one among all of us.

I wipe more tears away with my sleeve and reach under the bedding with one hand to pull carefully on her arm with the other, not wanting to look at her but knowing that I must. I slide her body gently out.

A gut-punch of disbelief, of horror and grief and confusion all mixed together.

Not Mia.

Not a body. A doll. Just a baby-sized doll dressed in a white sleepsuit, blue eyes staring up at the ceiling, tufts of synthetic blonde hair brushed neatly to the side.

I collapse back onto my heels, the relief rushing over me like an avalanche, blanketing me, a held breath bursting from my lungs. The relief is so powerful it's almost unbearable, a high more intense than any drug. Mia is not here, which means there is still a sliver of hope. I shift the rest of the bedding to double-check she's nowhere beneath it. No.

I go over to check Angela again. Her pulse is still there but the sheet next to her wound is soaked with blood. I pull out another clean sheet from a drawer and press it on, slide a cushion under her head.

The 999 operator is still on the line when I retrieve my phone.

'I've got to go,' I tell him. 'Second-floor bedroom, female victim in her seventies, critically injured. Please hurry.'

I hang up and lean down close to Angela's ear, hoping she can hear me.

'Hold on, Angela. I'm going to find Mia.'

It's what she would want me to do. What *she* would do, in my place.

I grab the shotgun and stand up. The smell of petrol is over-powering, sharp and oily and burning into my nostrils. Mia's nursery is soaked with it, the cot, the chest of drawers, dark splashes on the carpet. One spark and this whole room would go up like a bomb, everything ablaze within seconds.

So why hadn't it been lit?

I look into the other rooms on this floor. Spare bedrooms and a bathroom. All untouched. As far as I've seen, the nursery is the only room that has been turned upside down and soaked in petrol. Not methodically but fast, rage-fuelled destruction as he searched in vain for the one thing he'd come here to find. I stand in the middle of the debris, trying to make sense of it. There's enough petrol poured in her room to turn it into an inferno, her guardians dead or injured, and no sign of Mia.

So why not light the fire to cover up the crime?

Then it hits me.

Because he wasn't finished.

He hasn't found her. He *has* to find her, to be sure the job's done before he lights the match. Even a burned body would yield DNA, wouldn't it? Unless it was completely incinerated, and he could never be sure of that in a house fire. Too many variables. He can't risk leaving a body to burn. He has to be sure that no trace of her is ever found. Take the baby and burn the rest, the clothes, the sheets, the muslin cloths, the bottles of formula, anything that might hold a trace of her DNA. Extinguish all traces of her, as if she never existed.

But if he hasn't started the fire, he hasn't found her. I pray that I'm right. Had I disturbed him when I arrived a few minutes before? Had he fled before he could finish what he came here for?

I go across the hall into a spare bedroom. Check under the bed, behind a desk. Nothing.

The urge to shout Mia's name is almost overwhelming, but I can't risk it. Instead I will search every inch of this mansion if I have to.

Think.

Angela was doing what Kathryn did when she got off that train five days ago. Drawing the danger away from Mia. Away from the baby. Right from when Mia was born, Angela had been doing exactly this – consciously or otherwise. That was why the nursery was on the top floor of the house, rather than next to their own bedroom on the first floor, or next to her mother below that in the annexe. They had done what parents have always done, put the precious child in the topmost branches of the tree, to be further away from predators on the ground. In their walled estate in the middle of the countryside, as far away as possible from a predator they knew was out there. But it hasn't been far enough.

I turn to face the stairs and drop into a kneeling position, the shotgun tight into my shoulder. Close my eyes and listen for five seconds. Ten.

There. Was that something? I stay perfectly still, my breath held, turning my head slowly from side to side. For a moment I think my ears are playing tricks. Then I hear it again, faint, muffled, almost inaudible. But unmistakeable.

A cry.

64

I run to the bedrooms at the end of the hall. Two doors opposite each other, both ajar. I push the right-hand one open, looking all around for the source of the noise. A double bed, untouched. A dressing table and stool. A big oak wardrobe. Empty. I drop to all fours and look under the bed. Nothing.

Across the hall, the other room is a mirror image of the previous bedroom save for two twin beds rather than a double. The beds are covered with yellow and black tartan blankets, flat and untouched, nowhere to hide a baby. No ottoman base, nowhere that might open to reveal a hiding space. There is a slatted door into a walk-in closet, empty rows of hangers, old shoe boxes stacked high against the wall. None of them big enough.

She's not here. Did I imagine it? No, *no*.

The noise comes again. Muffled, again, and I feel helpless frustration start to boil up inside. Mia is close by, I *feel* her. In a roof space? There's no trapdoor to the attic here, not in this room anyway. Memories strobe through my mind. Images of Mia in her cot yesterday, Angela opening the blinds in her room, warming a bottle of milk in the microwave, telling me about her daughter and her granddaughter. Angela wasn't at all what I expected, very down-to-earth despite how far she'd come from her own upbringing. Or perhaps, because of it. Her soft Liverpool vowels pushing through a little stronger when she talked about her own bedroom, as a young girl growing up.

Two in each bed and the littlest in the bottom drawer.

My eyes are drawn to a chest of drawers taking up one half of the far wall, solid dark oak with four wide drawers. An oval brass-framed mirror above it on a stand, cream lace doilies and porcelain figurines beside it.

I pull open the bottom drawer.

Mia stares back at me, big blue eyes glistening with tears, blinking against the sudden light. She gives another startled cry and I feel as if my heart is about to explode with relief.

'Hey, you,' I say, feeling the weight of tears behind my eyes again. 'Hello Mia.'

She is lying on a soft white blanket, one half of the drawer cleared to make a little nest big enough for her to lie in. She has a yellow muslin cloth clutched in one little hand, damp from where she has been sucking it. I pick her up, blanket and all, and lay her gently onto the carpet, turning her this way and that to check for any blood, any cuts or signs of injury, but there's nothing obvious. I wipe her tears gently away and her small hand closes around my finger.

'Come on, little one,' I say. 'Let's get you out of here.'

I sling the shotgun over my shoulder, wrap Mia up in the blanket and carry her down the back stairs. They must have been designed for use by the domestic staff back when the house was first built, they're much narrower and darker than the main staircase that leads up from the hallway. The back stairs run all the way down the rear of the house with only a few windows, the bottom section deep in shadow. I stop halfway down to listen for any other noise, any sign that Church is waiting for me in the scullery below, but hear nothing apart from Mia's low gurgling and snuffling. Now I have her, safe, unharmed, my only thought is to get her out of here as fast as possible. But there is one more stop I have to make before we can leave.

I reach the bottom of the stairs and creep through the scullery, converted into a walk-in larder, its walls lined with shelves and cupboards. To the right is the main house, to the left, the annexe. I slip left and creep down the corridor, the creaking of wooden floorboards horribly loud in the silence. I unsling the shotgun from my shoulder and hold it one-handed, the stock tucked against my elbow, finger on the trigger. The door to the room at the end of the corridor is closed. Zoe's room. Dominic Church's ex-wife. I have a horrible, sick feeling in my stomach that he will have taken his revenge on her, too, finished off what he started a year ago while she lies helpless in bed.

I push open the door to the white room.

Zoe's here, her head turned slightly to the side, wires and machines and clean white sheets, the monitor next to her bed still beeping its slow and steady rhythm, her body somewhere between life and death. No wounds, no sign of injury. She seems the same as she was yesterday.

'I have to take Mia away from here,' I say, standing by her bed. 'I'm sorry, Zoe.'

If there was a way of taking her with us, I would. But she needs the machines, she needs this room. I check the machine's monitor.

Her pulse seems regular, no alarms or warning messages. The police will be here soon and—

A reflection in the glass of the monitor. Movement. A flash of something in the garden behind me. A figure?

I turn, dropping into a crouch by the bed to scan the windows that give out onto the lawn, cold creeping over my skin. My phone rings in my pocket and I flinch in alarm, laying the shotgun on the floor to snatch it up with my free hand, still clutching Mia in the other.

Stuart's number shows on the display.

'Ellen.' His voice is tight with worry. 'Where are you?'

'I'm here, at The Grange, you have to get everybody here as fast as—'

'I told you to stay at the hotel!' It's almost a shout. 'We diverted the team, we had a strong positive sighting on the target but it turned into nothing.'

'He shot them both, Stuart.'

There is a stunned silence before he replies. 'Who? What are you talking about?'

'Gerald Clifton's dead.' I take a shuddering breath. 'And Angela's in a bad way, she needs paramedics here right now, I called an ambulance but they need to hurry.'

'Ellen,' he whispers, 'you need to listen to me and this time you need to do what I tell you. You have to trust me. Can you do that?'

'Yes.'

'We've got a new trace on Holt, he's just switched his phone on again and we've been able to triangulate the signal. Ellen, listen to me very carefully: he's *there*. He's still in the house. You have to get out. *Now*.'

65

I creep through the house, shushing Mia on my shoulder, freezing at every sound, my eyes scanning every door and window we pass by. The name drumming in my head with every step, over and over again. *Detective Sergeant Nathan Holt.* I have this powerful sense that he is watching me, stalking me, ready to strike when we're within sight of escape. The keys to the Mercedes estate are in a bowl by the front door: it has a car seat for Mia and it's faster and bigger than my Citroën. I sprint out onto the drive feeling horribly exposed, tear open the rear door, strap her in and scoot around to jump into the driver's seat in front. Every moment I'm expecting to hear the crunch of gravel, an angry shout, a gunshot.

Go.

It's only as I'm accelerating down the drive in a spray of gravel that I realise the black saloon car parked there earlier has gone. But I don't have the headspace for that right now, I've promised Stuart I'll drive straight to police HQ without stopping and meet him there. He texts telling me he'll meet me in the visitor's car park, that I shouldn't stop for anything or anyone, and I send a thumbs-up in reply.

The urge to put my foot to the floor is strong, to let the big Mercedes engine rip and get there as fast as possible. But I'm acutely aware of Mia strapped into her car seat next to me, a new vulnerability in traffic that has me second-guessing every other driver in case they're going too fast or coming too close. I keep looking over at Mia to check she's OK in the bulky rear-facing seat, but she seems quite content to suck on a corner of her cloth and gaze out of the window at the dark clouds racing by.

Relief starts to ease through me as I leave the Buckinghamshire countryside behind and hit the outskirts of London, the comforting familiarity of city streets and buildings and *people*, of safety in numbers. I have kept my promise to Kathryn.

Safe now. Safe now.

As I'm coming into Pinner I pull up at a red traffic light and my phone buzzes with a new message from an unrecognised number.

Remember the abandoned studio complex? Go there now. No police, no calls, no diversions

I turn in my seat, half-expecting Holt to be sitting in traffic behind me or watching from across the street, phone in his hand. But I can't see him. I fire off a quick text in reply.

Why would I do that?

I'm pulling away when my phone buzzes again in my lap. Another text, no words, just an image, a close-up picture of Noah's face. His Spiderman glasses are gone. He looks serious, wide-eyed.

Terrified.

The angular black muzzle of a pistol is held at his temple by an unseen hand.

I swerve across the lane, an oncoming taxi missing me by inches and leaving a frenzy of angry hoots in my wake. *Noah*. My stomach turns over and for a moment I think I might be sick, swallowing back acid in my throat. An unwelcome memory returns, the last words Noah had said to me on Friday as he traced a shape over his little chest.

Cross my heart and hope to die.

Another message arrives seconds later.

Bring the baby to studio 7 and we can trade. Or you can let him die. Your choice.

I can't drive. I can barely see, the picture of Noah's terrified face burned onto my retinas. I pull over into a bus stop and sit for a moment, trying to control my breathing and the galloping, crashing of my heart.

My godson. My best friend's son, her firstborn, a child I have known since the day he came into the world. Not my blood, but as close as I'll probably ever get. Tara's sweet, serious six-year-old, who somehow finds himself weighed in the scales with the baby now dozing in the car seat behind me. A stranger's baby, an infant I promised to protect. Another innocent, a child I have saved from mortal danger. Can I really give her up now? Can I make that choice?

There is no right answer to this. No good outcome. I send a reply, the only words I can summon to mind.

Don't hurt Noah

> *What happens to him is entirely up to you, Ellen*

I put my head back against the headrest and take one last look at Mia. Her eyelids are heavy as she drowses in and out of sleep, her little cheeks pink and rounded like summer apples. Finally, I tear my eyes away from her and send a reply.

On my way

> *Hurry. You call the police, he dies*

I put the new address into the satnav on the dashboard and pull out into traffic again, hands clenched tight around the steering wheel. The satnav says the studio complex is 2.2 miles away, a mile further than the police station. I follow the directions on autopilot but my mind is elsewhere, scrambling, racing, trying to think of a third solution to this impossible equation. But I can only see two: Noah or Mia. Mia or Noah. It's that simple.

And by the time I'm pulling into the deserted car park, driving through drifts of leaves and rubbish, I know what has to be done.

My phone rings in my lap.

'What's happened?' Stuart says before I can speak. 'Why are you not at the station? You should be here by now.'

'I can't talk at the moment.'

'Just park up in the visitors' area, I'm going down there now, I'll wait for you.'

'I can't, Stuart. Not anymore.'

'What? I don't understand, Ellen, what's going on?'

I glance at the shotgun in the passenger footwell beside me. 'I'm sorry, Stuart. There's something else I have to do first.'

'Tell me what's—'

I press end and put the phone on silent, driving to the far end of the car park, to the rear doors that I ran out of five days ago. I kill the engine, sitting for a moment in the silence. Preparing myself. Running through it all in my mind.

Mia is dozing again, the motion of driving has lulled her into a contented sleep. I wish more than anything that we could be driving into the police station right now, into safety. For both children to be out of harm's reach. But it can't be.

No. This is the only way.

I make one more call, then spread out the big white blanket on the back seat, to get ready for what I have to do.

'I'm sorry, Mia.' I brush away a tear and reach for the straps of her car seat. 'I'm sorry.'

*   *   *

The studio complex is just as I remembered it. A cavernous empty shell, the windows milky and crusted with dirt, long wide corridors rich with the smell of mildew and decay. Stacks of plastic chairs, abandoned. Open doors to offices still full of furniture like a *Marie Celeste* beached on land, an oversized relic of an earlier age, waiting too long for new tenants who will never arrive.

With the baby swaddled loosely in a blanket against my right shoulder, I hurry down corridors, deeper into the complex, following faded signs to studio seven. Turning first left, then right, then left again. I'm greeted by a hint of smoke in the air from the fire set by Dominic Church the last time I was here. Finally I reach a heavy double door with the number seven stencilled on it in faded grey type. I pull the door open, heaving against its weight, and peer inside.

Darkness. I wait for my eyes to adjust, slowly making out shapes on the far side of the big room. A stage set, maybe? A man? Noah? I step into the room and the big door swings shut behind me with a *thump* as almost total darkness returns.

The air is cooler in here but it's stale, fetid, as if it has been trapped in here for years. A coldness creeps over my skin, sweat clammy against the fabric of my top.

'Hello?'

The word echoes up and away from me, bouncing off a high ceiling before fading to nothing. I use the torch on my phone to cut into the dark. The studio is huge, at least a hundred feet square, everything painted black. A low catwalk runs into the centre, linking to a stage on the far side. I walk slowly towards it, my shoes clicking on the hard black floor.

'It's Ellen Devlin,' I say, my left hand going protectively over the blanket. 'With Mia, just like you wanted.'

There is no answer. I keep walking, up the three steps onto the stage where long black curtains fall from ceiling to floor.

'Where's Noah?' I say. I'm desperate to see him, to be sure he's still OK. 'Where is he?'

No answer, and then—

Light. In a split second the room is flooded with a hundred blinding lights, filling every corner with dazzling brilliance, a hundred bulbs at once, a thousand, filling the room with brightness that forces me to screw my eyes shut and cover my face with a hand. As my eyes slowly adjust, white flashes still dancing across my pupils, I make out a high ceiling filled with metal tracks and gantries for stage lighting, all of it trained on the stage. I squint, and a figure emerges from the dazzling glare on the other side of the studio.

A shape, an outline. A man.

'Hello Ellen,' he says. 'Good to see you again.'

66
Kathryn Clifton

- BEFORE -

The woman's name was Ellen.

She looked kind. Capable. Like she knew what she was doing, where she was going in life. Kathryn studied her across the little train table, this tall woman in the seat opposite, gazing down at Mia as if she was the most amazing thing in the world. Which she was, of course. Her niece, the miracle baby, all she had left of her big sister, like Zoe had been reborn and given another chance.

Kathryn's phone buzzed with another text.

He must be tracking you, following in a car

She looked at Mia again and felt another lurch of panic, shivery and cold right down to her feet. She knew the stakes: if he caught Mia, he would kill her and her body would never be found. That was why Kathryn had taken her, why she had run. *If he's tracking me*, she thought, *maybe I need to give him a trail to follow. A trail that leads him away from Mia.*

She couldn't leave Mia with just anyone. But maybe she could leave her with this woman. Ellen. She looked smart, sensible, *normal*, as if she would do the right thing. Mia would be safe with her, just for a little while. Not even half an hour. It was either that or get caught – both of them – and that was not going to happen. Kathryn could not allow it to happen. She would be a decoy instead.

Time was running out.

Stay on the train or get off.

Stay on or get off.

On or off.

Now or never.

Kathryn could feel her heart tear a little at the thought of what she was about to do. She made her decision and fired off another text, the replies dropping in seconds later.

Do it

I should get to Marylebone in time to intercept

Be careful

Kathryn found a biro in her bag and a sheet of paper, a delivery note. She turned it over and began to write, watched her hand forming the letters.

Please protect Mia
Don't trust the police
Don't trust anyone

She folded the paper once, wrote Ellen's name on the front and tucked it back into her rucksack.

Do it now. Before you change your mind.

'Would you be all right with Mia just while I take this call? It's . . . urgent.'

'Sure,' Ellen said, smiling down at the little bundle in her arms, Mia's tiny hand wrapped around her index finger. 'Go ahead, we'll be fine for a minute.'

'I'll just be down there.' Kathryn gestured over her shoulder, down the carriage. 'I'll be back.'

Ellen looked up again, her smile fading.

'Kathryn, are you sure you're all right?'

'Yeah.' Kathryn got up out of her seat. 'Thank you, I won't be long.'

She reached out a hand and touched her fingertips gently to the baby's head, praying that this would all be over the next time she saw her sister's beautiful baby girl. The panic was making her hands shake and she wondered if Ellen had noticed it. *Just go.*

She walked to the end of the carriage and stood by the door, calling for a taxi to pick her up from the station as soon as possible. It seemed to take forever for the train to slow, to pull in and stop, and she was first to step onto the little platform at Seer Green. Thrusting her hands into the pockets of her coat, she hurried away from the train. She couldn't look back. If she did, she might change her mind. But there was a tapping on the window as she walked past, Ellen's face a picture of confusion, still cradling Mia in her arms.

'Sorry,' Kathryn mouthed silently at her.

She turned and hurried away down the platform with a handful of other passengers, through the barriers and out into the car park at the front of the station. There was a pull-in for taxis in the corner, a chain-link fence separating the car park from the platform and the track. She called the taxi firm again to be told – again – that a car was on its way to her.

From here she could see the train as it pulled out of the station, engine grumbling, moving off as it headed south-east towards London. Kathryn felt her veins bubbling with panic, her knees almost buckling beneath her. *Oh God, have I done the right thing?* She couldn't take her eyes off the train as it moved away, picking up speed, carrying Mia further away from her with every second. She was still watching the end of the train recede into the distance as a car pulled in behind her. The sound of an engine, a door opening, footsteps on the tarmac.

She turned. Not a taxi driver. A familiar face, his eyes widening in surprise for just a moment as he saw she was alone.

Just her.

No baby.

But he recovered quickly, moved closer to block her escape. In his gloved hand, the glint of something metallic.

'Hello Kathryn.'

'You,' she said.

67

Detective Inspector Stuart Gilbourne faces me across the studio.

A white one-piece boiler suit covers his clothes and he has plastic overshoes on his feet, an angular black pistol held low at his side in one latex-gloved hand. He looks calm, composed. In control.

'You,' I say, nausea rising up from the pit of my stomach. 'You're the Ghost.'

He gestures at me with the pistol. 'Put Mia on the floor and take three steps back.'

'Where's Noah?' I say, clutching the baby tighter to me. 'What have you done to him?'

'He's fine.'

'Bring him out, show him to me.'

'All in good time, Ellen.' He gives me a small, cold smile. 'Thanks again for last night, by the way. I really enjoyed myself.'

I feel dizzy, sick, bile burning the back of my throat. There are a dozen things I want to say, a hundred things. I want to scream, shout at him, hurt him, make him feel a fraction of the anger and fear and betrayal and shame pulsing through me at this moment.

'You bastard,' I say. 'You used me, to get to Mia.'

'I did what I had to do.'

'Angela was right about the Ghost.'

'Half right,' he replies. 'She just picked the wrong horse.'

'That's why Kathryn told me not to trust the police. She knew one of you was dirty but you'd spun her around so much by that point that she didn't know which way was up. You or Sergeant Holt. Or maybe both of you together.'

'The top brass had started to have suspicions. They'd ordered my own partner to keep tabs on me, can you believe that? So Nathan had his own agenda.'

I shake my head. 'That was the reason why Holt wanted to get a DNA swab from her right at the start, wasn't it? In case you tried to mess with the results. Maybe switch the sample, replace it with someone else's so the DNA didn't connect to you. He wanted to get an untainted sample, independent of anything you might do. But you still managed to intercept it.'

Gilbourne shrugs. 'I'm his boss.'

'Why did you kill those women, Stuart?'

'First things first,' he says, raising the gun to point at me. 'Put the baby on the floor. *Now.*'

'Not until you tell me.' I don't move. 'Sienna Parker, the first victim. Why did you kill her?'

'Why do you think I'm going to tell you that?'

'Because you're proud of getting away with it. Because it shows you're smarter than all your colleagues, your forensics people, the boss who thinks you're past it.'

He studies me for a moment, as if weighing up what to tell me. He lowers the gun a fraction, a smile flickering at the edges of his mouth.

'Sienna was a greedy whore. And I mean that literally. All I ever wanted to do was keep working, keep on top of things. Stay sharp, like I used to, put in the long hours and the all-nighters. But as you get older it gets harder, you find you need a little bit of extra help to keep your energy levels up. A little bit of a pick-me-up now and again.'

'It wasn't Holt who worked on that task force, was it? Human exploitation?' My mind is spinning, tumbling. 'It was you.'

'You're a smart cookie, Ellen. I knew Sienna from back in the day, knew she could sort me out with some Dex when I needed it.' Seeing my confusion, he adds, 'Dexamphetamine. Drug of choice for pilots, soldiers, people who have to keep going no matter what. Sienna sold to me for a while but then she got greedy, decided to try blackmailing me. Unfortunately she'd also told her best mate Louise, who'd dropped a few hints to the pretty little outreach worker who was trying to get them both off the streets.'

'Zoe Clifton.'

'The other two were lowlifes, scum. But it was a shame about Zoe.'

'A shame you didn't finish her off, you mean.'

'Wouldn't have been necessary if Sienna had kept her mouth shut in the first place – it was her fault, really. I knew I had to close it off, nip it in the bud.'

'So the whole thing was a cover-up?'

'You don't understand.' His voice rises as if he's struggling to stay in control. 'If it had got out, I would have lost every-thing. Career, pension, reputation, freedom. Scumbags I've put in prison making new appeals, my convictions quashed, a *lot* of nasty bastards back on the streets.' He opens his left hand like a flower. 'Everything gone, just like that. All those years of service, and for what? Because I was trying to do the best job I could? It was unfortunate, but necessary – Sienna didn't really give me any choice.'

'All this, because you're an addict?'

'Because I've given my life to this job!' he shouts. 'I'm a good cop who's done a few bad things, that's all. But for the right reasons.'

The studio lights are hot on my skin but I feel frozen, chilled to the bone. 'You killed them and made it look like some serial predator attacking vulnerable women, only you knew how to avoid leaving DNA evidence behind. You've got decades of experience with evidence. And once you'd dealt with them, you had to find out whether Zoe was a threat as well.'

'I had to find out what she knew.'

'So you got close to her. Just like you got close to me.'

'I didn't *plan* to get involved with her, certainly didn't plan to sleep with her. But one thing led to another, you know how it goes. Apparently some women can't resist my charms.' He gives me a crooked smile. 'Isn't that right, Ellen?'

'You were the man Zoe was seeing, but she found out what you'd done, didn't she?'

'One mistake, that's all it was.'

'How did she find out?'

'I was planning to track down Sienna's dealer, get some pills off him when things had calmed down. So I kept her phone. *Stupid.*' He shakes his head ruefully. 'One night Zoe's at my flat, we've both had a few drinks. She's looking for a charger and she finds Sienna's phone instead, recognises her stupid bloody butterfly-pattern phone case. She puts two and two together, we have a row and she storms out.'

'So you had to silence her too. Except when you attacked her, you didn't finish the job, did you?'

Gilbourne shrugs. 'Best laid plans, and all that,' he says, his voice back under control. 'It only takes one piece of bad luck to trip you up. Zoe's never going to wake up from her coma, but if they ever made a DNA match from Mia it would put me right in the hot seat as number one prime suspect, and then everything I've ever achieved would start getting pulled to pieces.'

I remember what Angela had told me yesterday about the search for Zoe's boyfriend, the nameless man who had somehow evaded detection and faded into the background after she was attacked and left for dead.

They investigated, they pulled her private life apart, but they never came up with a name.

Of course they didn't.

'You investigated your own crimes,' I say. 'Tried to set up Dominic Church as your fall guy, paint him as some angry ex-husband out for revenge. When that didn't work, you moved onto Leon Markovitz, a disgraced journalist who'd been pushed over the edge, before dropping just enough hints about DS Holt to put him into the frame too. How were you going to tamper with Mia's DNA results? Which one of them were you going to frame?'

'Doesn't matter now, does it?' He shrugs. 'Now I've got you. The baby disappears and we have a brand new narrative, a story to fit everything into. Or at least muddy the picture enough to make sure no one can ever put the pieces together.'

'They won't believe you.'

'I think they probably will. Decorated veteran of the Met versus a deranged divorcee cat lady desperate for a baby at any cost? Get real, Ellen: you're the perfect patsy. I suspect you've been good enough to bring along the murder weapon used on Mr and Mrs Clifton as well, haven't you? Where is it?'

My stomach drops. *The shotgun.* I picked it up next to Gerald's body and assumed it was from his own gun cabinet, that he had been defending himself. Wrong again. I glance at my surroundings, at the lights, the stage, the set. A TV studio, an apt place for the fiction I have unwittingly helped him create.

'It's in the car.'

'You took her Mercedes, didn't you? Because of the car seat.' He smiles when I nod an affirmative. 'Good. So we've got the murder weapon covered in your fingerprints, which will be found in the car you stole from the Clifton house after killing them and taking the baby. Where on earth had they hidden her, anyway?'

'In a chest of drawers,' I say in a monotone. 'You shot them both and set me up to take the fall for it. You knew I'd drive out there, find it all.'

'Rather neat for a Plan B, isn't it? Plan A had Kathryn doing all the legwork. I got her just nervous enough so she'd take the baby out of that house, but by then she was so confused she didn't know who to trust. Dominic Church was so paranoid he convinced her that someone was tracking her phone – he was right, actually – and that she was about to get caught. Then she had the crazy idea to hand the baby to a stranger and that was when *you* got involved.'

'You killed her too, didn't you?'

'What do you think?'

'I think you're a manipulative psychopath.'

He smiles. 'That's not what you said in your hotel room last night.'

I feel a hot bloom of anger in my chest as I think of the hours we spent together, of the secrets I've shared with him, of taking this man into my bed.

'Where's Noah?' I say again, fighting to keep my voice steady.

'He's safe and sound.'

I study him, the confident smile, the unkempt hair, the scattering of stubble across his jaw. The tiniest twitch at the corner of his eye.

'He's not here, is he?' I say. 'You're bluffing. The picture's a fake.'

He raises an eyebrow, gives me a little nod of respect.

'Very good, Ellen.' He takes a plastic cable tie from his pocket. 'My own little deepfake image, but amazingly realistic, wasn't it? Thought it might come in handy if you needed persuading at any point during these proceedings. All warfare is based on deception, right? Didn't they teach you that one in the navy?'

'This isn't warfare, it's murder.'

'What's the difference? Now put the baby down and take three steps back, like I asked you to already.'

'Then what?'

'It's time for you two to exit stage left, in a puff of smoke.' He raises the gun again. 'I'm not going to ask you again.'

I bring my arm up instinctively across the blanket as if I can protect the baby from a bullet.

He brandishes the cable tie in his left hand.

'Time for you to disappear. Both of you. Now put Mia down on the stage and hold your hands out to me, wrists together.'

'No.'

'*No?*'

'You can have me, but not her.'

He cocks the pistol's hammer back, raising it so the blued steel muzzle is level with my eyes. 'I'm taking both of you, Ellen, that's just how this is going to work.'

I raise myself up to my full height, blood pounding in my ears, rolling onto the balls of my feet.

'OK then,' I say. 'You want her? You can have her.'

I gather the baby in the blanket and throw her at him.

68

He stumbles backwards, flailing a hand at Mia's thick white blanket, his eyes widening in alarm at the baby rolling out of its folds, the cutest blonde baby in a white sleepsuit with perfect little fingers, silent and smiling as she falls out of the blanket and her head hits the stage with a *smack* of plastic. The doll only fools him for a second but I'm already fumbling for the shotgun hanging on its strap beneath my raincoat, my right hand grabbing for the smooth walnut stock, left hand raising the barrel, heart smashing against my ribcage.

Too slow too slow.

I flinch at the explosion of a gunshot close to my head, the *crack* of a bullet passing an inch from my left ear, and then I have the shotgun up and levelled at his chest and he's staring at me in alarm, each of us with our guns trained on the other.

'Put it down!' he shouts. 'Put it down or I'll shoot!'

'You pull that trigger again and I'll do the same. We both lose.'

'What have you done with the baby? Where is she?'

'Somewhere safe.' My palms are damp with sweat. 'I wasn't going to risk another life by bringing Mia in here.'

'What the hell is wrong with you? Have you got a death wish?'

The lights are behind him, dazzling me, making me squint.

'*Deception*, Stuart. Just like you said.'

He lets out a heavy breath, shaking his head. '*Christ*, you're impossible.'

'That's what my husband used to say.'

He laughs, a short maniacal hoot, and just for a second I see a glimpse of the madness behind his eyes. The blank space. The evil.

'Why don't you lay the gun down nice and slowly, Ellen. So we can talk about this like rational adults.'

I keep the shotgun tight into my shoulder, levelled at his chest.

'I don't think so.'

'Well then, it looks like we've got ourselves a stand-off.' His smile fades, the pistol in his hand steady again. 'So you'd figured out it was me before you walked in here, had you?'

'Almost, but I had to be sure. I had to *know*.'

'And now you do,' his voice is thick with sarcasm. 'Does it make any difference to anything? No.'

'Ever since I met you, Stuart, it's been nagging at me. I couldn't work out how a twenty-four-year-old woman had managed to out-wit a veteran police inspector with all the resources at his disposal, how she'd managed to evade you, make a run for it taking Mia with her when the baby was so crucial to the investigation. Today, as I was driving back from The Grange I thought you'd been using Mia as bait, to draw out the Ghost, wait for him to make his move so you could catch him. It was almost like you *let* her go, because you needed Mia out in the open. You needed her out of that house, away from her protectors. Kathryn knew something was going on and you let her run, tracking her phone and not realising Holt was tracking her too with a device hidden in a toy he'd given to Mia.

Then I realised: you used Kathryn the same way you used me. To get to Mia, get her out in the open where you could make her disappear. You needed a scapegoat, a middle man, and you knew I'd go to the house this morning if I thought Mia was in danger – that's why you phoned to tell me. You knew I wouldn't stay put in the hotel.'

He studies me with renewed interest, maybe even grudging admiration. 'When poachers take a herd of elephants, they shoot the young first because they know the adults will gather around the bodies, making themselves an easier target. You played your part very well, Ellen. When you told me your Libya story last night, I knew you'd be perfect for it.'

'You bastard.'

He shrugs. 'Whatever.'

'I couldn't understand the break-ins at my house either. Whoever came into my house on Wednesday night thought I wasn't going to be there – that's why they bolted when I came downstairs. I couldn't work out why they thought the house would be empty. Then I remembered I'd said in the police station that I'd be going to stay with a friend. Only you, and Holt and my solicitor were in that interview room. That's why you broke into my house on that first night – you thought I wasn't going to be there. But I changed my mind. So you had to come back the following day.'

'Go on. Why?'

'To gather up anything of Mia's that I'd kept, that might have her DNA on it. That's why you took all the baby stuff, in case any of it was hers. Even that first time you questioned me, you were very keen to be sure I'd surrendered everything belonging to Mia.'

'The break-in could have been Holt.'

'No. When you came to my hotel last night, it was to find out what Angela Clifton had told me, how much she suspected. But you also thought you'd do one last check through my stuff. Mia's muslin cloth I'd been keeping in my handbag, it had her saliva on it. I couldn't find it this morning, because *you* took it.'

'This is why we're here, is it? Because of a stupid cloth?'

'We're here because you've killed four people, Stuart, and tried to kill two others. Because you started with one murder and you couldn't stop. You've tried to conceal what you've become, when the truth is you've become everything you've always hated.'

'It's all so simple for you, isn't it?'

'At The Grange when you told me Holt was still there, it was you, wasn't it?'

He shrugs again, as if the answer is obvious. 'So, is a rescue party on its way?'

'I don't need rescuing, Stuart.'

'So it's just me and you for the time being?' he says, inching forward. 'Together again.'

'Just the two of us.'

'You think you're going to shoot me, do you?'

'If I have to.'

He shakes his head. Emphatic. 'You're not going to pull that trigger, Ellen. You're a good person, you don't have it in you.'

A memory of Dominic Church's words comes back to me. *Two types of people in the world: those who will pull the trigger, and those who won't.* Way off in the distance I hear the faintest rise and fall of a siren. Help's coming, DS Holt's coming, but he won't be here soon enough. There is only one way for Gilbourne to be safe now, to be able to tell his story, spin his own lies without challenge: if I'm dead before Holt arrives.

And there is only one way for Mia to be out of his reach and safe, *truly* safe: for Gilbourne to be gone.

'It's a funny thing, Stuart, but people keep telling me that.'

'And what did you say the last—'

I jerk the trigger.

There is a punch of savage recoil in my shoulder and in the same moment a horse-kick of pain in my chest, a brutal smashing blow and a flash of brightness in the air between us as both guns go off at once. And then I'm flat on my back and there is pain *everywhere*, waves of agony crashing over me like surf on a beach, every nerve ending alight with pain.

I lie there for a few seconds, all the air pounded from my lungs, crying out as I raise my head. Gilbourne lies motionless a few feet away, his overshoe-clad feet pointing at the ceiling. My raincoat is splashed with red. The doll lies discarded on the floor between us, its unblinking blue eyes fixed on me with a lifeless stare. I think of Mia sleeping in her car seat outside, a note tucked under her foot, scribbled on a scrap of paper in the moments before I ran into the studio with the doll in my arms.

Please protect Mia. I think Gilbourne is her father. I'm sorry – E

She is the one good thing in all of this, and she will be safe now.

Not hunted anymore. Not hidden away. Free.

I let my head fall back to the stage, looking up at the blinding brilliance of hundreds of lights arranged in rows above me. I take a breath, wincing against a fresh wave of pain. The coppery taste of blood in my mouth.

The lights above me are dimming now. Receding.

Fading into darkness.

THREE MONTHS LATER

69

The day is dry and bright and icy-cold, trees bare under a cloud-less December sky, the high street busy with shoppers making the most of the good weather in the last few days before Christmas. Mia sits in her pushchair, chewing enthusiastically on a bright yellow teething ring with bunny ears. She's dressed in a white padded romper suit, with a blanket across her lap and a knitted bobble hat pulled down over her ears, wrapped up and cosy, her cheeks ruby red.

I smile as I see her, making my way over to a table by the window of the café.

'She's getting big,' I say to Dominic.

'Sitting upright,' he says. 'She'll be crawling soon.'

Mia is in her pushchair, with Dominic at her side. On her other side is Barbara, her great aunt, who's been helping to take care of Mia while Angela follows the long road of rehabilitation from her injuries. A sprightly sixty-something with an uncanny resemblance to her older sister, Barbara holds out her hand and I shake it.

'Nice to meet you at last, Ms Devlin.'

Dominic pushes a cup towards me as I sit down. 'It's good to see you again, Ellen. How are you feeling?'

'Much better, thank you.' I unzip my jacket, the warmth of the café a welcome contrast to the crisp winter cold outside. 'Feel like I'm pretty much back to normal. The physio has been good and the doctors seem to think I'm doing OK.'

It's true, but luck was on my side too: Gilbourne's bullet missed an artery by half an inch – clipping my lung instead. A fraction higher and I would have bled out long before help could arrive. Instead, the wound had left blood leaking into my lung as I lost consciousness, DS Holt arriving minutes later with other officers and paramedics. Gilbourne was already dead, the shotgun lethal at point-blank range as I knew it would be.

A storm of publicity about the rogue policeman-turned-killer has still not abated, the official inquiry only recently announced. Leon Markovitz finally got the big scoop he'd been chasing, the huge story to prove the doubters wrong, a worldwide exclusive that I agreed to help him with.

I give Mia a wave. 'So nice to see this little one again.'

She continues to chew on her teething ring, giving me a gummy smile.

I take a sip of my drink, the hot chocolate warming me, and Dominic tells me more about Mia and all the things she's been learning to do in these past few months. He's not a blood relative but he's keen to spend as much time as he can with her, to be part of her life. He's made peace with Angela and started to put his life back together again, the cloud of suspicion that had hung over him for a year finally lifted – his supposed criminal record, I know now, was just another part of Gilbourne's tapestry of lies. Dominic, Angela and Barbara will all be together for Mia's first Christmas and I can tell it means a great deal to him as he starts to rebuild and look to the future.

Barbara goes to the counter to ask about heating Mia's bottle of formula milk. I lean forward, lowering my voice a little.

'Why didn't you tell me, Dominic, when we first met? Tell me what was really going on?'

'Because I knew that sooner or later you were going to end up talking to the police, and I wanted them to have as little information as possible.'

'So you kept me in the dark.'

'I did what I had to do, to keep her safe. Both her parents are gone now, only her grandma left. And me.'

'She has her mother. She has Zoe.'

'You know what I mean. She needs someone who can look out for her as she grows up. I can do that.'

I nod slowly, catching his eye for a moment before looking away. I've been wondering whether to tell him, whether it would feel right, but now we're face to face I know I can't keep it a secret.

'What?' he says finally.

'There's something I wanted you to see.'

I've been carrying it around with me for the last few days, taking it out and looking at it every hour or so. Studying it last thing at night, and first thing in the morning. I take it out of my purse now and slide it across the table. A single sheet of A4 paper, folded over twice, already starting to crumple at the corners. A new world opening up in six short paragraphs.

Dominic unfolds the paper and reads the text. When he looks up at me, there is a broad smile on his face.

'Is this . . .' He trails off.

'Yes,' I say. 'It's the first stage, anyway. But I thought it was time to move on, get on with my life, do what I needed to do.'

'That's brilliant, Ellen, I'm so pleased for you.'

'According to the agency there are more hurdles to jump, but they say I'm potentially a good fit for adoption and they have kids they're looking to place. Maybe as soon as summer next year, if I'm lucky.'

'Boy or girl?'

'I don't mind. Either would be amazing.'

He reaches a hand across the table, gently touches my arm. 'And how do you feel about it?'

'Excited,' I say. 'Still not really believing it's true. Scared, too.'

'You, scared?' He gives me a grin. 'I didn't think you were scared of anything.'

I shrug, take another sip of my hot chocolate. 'Worried that I'll mess it up, I suppose.'

The few times I've been pregnant, I had always been terrified I would lose the baby. And now, buried beneath the joy and excitement and expectation of finally having my own little family, there is still a tingle of concern about whether I'll make the grade when that dream finally comes true.

'I think you'll make a fantastic mother,' he says. 'A tiger mother, in a good way.'

'How do you know?'

Dominic touches a hand to the fading scar on his cheekbone. 'Because I've seen you in action, Ellen Devlin. I know.' He smiles. 'Trust me.'

Acknowledgements

As I write these words, I've just discovered that my books have sold more than one million copies in the UK. This feels like an astonishing, unimaginable number and I still haven't really got my head around it, if I'm completely honest. I still remember very clearly being a debut author in January 2017, not sure how my first thriller would be received, wondering whether it might be a one-off. A fluke. To find myself three novels later with one million copies sold is basically a dream come true.

And so to *you*, for reading this book and hopefully some of my others, I just want to say a huge thank you for being a part of the last four years.

Of course, another key part of the journey has been having a brilliant publisher and I consider myself very lucky to have found a home at Bonnier Books. A big thank you to my editor, Sophie Orme, for her insight and expertise and for always asking the right questions. Thanks also to Kate Parkin, Katie Lumsden, Felice McKeown and Francesca Russell, for all their hard work on this and previous books.

I wrote *Trust Me* during the spring and summer of 2020, before and during the first national lockdown. With my wife working from home, my daughter returned from university and my son having school lessons delivered online, the house was a lot more lively (in a good way) than during an average pre-lockdown writing day. But it also meant they were always on hand when I needed to talk things through on the story that they first knew – before I even wrote the first chapter – as *The Baby*. So thanks as ever to Sally, Sophie and Tom for their thoughts, ideas and input into the process.

I'm very grateful to Chris Wall of Cartwright King Solicitors, for his legal advice (if I ever get arrested, I will definitely be giving him a call). And to Chief Superintendent Rob Griffin of Nottinghamshire Police for answering all my questions, even the really weird ones. Thanks also to Dr Gillian Sare, for advice on medical matters and the use and abuse of drugs like dexamphetamine. Naturally, any errors or omissions in the areas of law, policing or medicine are down to me.

I found a non-fiction book by Kate Bendelow – *The Real CSI, a Forensic Handbook for Crime Writers* – very useful, with details of this story that touch on crime scenes and evidence collection. I drew inspiration from another book, *Living the Life Unexpected* by Jody Day, who writes with extraordinary insight into childlessness in a way that helped to inform aspects of Ellen's story. I was also inspired by a podcast on Audible, *Evil Has a Name*, which explored a series of notorious crimes that went unsolved for years until a breakthrough using DNA.

Last but certainly not least, a heartfelt thank you to the stellar team at the Darley Anderson Agency, Mary, Sheila, Kristina, Rosanna, Jade and Georgia. This book is dedicated to my agent, Camilla Bolton, who took a chance on me when I was unpublished, and whose skill, knowledge and instincts for a good story have made me a better writer ever since. I'm glad you're in my corner.

A message from T.M. Logan . . .

Hello!

Thank you for picking up *Trust Me*. I hope you enjoyed it.

I first got the idea for this story at an ice hockey match. Sitting a few rows in front of me was a young family, including an incredibly cute baby – just a few months old – who couldn't stop grinning at everyone around her. I wondered in an idle moment whether I could still cope with looking after a small baby, as both my children were teenagers by this point. Would I still know what to do and how to do it? Would it all come back to me?

Then I wondered what I would do if I had no choice, if the baby was left with me and the mother disappeared . . .

And how about if I had *never* had that responsibility before, but had always yearned for it? If I had wanted a child for years but it had never happened? That was when Ellen popped into my head: a capable, resourceful individual who has reached a turning point in her own life. Where did her name come from? The truth is, I'm a huge fan of the 1986 movie *Aliens* and I was channelling Ellen Ripley as I wrote her chapters, finding herself in this dangerous situation and determined to protect a stranger's child at all costs. She was a part of the inspiration for Ellen Devlin and how *Trust Me* found its way onto the page.

My next psychological thriller starts with a small white lie.

The kind of lie you might tell to keep your child out of trouble – especially when he begs you to confirm that he came home early last night and has been up in his room ever since.

And so you back him up. You give him an alibi. Instead of telling the truth: that he actually crept in at 3 a.m., clothes streaked with mud and bruises on his face. Fear in his eyes and a plea in his voice you've not heard for a long time. *Please, Dad.*

But sometimes a small white lie can be the most dangerous thing in the world.

Because five teenagers went into the woods last night.

And only four came out . . .

This new novel will be published in 2022, and I can't wait!

If you would like to hear more about my books before then, you can visit www.tmlogan.com where you can become part of the T.M. Logan Readers' Club. It only takes a few moments to sign up, there are no catches or costs.

Bonnier Books UK will keep your data private and confidential, and it will never be passed on to a third party. We won't spam you with loads of emails, just get in touch now and again with news about my books, and you can unsubscribe any time you want.

And if you would like to get involved in a wider conversation about my books, please do review *Trust Me* on Amazon, on GoodReads, on any other e-store, on your own blog and social media accounts, or talk about it with friends, family or reading groups! Sharing your thoughts helps other readers, and I always enjoy hearing about what people experience from my writing.

Thank you again for reading *Trust Me*, I really do appreciate it.

Best wishes,
Tim